DEBORAH CALLING

A Novel

Book of Deborah 2

Avraham Azrieli

ISBN: 978-1-953648-05-1

BOOKS BY AVRAHAM AZRIELI

Fiction:

The Masada Complex
The Jerusalem Inception
The Jerusalem Assassin
Christmas for Joshua
The Mormon Candidate
The Bootstrap Ultimatum
Thump
The Elixirist
Deborah Rising
Deborah Calling
Deborah Slaying
Deborah Striking

Nonfiction:

Your Lawyer on a Short Leash – A Guide to Dealing with Lawyers
One Step Ahead – A Mother of Seven Escaping Hitler's Claws

Author Website:
www.AzrieliBooks.com

For Fiona with love.

DEBORAH CALLING

1

Deborah lay among the rows of sleeping men under the thatched roof of the pavilion. Every time she dozed off, one of the slaves would grunt, snore, or break wind, jolting her awake again. Her blistered hands and feet throbbed under the bandages, and her freshly shorn scalp itched against the rough straw mat, which did little to soften the hard earth. She had acclimated to the stench of the tannery during her first day of work, but the men's body odors grew fouler in the still air of the night. Would she also reek like that once she had succeeded in transforming into a man? The thought made her smile in the dark.

Eventually, her exhaustion won over, and she fell asleep.

In her dream, Deborah rode an eagle through a flawless blue sky. The clear air caressed her face and filled her long hair, which fluttered behind her like an orange cape. She held on, her freckled arms as white as the feathers on the eagle's neck. The wind whistled under the vast wings, which swayed gently. The eagle's back was as soft as a pillow, yet firm underneath, supporting her weight with ease. She felt free and happy. She was safe.

A harsh bump jolted her. Deborah clutched the feathers while the eagle flapped its wings rapidly to regain altitude. They hit another bump, harder this time, and then dropped, pulled downward by an invisible force. The blue sky was gone, replaced by thick clouds. The rushing air no longer whistled, but became a hoarse whisper.

"Stay quiet, or I'll kill you."

Another bump from behind made the eagle, clouds, and wind disappear altogether. She was back on the ground among the slaves, lying on her side in a fetal position while someone clung to her from behind like a spoon. A heavy hand pressed down on her shorn scalp, the palm as rough as untreated cowhide. An arm circled her chest, pressing hard.

Deborah tried to speak, but couldn't.

"You're a pretty one," a man whispered.

She strained to get free from his grip.

He threw a leg over, pinning her down.

She groaned.

"Hush, girl." His lips pressed to her ear, exhaling rancid breath.

She forced the words out of her mouth. "I'm a boy!"

"I know what you are."

She twisted her body to roll away.

He held her in a tight vise, making it hard to breathe, and his hand snaked down between her legs.

A scream crawled up her throat, but she held it back, fearing exposure and humiliation.

He grabbed her crotch and sniggered. "Where is it, boy?"

Deborah turned her head and faced him nose to nose. The faint glow of the torch from the far end of the pavilion illuminated a familiar face: One Eye, the Philistine slave who had tried to expose her earlier that day, when her menacing husband, Seesya, had raided the tannery, searching for her. Only the intervention of Petro, the slave in charge of their workgroup, had saved her from capture and certain death.

One Eye locked his lips to hers and stuck his tongue into her mouth.

Deborah convulsed with disgust and bit down on his tongue.

His head jerked back, and he wailed.

Taking advantage of his momentary distress, she butted his nose with the side of her head. He cried out again, rolled off her, and punched the side of her abdomen once, twice, and a third time. She gasped for air, paralyzed with pain. One Eye got on top of her, locked her arms down with his knees, and struck her head with a clenched fist.

Awakened by the commotion, the slaves around them sat up to see what was happening.

One Eye landed another fist, and another.

None of the slaves interfered.

Her vision fogged up, darkness creeping over her.

The blows stopped abruptly, and One Eye fell over to the side. Petro's face appeared in the fog over her. The group leader, who had introduced her to the tannery work that morning, said something, but she couldn't comprehend his words.

One Eye lurched to his feet and punched Petro.

Deborah crawled away while more slaves hurried over to watch the fight. She reached one of the stone pillars that supported the roof of the pavilion and pulled up to a sitting position, her back against the pillar.

The crowd laughed and jeered as the fight migrated out of the pavilion toward the rows of soaking tubs, which were filled with a mix of river water, urine, and feces. Someone brought over a torch, and the slaves circled Petro and One Eye, egging them on.

Taking deep breaths, Deborah began to recover. She wiped her exposed head with the slack bottom of her sleeveless shirt. For a moment, she longed for her lush hair and its comforting softness.

The chanting died down.

Leaning on the stone pillar with her bandaged hands, Deborah rose to her feet shakily and tried to see what was happening.

The crowd hooted.

She stumbled forward, pain flaring up in her bandaged feet, and pushed through the men.

One Eye had somehow forced Petro down to his knees, facing away, bent over, his right arm twisted behind his back. One Eye used his weight as a lever to bend Petro's arm further. It was obvious he was trying to break it, and the pain must have been awful, but Petro didn't utter a sound. He pressed his free hand to the ground in front of him as an anchor. One Eye shouted a string of curse words while pushing forward with great effort. Petro put his head in, chin to the chest, and straightened his legs abruptly, rolling forward. One Eye fell on top of him. They became a tangled web of arms, legs, and jittery hands hitting, scratching, and clawing.

The crowd cheered, the circle shifting left and right to give the two men room to tumble this way and that. At one point, Petro managed to hold on to One Eye from behind in a manner not much different from how Deborah had been held only a short time earlier. One Eye tried to wriggle away, but Petro had him in a neck lock, blocking his airways. One Eye tried to wrench off Petro's hold, but couldn't. He was suffocating.

The crowd shouted and clapped as the fight seemed to reach its climax.

In a fit of desperation, One Eye stood up, his legs carrying the combined weight of both men. He stumbled backward, his foot caught on the lip of a tub, and the two men fell in.

No cowhides were soaking in that tub at the moment, but it had been filled up in preparation for the next day. The nasty brew of human waste did wonders for softening animal skins, but for the two submerged men it must have been horrific. The spectators roared with laughter when One Eye's head popped up, his face smeared with feces. He wiped his face, spitting and cursing as he tried to stand up. Petro emerged a moment later, leaped onto One Eye's back, and the fight was on again. Whereas all the male slaves crowded around the tub, none of the women came out of their pavilion, which stood at the downstream end of the tannery.

The two men in the swirling tub punched and kicked each other, but their blows were mostly off target as they repeatedly lost their footing and plunged underwater. Splashes of water and human waste sent the spectators jumping back with cheerful howls. Glancing at the gate, Deborah expected the guards to rush inside and impose order, but the gate remained closed, and there was no sign of the guards.

As the vigor of their assaults declined, One Eye managed to land a hard fist on Petro's forehead. The group leader clutched his head, tumbled back, and sank yet again into the grimy water. Deborah expected One Eye to jump in and finish off his opponent, but he waded to the side and grasped the lip of the tub. The slaves booed while he attempted to climb out of the tub.

Petro emerged from the dark liquid, wiped his face, and saw what was happening. He hopped onto One Eye, who held on to the lip of the tub for another moment, before his fingers slipped off. The two men fell back, sunk in briefly, and reappeared with Petro on top, pushing One Eye's head underwater.

The slaves chanted, "Petro! Petro! Petro!"

The group leader's wet face was taut with resolve as he held his struggling opponent underwater. Only One Eye's feet were visible, kicking frantically.

"Petro! Petro! Petro!"

Suddenly, the slaves' cheers fizzled out.

Voices from the back whispered, "Master is coming!"

A hush fell over the tannery, broken only by the splashing of One

Eye's feet.

Deborah turned to look.

Kassite approached from the direction of his house, which stood on stilts near the riverbank upstream. A night robe covered his lanky figure, and his bushy white hair stood out in the darkness.

The crowd of slaves parted, letting him through, bowing their heads.

His leather boots pressed into the wet sand with uneven squishy sounds, produced by his limping.

Petro looked up from the tub. One Eye's bare feet thrashed, raising a ring of brown foam.

The slaves watched in rapt silence, gazes alternating between Kassite and the tub.

With a flick of his wrist, Kassite made his wish clear.

Petro lifted One Eye out of the water and dragged him to the edge of the tub. Several slaves pulled One Eye out and pounded on his back until he quivered and let out a projectile of vomit, followed by a fit of coughing.

Kassite's eyes searched around the circle and found Deborah. She realized that he somehow knew she had been the cause of the fight.

Petro climbed out of the tub and bent over, panting, while mucky water dripped from his sleeveless shirt.

With another flick of his wrist, Kassite sent all the slaves back to the pavilion, where they lay down on the straw mats and closed their eyes.

Deborah stayed put.

Kassite limped over to the riverbank at a spot halfway between the two pavilions, where the light of the torches barely reached. Petro supported One Eye as they hobbled over and stood before Kassite. Deborah followed them, walking cautiously on her bandaged feet.

"You broke my most important rule," Kassite said. "Do not fight!"

"I'm sorry, Master," Petro said.

One Eye only grunted.

"He attacked the new boy." Petro pointed at Deborah. "When everyone was sleeping, he hit Borah."

Kassite looked at her, and she nodded.

"I had to protect Borah," Petro continued. "You put him in my group."

"That is correct," Kassite said. "Group leaders are responsible for their men."

One Eye sat down on the ground, coughed hard, and spat. "Borah is not a boy," he said.

Kassite looked down at him. "What did you say?"

"Borah is not a boy." He spat again. "Borah is a girl."

There was a long silence.

"A girl?" Kassite chuckled. "What gave you this idea?"

Coughing some more, One Eye pointed at Deborah. "Her husband came here today, when you were away. I tried to tell him, but Petro threatened to poke out my eye."

Kassite turned to Petro.

"I had no choice, Master," Petro said. "He wouldn't stay quiet, and if the Hebrew men had noticed our argument—"

"Borah is a boy," Kassite said. "That is it."

"I felt her breasts." One Eye pantomimed grasping Deborah's chest. "They're small, but she has them. And I also know what she doesn't have." He patted his crotch and smirked.

Kassite held up a hand. "Have you told anyone else about this?"

One Eye shook his head.

"No harm done, then. Now, are you two done fighting?"

"Yes, Master," Petro said.

One Eye shrugged.

"You stink like the latrines." Kassite sniffed and twisted his face. "Go in the river and clean up thoroughly."

Petro supported One Eye, who got up slowly, groaning. As they entered the water, Petro glanced over his shoulder at Kassite, who pointed a thumb down.

Venturing deeper into the river, Petro stepped behind One Eye, put a lock on his neck, and hopped onto his back, forcing him underwater. They disappeared in the dark water.

Shocked, Deborah stepped closer to the river's edge and pointed her bandaged hand at the water, which boiled up with their struggle. "Master!"

"You started it," Kassite said. "Go in and help Petro finish it."

She took another step, the water lapping at her toes, and stopped. In her mind, she heard the Hebrew boys reciting the Ten Commandments at the small temple courtyard back in her hometown of Emanuel, and the words emerged from her lips without forethought: "Do not kill!"

After what seemed like a long time, Petro's head appeared above the water while he continued to hold One Eye below. Their battle sent circular waves that spread in quick succession on the surface of the slow-moving river.

"Go help him," Kassite said.

"Do not kill!" she repeated.

A bare foot jerked out of the water, and the heel kicked Petro in the head. He yelled in pain and dropped sideways into the water.

Kassite gestured, urging her into the water.

"God forbids killing!"

The two men rolled several times, alternating for quick, desperate gasps of air.

"Does your god allow girls to become boys?"

The question confused Deborah. "He said nothing about that."

"He made you a girl."

The underwater rotating ceased, and neither of the men was visible.

"He forbade killing—for girls and for men, it's forbidden."

"A man kills when killing is necessary. Go!"

Deborah took another step into the water, which by now had completely soaked the bandages on her feet. The boys' voices kept ringing in her head: "Do not kill!" She wanted to proceed, to obey Kassite as she had vowed to do, to show him that she could muster the will to act as a man, but her legs refused to move forward.

Kassite sneered.

The surface of the river gradually calmed down.

Deborah watched with growing alarm. Were they both dead?

Petro's head appeared, and he turned to face Kassite, nodding once.

A moment later, One Eye's motionless body surfaced, facedown. The lazy current carried it downstream.

Petro came out of the river, breathing heavily. He bowed before Kassite and walked to the pavilion.

Her hand pressed to her mouth, Deborah stared at the river, where One Eye's body dissolved into the night.

"It was necessary," Kassite said. "He could have told other's about you."

"Do not kill," she whispered.

They stood in silent, looking out at the dark river, now completely quiet and still.

"He lost his eye while building my house." Kassite gestured at the stilts-supported house up the riverbank. "Another slave dropped a hammer on him. Took a month to recover, almost died, but he went back to work without complaining."

Clearing her throat, she said, "I'm sorry, Master."

"Me too," he said. "I will not kill another worker because of your failure."

"It won't happen again."

"If a man with one eye saw through your act, how long before others do?"

She hung her head. Kassite was the mythical Elixirist, and after all she had gone through to find him and obtain his agreement to help her become a man, here she was, less than a day later, disappointing him.

"The Male Elixir I gave you yesterday," he continued, "will help you transform only if you do what you're supposed to do in order to change. Remember my advice?"

"Yes, Master," she said. "Imitate until you mutate."

"Then imitate better, or you'll never mutate."

Kassite walked up the riverbank back to his house. Deborah went to the men's pavilion, where all the slaves were already asleep. She lay down on her straw mat, relieved to take the weight off her burning feet, and closed her eyes.

A moment later, she opened her eyes and checked that no one was sneaking up on her. She trembled at the memory of One Eye's coarse lips pressing against hers, of his bare feet writhing in the tub, and of his motionless body floating downriver, shrouded by the night. Had other slaves sensed her femininity? Was someone lurking in the dark right now, waiting for her to fall asleep, preparing to attack her?

Deborah glanced over her shoulder and met Petro's gaze. The Philistine slave pointed at his eyes and at her to indicate that he would be watching over her. She felt better, remembering how he had defended her against One Eye. It was comforting to know that someone was ready to protect her.

Resisting the urge to glance again at Petro, Deborah took a deep breath, trying to calm her nerves. Did Petro believe that she was Borah, a boy slave, or did he know that One Eye had been right? Was Petro her defender, or did he pose a new and bigger risk? There was no way to know for sure, but she had to believe that he'd meant what he said earlier to Kassite: "I had to protect Borah. You put him in my group."

She recalled with a pang of fear the way Petro had drowned One Eye in the river without hesitation. Would he not kill her the same way if Kassite changed his mind and pointed his thumb down behind her back?

Curled up in a fetal position, Deborah hugged her knees to her chest and fought off a tremor. She missed her few belongings, especially her father's fire-starters, which she liked to hold, one stone in each hand. In the tannery, however, Kassite allowed the slaves no personal possessions. The sack that held her meager belongings had remained at his house. The men around her snored, grunted, and passed wind, each sound reminded her of the mortal danger another exposure of her gender would bring. Unable to resist, she glanced back over her shoulder. Petro's eyes were shut. He was no longer watching.

The tremor returned. It swelled into outright shaking. Her teeth began to chatter.

Anger rose inside her. Why was she wasting precious sleeping time on foolish doubts and fears? How could she survive the hard labor in the tannery without rest? None of the men around her would spend a single moment on self-pity at the expense of sleeping—that's something she should imitate!

Deborah pushed the memory of One Eye's attack and his floating dead body out of her mind. She imagined the eagle flying above the clouds through a clear blue sky. The shaking declined, her breathing slowed down, and her eyes closed.

2

From high above, the town of Emanuel seemed small, a hillside village encircled by stone walls. It grew larger as they descended in circles through the clear sky. Deborah held on to the white feathers on the eagle's neck and squinted in the rushing wind. Below, a crowd gathered near the gates of the town, across the road from the fairgrounds. Everything looked different from this vantage point, but Deborah recognized the event with a jolt of sorrow. It was the trial of her sister, Tamar, whose thick locks of orange hair glistened in the sun as she slipped, feet first, into the Pit of Shame in preparation for the stoning. Deborah saw herself below, sitting with the other maidens of Emanuel in a large circle around the Pit of Shame, forced to watch the execution of a young wife convicted of whoring—only because on her wedding night her bedcloth had shown no bloodstains.

Judge Zifron of Ephraim, the ruler of Emanuel, sat on the platform across from the elders, who had declared the guilty verdict. Next to the judge stood the priest, Obadiah of Levi, in his white robe and bejeweled breastplate. The judge's son and heir, Seesya, who had accused his new wife, stood at the head of a queue of men by the pile of stones, ready to throw the first one.

Deborah looked at her hand, clutching the eagle's feathers, and saw the ring that Seesya had pulled off Tamar's finger and put on hers, betrothing her to be his next wife after her sister's death. She shut her eyes, refusing to watch the horror of Tamar's stoning again. Bending to rest her cheek against the eagle's neck, she wished it to fly away.

When Deborah opened her eyes, the sun was gone. A crescent moon and countless stars illuminated the night. The eagle descended to a solitary palm tree, reached down with its talons, and clutched the thick fronds. She recognized her family's one-room house, which had been neglected since her parents' murder the year before. The surrounding fields and orchards were cultivated, because Palm Homestead was now in the hands of the house of Zifron through Seesya's marriages to Tamar and Deborah.

"It's all a big lie," Deborah said to the eagle. "Seesya is not entitled to our inheritance."

Tilting its head, the eagle seemed to question her statement.

"He failed to consummate the marriage," she said. "He didn't possess either of us in his bed. My poor sister—of course she didn't bleed. And then, based on his false accusation, they stoned her. But on my wedding night, I tricked him with cow's blood and saved myself from Tamar's fate. He got so mad that, later in the night, he tried to kill me with his own hands."

The palm tree swayed under them.

"And this tree you're holding on to," Deborah continued, "it bears my name."

The eagle's ears perked up.

"It's true," she said. "My father named it Deborah's Palm after he had seen me in a dream sitting under this tree and delivering Yahweh's message to the Hebrews. I'll be God's prophet, like Moses and Joshua."

The eagle shifted position at the edge of the fronds, which bent under the weight.

Looking down, she recognized herself again, standing in the dark with her friend Barac and his father, Abinoam. They had fled Emanuel in the middle of the execution when Barac's refusal to cast a stone at Tamar drew Seesya's ire.

Deborah was too far up to hear their conversation, but she remembered it clearly. Barac was telling her the story of a mythical Elixirist, who had turned the women of Edom into men to take their dead husbands' place and drive away an Egyptian army. That's when she had realized how she could free herself from Seesya: find the Elixirist and convince him to help her transform into a man. Then she would return to Emanuel and fight to win back Palm Homestead.

The eagle took off into the night, which quickly became day, followed by another night. Deborah saw herself standing near the communal burial cave with Obadiah, whose priestly white robe stood out in the darkness. He had just smuggled her out through the town gates, hidden in his cart under a corpse. As she prepared to leave on her quest to find the Elixirist, Obadiah held his hands above her head, fingers parted in pairs, and recited the priestly blessing.

Riding the eagle, she watched herself, a lonely figure on the road below, as she walked through the night, took refuge when the sun came up, and was awakened by a caravan of Moabite traders, followed by Seesya's soldiers, who were soon hit by deadly arrows from the bow of Zariz, a Moabite boy.

Deborah watched the two of them riding together on Zariz's horse. He taught her how to control the reins and shoot arrows, and she drilled him in throwing stones at targets while blindfolded. Deborah smiled at the sight of them laughing carelessly, but then she remembered the derisive Edomite proverb he'd quoted: "Beware of the Hebrews, for their tongue is oily and their sword is invisible."

It was night again when Deborah saw herself collapse on the road near Shiloh, despairing at the futility of her quest. As the eagle flapped its wings, hovering in place, Deborah remembered how she had felt that night, a helpless girl, alone in the world, without hope. She reached down from the eagle's back to pat the girl's shoulder and tell her that Obadiah's blessing would come true, that Yahweh would help her find the Elixirist, who would agree to give her the Male Elixir and direct her through the long process of transforming into a man. Her hand almost touched the girl's shoulder when a bell rang loudly and she woke up.

3

Kassite was ringing a bell that hung from the edge of the pavilion roof. Sunrise painted the sky a pale red. Deborah was wedged between the slaves, some still snoring, others beginning to move about. She tried to get up, but a muscle cramp in her back made her groan and lie back down. Breathing deeply as the pain eased, she remembered last night's events and looked around for Petro. He was already up.

Her bandaged feet burned when she put weight on them, but not as badly as the night before. She removed the bandages from her hands and examined them in the daylight. The ointment had soaked in, the purple color had softened, and new skin had begun to emerge. Following the example of the other slaves, she folded her straw mat and added it to the pile at the end of the pavilion. She passed near Kassite, who was sitting in his chair, his wide-brimmed hat shading his face, his eyes on the piece of parchment he was holding.

The queue of waiting slaves at the latrines dissuaded her from even trying. She joined Petro and his group, which now numbered only seven slaves, at the storage area. The men picked up hammers and started pounding on chunks of limestone, which crumbled into small pieces and powder. Deborah imitated the way they used the hammers, the sound of their grunting, and the manner of their spitting when dust filled their mouths.

The crushed limestone was collected in a wooden bucket. Every time the bucket was filled, one of the slaves went to empty it over the hides in the row of five tubs she had filled yesterday with clear river water.

Her confidence grew, but so did her physical discomfort. The blisters reopened, setting her hands on fire. The muscles in her arms, shoulders, and back ached badly. She gritted her teeth and kept working.

Finally, Kassite rang the bell for the morning meal, and she put down her hammer with a silent sigh of relief.

After the meal, Petro checked her hands and gave her olive oil to rub on the blisters. He sent the others to continue pulverizing the limestone rocks and took her over to the tubs. He gave her oversized leather boots and told her to walk over the skins. Her weight pushed the skins deeper into the tubs, churned the water, and mixed in the limestone powder.

It was an easy task for the first hour, but the heat of the day, the odorous fumes from the human waste in some of the other tubs, and the swirling flies gradually brought Deborah near collapse. She kept reminding herself of the Male Elixir, which had coursed through her veins since the previous evening. The road to achieving her goal passed through this hard labor. The pain meant that her body was getting stronger and building up resilience—the first phase of her transformation.

The midday meal provided a much-needed respite, and Kassite's nod of approval injected Deborah with new energy. She returned to walking back and forth on the skins in the tubs, mixing in the limestone. A layer of clouds gathered above, hiding the hot sun, and a pleasant breeze came in from the river. She stomped the skins and watched her surroundings with keen curiosity.

The tannery was like a beehive, with the slaves hard at work on various tasks. No one stood idle. In the early afternoon, three oxcarts arrived from the direction of Aphek, piled high with fresh skins. Several groups of slaves left their work and went to help the oxcart drivers unload the skins. Kassite counted and wrote down numbers. When the oxcarts were empty, the drivers followed Kassite over to the curtained pavilions, where a group of women brought out finished leather products.

In addition to leather hides, Deborah saw coats, belts, and sandals, as well as horse harnesses and straps of various sizes. There were shields made of brown leather pinned onto wood, body armor pieces for the chest, back, and hips, quivers for arrows, sheaths for swords and knives, as well as the knee-high boots favored by soldiers. Everything was tied onto the oxcarts with ropes.

When the oxcarts rolled out through the gate and up the path to the main road, Deborah saw Kassite follow them on a horse. At the top of the path, he paused, turned the horse around, and surveyed the tannery from above. She thought his gaze lingered on her briefly, but it was hard to tell. With his dark coat and leather boots, mounted on a handsome horse, Kassite looked like a prosperous free man on his way to conduct business. The sight puzzled her. Wasn't his owner worried that Kassite might escape?

Deborah continued to step on the hides, pushing them underwater again and again. The churning water reminded her of One Eye's desperate struggle in the river and Petro's blank expression as he held his fellow Philistine below the surface until death arrived. How was it possible for a man to kill another while remaining so calm, showing neither reluctance nor remorse? Could she ever do such a thing?

Do not kill!

Vowing silently never to violate Yahweh's sixth commandment, Deborah raised her eyes from the tub to the sky above, pushed away the memory of last night's killing, and thanked Him for watching over her.

By sunset, when Deborah was near collapse, she saw Kassite return on his horse, followed by one oxcart, now loaded with sacks of wheat and barley, jars of olive oil, and baskets of fruit. The soldiers opened the gate, helped him dismount, and bowed to him as he went into the tannery. While a group of slaves hurried to unload the oxcart, Kassite limped over to the pavilion and rang the bell, announcing the evening meal.

4

The next morning, the group began the process of scudding, which involved the removal of the remaining fur from the hides, now softened up by the lime solution. They stretched the hides over wooden planks and scraped them with dull knives. The fur came off slowly, each hide taking half a day to complete. The morning and midday meals came and went, and the work continued. Between her blistered hands, lacerated feet, and cramped muscles, a fog of pain dulled Deborah's mind. She worked mechanically, no longer thinking, until the day finally ended. After the evening meal, she went over to the small canopy past Kassite's house. There were six cots, occupied by sick or injured slaves. One of the two Philistine women treated her hands and feet. They didn't speak a word to her.

The following day, Deborah continued to scrape fur off the hides. Her body ached and her eyes burned from the lime fumes.

A cry of pain startled her.

One of the slaves held up his forearm, which was bleeding. The knife he had been using rested on the cowhide, stained in red. He cried out again.

Deborah dropped her knife and went to him. She reached for his wounded arm, but he turned away, shouting Philistine words she didn't understand.

Petro came over, grabbed the man's arm, and pushed his hand away to look at the wound. It was a deep gash, bleeding profusely. Petro clasped the forearm with his calloused hand, covering the wound, and pulled the man up. Deborah held his other arm, and together they led him up the riverbank. The two women sprang into action. One of them fetched a bowl of water from the river while the other helped the injured man lie down on the ground. The women cleaned the wound, applied a thick paste from a jar, and wrapped the wounded arm in a cloth.

Each succeeding day Deborah woke up with her body in pain, inside and out, from her feet to the top of her head, which the sun had burned right through the soft remnants of her hair. The aches in her muscles and joints were real and nearly intolerable, but the suffering helped her understand the words of Miriam, the leper woman who had saved her in Shiloh: "Pain is the real gift from Yahweh, for without pain, there is no life." The pain saturating every part of her body meant that the Male Elixir was making her delicate bones sturdier and her muscles mightier. With every moment, this pain brought her closer to manhood, which for her was nothing short of the gift of life itself.

At the same time, she found herself growing more content than she had felt at any time since the day of her parents' murders the previous year. It was odd, because life at Judge Zifron's house, where she and Tamar had lived as orphans, had been much more comfortable than life at the tannery, and the work at Zifron's basket factory had been incomparably less arduous than the work she was doing here. Yet, despite the grueling work under the hot sun, the gory animal skins, and the grimy Philistine slaves, she felt whole again.

At first, Deborah credited this positive feeling to the physical changes—her growing muscles, coarser hands, and prouder posture, as well as her inner resilience, which grew by the day. But as she constantly observed the men around her in order to imitate them, she also noticed that they, too, felt content despite the hard work, harsh conditions, and total servitude. It occurred to her that the strict routine, clear authority, and repetitive tasks had something to do with it. Life in the tannery was free of confusion, regulated by the ringing of the bell and the cycle of multiple steps of treatment that transformed gory animal skins into fine leather. Each slave and every group knew what to do and when to do it. There was no need for discussion or new orders. The strict separation between men and women—even talking was forbidden—removed any risk of conflicts in that realm. In addition, the full stomachs and restful nights dulled any resentment the slaves might have felt, considering that many free men and women had little to eat and slept fitfully in fear of violence at their isolated homesteads or small villages. As a result, rather than begrudge the total deprivation of personal freedom, the slaves seemed to accept their fate, obey the rules, and avoid conflict. Above all, they uniformly showed unwavering reverence for Kassite.

Watching him for several days, Deborah gradually understood the reason. Kassite alone managed every aspect of life in the tannery. He rang the bell that regulated their lives, decided every detail of every stage of the work, assigned tasks to dozens of groups working simultaneously on large batches of hides in various stages of processing, and supervised the stitching, sewing, and fabricating of the final products by the women. Deborah also came to understand why Kassite required each slave, male and female, to bow before him after receiving each meal. By that simple gesture, they acknowledged him as the giver of their food and shelter—in essence, of their very lives.

Shifting to the next task—bating—tested her resolve. Together with another slave, she pulled from each latrine a barrel filled with a festering mix of urine and feces, carried it to the row of tubs, and poured the content onto the hides. Once this was completed, and the skins in the five tubs were covered with feces, she and the others had to stomp on them for hours in order to knead the dung and urine into the fibers of the hides. According to Petro, the bating made them pliable and more absorbent for finishing and dyeing.

Several times during that day, she bent over and vomited. The others laughed, patted her back, and told her that every new slave vomited during his first bating—a rite of passage that separated the novice from the veteran. Petro's attention to her hands and feet at the beginning, she realized, had been part of a well-established practice of easing a new slave into the challenging work while avoiding major injury or illness, which would cause disability and loss of a laborer for a day, a week, or altogether. But her visceral disgust at human waste was nothing more than a comedic moment for the others, and by the end of that particularly distasteful day, it made her laugh as well.

Once in a while, Kassite left the tannery on his horse, always in the direction of Aphek, either accompanying one or more oxcarts loaded with new products, or alone, returning later with skins of slaughtered animals or large quantities of food supplies. She never saw Orran of Manasseh visit the tannery he owned. Was the foul stench too much for the rich man? Was that the reason Orran entrusted all aspects of the operation to Kassite, rewarding him with a lifestyle befitting a free man? Did Orran know that the old slave managing the tannery was the mythical Elixirist from the land of Edom?

Drenching was the second-to-last phase in the preparation of the hides for final finishing as leather products. The group spent two days washing and scrubbing the skins in the river to remove all remnants of the lime, feces, and urine. Petro assigned Deborah to drain the tubs and refill them with fresh water. Lugging the cart with barrels from the river to the tubs was not as hard as the first time, and she didn't have to smear mud on her arms, legs, and face, because dipping in the river did not remove the layer of muck that had bonded with her white skin and gave her the dark complexion of a Philistine.

They put the hides in the fresh water and left them to soak. The next day, they shook the hides, spread a thin layer of salt on both sides—the final phase, called pickling—and pegged the skins to the inside of the perimeter fence.

That evening, the group ate together, sitting in a circle. Petro chanted a Philistine song as the men sipped their minty hot drinks. Deborah went to sleep with a smile.

5

In the morning, the group picked up a new batch of animal skins and began the process all over again. This time around, Deborah was able to keep up with the men. Her hands and feet had healed, her muscle cramps had faded away, and her body had grown stronger, giving her the resilience to work long hours before exhaustion slowed her down. Her Philistine coworkers treated her with bemused indifference, much as older brothers would with a skinny teen eager to do a man's job, except for Petro, who took time to show her how to perform each task more efficiently and nodded approvingly when she succeeded.

Deborah began to count the days, something she hadn't done during the first cycle. When the group finally pegged the treated hides to the perimeter fence, they had been working on this batch for eighteen days. That meant that her stay in the tannery so far had amounted to more than a month. She was pleased with the bulging muscles of her arms and legs, as well as the rough skin on her hands and feet, and continued to follow Kassite's advice to imitate the men's posture and mannerisms. Overcoming her own habits, especially with regard to personal hygiene, was challenging, but she resisted, and a layer of filth thickened on her skin like crusty armor.

That evening, Deborah picked up her food, bowed to Kassite, and lingered for a moment, making sure he couldn't miss the obvious changes in her physique. She remembered his strict rule not to speak to him unless spoken to first and hoped he would speak to her. He didn't.

She joined the group, and as they had done at the conclusion of the previous batch, there was relaxed camaraderie as they ate together and sipped the minty hot drinks from their cups while Petro chanted the Philistine tune, which was becoming familiar to her.

After the meal, Deborah saw Kassite walk to his house and cross the short bridge to the front door, which one of his servants held open. As if sensing her gaze, Kassite paused and glanced in her direction. For a moment, she expected him to beckon her over, but he turned away and entered his house.

The third batch of animal skins was slightly bigger, and the work had become more monotonous. Deborah knew what needed to be done and took initiative without waiting for Petro to instruct her. The foul odors of fresh feces and urine being stomped on no longer made her sick, and she was able to step in when the others needed help. When the group completed the process yet again and pegged all the hides to the fence for the third time, her satisfaction and sense of achievement overwhelmed any remaining physical pain and anxiety.

That night, after the meal, the group sat together and enjoyed the minty hot drinks and Petro's quiet chant. He smiled at her, showing broken teeth, and one of the other men patted her on the shoulder and said something in Philistine, which she now understood to mean: "Not bad for a silly boy." The others cheered, sharing the credit of training her. Deborah realized that she was the last of the group to accept herself as Borah, the new boy-slave, who had to learn the work and acclimate his young body to the hard labor and harsh conditions of the tannery. In fact, she was looking forward to tomorrow, when they would start to work on a fourth batch of hides together.

The next morning, Kassite summoned her immediately after he rang the bell at sunrise. She was still sleepy, wiping her eyes with one hand while holding the folded mat in the other.

"Good morning, Borah," he said.

She bowed.

"Have you learned the stages of preparing the skins?"

"Yes, Master."

"Put away your mat and follow me."

Kassite limped to the riverbank and waited until she joined him.

"Do you have any questions about the work?"

Deborah wanted to ask if he had noticed how far she had progressed in her transformation from girl to boy, but he clearly allowed only questions about the work.

"I have one question," she said. "I've lost count of the days of the week, but surely the Sabbath has passed several times, and yet we kept working."

He seemed surprised by her question. "We work every day, all year long."

"But the seventh day is the Hebrew day of rest."

"None of the slaves here are Hebrews. We have a few Edomites like me, but mostly they are Philistines, caught in battle and sold into slavery."

"Orran of Manasseh is a Hebrew. Our God, Yahweh, gave us Ten Commandments, and the fourth one is to observe the Sabbath."

"And?"

"A Hebrew must give all his slaves and livestock a full day of rest on the Sabbath."

"Rotting skins cannot rest," Kassite said. "We must keep the process going, or they will spoil."

"We could do the minimum required to prevent spoilage while most of the slaves rested on the seventh day. Isn't Orran concerned about God's wrath?"

"Our Hebrew owner gives generous gifts to other gods, who are less concerned with slaves than your Yahweh."

"And you?" She kept her voice quiet to avoid being overheard. "Don't you care about these people?"

"I feed and protect them."

"As any jailer would."

Kassite raised his eyebrows. "You like to argue."

"I like to find out the truth."

"Seeking the truth is a dangerous habit for a slave."

"I wasn't born to be a slave."

"Neither was anyone else here." He gestured at the slaves, rising from their sleep under the pavilion and getting ready for work. "But their gods were too weak to protect them from their enemies. The last thing slaves need is a weekly day of idleness to sit around and commiserate."

Having experienced the excruciating tannery work for weeks on end, she was shocked by his cold words, which implied subjecting the slaves to perpetual, nonstop hard labor for the remainder of their lives.

"Do not think of me as a brutal man," he said. "One day, when you are responsible for the lives of others, you will understand the first rule of governing men: idle hands trigger irritable souls."

Deborah wanted to ask him why he assumed that she would one day be responsible for the lives of others. Did he believe in the truth of her father's dream, which she had shared with him, that she would grow up to become Yahweh's prophet to her people?

He held up his hand to indicate the end of the discussion.

Despite her efforts to control herself, she blurted out the real question. "How long until I complete the transformation from girl to boy?"

Pursing his lips, Kassite didn't answer.

She bent her arms to show him her bulging biceps. "The work has made me strong and resilient. My tolerance for pain and capacity for hard labor are as good as those of any boy my age."

"I will be the judge of that. Besides, the path ahead is long: the transformation you seek requires three phases."

"I remember your explanation about the phases. This place has made me physically strong, but the next phase is about changing my character from female to male. How would this mind-numbing, monotonous labor of the tannery help me develop a man's character?"

"Do you doubt me?"

"No, Master, but I want—"

Kassite raised his hand again. "Enough with the questions."

"I only want to know how soon I can leave—"

"You cannot leave."

"Why? I already drank the Male Elixir, so it's only a matter of going through the process—"

"Only the first dose," he said.

Deborah wasn't sure she'd heard him right. "What?"

Around them, the tannery came to life as slaves began the day's work in earnest.

"Master!" She raised her voice. "What do you mean?"

"You heard me." He took a deep breath and exhaled slowly. "The Male Elixir also has three parts, corresponding to the three phases of transformation—physical strength, character, and body parts. When I determine that you have achieved the necessary physical strength, you may begin the second phase of transformation, evolving your character from the passive, temperamental, small-minded, and anxious female to the superior male character, which is—"

"Proactive, even-tempered, adventurous, and logical."

"There you go." He smiled.

"But you gave me the Male Elixir!" She remembered the foul smell and lumpy texture of the dark, bubbly liquid in the goblet. "I drank it!"

"That was only the first dose."

"Why didn't you tell me it's divided into three doses?"

"I am telling you now." He held up three fingers.

Her rage ignited like a clutch of dry leaves. "You lied to me!"

"Keep your voice down." Glancing around to make sure her outburst hadn't attracted attention, he pointed a finger at her. "Never accuse me of lying. You are an ignorant Hebrew girl, and if I had to tell you everything you do not yet know, I would be talking nonstop for ten years."

Deborah wanted to argue that hiding a crucial fact amounted to lying, but his expression told her that further argument would be futile. He had tricked her, but there was nothing to do about it. She was totally dependent on his willingness to continue helping her.

"Do you remember your vow of total obedience?"

"Yes, Master."

"Wait here." Kassite turned and limped away. He passed among the slaves and selected six men, pulling them away from their groups. They followed him back to where she stood by the riverbank.

"This is Borah." Kassite placed his hand on her shoulder. "From this moment, he will be your group leader."

Deborah was shocked, but if they were wondering why Master had put them under the authority of a boy, none of them showed it.

Kassite pointed at a pile of fresh animal skins that had arrived the day before. "Get started."

With that, he left them.

The men looked at Deborah expectantly.

Taking a deep breath, she said, "Carry the skins to the river."

The men did as she told them, and a new cycle of work began, only that now she assigned tasks to a group of slaves in addition to doing her share of the work. It felt very strange, almost like a dream, but she fell into the role with surprising ease.

Unlike the Philistine men in Petro's group, who had dark skin and a strong, compact stature and ranged in age from twenty to about forty, the men in her new group were mature, at least over thirty years old, and shared a light complexion, with blue or gray green eyes, reddish or blond hair, and milky skin wherever the sun had not weathered it. Their sleeveless shirts revealed furry arms, reminiscent of Sallan, Kassite, and their servants. They spoke in a mix of Hebrew and Edomite words. At first, she worried about being the odd man out in this Edomite group, but from the moment she directed them to start moving the skins over to the riverbank, they showed her nothing but respect and diligence. She knew it wasn't her own authority that generated such obedience, but Kassite's directive that Borah was their group leader. Master's word was sacrosanct.

That night, sleep refused to come. Deborah was still resentful of Kassite for failing to tell her about the two additional doses of the Male Elixir she needed before reaching her goal. Could she trust him to provide the next dose when the time came? She was further puzzled by his decision to appoint her as group leader immediately after their argument. Did he believe in her capability, or was he setting her up to fail?

Deborah reflected on her first day as group leader, which had passed without incident. The Edomite men had followed her instructions and said very little. By sunset, they finished cleaning the skins and placed them in five tubs of fresh water. She could find no shortcoming in her performance as group leader. Perhaps Kassite did believe in her ability, but if he didn't, she would prove him wrong.

The man to her left snored heavily, and the one by her feet mumbled Philistine words in his sleep. She no longer noticed the odors of rotting skins and festering lime, but her sense of smell remained acute for other smells, which a hundred men, packed tightly together under one roof, produced aplenty.

Lying on her back, she tried to calm her mind by counting the long wood beams in the faint light from the single torch at the end of the pavilion. The beams supported a thick layer of thatch above but were exposed underneath. They were fairly straight and even, about twenty steps long, which was the width of the pavilion. Leather straps and ropes secured the ends of the beams to a frame of thick planks, which rested on top of stone pillars that were fixed into the ground every ten steps all around the rectangular pavilion.

Deborah counted fifty beams from end to end, the whole length of the pavilion. About halfway through the second round of counting, she fell asleep.

6

The eagle took off from the roof of the pavilion, passed over Kassite's house, and turned toward the setting sun. The giant bird easily soared, rising high above the Yarkon River, whose dark water and mild curves resembled an uncoiled snake. The high altitude gave Deborah sweeping views of the land, with checkered fields ready for harvest, orchards heavy with fruit, and lush pastures dotted with grazing cattle. The air didn't rush at her face, but stroked her like a gentle evening breeze. Over the distant horizon, the land and the sky merged into a belt of hazy azure, which she guessed was the Great Sea.

Deborah let go of the eagle's neck and extended her arms sideways, closing her eyes and surrendering to the sensual pleasure of weightless gliding in complete freedom and peace. But her pleasure was cut short when the air turned wet and chilly. She opened her eyes in alarm. The clear sky and setting sun were gone, replaced by a thick cloud. Had they reached the haze over the Great Sea, or had this cloud materialized suddenly out of nowhere? She could see nothing through the dense fog, which chilled her bones. A sense of doom overcame her. She leaned forward, her chest against the eagle's neck, her arms around it, and wished for the sun to return. At that moment, a bell rang nearby, and she woke up.

It was morning, and the commotion around Deborah chased away the ominous chill of the dream. She rinsed her face in the river and joined her group at the tubs, where they pulled the hides out of the water for the next phase of treatment.

The day passed in a frenzy of hard work, followed by similar days that varied only by the succession of tasks required to tame the rough animal skins into fine leather hides. Deborah worried constantly that she might commit errors and cause damage to the hides, or lose credibility with the men in her group. The nights were dreamless, though she kept hoping for the eagle's return and imagined going on another flight, enjoying the sun and warm air, not the cold, wet fog that had blocked off all view the last time.

The bleak ending of that recent dream continued to bother her. Had the fog been a warning of an impending disaster? Life in the tannery was hardly pleasant, but she was getting stronger and more resilient. Kassite had said that the Male Elixir would accelerate her transformation, and she could feel it happening with every additional day of hard labor. At the same time, she worried whether the dream had meant that her clear path would soon become foggy, or that her destination might not be a happy one, but a cold and dark place. She hoped that wasn't the case, but what else could the dream foretell?

One hopeful possibility was that the eagle's flight had been cut short by the ringing of the bell, and that the dream's true meaning would have become clear had it continued to its intended conclusion. Where would the eagle have taken her, had she not woken up? Deborah imagined flying out of the chilly fog to a warm, bright place, perhaps the coast of the Great Sea, where she would have rested on the warm sand while the rays of the evening sun soaked her muscular arms and legs—the arms and legs of a boy like Barac or Zariz, a boy on the cusp of manhood.

The days passed quickly as the group went through the liming and scudding, followed by the bating, which was still disgusting but no longer sickening.

One day, after the midday meal, while Deborah and her group were busy washing human waste off the skins in the river, Kassite summoned her.

"Clean up," he said, "and change your shirt." He gave her a fresh sleeveless shirt.

"But my group—"

"Give them instructions and meet me at the gate."

She went back to remind her group to change the water in the five tubs assigned to them. Choosing a spot upriver near Kassite's house, where the water wasn't dirty, she rinsed her face. After a stop at the latrines to change her shirt, she hurried to the gate.

Kassite was already mounted, dressed in his fine coat, wide-brimmed hat, and leather boots. He held the reins of a second horse—a gaunt male with bald spots and yellow teeth. The guards stood by, watching.

They obviously didn't recognize her as the girl who had come here over two months earlier, but they must have been wondering why Kassite needed company today. She hesitated, mindful of her slave shirt, bare feet, and exposed head. How could she leave the tannery like this, while he was dressed as a prosperous free man?

"Come on, boy," Kassite said. "I do not have all day."

Deborah reached up, grabbed the saddle horn, and mounted the horse. She took the reins from Kassite, leaned forward, and patted the bony neck. The old horse followed Kassite up the path to the main road, where a loaded oxcart was waiting for them, its drivers resting in the shade.

7

The oxcart rolled slowly in the direction of Aphek. Kassite sped up, overtaking it. Deborah's horse broke into a healthy gallop, following close behind. After a while, Kassite veered off the road and into a field, raising a cloud of dust. Deborah clung to the saddle, fearful that the old horse would trip and throw her off, but it slowed down and stepped off the road cautiously.

"That was good." She rubbed its neck. "We're going to get along very well."

The horse whinnied.

"Do you have a name? No? Then I'll call you Soosie." The word meant "my horse" in Hebrew, and when the long head rocked up and down, she laughed. "You like the name, don't you? That's it, then. You're Soosie!"

Up ahead, Kassite stopped his horse in the shade of a tree and turned to watch the road. She came up next to him.

"Not bad," he said. "Controlling an unfamiliar horse is not easy."

Deborah shifted in the saddle, and Soosie snorted.

"You ride as well as any young man."

She sat upright, filled with pride.

"Have any of the slaves showed suspicion of you? Looked at you strangely?"

"No, Master."

"Your group members? Any hint of doubts about you being a boy?"

She touched her hair, which had begun to grow back. "None."

"It is easy to deceive people, is it not?"

"Why?"

Kassite chuckled. "Because people do not see what is right in front of them when they expect to see something else—as if there were a sieve between their eyes and their mind that filters out what does not fit their expectations and fills the blanks with what does."

His words made Deborah uncomfortable. Until now, she had been completely preoccupied with her own survival under the pressure of hard labor, physical pain, and the loneliness of keeping the secret of her gender from the others. But his disdain for their gullibility reminded her that pretending to be a boy amounted to deception, which the two of them were perpetrating on the slaves. Her father had said often, "Lying is a sin in the eyes of Yahweh." Kassite, however, gloated at the success of their deception. Was he also proud of lying to her about the Male Elixir? Should she worry that his promise of help was deceitful altogether? Was his true intent to keep her as a slave indefinitely?

"You are doing a fine job with the group," he said. "I have been watching."

"The men obey me only because you told them to. Otherwise, they'd never take orders from a boy of fourteen."

"They would not take orders from a grown man either, unless I told them to."

"How do you do it—control all the slaves without making them afraid?"

"Oh, they are afraid. They are very afraid."

"Of the guards?"

"The guards?" He laughed. "The guards are paid to protect us from marauders who might lust after the women or the leathers."

"Then what are the slaves afraid of? There isn't a single whip in the tannery."

"You do not need to flog a man or cut his flesh to make him afraid. It is enough to convince him that the consequences of disobedience will be unacceptably painful." Kassite gestured at the area around them. "This is what they are afraid of. They are strangers in this land. The Hebrew tribes hate the Philistines even more than they hate each other, and the Canaanites are no better."

"The slaves are afraid you'll let them go?"

"Correct. When I expel a disobedient slave from the tannery, Orran sells him off for work in the fields or the quarry pits, doing hard labor for meager bread and constant whipping. Or worse, rents him out to a rich judge in one of the Hebrew towns, where he will suffer injuries or a violent death." Kassite sighed. "I had to do it a few times early on, but the rest of them learned the lesson. If they work hard and follow my rules, I take care of them—give them food, shelter, and safety—and treat them fairly."

"But they have nothing of their own," she said. "They share sleeping mats, drinking cups, everything. Why don't you let them at least keep a trinket from their home country?"

"If you own nothing, there is nothing for you to fight over."

"And their gods? Why can't they have a small figurine to give them comfort?"

"Gods may give occasional comfort to a person in distress, but they always give everybody plenty of excuses to fight each other. The last thing I need in the tannery is a bunch of competing gods."

Deborah was unsatisfied with his answers. It troubled her that she couldn't understand how he alone controlled over two hundred slaves with such ease.

"It seems cruel, but it is necessary," Kassite said. "Over the past eighteen years, building up a large tannery, I have learned from my mistakes. I know what has to be done and what should never be allowed."

"You made mistakes?"

"Only the dead make no mistakes. A leader makes decisions and takes actions, and therefore cannot avoid some mistakes and failures. The difference is that a weak leader bemoans past mistakes and wallows in failures, whereas a wise leader learns from mistakes and draws strength from failures."

"What's the worst mistake?"

"To allow uncertainty and confusion. Experience has taught me to keep my doubts and ruminations to myself while setting unambiguous rules and clear expectations for my workers. And after all this time, I know what rules they will understand and obey, and what expectations they can meet realistically. That is how I get results from the slaves and respect from my owner."

"But you're still a slave," Deborah said.

Kassite glanced at the road, back where the oxcart would soon come into view. "I am an old man," he said. "The life I have made for myself in the tannery is better than the life most free men would ever dream of achieving. I am content."

"Don't you want to be free again? Go back to Edom?"

He shook his head.

"Your old friend Sallan wants to go home."

In a tree nearby, birds chirped, breaking the silence. Deborah held her breath, dreading his reaction. Back in Emanuel, Sallan—the old Edomite slave who ran the basket factory for Judge Zifron—had confirmed the story Barac had told her about the mythical Elixirist turning men into women. Sallan had also told her that the Elixirist's real name was Kassite, that they had last seen each other eighteen years earlier when they were sold off to different owners, and that the slave dock in Shiloh was the place to begin her search. In return, she had vowed to go back to Emanuel after finding Kassite and help Sallan gain his freedom from the judge's ownership and return to his Edom. When she had actually managed to find Kassite and told him what she had promised Sallan, Kassite became very angry and said, "Sallan was not relying on you to obtain his freedom. He was relying on me." Now, two months later, she watched his face, but saw no anger.

"Sallan has many reasons to return to Edom," Kassite said. "I have none."

The oxcart appeared around the curve, where the road hugged the slopes over the river. It moved slowly, raising only a whiff of dust in its wake.

Deborah waited for him to elaborate.

"It is true, though, that I long to see Sallan again, to embrace my dearest friend and hear his roaring laughter. But having lost one foot and both ears as punishment for trying to flee our original captors, I find escape to be a frightening idea. That is why, when I learned many years ago that Sallan had died, my grief was mixed with relief, because there was no longer a pressing reason for me to escape from this comfortable existence, even if I could."

"But now you know he's alive."

"And I am torn." Kassite prodded his horse to walk back toward the road. "The consequences of an escape could be unacceptably painful."

"That won't happen." Deborah shook the reins, and Soosie followed.

He paused and turned to face her. "What did you say?"

"We won't get caught."

Kassite ruffled his horse's mane. "I am like this horse. I know my place in the hierarchy of power. You, on the other hand, are young and therefore blind to the real complexities of the world."

She wanted to argue, but he stopped her with a hand.

"I admire your determination," he said. "But it is not enough to be determined when reality dictates the results from the outset."

"Yahweh dictates the results," Deborah said. "He's been at my side since the night I escaped Emanuel. How else could I have survived to reach this point?"

"You have been lucky," Kassite said. "Relying on luck in the future, however, would be pure folly. Orran of Manasseh would not sit back and allow me—his source of wealth—to disappear and be gone. He would send his men on fast horses in every direction until they found me and chopped off my good foot so I could no longer run away. I would be back where I belong, a crippled old slave who earns piles of silver coins for his owner."

They stopped their horses at the edge of the field and watched the oxcart proceed slowly up the road. Butterflies flew about, birds fluttered in the trees, and a slow breeze kept down the heat, but the peaceful surroundings did nothing to calm the panic that gripped Deborah's chest. What was he saying? That he wouldn't help her free Sallan? It didn't matter. She would keep her promise to Sallan either way, but would Kassite keep his promise to her?

Taking a deep breath, she asked, "You're still going to give me the rest of the Male Elixir, right?"

"The second dose, yes, when you are ready."

"How long?"

"As long as it takes." Kassite urged his horse forward, but kept his eyes on her.

Deborah kept pace with him. "Not too long, I hope. Sallan is waiting."

They rejoined the road and followed the oxcart slowly. Aphek wasn't far ahead, and the road meandered closer to the river.

"He has been waiting for many years," Kassite said. "A little longer will not make a difference."

"After so much time, the wait could be even harder—"

"He will wait!"

She was taken aback by his snap response.

"Escaping would be suicidal for me," he said, "and disastrous for the workers."

"You mean the slaves?"

"I have a responsibility."

"But you're also a slave."

"For Orran, I am a slave, but not for the men and women in the tannery. Master is what I am for them, all-powerful and benevolent. A father is responsible for his children, do you understand?"

"They are not children."

"Without me, there would be chaos—fighting, raping, rioting—and Orran would send soldiers, slashing with swords and stabbing with spears. If I left, the tannery would become a slaughterhouse!"

His anger did not alarm her this time, for it opened a window into his soul, showing that he was good and noble.

Further up the road, Deborah saw two fishermen out on the river. They stood on a raft, casting a net into the water. It was a small raft, barely big enough to hold the two of them, made of wood beams, stacked against each other and tied with leather straps to a frame of planks. It was crude, but its construction tickled her memory. As the horses paced around a curve in the road, she turned her head back for a last look at the raft, and made the connection.

"Wait!" Deborah turned Soosie and trotted back to the point nearest to the raft in the river. "Look!"

Kassite followed her. "Look at what?"

"The solution to our problem." She shook with excitement. "There it is!"

"What problem?"

"You don't want to abandon the slaves in the tannery because they depend on you for their lives, correct?"

He nodded.

"Back in Emanuel, Sallan told me that powerful men approach every challenge by developing a strategy."

"Did he tell you what the word means?"

"Strategy is what men of power and wealth use for self-preservation. When a situation comes up, they look at all the facts, figure out what they can use for their advantage, and come up with solutions that promote three things: their safety, their fortune, and their power. Strategy is the reason they rule the world, whereas everyone else submits to them, works hard for them, and pays them taxes"

Kassite chuckled. "Have you memorized everything he said?"

"Only what seemed important."

"Sallan is correct, as always. Do you have a strategy?"

"Look at this raft." She pointed. "What does it remind you of?"

He looked for a long moment. "My father took me to the Sea of Reeds once. After he delivered a load of copper to his Egyptian customers, we spent the afternoon fishing. It is a nice memory, one that I often visit in my mind."

"Let me give you a hint. When you sit in your chair at the tannery and look up, what do you see?"

He touched the front edge of the brim of his hat. "I see this."

"No, above the hat."

"The pavilion roof?"

"That's our strategy," Deborah said. "Turn the roofs into rafts, and all the slaves will float downriver across the Coastal Plain, out of Hebrew land, and all the way to safety among their Philistine people."

"Very clever." Kassite looked at her with an expression that bordered on admiration. "You already think like a man."

"Girls aren't stupid."

"It is not a matter of stupidity, but of destiny. Women exist to keep the home—make food, sew clothes, bear children, care for infants. That is why the gods made women fit for domesticated submission—passive, temperamental, small-minded, and anxious. Men, on the other hand, exist to fight and hunt, which is why we are proactive, even-tempered, adventurous, and logical. We think big—traveling far, taking risks, winning battles, conquering."

Deborah knew which of the two paths she wanted to follow: Hunt! Travel! Seek adventure! Win battles and conquer! One day, she would battle Seesya and take back what he'd stolen—Palm Homestead!

As if he could read her mind, Kassite shook a finger at her. "My Male Elixir is working fast—and it is only the first dose."

Deborah shrugged, hiding her pride.

"Tell me the rest of your strategy."

"We'll do it at night," she said. "The slaves will float down the river to Philistia, and you and I will ride to Emanuel. Word of the escape will reach Orran late the next day, but he won't know about the rafts. He'll send his soldiers chasing after two hundred slaves on every road leading from here to Philistia, then in other directions, then into the hills and anywhere else he could think of. Only when his soldiers return empty-handed, Orran might realize what had really happened, but it would be too late to chase the rafts. He might also realize that you had run away to Edom, but it would be too late for that, as well."

"Orran will not wait. He will send soldiers after me as soon as he finds out about the escape."

"Why chase you when the tannery is empty and all the slaves are gone?"

Kassite pointed to his head. "Knowledge is not sold at the slave market."

"Neither is freedom, and finding us on the roads won't be easy."

"It is not only about the risk of getting caught. After all I have done to build the tannery, how could I destroy it?"

She stared at him in disbelief.

"I know," Kassite said. "The tannery is not mine. Why should I care if nothing is left of it? Still, your plan is deficient because, as you said before, a rich man always comes up with a strategy to meet his selfish goals, and Orran is very rich. I know because I made him so. He will send soldiers after me as soon as word reaches him about the escape."

Deborah thought for a moment. "Not if he believes the slaves killed you before escaping."

Kassite laughed. "You are truly devious, young woman."

"Young man, not woman."

They came around another bend in the road, and Aphek appeared up ahead. From this vantage point, the city looked grand and imposing, rising over the riverhead and the narrow gorge. The walls were tall and massive, and a giant palace with its own fortification walls and guard towers dominated the center of the city. Deborah noticed that the whole roof of the palace had caved in, and that a wing had collapsed, the remains charred by a fire.

Deborah pointed. "What happened to the palace?"

"It has been like that for many years," Kassite said. "The Egyptian governor used to reside here until the Great Famine, maybe twenty or thirty years ago."

"The Egyptians ruled here?"

"The pharaohs ruled this region for many centuries, but now they have their own problems with the Philistines and other sea people. In fact, we are riding on a road the ancient pharaohs built. They called it The Sea Highway." Kassite turned his horse around. "If you ride back down the road, past the tannery, south to Gaza and the shores of the Great Sea, and west along the edge of the Sinai Desert, you will eventually reach the great Nile River and the pyramids."

"I'd like to see the pyramids one day."

"Maybe you will." He turned his horse back in the direction of Aphek. "Riding north, past the river gorge, the road goes through the land of Manasseh all the way to Megiddo and Hazor, where the Canaanite king, Javin, rules over the other Hebrew tribes with an iron fist. From there, you could circle the Sea of Galilee and travel up to the great mountains of Lebanon, where cedar trees grow taller than ten houses stacked up one on top of the other. All of it was once under the mighty Egyptians. No king could stand up to their power, and no nation could resist being subjugated to the pharaoh."

"Except for your nation, because you helped the king of Edom defeat the Egyptians by turning the women into soldiers."

Kassite stabbed his knees into the horse's ribs and sped up. Deborah prodded Soosie and caught up with him.

"Let me tell you a rule to remember," he said over the noise of the trotting horses. "Winning one battle does not ensure a lasting freedom. You have to win every battle, again and again, for as long as you wish to remain free."

They rode up the last section of the road, passing through the checkpoint at the gorge, where the guards waved them through. Kassite's words replayed in her mind. Deborah sensed that he had spoken not only about the battle won by the women of Edom, but also about his own experience of a lost freedom and a long slavery, as well as about her struggle for freedom from Seesya, the house of Zifron, and the curse of womanhood. *You have to win every battle, again and again, for as long as you wish to remain free.*

8

The fairgrounds near the gates of Aphek had not changed since Deborah had passed through during her search for Kassite, but she had changed. Walking through the busy marketplace behind Kassite and the oxcart, leading Soosie by the reins, she felt strong and confident, even though her feet were bare, her body was clad in a slave's long shirt, and her cropped hair was exposed. She looked around curiously as dozens of vendors peddled their wares to shoppers, who were dressed in a variety of fashions and spoke various languages.

Orran of Manasseh's large shop was filled with customers. The oxcart drivers unloaded the products, and the man at the desk gave Kassite a bulging purse.

Deborah followed Kassite as he visited several vendors, who invariably welcomed him with big smiles and deep bows. He bought bags of flour and barley, jars of wine, honey, and olive oil, as well as large baskets filled with dates, figs, pomegranates, lemons, and carobs.

Outside the fairgrounds, the oxcart drivers stopped in the shade of a tree to secure all the goods with ropes. Kassite limped to the edge of a steep slope overlooking the head of the river.

Fed by the springs at the foot of the Samariah Hills, the fast current of the Yarkon River gushed through the narrow gorge below. Several Hebrew boys were shooting stones with slings off the edge of the steep slope. Only the tallest among them managed to shoot close to the opposite bank. Kassite engaged the tall boy in a brief conversation and gave him a silver coin in exchange for the sling.

Kassite waved Deborah over, handed her the sling, and said to the boy, "Show my slave how to use it."

"Slaves aren't allowed to use weapons."

"Use it?" Kassite chuckled, shaking his head. "I just want him to know how it works so he can start making slings for me in my tannery."

Deborah examined the sling. It was a simple weapon, with an open leather pouch about the size of a hand. At each end of the pouch was a cord as long as her arm, which made the whole sling more than twice the length of her arm. The cords were woven of plaited flax or some other twine. One cord ended in a loop, and the other terminated in a leather tab.

The tall boy borrowed a sling from one of his friends. He threaded the two middle fingers of his right hand in the loop, bending them to prevent the loop from slipping away, and held the tab between the forefinger and the thumb of the same hand. The pouch dangled below. With his left hand he picked up a stone and set it in the pouch. The weight of the stone held down the pouch, causing the cords to straighten. He suspended the sling under his right hand, the pouch hanging down by his leg, almost touching the ground.

"First, you test the weight of the stone." He swung the pouch gently back and forth like a pendulum. "Then you make sure no idiot is standing too close behind you."

His friends sniggered and fell back.

"I will give you another coin," Kassite said, "if you can reach the other side."

The boy accepted the challenge with a quick nod. He leaned forward slightly, gazed at the opposite bank of the river, and rotated his arm. At the top of the second rotation, he let go of the tab, which released one cord, allowing the stone to fly out of the pouch. It soared in a perfect arch over the river and landed in the shallow water near the bank.

His friends groaned with disappointment.

"Go on, Borah," Kassite said to Deborah "Your turn."

She had watched the tall boy and memorized what he had done. Now she repeated the same steps. Hooking two fingers in the loop, she pressed the tab between her forefinger and thumb, placed a stone in the pouch, and let it dangle down freely. She leaned forward, gazed at the opposite side of the river, rotated her arm once and, as the stone reached the apex halfway through the second rotation, let go of the tab.

Her stone came out too late, flew downward, and fell into the rushing water at the bottom of the slope, about forty steps below where they stood.

The Hebrew boys laughed, and one of them yelled, "He can't do it."

"He throws like a girl," said another.

The tall boy grinned. "What do you want? He's a stupid slave."

Her face burning, Deborah turned to leave.

"Try again," Kassite said, pulling a coin from his purse and holding it up. "Go ahead."

The boy searched the ground, selected a stone, and set it in the sling. His shot, however, was only slightly better than his first, hitting the edge of the water on the opposite side. The other boys shouted with exaggerated disappointment.

Deborah took her time to find a stone that was slightly larger and rounder than the previous one. She repeated the steps methodically, including the one step she had missed in the first attempt—swinging the pouch slightly back and forth to test the weight of the stone. She knew how to throw a stone by hand better than most boys, and the sling, she realized, had the effect of extending her arm to double its length and, therefore, double the power. Her mistake had been to release the tab too late. She would not repeat it.

The Hebrew boys quieted down, watching her.

Deborah chose a spot on the other side of the river, where the tip of a boulder showed through the grass on the opposite slope.

"What's he waiting for?" The tall boy snorted. "Let it splash, slave!"

She focused her gaze on the tip of the boulder and imagined that it was the head of the tall boy. She rotated the sling once, and on the second rotation released the tab just before the stone reached the apex.

It flew in a long arch, over the water, and pounded the slope near the tip of the boulder.

The boys were stunned, but Kassite laughed and clapped his hands.

"Great shot," one of the boys said.

Another one poked the tall boy. "He's better than you."

"Ouch," a third boy said. "Beaten by a dirty slave."

"Dirty and smelly," the tall boy said. "Time for a bath!" He stuck his leg in front of Deborah and shoved her.

She fell forward and rolled down the steep slope, gaining speed. She groped for a rock or a shrub, but caught nothing that could stop her. She landed in the water. It was shockingly cold, and she swallowed a mouthful before her feet found the bottom. She kicked hard, and her head popped out of the water. Coughing badly, she tried to stand, but the swift current toppled her. She was underwater again, but this time she managed to keep her mouth shut.

When she came up again, slapping the water desperately, the sling was still in her right hand. The rushing water swept her downriver, indifferent to her frantic struggle. Coughing hard again, she saw the riverbank only a few steps away, but she didn't know how to swim, and her feet couldn't reach the bottom.

The current flipped her over, her face down in the water, then turned her back up again. From the corner of her eye she caught sight of Soosie, sprinting along the top of the slope. She managed to inhale and tried to yell, but the water flipped her over again and kept her down. She held her breath, kicked, and flailed her arms, but the water held on tightly, cold and uncaring. She begged Yahweh to help her as the yearning for air grew more and more intense. She wanted to open her mouth, but knew that breathing in would not bring air and relief, but water and death.

At last, she saw her parents' faces, glowing with kindness and love, and she started to open her mouth to let the water in, but a glimpse of Barac's face came to her—not dead, as she had imagined him since Seesya had bragged about playing ball with Barac's head, but very much alive, his brown eyes wide with alarm, his mouth closed, lips pressed together as if telling her to do the same.

With a final burst of frenzied kicking, Deborah managed to raise her head above water, but only halfway, not enough to take a breath. To the right, through the mist of water over her eyes, she saw the blurred vision of a horse splashing into the river. The current pulled her down again with a force she couldn't resist. As her face went below the surface, she bent her right arm and straightened it to pitch the tab-end of the sling toward the riverbank while her fingers remained hooked in the opposite, loop-end of the sling.

The river sucked her deeper, and she held out her right arm, wishing it to grow longer.

Nothing happened. Darkness engulfed her.

The sling tugged at her bent fingers.

She kept her grip.

Another tug, as slight as the first.

Was she imagining it?

A third tug, this one harder, then another, violent, trying to yank the sling away. Her two fingers hurt as the leather loop cut through them, but she refused to let go. Her whole arm twisted, threatening to tear out of her shoulder. She held on against the unrelenting force of the water. A moment later, her head popped above the surface and she inhaled, her tight throat producing a thin shriek.

Soosie, in the water up to his chest, his teeth clenched on the other end of the sling, dragged her toward the shore. Her feet found the bottom, but Soosie continued to pull her up the riverbank and out of the water.

Deborah coughed hard, spitting water and bile. She began to tremble.

Kassite arrived and covered her with his coat.

The trembling made her teeth chatter, and she continued to cough, her throat burning. She felt Soosie licking her face.

"One thing is obvious," Kassite said. "Even the horse is smitten with you."

Soosie whinnied.

9

That night, Deborah slept with the sling tied around her waist, the cords knotted at her belly button and the pouch flat against the small of her back. Personal possessions were strictly forbidden, but after her brush with death at the river earlier, Kassite said nothing when she secured the sling under her wet shirt.

In the morning, when the bell woke her up, Deborah expected him to summon her, but he didn't even look in her direction before returning to his house. She went to wash her face in the river and lingered there, glancing at the short bridge that connected the riverbank to his front door, hoping he would reappear.

There was only so much face-washing she could do while everyone started working. Her group was already at the tubs, where the hides had soaked in fresh water overnight. It was time to proceed to pickling.

She had noticed that two of the men, Antippet and Patrees, always ate together and slept beside one another. Deborah wondered if they were brothers. Taking an opportunity to let them work as a team, she sent them to fetch the salt.

The group pulled the hides out of the water, covered them with salt and pegged them to the inside of the perimeter fence to dry. The work continued until the bell rang for the morning meal.

Deborah took her food and bowed to Kassite. He nodded and turned to the next slave in line. Disappointed, she sat under the pavilion and ate.

The same thing happened at the midday meal, except that she no longer felt slighted. Kassite knew that she hid the sling under her shirt in violation of his rules, and his silence was a form of recognition, even of respect. Soon, he would declare her ready for the second dose of the Male Elixir.

After all the slaves had received their meals and bowed to Kassite, he limped to the gate, had his horse brought up, and rode off alone in the direction of Aphek.

They worked until sunset. In Kassite's absence, one of his servants rang the bell for the evening meal and returned to the house on the river.

Each slave carried his food and cup of hot drink to the pavilion, bowed to Kassite's empty chair, and sat on the ground to eat. When the men were done, the women came over to collect their meals.

In the twilight, Deborah noticed many of them glance at the gate, which remained closed. She understood their anxiety. The last time Kassite had been late to return was the day Seesya and his soldiers raided the tannery.

The slaves sipped their hot drinks and conversed in hushed voices. They went to wash the cups in the river and returned them to the storage area. Darkness descended, and a torch was lit at each of the two pavilions. Some slaves lay down to sleep, and Deborah did the same. Many others remained awake, including her group of Edomite slaves. They sat outside the pavilion, chatted, and sang melancholy songs.

Finally, when sleep continued to elude her, Deborah went over to where the men of her group were sitting.

"We have to work tomorrow," she said. "Get your mats and go to sleep."

No one moved.

Nearby, a slave she didn't know said, "Go away, boy."

"It's late," she said. "Time for sleep."

"Who are you to give orders?"

"That's right," another one yelled. "Shut up and wait for Master to return!"

Many voiced their agreement.

She looked at Antippet and Patrees. "Get your mats and go to sleep."

The first protester got up and advanced toward her. He was short and stout, and spoke with a heavy Philistine accent. "Sit down, boy, or I'll knock you down!"

Antippet and Patrees stood quickly and faced him.

The other Philistine slaves got up, the rest of her Edomite group joined Antippet and Patrees, and everyone clenched their fists, ready to fight. The flickering lights from torches made the men seem even more menacing.

She felt her knees buckle, and a familiar choking sensation rose in her throat. What had Zariz said about that? "Listen to your fear, but don't let it control you."

Taking a deep breath, Deborah stepped forward, bypassing her group of Edomite protectors, and faced the mob of angry Philistine slaves. "Master forbids fighting," she said with a voice as deep and as commanding as she could manage. "Master set up a routine for us. After dinner, we go to sleep. Master expects it!"

Her adversaries grumbled in protest.

"Master will punish you," she declared with feigned confidence. "He'll send you to Aphek to be sold off!"

They quieted down, but the first Philistine slave to protest, who now stood at the head of the men, yelled, "Who is this boy?"

"You!" Deborah pointed at him. "You'll be the first to go!"

He laughed, but it rang hollow.

Antippet and Patrees walked to the pile of straw mats. The rest of her group did the same, and she saw Petro leave the group of Philistine slaves and walk over to collect a mat. The others gradually followed, and everyone settled down to sleep.

Deborah waited until the last slave was lying down quietly. Soon, no one was awake. She lay down, closed her eyes, and listened to the usual sounds of snoring, grunting, and passing gas. The confrontation with the slaves replayed in her mind. Why had she spoken up? Why had she taken such a risk, knowing that Kassite was not there to defend her? She recalled the Philistine slaves shouting at her, their fists clenched, their faces twisted in anger as they advanced, eager for violence.

Her legs began to tremble. She hugged her knees to her chest, taking deep breaths, trying to stop the shaking, but the battle was lost, and her whole body shook uncontrollably. Her eyes filled with tears and, despite her efforts, she broke down and sobbed, her face buried in the crook of her arm for fear of waking up the men lying beside her. She tried to push away the memory of the angry confrontation and think of the future, of leaving this harsh place as a young man, free and strong. It won't be long, she told herself, remembering the quote from the High Priest: "When you pursue your True Calling, God provides the shortcuts."

Her sobs waned, and she wiped her face with the tail of the long shirt.

An odd tapping noise came from outside the canopy.

She sat up and looked around, trying to locate the source of the sound. The tapping was slow at first, but sped up quickly.

Rain!

She went to the edge of the pavilion and stuck her hands out with the palms turned up to catch the drops. The rain grew heavier. She stepped out from under the thatched roof and raised her face to the torrent of fresh drops, letting the water run down her face and body and wash away the layer of dust and grime. It hadn't rained since before Tamar's stoning, and the air filled with the biting aroma of a first rain.

Completely soaked, Deborah stepped back under the pavilion. She brushed the water off her face and short hair, shook the long shirt, which stuck to her body, and stood silently, watching the downpour.

The heavy rain blurred the opposite side of the tannery, and the torch at the end of the women's pavilion was reduced to a hazy point of light in the darkness.

Back on the sleeping mat, the moist fragrance reminded her of better days. Lying on her side, she rested her head on her folded arm and conjured images of Tamar and their parents, of happy times together at Palm Homestead. Deborah imagined that she was back there, among the loving family she'd once had.

10

The pain woke Deborah woke up. She rubbed her lower abdomen, trying to decide whether to hurry to the latrine. It was still dark. The path to the latrine would be slippery after the rain. She changed position, and the pain eased up. Around her, everyone was asleep. Unlike most nights, which were hot and humid, a cool breeze carried the scents of soggy earth and wet vegetation.

The pain worsened, and she sat up in alarm. She felt dampness between her legs. Her first thought was that her undergarments hadn't yet dried from the rain, but when she touched the dampness and held her fingers up to the dim torchlight, she saw blood.

Deborah groaned, not because of the physical pain, but because of the crushing disappointment. She recalled Seesya touching his saddle and holding up his hand, red in the light from the torches, his voice mocking: "Look at this! From a stupid girl to a stupid woman!" She had hoped that the first dose of the Male Elixir would not only accelerate the growth of her muscles and physical resilience, which it had done successfully, but also cause her body to shut down that single most explicit manifestation of womanhood.

This is the last time, Deborah told herself. Never again!

With the long shirt bunched up between her legs, she tiptoed through the tight mass of sleeping men, careful not to step on anyone. The infirmary was upstream, just beyond Kassite's house, but halfway there, the pain made her stop. Bent over, she pressed on the area where the pain centered and waited for it to ease. Meanwhile, she considered what to tell the two women in charge of the infirmary. As groggy as they might be, waking up suddenly in the middle of the night, would they miss the real cause of her bleeding?

She changed direction and went to the river. Stepping into the water up to her thighs, Deborah shuddered from the cold. Everyone was asleep, but there was always a risk that one of the slaves would get up to relieve himself, which at night most did at the river's edge rather than risk the walk to the latrines. She quickly removed her undergarment, rinsed it well, and cleaned her private parts as best she could.

With her wet undergarment back on, she stepped out of the water. Going back to sleep was tempting, but if she bled again and one of the slaves noticed it, the result would be nothing short of disastrous.

Kassite's house was dark. Deborah stepped from the muddy riverbank onto the short bridge, which swayed and squeaked.

She knocked on the door, and one of the servants opened it, holding a small oil lamp. He wore only a loincloth, and his smooth chest was ghostly white.

She cleared her throat. "I need help."

He showed her in, closed the door, and went to the bedroom.

A moment later, Kassite appeared.

Deborah was filled with relief. "You're back!"

"Barely." He hopped on one leg, supported by the servant, and sat in a chair. Under the bottom of his robe, his left leg ended above the ankle. "This is an odd time for a visit."

"I had no choice."

"What is it?"

Deborah pointed at her crotch. "I'm bleeding."

"Ah. Your female side is fighting back."

"I was hoping it wouldn't happen with the first dose already working in my body."

"At least we know for sure that you are not pregnant."

Her face flushed. "That would be impossible."

"There." He pointed at a cabinet. "Take one of my servants' loincloths. The female slaves use a similar thing."

She opened the cabinet door. Folded clothing items were neatly arranged, including at least twenty linen loincloths.

"Put it on as flat as possible," he said. "And make sure your long shirt fits over it normally."

With her back to him, she lifted her long shirt, lowered her wet undergarment, and tied up the loincloth.

When she turned back, he was watching her.

"I like the way your thighs look," he said. "Come closer to me."

She shook the long shirt to loosen it off her wet body and stepped toward him.

Kassite leaned forward and reached for her.

She jumped back.

"Do not flatter yourself." He chuckled. "I have all the flesh I desire, and there are plenty more who would rejoice at the opportunity."

Embarrassed, Deborah stepped closer.

Pressing her thighs and biceps, exposed by the sleeveless shirt, he nodded in approval. "You are getting stronger. Show me your hands."

She did.

He touched the rough skin that had grown over the blisters and nodded in approval. He pointed at her feet, and she lifted each one to show him the soles, which had thickened and become black.

"Very good," he said.

"The women at the infirmary helped me with the blisters, but I couldn't go to them with my female bleeding."

"You are changing faster than I anticipated."

"It's been many weeks since I drank the first dose."

"And it is working perfectly."

Deborah stopped herself from asking again when he would give her the second dose. Appearing too eager, she feared, would show femininity and make him think she wasn't ready yet.

"Give me the sling," he said. "I want the craftswomen to make a few copies."

She reached under her long shirt, untied the knot, and gave him the sling.

"Your shooting match against the Hebrew boy was impressive, both in distance and in accuracy. It exceeded my expectations."

"A lucky shot," she said.

Kassite shook his head. "Nothing to do with luck. It showed that you have the capacity to become a killer when necessary."

"A killer?" Deborah took a step back. "I'm not a killer."

"When circumstances force a choice between getting killed and becoming a killer, most men fall apart, beg for their lives, or start weeping like children, whereas the truly brave harden up with firm resolve, total focus, and icy determination to kill."

"I'm not a killer," she repeated.

"When you looked at the tip of that boulder on the other side of the river, what did you imagine seeing?"

She lowered her eyes.

"You imagined the head of the Hebrew boy, did you not?"

Deborah nodded, embarrassed.

"Elixir-making," Kassite said, "is not only about mixing exotic ingredients. It is about knowing human nature, seeing what is in a person's heart, and identifying their true desires. Do you understand?"

The Elixirist in him was speaking now, not the old slave who had managed to carve himself a comfortable life amidst the misery of a tannery. She was trying to comprehend what he meant. Was he able to see what was in her heart? Did he know what she was thinking? Could he tell that she doubted his honesty and questioned the value of his promise to help her?

"No shame in justified rage," Kassite said. "That boy's mockery was foul, and you wanted to kill him. In your head, he became the target. Correct?"

"Yes, I imagined his head where the boulder was, but only to help me focus my anger. I would never shoot a stone at a boy for real."

"You have it in you, girl." He chuckled. "Don't forget this experience. Deadly focus is a rare quality, even among men, most of whom are mere shadows of masculinity."

"Obviously, I'm not a man." She gestured at her crotch. "And I'll need a fresh loincloth in a few hours."

"After the morning meal, come in and put on a clean one."

"Here? At your house? During daylight?"

"The time for caution is over. We will be leaving this place very soon."

Deborah was already at the door, but his words stopped her. Had she heard him correctly? Turning back to face Kassite, she saw his expression and knew he wasn't joking.

"What changed your mind?"

He rose slowly, leaning on the table for support. "Orran changed my mind."

"You went to Orran?"

"He is my benevolent owner. After eighteen years of loyal service, having built for him a great tannery and much wealth, I naively hoped that gratitude would make him grant my wish."

"What wish?"

"I traveled to his homestead, north of the city, and asked him to let me go home to Edom and spend my few remaining years among my people. I promised to train a new master, of course, and make sure the tannery continued to work smoothly. It is a reasonable request, is it not?"

"What did he say?"

"He laughed."

"That's it?"

"There was an explicit warning, too. Look here."

Kassite pointed at his right leg, above the ankle, where the skin was scraped off in a tidy circle all around the leg. It looked like a moist red ring, and when Kassite put his legs next to each other, she could see that the ring marked his good leg at the same height where his left leg had been amputated.

Deborah gulped, shocked by the sheer cruelty of it. "I don't understand," she said. "Also with Sallan. Why would an owner maim a good slave, or a horse, or a cow?"

"Or a woman."

"Yes," Deborah said. "A woman, too."

"Remember strategy?" Kassite said. "A slave who can read and write, add and subtract, buy and sell, and manage the workers in a factory, doesn't need good feet. In fact, they can get in the way of obedience by enabling an escape. For a rich owner, it would be good strategy to chop off the feet of such a valuable slave.

11

Deborah and her group worked for two hours before Kassite rang for the morning meal. It was enough time for them to salt another batch of hides and peg them up on the inside of the perimeter fence. She was puzzled to see female slaves come out of their curtained pavilion and take down many hides that were clearly not dry yet, especially after last-night's rain. The women took the hides into their pavilion. Deborah wondered what they were doing there, and why.

She collected her meal and bowed before Kassite.

"Good morning, Borah. Are you well?"

"Yes, Master. The pain is gone."

"Excellent. Are you ready?"

"Ready?"

He held up a wooden goblet.

It took her a moment to digest this unexpected surprise. "Yes! I'm ready!"

Kassite handed her the goblet.

It smelled of rotten eggs and spoiled meat, but it didn't repulse her as the first dose had. She pulled back her shoulders and stood straight as a proud young man. By giving her the second dose of the Male Elixir, Kassite was implying that she had completed the first of the three phases of transformation: "Building the physical strength of a boy means not only growing muscles, but also developing resilience, tolerance for pain, and capacity for hard labor." Now it was time for the second phase—developing a masculine character. She again recalled Kassite's words: "You will have to change your character from the passive, temperamental, small-minded, and anxious female to the superior male character, which is proactive, even-tempered, adventurous, and logical."

"Go on," he said. "Drink it."

Right there, with other slaves watching curiously, she tilted the cup and drank all its content.

The second dose was thicker than the first one and tasted even worse. It contained floating chunks of unidentifiable origin, which were hard to swallow and left a sticky coating on the inside of her mouth. The odor now resided in her palate, filling her nostrils from within. She gulped, and some of the elixir came back up, making her gag, but she swallowed and kept it down.

Sitting under the pavilion with her meal, Deborah ignored the slaves' curious glances, sipped water, and took small bites of food, which calmed her stomach.

After the meal, she went to Kassite's house, put on a clean loincloth, and tossed the blood-soaked one through the window into the river. She hoped that this was the last time she would experience female bleeding. Once she completed the second phase and satisfied Kassite that her character had transformed, as well, he would prepare the third and last dose of the Male Elixir, which would cause her private parts to actually change, propelling her over the final barrier into a complete male in every respect. Though she had never seen a naked man, she assumed it couldn't be much different from that of male animals. The idea of growing a male organ made her cringe, but it was a price worth paying for a life of freedom and independence that Hebrew men took for granted.

Work continued as usual for the men, but the women remained inside their curtained pavilion. After the midday meal, as Deborah's group returned to work, Kassite summoned her. Seated on his chair in the empty pavilion, he gave her the original sling back, as well as six identical new slings.

"Teach your group how to use these." He pointed at the riverbank. "Shoot out over the water."

"Yes, Master." She took the slings. "May I ask a question?"

Kassite nodded.

"What about the rule against slaves and weapons?"

"Girls and weapons, too, yet here you are." He chuckled. "You must make up your mind about rules, one way or the other. Do you prefer conforming or rebelling?"

Deborah didn't know how to answer.

"Questioning, I guess, is what you prefer most." Kassite patted her shoulder. "Here is why I would like you to teach your group to shoot. Antippet, Patrees, and the other four are Edomite men, like me. They cannot escape with the rest of the slaves to Philistia—it would be worse there than here for them. They are strong and loyal men who will be useful on the journey to free Sallan and then on to our homeland."

"Do you have a plan for freeing Sallan?"

"I am working on it. Go teach them the art of the sling. Our lives may depend on it."

Deborah glanced at the gate. "What about the guards?"

"They are busy with a barrel of good wine I gave them. The potent herbs I mixed in will soon put them to sleep, blessed with the sweetest of dreams."

She laughed, wondering what kind of herbs would cause grown men to fall asleep and have sweet dreams. Then again, Kassite was the Elixirist, and if he could turn women into men, surely he could put men to sleep and give them sweet dreams.

Deborah paused at the door. "We still have a few hides to wash and pickle. Left in the tub, they'll be ruined."

"You are worried about ruining a few animal skins?" Kassite opened his arms wide. "This whole place will be ruined tonight."

His words kept ringing in her ears as she gathered her group at the water's edge and demonstrated shooting the sling. The Edomite slaves were hesitant at first, watching Deborah with awe as she rotated the sling and shot a few stones over the water. They kept glancing toward Kassite, who was busy giving instructions to a group of women slaves near their pavilion. Deborah passed out the new slings and showed each man how to hold the tab and loop, size up a stone to fit in the pouch, and prepare to shoot.

They started practicing. Once they overcame their initial hesitation, they proved to be enthusiastic students, quickly improving their skills. Antippet and Patrees competed with each other, and their stones hit the water at close increments, gradually reaching further. Meanwhile, Deborah improved her own skills with repeated shots until her stones flew in perfect arcs over the whole width of the river, landing on the opposite bank, over two hundred steps away.

The other groups of slaves, working at the tubs or scraping hides on the ground, paused to watch. With the sun descending, many of the men left their work and wandered closer to Deborah and the six Edomite men, who kept picking up stones and shooting them over the water.

Satisfied that she could reach the other side every time, Deborah began to work on her aim. She selected a large mound of sand as a target. When her shots landed there consistently, she chose a smaller target—a tree stump at the edge of the vegetation above the opposite riverbank. She missed it four times, and by then everyone was watching her, having figured out what she was trying to do.

Finding herself at the center of attention, Deborah wanted to stop, but Antippet was ready with a stone for her, holding it forth with a grin that contained equal parts glee and encouragement.

She shook her head, but he insisted.

"Take it, boy," he said. "Maybe you will get lucky now."

The word "boy" grated on her. It was the first time any of the Edomite slaves in her group had shown her disrespect.

Deborah took the stone and set it in the pouch. She stepped to the edge of the water, hooked two fingers in the loop, and grasped the tab between her forefinger and thumb. The weight of the stone pulled down the pouch, which swung gently by her ankle. Her eyes found the tree stump on the opposite side of the river. She tried to concentrate, but couldn't ignore the murmuring of the hundred set of eyes focused on her back. Her body tensed, and she struggled to take a deep breath. There was no way she could hit the small target she had foolishly chosen. In fact, she doubted her ability to shoot this stone across the river.

A few of the men cackled and made derisive comments in the Philistine language. Anger bubbled up inside her, and she recalled the Hebrew boys at Aphek, calling her a "dirty slave." She had beaten the tall Hebrew boy, and she could do the same now.

Leaning forward, Deborah focused on the tree stump, conjuring the tall boy's face from memory. It was a vague image, perhaps because there wasn't enough rage left in her against that boy. And as she stared hard at the tree stump, Seesya's face started to emerge, framed by oily black hair that went down to his shoulders. His lips were severed diagonally by the red scar, giving him a permanent ugly smirk, and she could hear his voice, slick with venom, when he had shown her Barac's knife and said, "My soldiers took it from your friend, Abinoam's boy, before we chopped off his head and kicked it around like a ball."

Her fury exploded in a burning, hate-filled determination to kill Seesya, right there and then. The sling whistled as it sliced through the air by her ear, rotating one and a half times. The stone shot out from the pouch, flew over the river, and hit Seesya's face, which disappeared as the dry tree stump exploded into many small pieces.

The slaves cheered, and the Edomite group surrounded her, laughing and pounding her back. She managed a smile as her mind struggled to clear away the fog of murderous rage, which slowly faded, leaving her weak and slightly nauseated.

Kassite limped over from the pavilion. "That was an impressive shot," he said. "You are an exceptional—"

"Boy," she interrupted, afraid he'd say "girl."

"Exactly," he said. "An exceptional young man."

"Thank you, Master."

He paced up the riverbank, leading her away from the others, and asked, "Whose face did you imagine as your target this time?"

"Seesya, son of Judge Zifron." Deborah felt her anger heat up again. "He had my sister stoned to death soon after marrying her, and later, he boasted of murdering my friend Barac and kicking his head like a ball!"

Kassite put a finger across his lips, hushing her.

"I'm sorry, Master," she said, more quietly, "but the thought of him makes me furious and I can't control it."

"Controlling your rage is wasteful."

"Why?"

"Rage is a very useful thing to have."

"I don't understand."

Kassite looked out over the water, taking his time to choose his words. "Rage is like a mighty stallion, an explosive force of nature. If you fail to tame it, the result can be deadly, but if you harness it wisely, it will carry you over the highest peaks, trample your enemies to oblivion, and deliver you through the toughest battles, all the way to the ultimate victory your heart desires."

The sun touched the horizon far down the river, the reddish glow reflecting on the surface of the water. Kassite rang the bell, and the slaves lined up for the evening meal. The men ate under their pavilion while the women took their food back to their curtained pavilion. Everyone ate quietly, watching Kassite with tense anticipation.

Immediately after the meal, Kassite summoned the group leaders, including Deborah, and told them that everyone would be leaving the tannery for good this night. He didn't provide an explanation or take questions, but proceeded to assign tasks to each group, except Deborah's. He nominated Petro to lead the two rafts down the river to the coastal territory of the Philistines.

When the group leaders went back to inform the men and women of the plan, Deborah expected cheers or cries of shock, but the group leaders allowed none of it and put their subordinates to work promptly.

Kassite sent Deborah with her six Edomite group members to tie up the sleeping guards. "Don't harm them," he said.

The eight guards were lying on the ground under a big tree near the livestock corral, snoring loudly. An empty barrel of wine lay on its side. Their leather armor, swords, and spears were on the ground nearby. The Edomite slaves gagged the first guard before he could raise the alarm, tied him up, and blindfolded him. They did the same with each of the other seven guards, dragged all of them into the livestock corral, and placed them on the ground in the middle, surrounded by the animals.

Deborah found the old horse she had ridden to Aphek. "How are you, Soosie?"

The horse licked her face, making her laugh, and followed her into the tannery. She found a piece of bread by the oven. "Here you go," she said. "I'll see you in a little while."

The Edomite slaves led the other seven horses, as well as one goat, into the tannery and closed the gate. Deborah, meanwhile, went to Kassite's house. When she took off the loincloth, it was clean. Her female bleeding was over, and not a moment too soon.

Under the light of torches, the slaves knocked down the stone columns that supported the roof of their pavilion. They stripped the thatched top and cleaned the beams until the whole roof looked like a giant raft, fifty steps by twenty. Kassite directed them to attach additional crossbeams and planks, fortifying the structure to keep it from buckling. The horses were fitted with harnesses and ropes and dragged the roof into the water. Everyone held their breath, and when the roof stayed afloat, they cheered.

At the women's pavilion, the female slaves took down the side curtains and cut them into pieces, which they adjusted as makeshift robes over their long shirts. They had spent the day fabricating sandals for everyone, as well as coats and hats for the men, using hides taken down from the fence. None of it was refined, considering the unfinished tanning process and the speed with which the women had made everything, but it was enough to help everyone resemble free men and women.

For Kassite's two servants, Deborah, and the six Edomite slaves, the women had made sets of leather armor and boots.

The slaves toppled the women's pavilion, stripped the thatch from the roof, and strengthened it with additional crossbeams and planks. With men and horses pulling together, the second raft was soon in the water, secured to the first one with ropes. Kassite directed the men to bring food from the storage area near the gate and load it onto the rafts. The two women from the infirmary packed up their jars and bottles of potions and ointments, as well as bandages and cots for the injured men currently lying there. A group of slaves carried everything to the rafts.

Late into the night, the work was finished and the rafts were ready. The slaves lined up at the riverbank. Kassite's chair was brought over, and he sat down with a purse in his lap. Each slave bowed before him, accepted a silver coin, and boarded the rafts. Many wept softly as they sat down for the journey. Deborah understood why they cried. It wasn't sorrow or regret, for they were clearly happy to go free, but the sadness of separation from Kassite, who had been like a father to them—strict and demanding, yet fair and generous. Within the world of the tannery, despite the hard work and rough conditions, each one of the slaves knew that Kassite, in his own way, loved them.

Petro waited until all the men and women had boarded the rafts. Rather than bow, Petro knelt before Kassite and kissed his hand.

"Thank you, Master," he said in a broken voice.

Kassite helped him to his feet. "May the gods watch over you until you reach safety."

With Petro standing at the front of the lead raft, a few men took positions at the corners of the rafts and used long planks to push off in the shallow water.

Kassite limped to the water's edge.

The rafts moved very slowly toward the middle of the dark river. Seated shoulder to shoulder, the men and women stared at the shore, their eyes on the tall man with the wide-brimmed hat and bushy white hair, his hand held up for a last farewell.

Soon, the current took hold of the rafts, and they headed downriver, away from the light of the torches, into complete darkness.

12

Deborah followed Kassite, his two servants, and the goat to his house.
The servants helped Kassite take off his coat and hat. They spread the
coat on the bed and stabbed it with a knife in many places. They cut off
several locks of his white hair, placed them in his hat, and laid it down
on the bed with the coat. One of the servants held the goat above the
bed, the other one sliced its neck, and the blood poured all over the
perforated coat, the hat, and the locks of hair. When the blood ran out,
the servant threw the goat into the river.

Kassite put on a new leather coat, which reached below his knees,
and a white leather hat. He bowed before the copper effigy of Qoz and
murmured a prayer. With a last look around the house, which had been
his home for many years, Kassite sighed and limped outside. Deborah
could hear the bridge creaking under his weight.

One of the servants wrapped Qoz in a rag and carried it outside.
Deborah collected her sack, which had been at Kassite's house since she
arrived at the tannery, and reached into it. She took out her father's fire-
starters and pressed one stone to each of her cheeks. Standing at the
window, looking out at the dark water, she drew strength from the
stones and the memories they carried.

When she went outside, the Edomite slaves were changing into
leather armor that covered their chests, backs, and hips. They donned
leather helmets, strapped on the guards' short swords, and tied the
spears and shields to the saddles.

Similar outfits awaited Deborah and Kassite's two servants. Patrees
helped her tighten the straps over her shoulders, connecting the front
and back pieces of the armor. Her breasts hurt from the pressing leather.
The helmet, which was too big for her head, would have fallen off if not
for the chinstrap. A belt carried the sheathed sword and the sling, which
was attached with a simple knot that was easy to undo. She paced back

and forth to adjust to the rigid outfit. The whole thing felt stiff, awkward, and utterly strange. She wanted to pull everything off and put the slave's long shirt back on, but reminded herself of Kassite's advice: "Imitate until you mutate!"

The men loaded two of the horses with piles of fine leather hides. The remaining six horses were fitted with waterskins, as well as baskets of dates, figs, and carobs for the journey.

Soosie sniffed her leather armor, rocked his head, and pulled his lips back in a toothy grin. She tried to mount the horse, but her new leather boot slipped out of the stirrup and she fell to the ground, flat on her back. Patrees hurried over to help her, but Deborah quickly got back on her feet, grabbed the saddle horn, and got on the horse, her face burning, which she hoped wasn't noticeable in the dark.

Antippet held the gate open while Kassite led the way out. Deborah followed him up the path to the main road. The others rode two to a horse, followed by the two packhorses with the leathers. A crescent moon illuminated their way.

Kassite paused at the top of the path and turned his horse around while the rest of them gathered around him. Deborah brought her horse next to his. Below them, the tannery was lit by a few torches, which had been left burning. The river was black, the opposite bank invisible.

"Eighteen years," Kassite said. "I have built the biggest tannery in the land, and now it is dead."

"Maybe not," she said. "Orran can buy new slaves and restart production."

He didn't seem to hear what she said. He turned his horse and headed down the Sea Highway, away from Aphek. She prodded Soosie and caught up with Kassite. "Do you know the way?"

He turned his head in her direction. "Did you say something?"

"Yes. I was asking—"

"My hearing is not good at night," he said. "You want to know the plan, is that it?"

"Yes." She wondered why his hearing was impacted by the time of day, or night.

"Over the years," he said, "I have spoken with many travelers. This road passes through no village or town for a while, only isolated homesteads inhabited by Manasseh tribesmen, who would not bother an armed group of riders like us. But we should not cross into the territory of the Hebrew tribe of Dan, whose men favor thievery and skirmish over toiling the land. We will take another road, about five hours from here, near the ruins of a village, and head east, back to the Samariah Hills. If we follow it for a day, we will reach Bethel. Then we'll ride north to Emanuel, coming from the south, as if we had traveled all the way from Edom. That is the plan."

Deborah wished he would say more. What was the rest of his plan? What would happen when they reached Emanuel? How did he plan to obtain Sallan's freedom from Judge Zifron and get away from Emanuel without falling prey to Seesya and his soldiers? Was he going to buy Sallan's freedom? The price would be huge, considering Sallan's essential role in the basket factory.

The thought of seeing Seesya again made her shudder. It was unthinkable. Rather than enter Emanuel, she would hide in the hills while Kassite somehow managed to get Sallan out. Would staying away from Emanuel constitute a breach of her oath to Sallan? She didn't think so, because she had caused Kassite to go to free Sallan. In fact, her presence in Emanuel might destroy any chance of liberating Sallan, no matter what Kassite's plan was.

They kept going at a steady trot for several hours, stopping briefly to drink and tighten the ropes that held the leathers to the packhorses. The land was thick with trees and bushes wherever a farmer's plow had not passed. The homesteads along the way were dark and quiet, except for an occasional dog barking.

With first light, they saw the charred remnants of a village near the road. Where vibrant life had once flourished, there was nothing but ruins. Deborah noticed the round wall of a well, but when she rode over and glanced inside, it was filled with rocks.

They turned off the Sea Highway onto a smaller road, heading toward the sliver of sun that peeked over the rocky ridges. During the morning, the road took them across the plains and into the foothills. It narrowed, forcing them to ride single file as they climbed the western face of the Samariah Hills. The vegetation grew sparser, the breeze died off, and the sun beat down on them with growing ferocity. The horses slowed down, their heads hanging low to the ground, but Kassite kept going. Every time the meandering road crested a vantage point, he shielded his eyes and peered at the plains below, where any pursuers would be visible.

When the sun reached its apex, the heat of the day weighed down on them heavily. One of the packhorses stumbled and almost fell. Kassite relented and led the group off the road to a shaded crevice.

The Edomite slaves gave the horses water while Kassite's servants put out bowls of figs, dates, and chunks of bread. After eating, Kassite lay down in the shade and closed his eyes. The others did the same. Soon, they were snoring.

Deborah, however, could not rest. Unlike Kassite, she wasn't worried about Orran's soldiers—not yet anyway. Her mind was plagued by what was coming next. She imagined reaching Emanuel the next day, facing the stone walls and armed sentries. Was Tamar's body still hanging from the Weeping Tree? It would be impossible to see her beloved sister's remains and not burst into tears, which could lead to exposure and humiliation, or even death. Would Kassite agree to let her hide in the hills while he and the others entered Emanuel to free Sallan?

Deborah imagined herself arriving in Judge Zifron's courtyard, dressed in a soldier's armor, boots, and helmet, with her short hair and calloused hands. Her appearance had changed, but how long would it take for someone to recognize her as the girl they had known? And if they caught her, what would she say? That she was no longer that girl, that she was halfway to becoming a young man? Was there any doubt how they would react? All of them—Seesya and his soldiers, Judge Zifron and his younger sons and wives, even the priest, Obadiah of Levi—they would look at her as if she had gone completely mad. They would laugh at her, lock her up, and determine her punishment as befitting a wife who had struck her husband and run away.

Unable to sit still any longer, Deborah walked over and fed Soosie a few carrots. She found the sound of his chewing and the smell of dust and sweat that came from him strangely soothing. There was no use letting her fears overwhelm her. Rather, she had to find a way to survive the next two days. How would Kassite manage to obtain Sallan's freedom? She had to convince him to forgo any direct approach. They should camp out of town and send one of the Edomite slaves into Emanuel with instructions to find Sallan and smuggle him out, and they would gallop south as far as possible before the alarm was raised. It was a crude plan, and she expected Kassite to ask many questions, but did he have a better plan? How could he, having never visited Emanuel, met Judge Zifron, or faced the wretched Seesya?

The sound of distant horses made her pause and listen.

The riders were getting closer fast. She guessed there were at least twenty horses, maybe more.

She ran to Kassite and shook his shoulder. "Men are coming. Maybe soldiers!"

Within seconds, everyone was up. They pulled the horses deeper into the crevice, out of sight from the road.

The drumming of hooves grew louder.

Kassite held on to a boulder as if he were about to faint. The others huddled close together, pale with terror.

Deborah took a deep breath, forced a smile onto her face, and untied the sling from around her waist. She signaled to the Edomite slaves to get their slings out, as well. She knew that their only chance against real soldiers would be a surprise attack with a barrage of stones. If it came to swords, they were as good as dead.

She collected a fist-size stone from the ground, fitted it into the pouch, and glanced to make sure the men did the same.

Staying close against the side of the crevice, she advanced toward the road. Behind her, the men readied their slings.

The riders came downhill fast and passed from right to left in front of the narrow crevice, raising a cloud of dust. They concentrated on the narrow, rock-strewn trail, and none of them noticed Deborah and the men. Behind the riders, tied in a long chain, horses and donkeys kept up despite being loaded with goods. They continued down the meandering road, the sound of their hooves fading away.

Kassite mounted his horse and advanced toward the road.

"They weren't soldiers." Deborah tied the sling back around her waist. "I think they were marauders on the way back from raiding a village in the hills."

"How could you tell?"

"I saw blood on their shirts and spears. A raid would also explain the additional animals and packages of goods."

"You are observant. That is good." He paused, thinking. "Did they carry a flag?"

"Yes. It was light blue."

Kassite stared down at her from the horse. "And?"

"It was hard to see," Deborah said. "I think there was a drawing of a snake on it."

"Ah." He rubbed the horse's neck. "The Hebrew tribe of Dan, is it not?"

She was embarrassed to admit that Hebrew tribesmen could stoop to bloody robbery. "At least we know they weren't Orran's soldiers."

"There are plenty of other dangerous men to fear."

She stood close to Kassite's horse, looking up at him, her voice low. "Speaking of dangerous men, what's your plan for freeing Sallan?"

Sitting back in the saddle, Kassite thought for a long moment. "Knowing Sallan," he said, "a strategy has already been set in motion, ready for us to pick up and run with."

"How can you be so certain?"

He smiled. "My old friend is a master of the long game."

Before she could ask him to elaborate, Kassite urged his horse forward and rode out of the crevice, turning right in the uphill direction. The rest of them followed, and Deborah rode in the rear of the group, pondering the term "long game" and the idea that Sallan had been confident enough in her ability to find the Elixirist and enlist his help that he would set a strategy in motion to prepare for their arrival in Emanuel.

13

Higher up in the Samariah Hills, they rode by a small village that was still burning under a cloud of smoke. Dead bodies of bearded men, naked women, and slaughtered children lay all around. A pole bore the flag of Benjamin—a gray wolf against a multicolored background—oddly unharmed among the destruction. Deborah wanted to stop and bury the bodies of her fellow Hebrews in accordance with Yahweh's law, but Kassite kept going, and she knew he was right to do so, considering the risks.

They arrived at Bethel shortly after sunset and set up camp at the edge of the fairgrounds, which was sparsely occupied by travelers and merchants. There were no walls around Bethel, only heaps of rocks, shallow ditches, and a gateless entrance guarded by a few soldiers and marked with the flag of Benjamin.

The Edomite men unloaded everything from the horses and fed them. Deborah used her father's fire-starters to get a small blaze going. Kassite's servants prepared a meal of warm oatmeal, apples, cheese, and bread, which they sprinkled with olive oil.

Kassite unwrapped the effigy of Qoz, placed it on a rock, and served it a plate of food. All the men knelt on the ground, facing Qoz, their heads bowed.

"We thank you, Qoz," Kassite said, "supreme master of the world, for the food that you deign to share with us, as well as for guarding us on our escape from slavery. May you keep us safe until we reach our home in Edom."

The hot drink after the meal was rather bland, lacking the minty bite of the evening drink served in the tannery, but it nevertheless was comforting. Exhausted after two days without sleep, they lay down in their clothes and boots, forming a circle around the horses and the pile of valuable leathers. For the first time since before arriving at the tannery, Deborah had her old blanket for cover and her sack for a pillow. It smelled of the tiger tail stuffed inside, and she fell asleep immediately.

In the morning, Kassite instructed everyone to clean up as best they could. The men gathered around the well, poured water on each other, and scrubbed their arms and legs. They used a sharp knife to shave their cheeks. While Deborah's cheeks didn't need shaving, she was concerned about her hair. It had been more than two months since Kassite chopped it off on her first day at the tannery, and the stubble had grown to about half the length of her pinky. She knew that its color, as orange as freshly peeled carrots, stood out even among the Edomites' fair complexions. If her helmet fell off, someone in Emanuel could recognize her.

She approached Antippet, who was the last to use the sharp knife. "I need you to shave my head," she said.

He seemed surprised. "We're not slaves anymore."

Deborah hesitated. He was right. Cropped hair, together with sleeveless shirts and bare feet, was a mark of slavery.

Standing nearby, Patrees heard the exchange and said, "Do what Borah says."

"Right." She pressed her fingers to her head and scratched hard all over. "It's too itchy."

Sitting on a rock, Deborah feigned indifference while Antippet rubbed water into her hair and ran the blade against her scalp. She thought of happier days back at Palm Homestead, with her sister and parents still alive. Every Friday afternoon, their father brought into the house a large bucket of water and put hot stones from the oven in the water before going outside. Their mother, Raquellah, from whom the girls had inherited the lush orange hair, washed and braided their thick locks the same way she did her own. When they were done, she always called in their father, Harutz, who was unfailingly pleased with the results. Shutting her eyes, Deborah remembered her mother's quick fingers, gentle yet efficient, tugging and straightening as she interwove the long sheaves of hair.

The memory was cut short when Antippet's wet hands patted her scalp, now completely smooth. "It's finished," he said.

She scooped up water and splashed her face, washing the tears away before anyone noticed.

The men put on their armor and loaded the horses. While they were getting ready, Kassite the leather hides and bought two additional horses, as well as various copper tools and trinkets, which he had the men wrap up and secure to the horses. Deborah understood why the leathers had to go. News of the mass escape from the tannery near Aphek was bound to spread, and a group of men traveling with two packhorses loaded with fine leather hides might cause suspicion. Copper, on the other hand, was Edom's best-known commodity.

While she was adjusting Soosie's saddle for the ride, Deborah noticed a caravan leaving the fairgrounds and starting down the road south. She saw a few women and a gray-haired man in a multicolored coat. Next to him rode a boy with black hair, a quiver of arrows on his shoulder. She felt her heartbeat suddenly accelerate.

Zariz!

Deborah was paralyzed with shock. She had met Zariz and his father's caravan on the first day of her escape from Emanuel, months earlier, when only Zariz's mastery with his bow and arrows saved her from Seesya. And here they were again—on the very day she was returning to Emanuel, having succeeded in her quest for the Elixirist!

She hopped on her horse and took off, chasing after the caravan, which trotted away at a good pace. Behind her, Patrees yelled something, but she didn't look back. She had to reach Zariz, to see his face and be warmed by his smile.

Leaving the fairgrounds, she reached the main road and pulled hard on the reins to direct Soosie, whose rear legs lost traction as they made the turn, barely regaining balance. She prodded the horse forward, shaking the reins, kicking in with her heels.

As Deborah raced after the caravan, the women heard the pounding of hooves and looked over their shoulders. She passed them at full speed, pulled hard on the reins, and swiveled around to face the caravan, engulfed in a cloud of dust.

"Zariz!" She waved a hand in front of her face to clear the dust. "It's me!"

The lazy breeze slowly cleared the air, revealing their faces. Deborah rubbed her eyes and peered at the boy with the black hair. The face that looked back at her had neither the refined features nor the bright smile she remembered.

It wasn't Zariz.

"What do you want with us?" The gray-haired man had a brown, weathered face, and his voice was tense. "We're honest merchants."

Despite the crushing disappointment, she kept her posture up as she imagined a real soldier would. "I mistook you for an old friend. Go in peace."

He bowed his head and urged his horse forward. She moved aside and let them pass.

At the campsite, the men stood behind Kassite, watching her approach. Some of the people in the fairgrounds looked on curiously.

She dismounted Soosie and resumed checking on the straps and knots on the packhorses as if nothing had happened.

Stepping very close to her, Kassite said quietly, "Drawing attention is dangerous. What has gotten into you?"

"I thought they were the Moabites who helped me on the way to Shiloh."

"It is about a boy, is it not?"

Deborah's face flushed with shame. The mere sight of someone resembling Zariz had caused her to cast off all masculine strength and posture, instantly regressing to the foolish girl she had once been.

"It was a mistake," she said. "Won't happen again."

The Edomite men mounted their horses. They had all the trappings of well-equipped soldiers accompanying a prosperous merchant, Deborah noticed, but they didn't carry themselves as soldiers. Slumped posture and evasive eyes marked them as hired laborers or submissive servants, rather than soldiers ready for action.

Gathering everyone close, Kassite said, "Today we ride to a town called Emanuel, where an old friend needs help regaining his freedom. This is still the land of the Hebrew tribes, and our owner's soldiers might soon begin to chase us. You must stay together, speak to no one, and do only what I order you to do—nothing more, nothing less." He pointed at Deborah. "Watch Borah and imitate him: shoulders back, chin up, and eyes gazing straight ahead!"

Deborah kept a blank expression, but behind it, she rejoiced that Kassite was using her as an example for the men. She hoped he considered her hasty chase after the boy as a minor stumble and not as evidence that she was failing to transform her weak female character into a proactive, even-tempered, adventurous, and logical male character.

As they prepared to leave, several young women passed by, carrying water jugs on their heads. The Edomite men turned to watch the women. Kassite, who was already on his horse, clapped his hands and beckoned the men to hurry, which they did, eyeing the women one last time.

With the morning sun rising over their right shoulders, the group took the road north toward Emanuel. Each one had his own horse now, and they rode at a steady pace behind Deborah and Kassite, who looked regal in his long leather coat and white leather hat.

He turned to her. "Why do you stare at me?"

"I'm sorry, Master."

"Answer my question."

"You seem different," she said, embarrassed. "Like a judge, or a high priest."

Kassite laughed. "I am grateful for your flattery."

"You're welcome, Master." She was tempted to take advantage of this moment of levity to ask about the third dose of the Male Elixir, but held back, knowing that his answer would be the same as when she had asked about the second dose: "When you are ready."

He looked at her with a knowing expression, as if he'd guessed what was going through her mind. "Your progress pleases me," he said.

Deborah nodded and looked ahead, her heart swelling with joy and relief.

"Did you notice their lascivious staring?" He gestured with his thumb over his shoulder at the Edomite men riding behind.

She nodded again.

"They do not look at you that way." He chuckled. "They have no idea what you really are, do they?"

"I don't think so."

"My Male Elixir is working exceptionally well, not only due to its potency, but also because you are an excellent customer. You want it to work and are doing what is required."

"I have to succeed," she said. "There's no other way for me."

They rode in silence for a few moments.

"It's odd," she said. "I don't recall the men staring at the women in the tannery."

Kassite gave her an appraising look. "You know man's nature."

"It's not much different from that of male horses and donkeys."

"True, but my tannery would not have functioned peacefully with all the men fired up with lust for the women. Something had to be done about all that masculine libido, yes?"

They rode in silence for a few minutes.

"It's the evening meal," she said, making the connection. "You had the cooks put something in the hot drinks every night—the opposite of a love elixir!"

"It worked, did it not?"

"Not for One Eye."

"Perhaps it was your exceptional allure." Kassite grinned. "We will never know the answer."

"That's why last night's drink tasted different."

"We are not in the tannery anymore."

Glancing over her shoulder at the men, Deborah said, "I would've continued to give it to them, at least until we conclude our business in Emanuel. Is it difficult to find the ingredients to make the lust-killing potion?"

"Every elixir is a complex undertaking, an art, really." Kassite paused, the way he often did, weighing his words carefully, and continued in his slow manner of delivery. "Would you like to learn how to do it?" He smiled "It is a man's job, but you are no longer a woman, are you?"

Deborah knew he was mocking her again, but she didn't mind. His ability to mix an elixir that consistently, day in and day out, snuffed out men's most base urges was irrefutable proof that he was truly the Elixirist, capable of helping her become a man.

Kassite patted his horse behind the saddle, causing it to speed up. Without prodding, Soosie did the same, breaking into a steady gallop.

14

At midday, the horses slowed down under the beating sun. As they paced around a curve in the road, Emanuel appeared in the distance. Deborah pulled hard on Soosie's reins.

Kassite stopped beside her. "We have to go into town," he said.

"Why? We could send one or two of the Edomite men to get Sallan out in secret."

"That is not a plan."

"What is the plan, then?"

He gazed at the distant town for a long moment. "To find Sallan and follow his lead. That is my plan."

"Let me hide in the hills until you come back."

"You are the only one familiar with the place and the judge who rules it. I need you with me, or I might never come out of there alive."

"Someone will recognize me."

"You look nothing like the girl they remember."

She adjusted the helmet, which rubbed against her shaved scalp. "It's been only a couple of months."

"Our time is not measured in days or weeks, but in how far our experiences have changed us. A single day could count for a lifetime, whereas a hundred weeks might feel like time stood still."

Deborah couldn't believe he was philosophizing while she faced mortal danger. "That may be true," she said. "But under this leather armor, except for stronger muscles and a foul odor, I'm the same."

"Hardly the same." Kassite stared at her, the brim of his hat low over his brow. "Only your glorious eyes could give you away."

"My what?"

He chuckled. "That is the essence of your charm, that you do not realize the effect you have on others."

"Only on those with strange taste."

"Indeed." He laughed out loud. "Indeed!"

"Should I put my eyes in my pocket?"

"Maybe," he laughed again. "But seriously, whatever you do, do not look straight at one of your old acquaintances."

"That won't be easy."

"Simply keep your eyes squinted and your gaze away from the people who know you best. Do that, and no one will see the old Deborah in the young Edomite soldier named Borah."

She nodded, though she didn't share his confidence.

"Do you remember what I told you about how easy it is to deceive people?"

Deborah thickened her voice and imitated his slow, deliberate manner of speaking. "They do not see what is right in front of them when they expect to see something else, as if there were a sieve between their eyes and their mind that filters out what does not fit their expectations and fills in the blanks with what does."

"Impressive." He clapped. "You are an attentive student."

"I told you I memorize things that could be useful one day."

"Then memorize this prediction: No one will recognize you unless you reveal yourself."

Deborah wasn't convinced. "I lived there for a year. They know me."

Kassite shifted on his horse, thinking. "I have an idea. Tell me, how far is your father's homestead from here?"

Surprised by his question, she shrugged. "About two hours by foot. Why?"

"When facing a fearsome barrier, think of your ultimate destination—the reason for your journey—and your fear will turn to fortitude."

His advice was logical, but as much as Deborah tried to conjure the image of Palm Homestead in her mind, her eyes refused to draw away from the sight of Emanuel in the distance, with its walls and gates and the memories of Tamar's stoning.

"Can you find your way there while avoiding the town?"

"Yes," Deborah said before thinking it through, and immediately wanted to take it back. Her breath quickened at the thought of seeing Palm Homestead again. She pointed at the hills east of the road. "I'd have to go around Emanuel, then head north."

"Go fast. We'll wait here." Kassite turned his horse and trotted off the road into a crevice, where a small tree provided meager shade. Everyone followed him, dismounted, and gave the horses water. "You two." He pointed at Antippet and Patrees. "Ride with Borah and do what he says."

Deborah rode up a dry streambed, followed by the two men. The afternoon sun was at their backs, giving her a sense of direction. The horses' shoes tapped the rocks, and the sound filled her ears as if amplified by a hundred. She breathed deeply and recalled how her Moabite friend, Zariz, had taught her to imagine the layout of the land in her mind. She closed her eyes and imagined the road north, passing by Emanuel, continuing for a while, until a ravine appeared on the right, where her father had always made the turn eastward toward their home. If she turned left soon and traveled parallel to the main road, she was bound to intersect with the same ravine and recognize the path she had known from childhood.

They emerged from the dry stream at the meeting point of two hills, where smaller creeks fed the stream during flash floods. She chose the one to the left, heading northeast, but paused and turned her horse.

"Make a column of rocks," she told the men, pointing at a spot that would be visible when they rode back. "Stand it up as high as your knee."

Antippet and Patrees dismounted, collected flat stones, and balanced them one on top of the other to create the column marker. Deborah nodded in approval, turned her horse, and continued on.

The dry creek split again, and she had them build another marker.

When they were far enough from Emanuel, she turned north over the hills, keeping the sun over her left shoulder. She made sure to leave stone markers in intervals that were visible from one another.

After a while, she was expecting to see the familiar ravine to appear behind the next hill, or the next, but it didn't, and her doubts began to grow. The two men must have sensed it, and while they obeyed her without question, they were slower to dismount and collect the stones for each new marker, glancing in her direction as if expecting her to change her mind and turn back.

Deborah kept going.

The ravine appeared out of nowhere, barely noticeable from the direction they were coming. Relieved, Deborah waited for the men to construct a marker before resuming her fast trot. From here, she knew the way.

As they got near, Deborah veered off the path and urged Soosie up a hill that bordered the fields on the north. Near the top, she dismounted, handed the reins to Patrees, and gestured for the two men to wait. Keeping low, she approached the crest of the hill until Palm Homestead came into full view.

The small valley was as beautiful as she remembered it. The fields and orchards surrounding the small house were lush and healthy, and the ageless olive trees clung stubbornly to the patches of soil on the surrounding slopes. The old palm tree towered over the house, its canopy wide and green as it had always been. Her father had named it Deborah's Palm after he dreamed of her sitting under this palm and delivering Yahweh's message to the Hebrews. Women didn't become prophets, everyone knew that, but her father's conviction that his dream would come true had fueled her quest to become a man—a man who would be entitled to inherit Palm Homestead and one day become God's prophet, delivering His word to the people under this palm tree, as her father had envisioned.

She noticed a narrow canal that sliced Palm Homestead in half. It looked like a sword wound across a warrior's chest, flowing with blood from his still-beating heart, only instead of red blood, the canal was white from the underlying limestone and running with water from the cistern, where two slaves worked the winch lever on the crosspiece, raising one bucket after another from the deep reservoir underground. The canal passed between the fields and disappeared behind the next hill, no doubt delivering the stolen water to other fields owned by Judge Zifron.

As her chest tightened with a bitter mix of sorrow and rage, Deborah gripped the hilt of the short sword at her hip, burning to run down the hillside and stop the men who were stealing her family's water. But she remembered Kassite's advice to harness her rage for the right moment. The slaves bore no responsibility for their owner's crime, and attacking them would only serve to expose her and ruin everything. The stolen water would be replenished by the underground streams that fed the cistern until the day she returned to Palm Homestead as its true owner, cover up the canal, farm the land, and serve as God's prophet to His people. That was her True Calling, and she would let nothing and no one stop her from reaching her destination.

Deborah retreated below the crest of the hill, mounted Soosie, and broke into a gallop. The two men caught up with her after a few moments, and she kept going at a fast pace, turning at each stone marker, until she found Kassite and the rest of the men in the crevice by the road to Emanuel.

Kassite gathered the men together and pointed at the town. "From now on, we will ride steadily and act with confidence. I am an important visitor from Edom, and you are my guards and servants. When we reach the gates, stay together behind Borah and me. Keep quiet, alert, and polite while I speak with the sentries."

The road straightened out as they approached Emanuel at a steady canter. Near the gates, Deborah tried to avert her eyes but couldn't help glancing at the Weeping Tree, where Seesya's soldiers had strung up Tamar's body by her feet after the stoning, for all travelers to see. Tamar was still there, or rather, what was left of her after the birds had picked off everything but the bones. A groan escaped Deborah's lips, and she put a fist to her mouth to silence it. She had hoped that Obadiah of Levi would find a way to take down Tamar and give her a proper burial, but it appeared that neither his guilt for participating in her unjust execution, nor his fear of Tamar's dying curse, had been enough to make him take the risk. Did Obadiah have no faith in the powers of Yahweh to protect the just and honorable?

Kassite looked at the bones, which swayed gently in the mild breeze. "There will be time for revenge," he said. "Months from now, or even years, but not today."

"Yes, Master," she said, her voice scratchy. "I will harness my rage for the right moment."

"Good. No matter what happens, do not act or speak, not even in response to a direct question. You are Borah, my soldier, nothing more."

They passed by the Pit of Shame. On the other side of the road, at the fairgrounds, merchants peddled goods and farmers sold fresh produce. Ahead, sentries guarded the open gates. Deborah noticed new poles, one on each side, bearing Ephraim's flag of a white ox against black background.

One of the sentries raised his spear. "State your business!"

"I am Prince Antipartis," Kassite said gravely. "I come in friendship from Edom to call on your leader, Judge Zifron, bearing gifts and seeking mutual trade."

The sentry bowed and gestured to the shaded side of the gatehouse. "Please wait here."

While they congregated in the shade, the sentry ran up the street, all the way to the top, and disappeared into the judge's courtyard.

Long minutes passed. The stench of smoke and garbage drifted from the shacks and tents of the poor at the bottom of the hill. Sweat made Deborah's leather helmet stick to her scalp.

A distant whistle startled her.

Up the hill, at the top of the street, the sentry signaled them to proceed.

The slow ride up the main street of Emanuel filled Deborah with dread. The memory of Seesya's oily hair and odorous breath made her shudder. She thought of how far she had come since the last time she went down this road, hiding in Obadiah's cart under the corpse of a woman Seesya had speared to death. Now she was riding on her own horse, wearing armor and carrying a short sword, a sling, and a spear while sporting hard muscles and a masculine attitude. If only Kassite's confidence in Sallan's foresight and preparedness would prove right, the day might end successfully. On the other hand, if Sallan had done nothing to prepare, things could turn ugly. Deborah knew that she would rather fight to the death than end up back in Seesya's hands.

15

They entered the large courtyard of Judge Zifron's house, which was busy with merchants who delivered farm produce and livestock, purchased baskets and food items, or pleaded their case with the judge at the opposite end of the courtyard. Deborah quickly scanned the area for Obadiah of Levi in his priestly white robe, but didn't see him.

Having stayed at Shatz Ha'Cohen's grand house in the holy city of Shiloh, Deborah found Judge Zifron's house less impressive now, but the sights, smells, and noises welcomed her with the familiarity of a place that had been her home for a whole year. She rode behind Kassite across the courtyard. On the right, the hanging straw mats were raised to let fresh air into the basket factory. It was full of workers, but the relative darkness inside made it difficult for her to recognize anyone.

They dismounted and handed the reins to the servants, who tied the horses to a long bar and gave them water.

One of the attendants announced, "Prince Antipartis of Edom!"

Judge Zifron waved away the men surrounding him, straightened his gold-laced coat over his protruding belly, and stepped forward, opening his arms. "Welcome! Welcome!"

"It is my great honor." Kassite towered over the judge as they embraced and kissed on both cheeks. He kept hat on and gestured at the horses. "We bring you gifts of fine copper from the land of Edom, with the blessings of our gods and the best wishes of our king."

Kassite's two servants untied the packages, carried them to a table, and arranged all the copper tools and trinkets in an orderly display. Kassite praised the quality of material and workmanship of each item.

Meanwhile, Deborah glanced around furtively. She could spot at least six of Seesya's soldiers, one at each corner of the courtyard, one at the exit to the street, and one more at the door leading into the main house. They paid no attention to her, as Kassite had predicted. Glancing into the horse stable, she was relieved to see only a few horses inside, indicating that Seesya was away.

She stepped closer to hear the conversation.

"Word has reached our land," Kassite said to the judge, "about the exceptional strength of the Zifron baskets and the abundance of flour and barley, as well as olives and figs, in your flourishing domain."

"It's true on all counts." Judge Zifron held a copper pot in his hand, turning it over to look closely before putting it down. A curved knife and a wine jug with a long neck also attracted his attention. "Very nice. We don't see Edomite merchants very often here."

"These are only examples," Kassite said. "Our mines produce plenty of copper and iron ore, and our artisans make the most excellent tools, dishes, and weapons. In fact, when it comes to weapons, we could extract enough raw materials from the ground in one year to make swords and spear tips for a whole army, as well as armored chariots for the king and his generals."

"Armored chariots?"

"Plated with copper and iron."

The judge leaned forward eagerly.

"Our beautiful land is rich for mining, but most of it too dry for farming."

"Plenty of fertile land here, I assure you." Judge Zifron waved his arms. "We recently gained ownership of a boundless cistern that will triple our tillable land and multiply our crops many times over."

Deborah knew that he was speaking of the ancient cistern at Palm Homestead, and as her anger heated up, she wanted to shout the truth at the top of her voice: "You didn't gain ownership, you stole it!" But she kept her lips pressed together, as she had promised Kassite, and harnessed her rage for the right time.

"Splendid," Kassite said. "If you are interested, we could satisfy your needs in copper and iron while you fill our shortages in produce and baskets."

The judge motioned to the servants to take away the gifts.

Kassite looked around. "And where is the factory that makes the famous Zifron baskets?"

"Please, follow me." Judge Zifron marched across the courtyard. "It's right here."

Everyone moved aside to make way. Kassite went with the judge while Deborah and the Edomite men followed behind. She squinted, her eyelids half-closed, as Kassite had told her to do, but no one paid attention to her anyway. And why would they? In height, she almost matched the Edomite men, and her slimness wasn't obvious under the leather armor. As Kassite had said, people saw her armor, helmet, boots, and sword, assumed she was a soldier, and filtered out anything that might contradict that assumption.

The basket factory hadn't changed since she'd worked there, with dozens of girls and women weaving baskets at the tables, tall haystacks on one end, and piles of finished baskets at the opposite end. She scanned the large room, but didn't see Sallan or Seesya's mother, Vardit, who usually worked there.

"This is very impressive," Kassite said. "Who runs this operation for you?"

"An excellent foreman," Judge Zifron said. "In fact, he is originally from Edom. I bought him many years ago at an excellent price, considering how well he's done for me."

"An Edomite slave?" Kassite looked around. "I would like to meet him."

Deborah held her breath, waiting to hear where Sallan was.

"Unfortunately, he's been ill lately, but my son is supervising the work in the meantime." The judge beckoned a chubby boy of about fifteen. "Come here, Babatorr, and meet Prince Antipartis of Edom."

Kassite tipped his hat.

Babatorr bowed respectfully, his cheeks red and his smile wide. Deborah recognized him. He was Judge Zifron's second-oldest son, born to one of the judge's concubines who had died years ago.

"Tell the guests about our factory," Judge Zifron told his son.

Deborah glanced up at the ceiling, wondering if Sallan was upstairs in his plush quarters, or had been sent somewhere else to recuperate— or worse.

"The process starts at this tub," Babatorr explained, pointing. "We dip single stalks of straw or flax in the Reinforcing Liquid, then braid and dry them here." He led the guests over to the long table, where young slave girls picked three stalks and braided them into a single strand.

"The strands dry overnight before they're ready for weaving." He pointed at the three round tables in the center, where dozens of women worked. "We make different types of baskets—about a hundred baskets a day, or more if there's a big order."

"Our copper mines require many baskets," Kassite said. "The workers have to carry the rocks and ore out of the deep tunnels, and the baskets they use now disintegrate after a few weeks of use."

"Our baskets are strong," Judge Zifron said. "They won't break."

"Then we can sell thousands of them to the mines every year." Kassite picked up a basket and looked it over. "And in the regular markets, where we sell grain and other goods, the buyers will buy the storage baskets from us at the same time."

"That's a lot of baskets," Babatorr said. "I'm not sure—"

"Yes," Judge Zifron said, "we can make as many baskets as you need, and our land holdings are growing to supply the wheat and flax twine, as well as flour and fruit. How will you transport the goods?"

"Packhorses," Kassite said. "They can make the trip from Edom in a couple of weeks, depending on the season and the sandstorms. That means that each of my caravans can be here every other month to deliver copper goods to you and pick up a shipment of baskets and produce for sale in Edom."

Deborah was mesmerized by the ease with which Kassite lied.

His face gleaming with greed, Judge Zifron rubbed his hands. "We'll have to agree on quantities and prices."

"That is not a problem," Kassite said. "Are you certain that your factory can increase production to meet our needs?"

"Capacity we have, as long as the profits justify the costs and the efforts."

"The profits will be plenty for both of us."

Judge Zifron grinned, tugging on the lapels of his coat, which was tight over his extended girth.

"By the way," Kassite said, "the liquid you dip the straw in, is that the reason your baskets are so durable?"

Babatorr nodded.

"Have you used it for a long time?"

Glancing at his father, Babatorr shifted his weight from leg to leg.

"Yes," Judge Zifron answered. "We've used the Reinforcing Liquid since we started making baskets about eighteen years ago."

"May I?" Kassite went to the dipping tub, put his finger in the liquid, and licked it. He smacked his lips, tilted his head, and breathed through his mouth a few times, blowing rapidly. "Interesting," he finally said. "Very interesting."

Judge Zifron looked at him, waiting for an explanation.

"In Edom," Kassite said, "we have a similar liquid in which we wash copper and iron ore before it is melted and molded. We call it the Strengthening Stew, and in rare times of grave peril, a man may even drink it to get a leg up in a coming fight."

"Drink it?" Babatorr twisted his face in disgust. "How could you—"
His father shushed him.

Deborah leaned forward, eager to hear. On her last night here, Sallan had made her drink a goblet filled with the Reinforcing Liquid, promising her that it would make her stronger on her quest to find the Elixirist. She had doubted its powers at first, but in retrospect, would she have succeeded without it, considering the terrible setbacks she had suffered along the way?

"It is a secret formula," Kassite continued. "Only pureblood Edomite men may learn the ingredients, their measures, and the correct order of mixing them to make the Strengthening Stew and ensure its full potency. The formula has passed from generation to generation for ages, all the way down from our forefather, Esau, the eldest son of Isaac."

"I'm familiar with the legend," the judge said. "In our Hebrew tradition, it was our forefather Jacob, the younger of Isaac's sons, who knew how to make the Strengthening Stew, but he sold it to his older twin brother, Esau, in exchange for Esau's firstborn birthright."

"In Edomite tradition," Kassite said, "Esau did not wish to sell his firstborn birthright to his younger brother for the Strengthening Stew, but was tricked into doing so by Jacob at a moment of weakness after a long day in the fields."

An awkward silence ensued.

"No worry," Kassite said, his face breaking into a wide smile. "After so many generations, how could we hold a grudge against blood relatives?"

Judge Zifron laughed, and his son Babatorr joined in, visibly relieved.

Dipping his finger again, Kassite licked it as one would lick honey.

"The taste of home," he said. "Magical. And you, young man," he addressed the judge's son, "you have not foolishly revealed the secret formula to anyone, have you?"

"No, sir," Babatorr said. "I don't even know how to—"

Judge Zifron clapped his hands. "Time for fresh air, and some wine, too."

Kassite followed the judge out of the basket factory, but paused and chuckled. "Let me guess," he said. "Your Edomite slave has kept to himself the secret of how to mix the Reinforcing Liquid. Am I right?"

Judge Zifron looked around uncomfortably. His eyes passed over Deborah without recognition.

"Well?" Kassite kept a wide smile on his face. "Am I right?"

"Yes," the judge said. "But as I said, he's not well right now."

"I may be able to help him feel better. Like every member of our extended royal family, I am versed in the healing arts."

After a brief pause, Judge Zifron relented. "Summon him," he said to his son.

Babatorr hurried up the stairs to the second floor.

"Clever boy," Kassite said. "You must be proud of him."

"He has a good head for business, which is fortunate, because his heart is too soft for battle. My firstborn, on the other hand, is a man of the sword—a fearless warrior, my pride and joy."

The reference to Seesya sent a chill through Deborah, and she prayed silently that he wouldn't return while they were still in Emanuel.

A few minutes passed.

Babatorr reappeared at the top of the stairs. Behind him, two boy-servants carried a chair in which a pale old man was sitting, a wool cap covering his head. As the boys came down the stairs, Deborah was shocked to recognize the shadow of a man in the chair. It was Sallan. His fine coat, which had fit snugly over his stocky figure when she saw him last, hung loosely on his thin frame. His reddish hair and the golden fuzz on his arms had turned completely white. His formerly ruddy complexion was now waxy and gray, like old parchment, and silver stubble covered his sunken cheeks. It was hard to believe that, during her short absence, the vigorous foreman had turned into a frail old man.

Deborah hoped to meet his light-blue eyes, but his head was slumped forward, his face toward the ground.

"This is the slave I mentioned," Judge Zifron said. "As you can see, he's recovering from a brief illness."

The boy-servants put down the chair and helped Sallan stand. He slowly raised his eyes and looked at Kassite. A fleeting smile crossed his face, masked by a fit of coughing.

"You're standing," Judge Zifron said. "That's good. A few more days, and you'll be back to work."

Sallan's knees buckled, and his servants had to support him.

"Look what an important guest we have," the judge said. "Prince Antipartis came all the way from your homeland."

Sallan straightened up with an effort. "Great pleasure," he said hoarsely. "An honor seeing you here, Prince—"

"Antipartis," Kassite said. "I am the king's cousin, four times removed."

"Yes," Sallan said, clearing his throat. "I recall Your Excellency."

The judge was pleased. "At least your head is in good health, remembering the prince after many years away."

Coughing again, Sallan said, "Few tall men in our land."

Kassite chuckled, adjusting his white leather hat. "And few who know the secret of the Strengthening Stew."

Sallan and Kassite looked at each other in silence.

Of all the men and women watching, Deborah was the only one who knew the dramatic emotional conflagration that must have erupted in the hearts of the two old friends, finally reunited after eighteen years apart. They kept their emotions hidden, but she could see the thin film of moisture over their eyes and hear the slight tremor in their voices. She feared that they were going to fall into each other's arms.

"Sallan," Judge Zifron said, "tell the prince what's wrong with you. He's a medicine man, too."

Sallan tried to speak, but couldn't. He coughed again.

"Take your time," Kassite said.

"What's wrong with me?" Sallan shrugged. "My body is being crushed by the jaws of Mott."

Everyone froze at the mention of the Canaanite God of Death, whose name no one ever spoke out loud for fear of tempting fate.

"Nonsense," the judge said. "You're getting better by the day."

"I will take a look," Kassite said. "Your hands, show them to me."

He held Sallan's hands and turned them this way and that.

"Now let me see the inside of your mouth."

Sallan opened his mouth.

"Wider," Kassite said, peering inside.

Everybody watched as he made Sallan turn so that light from the setting sun illuminated his gaping mouth.

"Open your eyes wide for me." Kassite peered into Sallan's eyes. "Look up and down. Left and right."

Sallan complied, and while everyone was focused on Kassite's examination of Sallan's mouth and eyes, Deborah noticed that he never let go of Sallan's hands, which he clasped so tightly that his knuckles turned white.

After a long moment, Kassite stepped back, and their hands detached from each other.

Sallan sat back down in the chair.

"Take him back to bed," Judge Zifron said.

As the boys lifted Sallan and began to turn, his gaze found Deborah and paused briefly. In his eyes she saw a glint of gratitude, for she had kept her promise to come back for him.

"Come, Prince Antipartis," Judge Zifron said. "Let us honor you with food and drink, as befits an important guest and a future trading partner." He led the way from the basket factory to the courtyard. Out of earshot of all the workers, he asked, "Can you help him? Give him medicine?"

Kassite glanced back through the open side of the factory. "Not likely, I am afraid."

"What's wrong with him?"

"There are many things that go wrong in an old man's body. I know it from personal experience."

"Me too," Judge Zifron said. "But he was in excellent health only a few months ago."

"Your slave knows the true condition of his body."

"You mean—"

"He is dying."

Kassite's words shot a bolt of sorrow through Deborah. She stood behind him, the leather helmet low over her eyes, her posture straight and alert as that of any soldier guarding his prince, but inside, she felt like crying.

A table was set up, and servants ran in and out of the kitchen with bread, meat, fruit, and wine. Supervising the preparations was Vardit, who issued commands and pointed her finger here and there with authority. A little more than a year earlier, when Deborah and Tamar had first arrived here, newly orphaned and badly frightened, she had taken them under her wing, providing them with kindness and guidance, helping them adjust to life at Judge Zifron's house. As the judge's eldest wife and the mother of his heir, Seesya, Vardit was first among the women in the house, though her status didn't protect her from the flogging she had received for failing to prevent Deborah's first escape. The memory of Vardit's back, the skin lacerated by the knotted lashes, was still vivid in Deborah's mind. She longed to greet Vardit and hug her, but looked away quickly to avoid being recognized.

"Before we eat," Judge Zifron said, "let me show you our food stocks."

They entered the dark storage room off to the side of the courtyard, where the ground had been dug up, creating deep silos in which baskets and clay jars held flour, barley, seeds, dates, dried figs, hard cheese, and smoked meat, as well as wine and olive oil.

When they stepped out, Kassite straightened his hat and declared, "You are blessed with true abundance. The gods have surely smiled upon you."

"They still do." Judge Zifron smirked. "This is only part of our stocks. We also have several storage barns down by the gates. We keep them full until it's the opportune time to sell. The foolish peasants, who plan poorly for the dry season, lose their crops and come here hungry, willing to pay any price we demand. Sometimes we get paid in land, can you believe it?" The judge laughed. "They give us their land for a few baskets of flour and a chunk of meat!"

"We have a saying in Edom," Kassite said. "Even the proudest son will sell his father's land to feed his own children."

"True, but foolish. Children die all the time, and a man can produce new ones easily, but losing the family's homestead is forever!"

Judge Zifron's words speared Deborah's heart, as if he spoke specifically about Palm Homestead, which he and his son had stolen from her family. Touching the sword hilt by her hip, she imagined how easy it would be to draw her sword and run it through the soft flesh of the judge's fat belly all the way in until the hilt sunk in and disappeared inside his guts, just as the Hebrew hero Ehud, son of Gerah, had done to the king of Moab, who had oppressed the Hebrews several generations earlier. Her vision fogged up from the stifling heat of rage, but she didn't move. Yahweh had commanded, "Do not kill!" Stabbing a man through his gut wasn't something she could do under any circumstances.

Judge Zifron and Kassite sat down at opposite ends of the table, which was loaded with bowls of food and jugs of wine. The judge's servants stood behind him, and Kassite's Edomite soldiers, including Deborah, stood behind him.

"Your hospitality," Kassite said, "exceeds all boundaries."

Tipping his head, Judge Zifron chuckled, clearly flattered.

"With your permission, I'd like to give thanks to Qoz before the meal."

The judge nodded.

One of the Edomite men brought over the copper effigy. Kassite served it a plate of meat, cheese, and bread.

"We thank you, Qoz," Kassite said, "supreme master of the world, for the food that you deign to share with us, as well as for our new Hebrew friend, the esteemed Judge Zifron. May you bless his house and keep us safe on our travels until we reach our home in Edom and make sacrifices at your temple there."

The judge raised a goblet of wine. "To life!"

Kassite raised his goblet. "To life!"

Playing the gracious host came naturally to Judge Zifron. He urged Kassite to try each of the dishes and kept filling his goblet with wine. Eventually, Kassite sat back and pronounced himself full to the brim. Only then were the plates of food passed around to the other men, who had stood around and watched their masters eat. Deborah was too nervous to eat much, but forced down a piece of meat to deflect suspicion.

Judge Zifron brought the conversation back to business. "Rest assured," he said, "that our production of baskets will not slow down. The foreman is a strong man. I believe he'll get better soon."

"May your words reach the ears of the gods," Kassite said. "In my humble opinion, short of a miracle your slave is as good as dead."

"In that case, Babatorr will take over. My son has spent the last few weeks learning every aspect of the production."

"With one fairly important exception, it seems."

Reluctantly, the judge nodded. "He hasn't yet learned how to make the Reinforcing Liquid. Perhaps that's why the gods brought you here today, my dear Prince Antipartis."

Kassite held his arms wide open. "What can I do? It is forbidden for an Edomite man to reveal the secret formula, especially to the descendants of Jacob."

Judge Zifron pursed his lips, his face reddening, until he couldn't hold back and slammed his open hand on the table. "I will not be held hostage by a bloody slave! When my eldest son comes home tonight, he will deal with the stubborn Sallan—torture him if necessary, until he tells us how to make the Reinforcing Liquid!"

The news that Seesya would be coming home that night made Deborah's chest constrict. She struggled to breathe and felt a tremor begin to build up inside her. With effort, she inhaled deeply, recalling what Kassite had said: "No one will recognize you unless you reveal yourself."

After the meal, the judge retired to rest. Kassite and his entourage were shown to the guest quarters on the second floor over the food storage. They took off their helmets and boots and lay down on straw mats, except for Kassite, who had his own room with a real bed. He covered his face with his hat and appeared to have fallen asleep.

Having waited a few minutes to let the six Edomite slaves-turned-soldiers and the two servants doze off, Deborah could no longer contain her anxiety. She went into Kassite's room and shook his arm.

He groaned and removed his hat from his face. "What is wrong?"

"It's a disaster," she whispered. "Seesya is coming back tonight, and Sallan is dying. We should grab him and escape right now. It's our only chance!"

"Did I not tell you to leave everything to me?"

"You don't know Seesya. He'll make Sallan reveal how to make the Reinforcing Liquid, or Strengthening Stew, whatever you call it."

"Sallan will not talk."

"Oh, yes, he'll talk. And talk. And talk. And then he'll die. There's no way Sallan can survive Seesya's violence!"

"You survived it."

She couldn't understand why he was so cool about it. "I survived because I wasn't an old and sick slave, and because I was lucky. I won't survive tonight, not if Seesya recognizes me."

"I thought we put those worries to rest." Kassite pulled himself up to a sitting position, his voice low but growing sharper. "No one will recognize you unless you reveal yourself to them, and the surest way to achieve that disastrous outcome is to lose your self-control like a stupid little girl!"

Deborah recoiled from his insulting rebuke, but after a fleeting urge to cry, her fury exploded. "You're calling me a girl? Why? Because I don't want to lose my foot, or my ears, or my freedom? Because I'd rather take action than submit and become a slave?"

Kassite's face paled. He glared at her, and she knew he wanted her to apologize, but he had been the first to offend, and she knew he would lose respect for her if she backed down.

Finally, he spoke. "Will you honor your vow?"

"Which one?" Deborah looked away. "I vowed to return here to help Sallan win his freedom, and I vowed to obey you, but I didn't vow to give away my life."

"That will not be necessary." Kassite sighed. "Your worries are valid and the risks are great. There is only one possible course of action, and it requires patience and cool tempers. If we try to snatch Sallan and run, our end will come swiftly. We are in enemy territory, and our only advantages are subterfuge and manipulation." He grasped her arm with his cool, long fingers. "I was wrong to call you a little girl. You have proven yourself to be braver and smarter than most men. I ask you to trust me—with your life, yes."

His words deflated her anger, but not her anxiety. He was right, of course, that the odds of surviving an escape with Sallan were small, but the thought of facing Seesya, even transformed and masquerading as she was, terrified her.

"Do you trust me?" Kassite asked.

"You were obviously wrong about Sallan."

"In what way?"

"Master of the long game?" Deborah opened her arms in

exasperation. "You expected him to prepare for our arrival, to set a strategy in motion so that we could follow his lead."

"Was I wrong?"

"He's dying!"

"Sometimes good fortune hides behind misfortune."

"What does it mean?"

"You will see." Kassite chuckled and gestured at the door. "Get some rest. We have a challenging night ahead of us. Fatigue and anxiety will not help us win the game."

"Do we have a chance?"

"A chance of getting out of here alive?" Kassite considered it for a moment. "I would say it is about one in three."

16

When Kassite, Deborah, and the men returned to the courtyard, it was lit up with dozens of wall-mounted torches that made the air reek of smoke and burning oil. A group of soldiers were unpacking loot and tending to horses, but there were no slaves or women in sight. On the table where Judge Zifron and Kassite had enjoyed a lavish meal earlier, Deborah saw an array of long knives arranged by size, including straight, curved, double-edged, serrated, and two-pronged blades.

Judge Zifron and Kassite sat in large armchairs on one side of the table, with the judge's servants and Kassite's soldiers in a half-circle behind the two. A scribe sat on a stool at the judge's feet, ready with a parchment, a bottle of ink, and a feather.

Seesya came out of the house and marched across the courtyard. He wore leather armor and muddy boots and held a half-eaten apple in his hand. A new sword hung from his belt, the hilt made of stamped silver and decorated with jewels. The point of the blade, protruding from the bottom end of the leather scabbard, was dark with dried blood. Deborah watched him through narrow eyes, her heart pounding in her chest. He stood at the opposite side of the table, took another bite from the apple, and tossed it. She wondered to what extent his ears had healed since she'd pounded them repeatedly with her father's fire-starters on the night of their wedding, almost three months earlier, but his oily black hair came down to his shoulders, hiding the ears.

"This is my eldest, Seesya," Judge Zifron said. "Son, meet our esteemed guest, Prince Antipartis of Edom."

Seesya bowed. "An honor."

Kassite nodded and turned to the judge. "I have given our business some thought," he said. "I will need samples of every type of basket your factory can make."

Judge Zifron used the tip of his boot to poke the scribe, who dipped his feather in the ink and wrote down a few words.

"That way," Kassite said, "when we arrive home in Edom, my men can use the samples to solicit orders."

"It shall be done." The judge glanced at the open side of the now-deserted basket factory, where Babatorr was standing. "Did you hear, Son?"

"Yes, Father."

Seesya glanced at Babatorr and smirked. "Go on, boy, weave some pretty baskets with the women."

The soldiers laughed, and Babatorr lowered his eyes.

"Once we have the orders," Kassite said, "my men will add it all up, and I will send a caravan from Edom."

The scribe wrote that down, too.

"Very good," Judge Zifron said.

The boy-servants carried Sallan downstairs in a chair, a wool cap pulled down over his ears, his coat buttoned up to his neck. The servants placed the chair in front of the table, facing everyone. Deborah was shocked again by how old Sallan appeared, with his waxy skin and silver stubble.

"The prices," Kassite said, "will have to be agreed upon in advance, considering that I will be making very large commitments—"

The judge held a hand up to stop him. "We'll discuss it, sure. It's all very good. Excellent."

Seesya leaned against the table, taking his time, touching each of the blades as if they were objects of desire. The courtyard grew silent and tense.

"Tell me, slave," Seesya said. "How are you feeling this evening?"

Sallan cleared his throat. "Repulsed and disgusted," he said weakly. "How about you?"

Everyone laughed.

Seesya's face reddened, and he touched the hair over his right ear as if checking that it was in place. "You think all this is a joke?"

"I'm resigned to my fate."

"We'll see about that." Seesya selected a long knife from the table. "We can start with this fine instrument—"

"Hold on," Judge Zifron said. "Even a slave deserves a chance to do the right thing."

Seesya held up both his hands in a gesture that would have signaled respectful deference to his father, if not for the long knife he was still holding, the blade glistening in the flames of the torches.

All eyes were on Sallan.

"Tell us," the judge said. "How do you make the Reinforcing Liquid?"

Sallan shook his head.

"Don't you want to go upstairs and rest peacefully in your bed? Have I not provided you with the most luxurious quarters of any slave in Canaan?"

"There has never been a slave more fortunate than I," Sallan said, his voice shaky. "There has never been a master more generous than you have been to me. The pain of refusing you is greater than any physical pain your son could inflict on my old body."

"Then don't refuse me."

"My body belongs to you, but my soul belongs to the gods. Long before I came here, back in my homeland of Edom, I took an oath before Qoz to keep the secret, which had passed down from my ancestors. Breaking such an oath on my deathbed would surely condemn my soul. How can you ask me to sacrifice that which is beyond the grave?"

Everyone contemplated Sallan's words for a long moment.

"You are not the man you were in Edom," Judge Zifron said. "You are a slave now. The oath you took as a free man was lost with your freedom. As your body belongs to me, so does what's inside your head."

Sallan grasped the edge of the table and pulled up, rising with difficulty, until he stood. His light-blue eyes focused on Judge Zifron. "If a master could really own what's inside a slave's head, we wouldn't be in this situation, would we?"

"Insolent!" Seesya stepped forward and raised his hand to strike Sallan.

"Stop," a thin voice yelled. "Don't hit him!"

Seesya paused and, with everyone else, looked around to see whose voice it was.

"Please, Father." Babatorr stepped forward, his pudgy face flushed. "The foreman is old and ill. We need him to teach me all the workings—"

"Shut up, boy." Seesya shoved Babatorr away and turned back to hit Sallan.

Judge Zifron clapped. "Let the slave speak."

Glaring at Sallan, Seesya stepped aside.

"Master," Sallan said, "I have given you many years of loyal service, the full extent of my talent and the full bloom of my creativity. The baskets carrying your name have reached far and wide. Isn't that enough to earn the small favor of a peaceful death?"

"Go and die in peace," Judge Zifron said. "Who's stopping you? And you know what? I'll even throw you a funeral befitting an Edomite prince!" He turned to Kassite. "What would that require?"

A slight smile of irony crossed Kassite's face. "A stone coffin," he said. "Comfortable shrouds made of white linen, a good weapon for protection in the afterlife, and a purse with coins to buy gifts for the gods."

"It shall be done," Judge Zifron said. "Anything else?"

"A procession," Kassite said. "There is always a big procession for a prince."

"No problem." Judge Zifron sat back, pressing his hand to his heart. "You have my solemn promise for a funeral as grand as one held for a prince in your homeland. Every man in Emanuel will be summoned to attend and made to cry in mourning. But first, you must tell us how to make the Reinforcing Liquid so that we can keep the factory going."

Sallan lowered his head. "I cannot."

"And I cannot let my basket business die with you." Judge Zifron raised his voice. "Didn't you just say that the baskets carrying our brand have reached far and wide?"

Sallan nodded.

"Aren't you proud of that?"

Again, Sallan nodded.

"Then how can you expect me to shut down the factory? You must give us the formula for the Reinforcing Liquid—I command you!"

Sallan descended slowly back into his chair.

Seesya stepped forward and looked at his father.

The judge turned to Kassite. "My apologies, Prince Antipartis, for subjecting you to this spectacle, but surely you can see that we have no choice."

"A choice," Kassite said, "is a privilege that one decides whether to exercise, or not."

Nobody made a sound while the judge tried to understand what his guest meant.

"My sympathies," Kassite continued, "are in conflict. On the one hand, like you, I carry the burden of feeding my slaves and mercenaries while suffering their constant impertinence and conniving idleness."

"That's right," Seesya said. "Disobedient, lazy bastards all of them."

His father nodded in agreement.

"On the other hand," Kassite said, "I am sympathetic to this particular slave's fidelity to an oath that I, too, hold sacrosanct. Maybe the Hebrew god is more lenient when it comes to breaking sacred oaths? No disrespect intended to my gracious host."

"None taken," Judge Zifron said. "Gods don't care about oaths taken by slaves, and this foolish slave leaves us no choice but to use force to extract from him what's ours."

"That is fascinating." Kassite put one long leg on top of the other, lounging back in a pose of relaxed pondering. "In my country, a legend is often retold about the ancient Hebrew prophet Moses, also called the Law-Giver, who led your tribes through our land on their exodus from Egyptian slavery. It is said that the Hebrews revere the law so much that they accept as their leaders judges, not kings or lords. Is that true?"

"Yes," Judge Zifron said. "That's our tradition."

"A wonderful tradition," Kassite said. "I was wondering whether Moses left behind a law about the extraction of a secret from the mind of a slave. Did he?"

Judge Zifron looked at his guest in surprise.

An awkward silence hung in the air.

"The law?" Seesya leaned on the table with both hands, facing Kassite. "As my father said, the law is that this slave belongs to us, including what's in his head—especially the formula required to make Zifron baskets!"

"My son is right." Judge Zifron shook his finger. "The law of theft applies here. By harboring our property in his head, this slave is guilty of stealing from us."

"And we know," Seesya said, "what the punishment for stealing is."

Seesya's soldiers hooted and stomped their boots.

Seesya picked up the smallest knife. "We'll start modestly, and then continue piece by piece for as long as the stealing continues."

Watching this, Deborah felt sick. It was surreal, a bad dream that would end when she woke up. But it was real, and she wished for Obadiah of Levi to show up in the courtyard and pound his staff on the ground three times to stop this evil from happening. She looked at the doors to the street, but Obadiah wasn't there. She adjusted her leather helmet on her head, which was damp with sweat.

Sallan closed his eyes and held one arm forward as if he knew what to do and had rehearsed it before. His lips parted, and a strange sound emerged. Deborah, standing behind Kassite, recognized it as an Edomite chant, similar to the songs Antippet and Patrees sang at night by the fire.

Seesya grasped Sallan's wrist and pressed down so that the hand was flat on the wooden tabletop. He placed the point of the knife between the pinky and the fourth finger.

The chanting was sad, but it was not fearful. The Edomite men around Deborah began to hum along with Sallan.

"Slave," Judge Zifron said, "this is your last chance."

Sallan continued to chant, his eyes shut.

Seesya looked at his father, waiting for the go-ahead.

"May I suggest something?" Kassite asked.

Sallan stopped chanting.

The judge turned to Kassite. "What is it, Prince Antipartis?"

"Now that your slave realizes the certainty of the painful consequences of his stubbornness, perhaps you should send him back to his quarters for the night to contemplate."

Judge Zifron's face lit up. "Perhaps I should."

"By morning," Kassite continued, "he might see the futility of resistance and give in."

"By morning," Seesya said, "this damn slave might be dead of his illness."

"That's true," the judge said. "And we might be left without the Reinforcing Liquid, though with plenty of regrets. No, he must talk now, or suffer the consequences."

Sallan resumed chanting.

With a quick downward thrust, Seesya brought the blade down.

Sallan's pinky rolled on the table, leaving a trail of blood.

Deborah covered her mouth, and everyone groaned. Sallan cried out once but then continued to chant.

Placing the blade between the remaining fingers, Seesya said, "Here goes the next one."

"Father," Babatorr pleaded. "Tell Seesya to stop!"

Judge Zifron waved his hand. "Go inside the house if you can't bear it."

Chanting meekly, Sallan swayed.

"Speak up, slave." Seesya held the knife with both hands, ready to press down. "One. Two."

The chanting stopped, and Sallan's head slumped.

Her eyes moist, Deborah tried to see if he was breathing. Let him live, she begged Yahweh silently. Her heart filled with admiration for Sallan, who was dying for an oath he'd taken in another country many years ago, whereas she could do nothing to keep the oath she had taken right here in this house only months earlier to come back and free him.

One of Seesya's soldiers brought a jar of water and emptied it on Sallan's head, reviving him.

Seesya grasped Sallan's right hand and pressed it in the puddle of blood on the table. "Maybe we'll speed things up a bit," he said, selecting a longer blade and placing it over the wrist. "Speak up, or lose your hand. One—"

Sallan began to chant again, though his voice was scratchy, as if he didn't have enough air to push through his vocal cords.

Deborah couldn't stand this any longer. She wished for a rock that would fit in her sling, for time to prepare the Edomite men for a sudden attack, for a chance to do something—anything! But the cool voice in her head pointed out that Seesya's soldiers outnumbered them five to one. What could she do to save Sallan without bringing death and destruction upon her, Kassite, and the Edomite men?

"Father?" Seesya looked at the judge expectantly. "Shall we?"

Sallan's voice strengthened, and his chanting grew louder.

Judge Zifron sighed. He raised his hand to signal his approval.

"Before you continue," Kassite said, "would you like me to take a look at the slave? The last thing you want is for him to die before you've managed to extract the information."

Judge Zifron gestured. "Go ahead."

Letting go of Sallan's hand, Seesya grinned, the scar causing his face to seem even more menacing. He smoothed his oily black hair down over his ears, and his grin faded, telling Deborah that her father's fire-starters had indeed left lasting injuries. She felt a mix of dread and satisfaction.

Sallan ceased chanting and opened his eyes.

Rising from the large armchair, Kassite took his time to fix his coat and straighten his hat. He went around the table, smiled graciously at Seesya, and took Sallan's hand, which dripped blood from the severed pinky. He pulled a piece of cloth from his pocket and bandaged the wound quickly.

Deborah was impressed that he'd come prepared.

Kassite repeated the examination procedure from before, peering into Sallan's mouth and eyes. He grunted, went back around the table, and sat in the armchair.

"Well?" Judge Zifron looked at him. "Can we continue?"

"Medicine is not an exact science," Kassite said. "And I am not an expert on torture. Perhaps he could tolerate a couple more amputations. More likely, he will die with the next one. You can try."

Seesya grabbed Sallan's hand and reached for the blade.

Sallan began to chant again.

"If I were you," Kassite said, "I would not do it."

The judge turned to him. "You wouldn't?"

"Do you know what he is chanting?"

"No."

"An Edomite funeral chant." Kassite said. "In my opinion, this man is literally at death's door. All he needs is a little push, and your son is about to grant him this last favor."

Judge Zifron signaled Seesya to wait.

Sallan stopped chanting and opened his eyes.

Deborah struggled not to cheer.

"Let me continue," Seesya said. "He'll talk before he dies. I guarantee it, Father."

Kassite laughed out loud.

Judge Zifron turned, surprised by the laughter.

"I am sorry." Tilting his hat, Kassite laughed some more. "If your son can guarantee such a thing, then he must be in possession of the divine powers of the Hebrew god. As a mere human, who am I to disagree?"

Acknowledging his guest's irony with a chuckle, Judge Zifron clapped. "That's it for today. We'll try again tomorrow. Perhaps he'll see reason."

Seesya held up the blade. "This is the only language slaves understand."

"I've made my decision, Son."

Lips pressed in anger, Seesya dropped the blade on the table and spat on the ground. "It's a mistake!"

A son hurling open criticism at his father was a crime punishable by flogging. Everyone in the courtyard froze, waiting to see what Judge Zifron would do, but he only shook his head and waved dismissively.

The boy-servants stepped forward to lift Sallan's chair.

"Wait," Seesya said. "I have an idea."

He grabbed one of the boys, bent him over the end of the table, and held him down. The boy faced sideways, his face a frozen mask of terror.

Seesya picked up a two-pronged blade, placed it against the side of the boy's head, and moved it forward so that the boy's ear was caught between the two prongs. With a quick jerk forward, he sliced the ear off cleanly and flipped the blade sideways, tossing the severed ear into Sallan's lap.

The boy wailed.

Sallan looked down at the ear in his lap and began to sob.

Seesya grinned. "No more chanting?"

His soldiers burst out laughing.

"Slave," Seesya said, "look at me."

Sallan raised his teary eyes.

"Ready to talk?" Seesya grabbed the boy's hair and turned his head to face the other way. "Or have another ear in your lap?"

Sallan wept.

Seesya sliced off the other ear.

The boy screamed and struggled to get away, but Seesya easily kept him down.

Shocked into numbness by this dramatic turn, Deborah watched in horror. Ear removal was sometimes a punishment for escaping slaves, but this boy had not escaped. Had Seesya's own injured ears given him the idea to do this? Was it her fault?

"Well, slave?" Seesya flung the second ear at Sallan, hitting him in the chest. "What do you say?"

Sallan continued weeping.

Seesya dropped the bloody two-pronged blade, not letting go of the writhing boy, and picked up a long double-edged knife. He held it vertically, pointing down at the wound where the ear once was.

"I'm going to push it through," Seesya said. "Very slowly. He'll feel it coming into his head like a mare feels her first stallion. And if you continue in this stubborn silence, I'm going to start carving up your other boy, piece by piece, starting with his most precious parts. Do you get the picture?"

Sallan watched him through a mist of tears.

Unable to stand it any longer, Deborah gripped her short sword and prepared to draw it from its leather scabbard.

"One," Seesya said. "Two."

"Wait." Sallan held up his bandaged hand. "Don't kill him."

"Are you going to talk?"

"Yes." Sallan looked at the judge. "Please, tell him to let the boy go."

Judge Zifron signaled his son to step away, and Seesya complied, pounding his chest while the soldiers cheered.

Deborah's hand let go of her sword. Behind her stoic expression, she was far from cheering, yet she was flooded with relief. She cared nothing for the Reinforcing Liquid, or the Strengthening Stew, whatever they called it. Let Judge Zifron have it. She took a deep breath and exhaled slowly. She felt sick over the boy's injuries, but the danger to Sallan was over. Once he told them what they wanted to know, they would have no more use for him and no reason to object if he asked to go home to Edom with the "prince." She almost sighed out loud, relieved that the chances of getting out of Emanuel alive had greatly improved.

17

Sallan's unmolested boy-servant washed the other one's wounds at the well and tied a rag around his head. Judge Zifron told everyone else to step out of earshot. Deborah and the Edomite men went to the other side of the courtyard and watched, but Kassite remained seated, and Babatorr was summoned back from the house to listen in. Sallan began to speak, the scribe wrote it down, and Seesya paced back and forth, tossing a short blade in the air and catching it by the hilt.

Watching Seesya and his twirling blade, Deborah's sense of relief and optimism began to fade. Why was he staying in the courtyard? Had he not succeeded in breaking Sallan's will and forcing him to reveal the secret? Wasn't he eager for a hot bath? For clean sheets on a comfortable bed?

Trying to guess what was on Seesya's mind was difficult, because she could never think the way he did, free of moral boundaries, unburdened by empathy for other people and, most incomprehensibly, unafraid of Yahweh's wrath. What evil plans lurked inside his dark mind?

She looked at Judge Zifron, who ultimately controlled Seesya's actions, either with explicit orders or by the default of silence. Did he know?

The judge sat back in his large armchair, his hands resting on his belly, fingers interwoven, and listened to Sallan explain how to make the Reinforcing Liquid. His expression showed neither satisfaction nor impatience, as if this whole episode were but a routine bump on his path to more riches and power.

Deborah recalled something Sallan had once said: "Powerful rulers and men of great wealth do not make decisions based on what's fair and just. When a situation comes up, they look at all the facts, figure out what they can use for their advantage, and come up with solutions that promote three things: their safety, their fortune, and their power."

She tried to put herself in Judge Zifron's shoes, as big as those shoes might be. He needed the secret formula for his fortune, but what about his safety and power? The facts were that Sallan, a mere slave, had refused the judge's order to reveal a secret, withstood torture to the point of mocking his master, and surrendered only after Seesya stooped to brutalizing an innocent boy. Sallan, Deborah realized, had made the judge look weak, diminishing people's fear and respect for him. Sallan's resistance made Judge Zifron less powerful and less safe. The only way to recover that power and respect was to punish Sallan severely.

The judge's strategy now became clear to Deborah. He'd had to cause Sallan to talk, using a combination of promises and pain, but there was no way he would let a defiant slave go free. The fearsome reputation of Judge Zifron and his son depended on it. That's why Seesya had stayed—he was waiting for Sallan to finish telling them how to make the Reinforcing Liquid!

She had to let Kassite know before it was too late.

Leaning close to Antippet, Deborah whispered, "Punch Patrees really hard!"

He looked at her as if she had gone mad. "Punch Patrees? Why?"

Patrees heard it and turned to them.

"Punch him," she said. "Do it!"

Antippet shook his head, but Patrees didn't hesitate and threw the first punch. Antippet hit him back, and they began to wrestle. Everyone in the courtyard turned to look, including the group around Sallan. Seesya said something, and Judge Zifron laughed. The soldiers and attendants around the courtyard joined the laughter.

Deborah didn't watch the scuffle, but stared at Kassite. She touched her mouth. He got up slowly and walked over. Deborah noticed that he was hiding his limp with a stiff, straight-backed gait.

The Edomite men quieted down and lined up at attention, including Deborah.

"What is this behavior?" Kassite glared at the men. "We are guests here!"

Antippet glanced at Deborah. "Borah told us—"

"It's not over," Deborah whispered without moving her lips. "They're going to kill Sallan."

Kassite looked at her lips. "What did you say?"

She stepped closer to him, keeping her voice low. "They will kill him."

His eyebrows creased, changing his expression to one of doubt and disapproval.

"He challenged them," she said. "They have to kill him."

"Execute a dying man?"

"They had no problem torturing him."

Kassite nodded. "He who assumes the worst about his opponent wins the conquest."

"We have to attack first. We'll have surprise on our side—"

"Do nothing without my explicit order."

Before she could argue further, Kassite walked back across the courtyard and sat down by the judge. "I should whip them more often," he said, shaking his head. "Worse than donkeys."

The judge laughed and motioned to Sallan to continue talking.

When Sallan finished, the scribe wrote down the last item on the list of ingredients and handed the parchment to Judge Zifron.

"Well done." The judge put down the parchment. "Bring us refreshments!"

His attendants sprang into action: some went to the kitchen, others to add wood to the fire and bring a barrel of wine. A few women appeared with bowls of fruit and cakes, as if they had waited out of sight for a signal. They knelt, holding forth the bowls before Judge Zifron, Kassite, and Seesya, who also sat down in a large chair that a servant had brought for him.

Deborah watched with relief as Seesya's soldiers cleared the blades from the table while he bit into a red apple and chewed with great relish. Sallan's boy-servants reappeared, one wearing a bandage around his head. They lifted the chair and carried Sallan to the basket factory. Kassite glanced at Deborah and smiled briefly. She felt foolish for having staged the fight between Patrees and Antippet. Didn't men panic sometimes? She hoped he wouldn't interpret the episode as an indication of her failing to acquire a man's character. In all fairness, she had proposed a proactive, aggressive course of action, hadn't she?

As Sallan and the boys were about to disappear into the basket factory, Seesya yelled, "Wait a minute!"

The crowded courtyard quieted down.

Signaling to his soldiers, Seesya said, "Take the slave and his two boys down to the gatehouse, chop off their heads, and stick them on poles."

Sallan looked at Judge Zifron. "You promised me that I could die in peace, that you'll throw a funeral for me with—"

"Shut up!" Seesya threw the half-eaten apple, hitting Sallan's chest. "Take him!"

"I made an offer." Judge Zifron picked a dry date from a bowl and bit into it, chewing while talking. "And I would have honored it, but you didn't accept my offer, did you? My son had to inflict pain on you and your servant to pressure you into obedience. Now you'll pay the price of insubordination."

The soldiers grabbed Sallan and the two boys and led them to the exit.

Deborah couldn't breathe. She stared at Kassite, waiting for him to make a move, but he didn't even look at what was happening. He peered into a bowl of sliced pomegranates and selected a piece, which he examined with keen interest while the soldiers took Sallan and the two boys out of the courtyard. She started moving forward to draw Kassite's attention, but he glanced at her, shook his head slightly, and returned to nibbling the pomegranate slice.

"Justice must be seen," Judge Zifron said. "Even when it's unpleasant."

"It is our burden." Kassite nibbled at the pomegranates slice. "This is delicious."

The women and servants reappeared as if they had been waiting for a signal and rushed to set the table with cloth and dishes, followed by jugs of wine, loaves of bread, and plates of meat. Deborah heard a familiar voice and turned to see Vardit issuing instructions at the kitchen door. Before Deborah looked away, their eyes met.

Vardit stopped talking.

Deborah turned away and held her breath.

Vardit resumed instructing the workers.

Relieved, Deborah exhaled. The look in Vardit's eyes had suggested a vague recognition, yet the disguise must have worked or Vardit would have rushed over to check whether her eyes had tricked her, or her missing daughter-in-law had suddenly reappeared in the form of an Edomite soldier.

Still busy with the pomegranate slice, Kassite beckoned one of his servants, who brought Qoz over and placed a plate of food before it.

Seesya stepped closer and peered at the copper effigy. "Are his eyes open or closed?"

Judge Zifron hushed him.

"We thank Qoz," Kassite said, "our god, supreme master of the world, for the food he deigns to share with us, as well as for the opportunity to witness the wisdom and justice of our Hebrew friends. May Qoz keep us safe until we reach our home in Edom and make sacrifices at the temple."

"I've heard about your sacrifices." Seesya laughed. "A traveler told me that your king keeps a giant copper god that wields a very sharp pitchfork, like this little one here, and you people impale a pretty girl on it once in a while."

"It is a thunderbolt," Kassite said. "Not a pitchfork."

"Thunderbolt, pitchfork, what's the difference?"

"That's enough," Judge Zifron said, smiling apologetically. "Please excuse my son's youthful impoliteness."

"Fortunately, ignorance may be cured by learning. Here is the difference, young man." Kassite looked at Seesya. "A pitchfork might be used for impaling girls, or hay, but a thunderbolt in the hands of our mighty Qoz controls light and darkness, whips up storms and rainfall, and delivers blessings and curses. And when insulted by thoughtless men," Kassite concluded, his voice rising, "Qoz might use his thunderbolt to strike with deadly force!"

The sharp rebuke brought silence to the courtyard, and everyone paused to watch.

"Go ahead, Son." Judge Zifron stood up. "Apologize to our guest."

"No insult was intended." Seesya touched the sharp points of Qoz's three-pronged thunderbolt. "I was only curious about the sacrifices. No girls for your god, then?"

"I did not say that." Kassite took another slice of pomegranate and nibbled on it. "There is no impaling, but on special occasions, when the king wishes to express the highest form of gratitude to Qoz, an offering is made of a beautiful girl, free of blemish and vice, who rejoices at being selected for such great honor."

Seesya rubbed his hands, grinning. "How's this offering done?

Sword? Fire?"

Judge Zifron sat down. "Let's eat."

"I'm only asking," Seesya said, "because I'd like to offer a certain girl as a gift to your god."

Kassite turned to him. "Who might that be?"

Holding her breath, Deborah knew what was coming.

Seesya dropped back into his chair and grabbed a jug of wine. "My runaway wife."

"Is she beautiful?"

"My mother thinks so." Seesya drank directly from the jug.

"Your mother is right," Judge Zifron said. "The orphan girl is quite fetching in a foreign, exotic manner."

"She makes me sick." Seesya slammed down the jug and spat on the ground. "As soon as I catch her, which won't take much longer, I'll send her with your next caravan, and you can give her to your mighty Qoz—impaled, speared, gutted, or burned, whatever your king fancies, doesn't matter to me."

Deborah felt her face flush, but she had more immediate worries. The soldiers were halfway down to the gatehouse by now, and Kassite had done nothing to save Sallan. It was up to her, she decided, and started moving toward the exit from the courtyard.

As he put down the piece of pomegranate, Kassite glanced casually at the parchment. "Your scribe writes beautifully."

"Thank you." Judge Zifron held it up. "I employ only the best."

"But the list is incomplete."

Deborah paused and listened.

"What?" Seesya got up and snatched the parchment from his father's hand. "How do you know?"

Judge Zifron held out his hand. "Give it back to me, Son, and sit down."

Seesya handed the parchment to his father and sat at the edge of his seat.

"Perhaps I am wrong," Kassite said. "It has been many years since I helped make the secret liquid, and I do not remember everything precisely, but I do remember at least two ingredients that are missing from this list."

"Which ingredients?" Seesya got up again. "Tell us!"

"I cannot tell you."

"Why not?"

"Because the same sacrosanct oath binds me, too." Kassite smiled. "You are not going to slice off my finger, are you?"

"Prince Antipartis!" Judge Zifron feigned horror. "You are our guest!"

Seesya was already on the move. He ran to the back of the courtyard, where the horses were tied near the stable, untied a great white stallion, and took off across the courtyard, causing several servants to drop bowls and trays.

Everyone remained quiet as the sound of hooves faded down the street. Deborah realized she had never seen a white horse before, free of even a single patch of black or brown. The beast must have been priceless, and she wondered whether Seesya's new sword had come from the same unlucky owner, who had probably lost those precious possessions together with his life.

18

They heard the drumming of hooves approach the house, and Seesya rode into the courtyard. He jumped off and handed the reins to a servant. "They're coming back," he said.

"To life!" Judge Zifron raised his wine goblet.

Kassite smiled. "To life!"

Seesya grabbed the wine jug and gulped directly from it

"That's a magnificent horse," Kassite said, his eyes following the white stallion as it was taken to the stable at the back of the courtyard. "Egyptian?"

"What else?" Seesya slammed the jug down on the table.

"That lying slave," Judge Zifron said. "After all the luxuries I've allowed him, that's how he pays me back—insubordination and lies. I should have remembered the old saying: Showing kindness to a slave is like putting a worm into an apple."

"I'll make him eat his own rotten flesh." Seesya made a slurping sound with his lips, making his soldiers laugh.

"Revenge can be very satisfying," Kassite said. "Even when its cost is excessive."

The judge looked at him. "But he'll reveal the secret first."

"How would you know if he is lying again?"

Seesya pointed at Kassite. "You'll tell us."

"Help you uncover our people's most precious secret? I have done too much already."

"We must have it," the judge said. "Without the Reinforcing Liquid, our basket business would collapse."

After a long pause, Kassite said, "If you are willing to forgo revenge, there could be a safer approach."

"There's nothing wrong with our approach," Seesya said. "Pain is the best extractor of information."

"Young man," Kassite said, "in this situation, pain will achieve nothing."

"You want to bet?"

"That would be imprudent. If you lose, the greatest source of your father's wealth will be lost with it. The only safe path is to convince your slave to reveal the truth of his own free will."

"Prince Antipartis is correct," the judge said. "The risk is too great. We should not harm Sallan any more."

Seesya stepped forward, drew his sword, and planted the point in the ground. "Father, let me do it my way!"

Judge Zifron waved his hand. "I've made my decision. No more violence."

"A wise decision," Kassite said. "I can see now why your people made you a judge over them."

The judge nodded with a smile.

"Among your many slaves, do you have an Edomite slave of reasonable intelligence?"

"Why?"

"An Edomite man may reveal the secret formula to another descendent of Esau, providing the recipient takes an oath of secrecy, as well."

"I don't like it," Seesya said. "We'll be beholden to yet another filthy slave."

"A valid concern," Kassite said. "You can always buy a new Edomite slave and make sure he also swears to secrecy and learns the formula from the first one."

"Go, Son," Judge Zifron said. "Ask the warden for our best Edomite slave and bring him here."

Seesya sheathed his sword and left.

Moments later, the soldiers entered the courtyard with Sallan and the two boy-servants. The injured one was bleeding through the bandages. He wobbled, almost fell down, and one of the soldiers grabbed him roughly. Two other soldiers supported Sallan, whose face was as white as bed linen. They put him in a chair facing the judge and Kassite. The boys sat on the ground.

Seesya returned with a man in a sleeveless long shirt and bare feet, not older than twenty, who immediately knelt before Judge Zifron. He had the reddish furry look of the Edomite men, with short light hair, and a frightened expression.

"Stand up," Judge Zifron said. "What's your name?"

"Sahir."

"Are you from Edom?"

Sahir nodded.

"This is my guest, Prince Antipartis, who came from your country. Do what he tells you to do, or you will be punished." The judge turned to Kassite. "Go ahead, Prince."

Deborah edged closer to hear.

"Other than my plans to buy and sell many sturdy baskets," Kassite said, "I am free of any personal interest here."

"Greed," Sallan said quietly, "is the most potent personal interest."

Judge Zifron glared at him.

"There is no offense in the truth," Kassite said. "Greed is indeed a strong motivation for any industrious man. I am not ashamed of it. And how about you, slave? What is your motivation?"

Sallan glanced at the two boy-servants. "To see my homeland once more before I die."

"And silver? Or gold?" Kassite's tone was mocking. "What else do you wish to extort from your master in exchange for the correct formula?"

"Nothing," Sallan said, "for I cannot reveal the formula to my master. My soul's eternal damnation is worth more than any silver or gold."

"But you could reveal it to another Edomite man who swears to secrecy, right?"

"Yes."

"And what would you demand in return?"

"Only what I've said." Sallan shrugged. "To see Edom as a free man before I die and let the boys go free there."

Deborah was in awe of their ability to keep up this hostile and deceitful exchange without once showing their true feelings for each other.

Kassite turned to the judge. "Will you agree, provided that the secret of the Reinforcing Liquid is revealed in full, to grant freedom to this old slave and his two boy-servants and allow them to return home to Edom unmolested?"

"I agree," Judge Zifron said. "You have my word."

Seesya hissed, but stopped when his father gave him a sharp glare.

Kassite made Sahir kneel before Qoz and take an oath of secrecy.

Rising from his chair with difficulty, Sallan walked aside with Sahir and told him how to make the Reinforcing Liquid. Sahir repeated each ingredient and every step, committing them to memory. Kassite went over and listened in. This went on for a while, with Sallan testing Sahir several times.

When it was over, Kassite rejoined Judge Zifron. "It is done," he said. "They will now go into the factory and practice making the Reinforcing Liquid together and review all the other aspects of making the baskets so that Sahir will be most helpful to your son Babatorr in all other respects of managing the factory."

Judge Zifron clapped. "Very good!"

"Will you now announce that you set these three free? I will take responsibility for them, as a favor to you, until we reach Edom."

The judge pointed at the three of them. "I hereby grant Sallan complete and irrevocable freedom and safe passage, together with his two boy-servants. Go back to Edom, and may the gods punish you for your insubordination."

Deborah was simultaneously weak with relief and elated with joy. By uttering these words, Judge Zifron had unknowingly brought about the fulfillment of her oath to help Sallan win his freedom. The price had been stiff, with Sallan's finger and the boy's mutilated ears, but the final result was nothing short of a miracle. She was in awe of Kassite's clever maneuvering and the straight face he had kept while diverging from the truth left and right, masking his love for Sallan at the height of Seesya's violence, when the risk of fatal and total loss had seemed certain. Even she, who knew Kassite's true feelings for Sallan, had not seen a trace of distress, concern, or outrage behind Kassite's facade of cool bemusement, as befitting a wealthy nobleman.

Sallan, his two boy-servants, and the Edomite slave Sahir bowed before the judge and went into the basket factory.

"A tiresome bunch, these slaves." Kassite sat down and exhaled. "But the result is satisfactory, is it not?"

"Excellent." Judge Zifron rubbed his hands. "How can I thank you?"

"May I suggest generous discounts on the baskets and food

commodities I will be ordering?"

They laughed while Seesya got up and left. He joined his soldiers, who sat on the ground around plates of food and ate with their hands.

That night, after the long meal had ended, Sallan and the two boys came to the guest quarters. The boys carried a heavy sack each while supporting Sallan, who was swaddled in his tiger skin even though the night was warm. He was no longer the powerful foreman of the basket factory. All his privileges and personal effects had been taken away. He was now a destitute old man, but he was free.

Patrees helped the injured boy sit down and gave him water, while Kassite invited Sallan into the inner room. Deborah took off her leather helmet, unbuckled the short sword, and followed them. She paused at the doorway, stunned at what she saw.

Kassite was on his knees, holding Sallan's hand to his lips.

As shocked as she was, Deborah had the presence of mind to shut the door behind her before the Edomite men witnessed this inexplicable sight—Master kneeling before the slave whose freedom he had just secured.

Sallan helped Kassite up, and the two old men fell into each other's arms, embracing for a long time. Deborah wasn't surprised by the expression of affection, having heard from Kassite about his love for the friend he had thought was dead. But still, why had he—the Elixirist!—knelt before Sallan?

Sniffling, Sallan turned to Deborah. "Thank you for keeping your promise. I owe you everything."

"And I owe you this." Deborah pulled the tiger tail from her sack and handed it to him.

Sallan laughed and pressed it to his face.

"And this, too." Deborah bent her arms to show him the new muscles. "Kassite has already given me two doses of the Male Elixir. Only one more, and my transformation will be complete."

"Impressive results for such a short time." Sallan touched her biceps. "You look completely different, especially with all your beautiful hair gone."

"Beautiful?" Deborah scoffed. "It used to look like an orange tree before the picking."

"And that's not a thing of beauty?"

"To be a man, I'd give up much more than my hair."

Kassite chuckled. "She is a motivated girl, is she not? At first, I expected her to give up quickly, but she stuck with it and worked harder than anyone I have ever seen. In two months she has become more of a man than any of them." He gestured at the door to the other room, where the Edomite men were getting ready for the night.

Deborah blushed. "When you pursue your True Calling, God provides the shortcuts."

"Where was your god today?" Kassite took off his hat and passed his fingers through his white hair, which was sodden with sweat. "I have not played a tougher game in my entire long life."

"You were incredible." Sallan hugged him again. "Cool and aloof, like a real prince of Edom."

"Am I not a prince?"

"You are! I almost burst out laughing when Seesya guaranteed that he'd make me talk before I died, and then—what did you say to the judge? Wait, I remember!" Sallan closed his eyes, quoting from memory: "If your son can guarantee such a thing, then he must be in possession of the divine powers of the Hebrew god. As a mere human—"

Kassite joined him, and together they chorused, "—who am I to disagree?"

They laughed heartily.

"That's when I thought that we'd won," Sallan said. "The judge was sending me back upstairs for the night, and I had the potion ready."

"I counted on that," Kassite said.

Deborah looked at him. "What potion?"

"The Death Elixir."

"Death?"

"Nearly," Sallan said. "It makes the body fall into a sleep so deep that it's impossible to detect any breathing or heartbeat. I was going to drink it before dawn and appear dead to all in the morning. Kassite would find a way to get hold of my corpse, and once out of Emanuel, revive me."

"What about your illness?" She was struggling to understand. "Is it the result of another clever elixir? The Sickness Elixir?"

The two men looked at each other and laughed again.

"Limestone powder in water," Sallan said. "The simplest potion of all, though it gives you an awful nausea."

"You've poisoned yourself with limestone?" She covered her mouth. "For how long?"

"I started taking small quantities as soon as you left in order to grow the illness slowly and prevent suspicion. That way, by the time you returned with Kassite, even Seesya wouldn't suspect trickery."

"How could you be certain that I would return with Kassite?"

"I didn't know for sure, but in my heart I sensed the strength of your resolve and knew that you wouldn't give up until you found the Elixirist and enlisted his help. My only enemy was time, which always carries the possibility of real death."

She grabbed his arm, alarmed. "Are you near dying?"

"We're all dying," Sallan said. "From the moment of birth, death is the most certain future event. For me, death was an enemy not because it might take me, but because it might take you, or him." He looked at Kassite. "That was my greatest fear."

Deborah didn't let go of his arm. "How do you feel? Are you in pain? Are you dizzy?"

"Yes," Sallan said. "I'm in pain, I feel dizzy, and I'm probably near death, but it's all under control."

She looked at Kassite. "Is he losing his mind?"

"Hardly," Kassite said. "Do you not remember our discussion of strategy?"

Deborah thought about the moments right after the band of Dan tribesmen had ridden by with their loot and she had pressured Kassite about his plans for rescuing Sallan. "I remember your words exactly," she said. "Knowing Sallan, a strategy is already set in motion, ready for us to pick up and run with. My old friend is a master of the long game."

"You said that?" Sallan kissed Kassite on both cheeks. "You know me better than any man!"

Kassite beamed.

"Wait a minute," Deborah said. "Poisoning yourself until you almost die—that's the long game?"

"That's part of it," Sallan explained. "I also cut down on food in order to lose a lot of weight, dyed my hair white, and made my skin dry and brittle by rubbing it with sand. When a man looks deathly ill, his eventual death is the natural result. That was the long game, and it would have worked. Judge Zifron already allowed me to retire for the night, but then Seesya came up with the idea to torture my servant. That was the weakness in my plan. Seesya's inventive cruelty exceeded my expectations."

"But you could have died," Deborah said. "For real!"

"The higher the risks, the greater the rewards. But don't worry. As I induced the illness, so will I induce a recovery."

"How can you be so sure? What if the damage to your body is permanent?"

"What choice did I have? I had to prepare, give my dear friend something to work with." Sallan patted Kassite's back. "And what a show you managed to put on. Every move they made, you were ready with a countermove—like a swordfight of the minds!"

"It's all a show for you?" Deborah looked from one to the other in disbelief. "A game?"

"A game, yes," Sallan said, "but not in the sense of frivolous fun, obviously. It was a deadly game of minds, and we had to keep our opponents ignorant of our true goal."

"Beautifully put," Kassite said.

"Beautiful?" Deborah struggled to keep her voice down. "Taking poison? Losing fingers and ears?"

"Think of our position," Kassite said. "Our opponents held all the power, whereas we were weak and on their territory. There was no price for Sallan's freedom, because Judge Zifron would never have let go of the engine of his wealth. Therefore, the game required that we prevent them from realizing our true goal of freeing Sallan. Faking death would have been ideal, but once that option became unavailable, we had to come up with a different strategy. We created a false prize—the Reinforcing Liquid, coupled with a fake crisis—Sallan's fatal illness."

"Unfortunately," Sallan said, "in a conflict with powerful opponents, those with power always try to win through brutality first, and you have to let them use force and spill your blood." He held up his bandaged hand with the missing pinky. "But when they realize that their might isn't enough to bring them victory, the door opens for a compromise. The key to success is to let your opponents win a fake prize, gain an empty conquest, and celebrate an illusory victory, while you win the real prize—in this case, my freedom."

"Do you see it now?" Kassite grinned. "We won, but the judge and his hothead son foolishly believed that victory was theirs. Brilliant, is it not?"

"It would be more brilliant," Deborah said, "if you hadn't lost a finger and your servant hadn't lost his ears."

Sallan's smile faded. "A shackled man who desires freedom should expect to pay a heavy price." He glanced at his bandaged hand. "It's not as bad as losing a foot."

"Or your head, which the soldiers almost cut off at the gatehouse."

"That was close," Sallan said. "But we pulled it off, didn't we? We're free!"

"We are not free yet," Kassite said. "That young man Seesya—he is pure menace."

"I'll set a watch schedule," Deborah said. "We'll be ready for him if he comes."

"You're guests here," Sallan said. "Even Seesya wouldn't dare to attack guests in his father's house."

Deborah hoped he was right.

"I'm already thinking of home," Sallan said. "I can't believe we're going back to Edom tomorrow."

Kassite smiled. "It has been a long time."

"I was wondering," Deborah said. "Aren't you afraid?"

"Afraid?" Kassite looked at her. "Afraid of what?"

"Sallan told me how the king locked you up after you saved his kingdom, and you only managed to escape because you helped a deaf-mute guard to hear and speak again. What if the king finds out that you're back?"

The two men looked at each other.

"That old king is dead," Sallan finally answered. "A caravan from Edom stopped in Emanuel a few months ago. They told me that the old king, Esau the Eighteenth, had died, and his son, Esau the Nineteenth, died shortly afterward. The current king, Esau the Twentieth, is very young, which means that he hasn't yet earned the confidence of his people or the fear of his enemies. If anything, the young king would celebrate the return of the Elixirist, whose role in driving away the Egyptians has become the stuff of legends."

Kassite nodded in agreement.

The explanation satisfied Deborah. "By the way, do you know what happened to the guard? Was he punished for freeing you?"

They glanced at each other and smiled.

"It is a long story," Kassite said. "I am too tired to discuss the past right now."

"Indeed," Sallan said. "It's time to think of the future." He sniffed the tiger tail one more time, bunched it up, and pushed it into Deborah's sack.

She put her hand out to stop him. "What are you doing?"

"It's yours now. You've earned it."

"We will ride off at first light," Kassite said. "I have already taken leave of Judge Zifron and told him that I would like to get some traveling done before the day's heat forces us to take shelter. He is expecting our first orders for baskets and produce to arrive in a few weeks."

"He shouldn't hold his breath," Sallan said, and the two men laughed and laughed until they were bent over, leaning against one another, tears flowing down their cheeks.

19

Deborah and the eight Edomite men took turns standing watch outside the guest quarters through the night. Except for the occasional servant or soldier going to the washroom and back to sleep, the night was uneventful. When the sky began to lighten up in the east, Deborah went to the firepit and collected soot, which she mixed with water and smeared on her face, neck, arms, and legs. As Kassite had said, her eyes were the only part she couldn't disguise. Glancing around the courtyard, she saw no one. Soon she would leave this house, and the danger of being recognized would pass.

Antippet and Patrees went to get the horses from the stable, including the two additional horses that Kassite had purchased from the judge—one for Sallan and the other for his boy-servants to share. The compound started to wake up, and slaves carried food supplies from the storage area to the kitchen to prepare the morning meal. Deborah and the Edomite men put on their leather armor and helmets, strapped on the short swords, and tied the slings to the belts. The spears and shields were secured to the saddles. When the sun peeked over the hilltops east of town, the group was mounted and ready to go.

A few kitchen workers came out with packages of food for the road, which were accepted with smiles and gestures of gratitude. Kassite led the way across the courtyard, followed by Deborah, the Edomite men, and Sallan with his boys. One of Seesya's soldiers unlocked the courtyard doors and stood aside. For Deborah, eager to leave this place, it was all happening too slowly.

Someone tugged on her leg. Deborah's first instinct was to look, but she willed herself to keep her eyes straight ahead. Whoever it was, though, didn't give up. A hand reached up and grabbed Deborah's arm.

Squinting, Deborah looked down.

It was Vardit. She held up a package of food.

Deborah accepted the package and urged Soosie forward.

"Good luck!" Following alongside, Vardit pulled Deborah's hand and kissed it. "I'll pray for you!"

Out on the street, riding behind Kassite, Deborah exhaled with a slow, audible whistle. The shock that Vardit had indeed recognized her was mixed with regret that she couldn't greet Vardit, who had been kind to her. Even that quick exchange could lead to disaster if Seesya found out that his mother had kissed the hand of one of the Edomite prince's soldiers and said, "I'll pray for you."

The houses along the street were coming to life. Doors opened, fires started in workshops, and goats came out to nibble on the shrubbery. Women swept their floors, cooked food, and tended their small vegetable gardens. Here and there, a baby cried, a dog barked, and a donkey brayed. The air was crisp, and a light breeze tilted the smoke columns above the chimneys.

Kassite led the way down the main street of Emanuel. Deborah wished they could speed up, leave Emanuel, and put some distance between them and the murderous young man who, in the eyes of the world, was her husband. Seesya had made it plenty clear the night before that he didn't like his father's concessions. The gates, which she could see all the way down at the bottom of the hill, were wide open and inviting. Once they left town, Deborah intended to urge Kassite to get off the main road and travel into the hills, where tracking them would be harder.

She glanced over her shoulder. No one was following them. In a moment, they would be out of Emanuel.

Thinking of the journey ahead, Deborah wondered how long it would be before she could come back and fight for her inheritance. She had no family or friends other than this group of Edomite men. They were going home, but for her, Edom would be a foreign land, far away from everything she knew. Should she go with them? Did she have a choice? To win back Palm Homestead and fulfill her father's vision of becoming Yahweh's prophet, she must first become a man. For this, she had to stay with Kassite until he gave her the third and final dose of the Male Elixir, which would complete the process of her transformation.

The first phase—the requisite body strength and resilience—had taken a long time to achieve, but she hoped the second phase—the

masculine posture and character—would be accomplished more
quickly. Perhaps in a few days, while they were still near the Samariah
Hills, Kassite would declare her ready and give her the third dose. Once
she drank it, Kassite had explained, her sex parts would mutate to male.

She tried not to think about it. That final change was the most
uncomfortable aspect of the transformation. Would the third dose also
flatten her breasts and sprout stubble on her cheeks? She touched her
smooth face, wondering how it would feel to be a young man with the
start of a beard on his face, whether it would be prickly like her late
father's, or soft like the early growth on Zariz's chin, or somewhere in
between, like the budding goatee Barac had sported, short and dark but
still too sparse to take seriously.

She felt a pang of grief for Barac, yet smiled at the thought of Zariz.
She longed to see him again, even though she knew it would never
happen. He was a young Moabite, devoted to his family tradition of
plying the trade routes, whereas she was destined to become a man, farm
her father's land, and deliver Yahweh's message to the Hebrews.

About two-thirds of the way downhill, horse hooves sounded behind
them. Deborah turned her head and saw a lone rider galloping down the
street, leaving a wake of dust. She resisted the urge to speed up and
escape through the gates.

The rider flew by the group and continued downhill. She recognized
him as one of Seesya's soldiers. Quickening her horse's pace, she came
along Kassite.

"Look!" She pointed. "We should try to—"

Kassite raised a hand to silence her.

The soldier reached the gates and yelled at the sentries, who closed
the heavy doors.

When the group reached the gatehouse, Kassite addressed the three
sentries and Seesya's soldier. "Good morning! We have a long way ahead
of us—"

"My master," the soldier said, "wishes to greet you before you
depart."

Was he speaking the truth, Deborah wondered, or had Seesya heard
of Vardit's odd behavior and become suspicious? Deborah exchanged
glances with Sallan. He shook his head subtly. She understood. They
were no match for a trained soldier and three armed sentries, and even

if they managed to beat them back, open the gates, and run for it, Seesya's band of soldiers would chase them down the road and catch them easily.

A few minutes later, at the top of the hill, a group of riders emerged from Judge Zifron's courtyard. They rode downhill, Seesya in the lead, mounted on the great white stallion. There were about twenty soldiers, some not yet fully dressed in their leathers, but all carrying their spears. They reached the gates and took positions across the road, facing the group of Edomites.

"Greetings, Prince Antipartis." Seesya rested his hand on the silver hilt of his bejeweled sword. "What's the rush?"

Kassite smiled, waving to the east. "The morning sun does not wait for slow risers."

"Indeed." Seesya patted his restless stallion on the neck. "I was told that one of your soldiers was speaking with my mother."

Deborah kept her eyes to the ground.

"That would be impossible," Kassite said.

"You!" Seesya advanced his stallion at Soosie, and the difference in size between them made Soosie look like a donkey. "How do you know my mother?"

Deborah looked at him, her eyes squeezed tightly. She hoped the leather helmet and the soot on her face would keep him from recognizing her.

"He does not understand," Kassite said. "My soldiers do not speak your language."

"What's his name?"

"This is Borah. He is a young soldier I recently hired in—"

"How does he know my mother?"

Kassite chuckled. "He knows nobody. Was your mother among the women who gave us food before we left? He was only thanking her."

"She kissed his hand."

"Women do strange things," Kassite said.

Seesya pulled on the reins, shifting his horse's head sideways, and advanced until he was beside Deborah. "Look at me, soldier!"

She kept her eyes squinted.

Reaching over, he poked her chest. "Look at me!"

Deborah opened her eyes and looked at him. She saw his red scar twisting with the movements of his lips, and the oily black hair swaying over his shoulders. His familiar odor—sour sweat and garlic breath—reminded her of the last time they were so close to each other, on the night of their wedding, when he had failed to consummate the marriage and proceeded to choke her almost to death, before she knocked him unconscious with her father's fire-starters. Deborah stared at him, her chest filling with hot rage.

Seesya slapped the leather helmet off her head, and it fell away easily, being too big for her. His eyes opened wide and he yelled, "Holy Baal and Ashtoreth! I'll be damned!"

Rather than exploding, she harnessed her rage with a strange calm and used it to do what had to be done. Lifting her outside leg over the saddle, as if preparing to dismount Soosie, she grabbed hold of Seesya's arm and threw her leg over, hopping onto Seesya's saddle behind him. She drew her short sword and put the pointy end to the back of his neck while grabbing his hair with her left hand and pulling back.

The soldiers raised their spears, aiming at her.

The Edomite men were too stunned to draw their swords.

"Open the gates," Deborah said, "or I'll kill you."

The sentries ran to the gates.

"Don't do it." Seesya slowly raised his hands. "Keep calm."

"Open the gates!" Deborah pulled harder on his hair, tilting his head further back, her blade nipping his skin. "Open!"

"Leave the gates closed," Seesya said. "She won't do it."

The soldiers moved their horses around, aiming the spears.

The Edomite men finally recovered. They drew their swords, formed a ring around Kassite and Sallan, and began to move as a group away from the confrontation.

"I'm warning you!" Deborah stubbed her heels inward, and the stallion snorted, moving forward. "Open the gates, or it's all over!"

"Put the sword down," Seesya said. "You can't go anywhere. If you hurt me, all your friends are going to die."

"I don't care!"

"Oh, yes you do, my wife. You care what Yahweh thinks, don't you?"

She could tell he was smiling, and pulled hard on his oily hair, making him groan with pain. "Tell them to open the gates," she repeated. "I have nothing to lose!"

"You'll lose Yahweh's favor," he said. "Remember the sixth commandment? Do not kill!"

She didn't answer, but shifted her sword from the back of his neck to his lower back.

"Listen, men," he said. "On the count of three, kill the Edomites."

His soldiers turned their horses and aimed their spears at the Edomite group.

"No!" Deborah pushed the tip of her sword under the lower edge of his armor. "I'll maim you!"

"And have the blood of innocents on your hands?"

"You'll be a cripple!"

"And you'll be a sinner."

She pulled even harder on his hair, but the risk of violating one of Yahweh's commandments was too great, and she couldn't bring herself to push the blade into him.

"On the count of three," Seesya said. "One! Two!"

With a shout of frustration, Deborah threw away her sword.

Seesya elbowed her hard, and she fell off the horse, hitting the ground, the air knocked out of her. Before she could rise, he dismounted and stomped his boot on her back, pushing her face into the dust.

"Son of Zifron," Kassite said, "tell your soldiers to lower their spears before someone gets hurt."

With a quick gesture, Seesya signaled his soldiers to stand down. "Tell me, Prince Antipartis. How did my rebellious wife end up in your service?"

"Wife?" Kassite made a feeble attempt at laughing. "You took this young man for a wife?"

Seesya lifted his boot and landed it hard on Deborah's kidney, immobilizing her. He pulled her up and tore the leather armor off her chest.

Exposed to the sun, Deborah's adolescent breasts were white, freckled, and bruised from the tight armor, but they were undeniably present—the healthy breasts of a young woman at the outset of her childbearing years.

The Edomite men, who knew her as Borah, uttered cries of shock and dismay.

She tried to cover her breasts, but Seesya punched her again, and she collapsed.

Soosie neighed and sprinted at Seesya, knocking him to the ground. The horse reared up, raising his front hooves. Seesya rolled aside, and two of the soldiers urged their horses forward to protect him. Antippet rode over and grabbed Soosie's reins.

"Damn horse!" Seesya got up and brushed the dust off his armor. "Do you concede, Prince Antipartis, or do I need to strip her completely in order to convince you?"

"I had no idea," Kassite said. "I hired him—well, her—a few weeks ago. I needed another soldier for security along the trade routes."

"Now you know that this is no soldier, but an ugly witch."

Kassite looked away. "Please cover her up."

"I don't think so." Seesya pulled off Deborah's leg armors, boots, and sling, tossing them toward the Edomite group. "This stuff is yours, but she's mine."

Patrees collected the items from the ground.

Barely able to breathe, Deborah couldn't resist as Seesya took a rope from one of the soldiers, tied her wrists up front, and held on to the other end of the rope while mounting his horse.

"I respectfully protest," Kassite said. "Let us bring this before your father. He should decide."

"She's my wife, not my father's. I'll punish her as I see fit."

Naked except for a loincloth, her mind clouded by pain and humiliation, Deborah tried to free herself, but the rope was too tight, and Seesya began to ride. She managed to get up and walk after the white stallion.

"Open the gates!" Seesya rode toward the gatehouse. "Open up!"

Deborah ran after him, the fresh morning air cool on her bare skin.

Outside the gates, he rode faster, and she kept running, aware that if she tripped, he would drag her along, causing her skin to rip.

He stopped by the Weeping Tree, right under the dry bones of Tamar, and tossed his end of the rope over a solid branch. One of the soldiers grasped the loose end of the rope.

"Keep it tight," Seesya said.

The soldier made his horse step back until the rope tightened, forcing Deborah's wrists up above her head. Another soldier handed Seesya a horsewhip. It had a solid wood handle and three thin leather straps with knots at the ends.

"No!" Deborah tried to free her wrists from the rope. "No!"

At the fairgrounds across the road, merchants and travelers saw what was happening and ran over to watch.

The rope chafed the skin of her wrists, tightening with her struggle.

Kassite, who had followed with the others, came down from his horse. "This is not acceptable—"

"Don't interfere," Seesya said.

"I must insist." Kassite stepped closer. "This is not the way to resolve an honest dispute between honorable men."

"Back up, old man!" Seesya aimed the whip at Kassite's face. "She's a crafty witch, which is why I assume you didn't know what she was when you hired her, but I could change my mind and tie you up right here beside her."

Kassite stepped back. "It is true that I did not know, but I paid good silver for three years of service, which means she is still in my employ."

"Your employ?" Seesya grinned as he raised the whip. "Then this discipline will benefit both of us."

The whip whistled, and the knotted straps hit Deborah's back.

She wanted to keep her mouth shut and not give him the satisfaction of hearing her cry, but the pain stunned her with its fiery intensity. She screamed, even as part of her was bewildered that such a sound could emerge from her mouth.

The whip whistled again, and the knots slashed her back as if serrated knives sawed her flesh.

She screamed again and tried to run forward, away from him, but the rope around her wrists pulled upward, causing her feet to lose contact with the ground, and she swung back by her arms while the whip whistled for the third time. It was worse yet, if such pain was even possible, and she heard herself howl in agony. Trying to run sideways to avoid the next slashing didn't help. He landed the whip sideways, the straps wrapped around her ribcage, and the knots tore at her chest. As she swung the other way, he did the same from the opposite direction, the knots ripping at her left breast. The agony made her chest contract, pushing all the air out of her lungs in a wail that faded into an airless, soundless scream, then darkness.

20

The eagle soared above the Sea of Salt. Deborah marveled at the colors of the surrounding mountains—soft brown in the west and rich red in the east, as if the kidney-shaped sea had been poured like thick glue over a giant seam that separated two different lands. Barac sat on the wing beside her, his smile bright, his eyes large, brown, and warm. The wind swept away his white cap and ruffled his black curls. The eagle banked to the right and up through the blue sky, then left and down toward the water. The sudden maneuvers were thrilling, and Deborah leaned against Barac. He put his arm around her and held her against his solid frame. They smiled at each other, but then a shadow came from behind, and a giant black crow stuck its beak into her back. Excruciating pain tore her out of Barac's embrace, and she wailed.

The blue sky disappeared, together with the eagle and Barac. Deborah found herself lying on the hard ground under the Weeping Tree. Someone was poking at the wounds on her back, igniting the pain, and she remembered what had happened before she lost consciousness. She cried again and tried to sit up.

"Easy, easy," a woman said from behind. "I'm treating your wounds."

Deborah glanced back.

"It's olive oil and herbs," Vardit said, showing her a clay jar. "The Edomite prince gave it to me—some kind of special medicine."

"Prince?" Deborah's mind was slow to comprehend. "What prince?"

"Your master, Prince Antipartis."

"Oh, him."

"He cares about you more than one would expect in this situation." Vardit caressed her shaved head. "Poor thing. What happened to you?"

Deborah shifted with effort. The ground under her smelled of urine. "I'm sorry," she murmured.

"It's not your fault." Vardit dripped more of the oily paste on the wounds and spread it with her hand.

Deborah groaned and took a few quick breaths. She didn't want to faint again. "How did you recognize me?"

"You're too pretty for a boy." Vardit smiled. "And those eyes—even when you tried to avoid me, I couldn't miss them. No other person has eyes like yours, as green as—"

"As vomit?"

"As fresh leaves after the first rain. Only your sister had such beautiful eyes."

"My mother did, too."

Vardit continued to rub the paste over the lacerations on Deborah's back and chest. The searing pain was overwhelming. Unable to hold back anymore, she wept.

"That's it." Vardit plugged the jar and wiped her hands with a cloth. "All done."

She pulled Deborah up to a sitting position and slipped a red robe over her head. Deborah tried to put her arms through the sleeves, but her wrists were still tied up front. The rope no longer looped around a branch above. It went from her wrists down to her ankles, binding them together, and from there, it slithered to the nearby tree and looped around the trunk. Flies swarmed her.

Three soldiers sat in the shade, their horses tied nearby. A group of children watched curiously from the adjacent road. Deborah looked around through the film of tears that the fresh pain had brought, and saw the busy fairgrounds across the road and the gates of Emanuel a short distance away, the black flags of Ephraim fluttering in the light wind. Above her, Tamar's skeletal bones dangled from a high branch.

One of the soldiers came over and untied her wrists. Deborah put her arms through the sleeves and adjusted the red robe over her exposed breasts and down to her legs. The robe stuck to her wounds, which flared up painfully. The soldier tied her wrists again.

"I must go back," Vardit said, "or there will be more trouble."

Deborah noticed Vardit's bruised cheek. "Did Seesya hit you?"

"I deserve worse, foolish woman that I am. If I hadn't approached you, none of this would have happened."

"A son hitting his mother is an abomination." Deborah cleared her throat, ashamed of her shaking voice. "Why does your husband allow it?"

"Why?" Vardit laughed bitterly. "Because I was born a woman. That's our fate, girl. I accepted it long ago, and so should you."

There was a remedy that could lift the heavy burden of that fate, but Deborah couldn't bring herself to tell Vardit about the Male Elixir. The judge's wife was too old for it, too far down the path of a wife and a mother, too entrenched in a life that required submission and obedience. Deborah remembered that Shatz Ha'Cohen, the High Priest in Shiloh who had handed her over to Seesya to be forced into marriage, had quoted what Yahweh had said to Eve in the Garden of Eden: "Always you shall lust after your husband, and he shall reign over you." Telling Vardit about the Male Elixir now would only make her realize that she could have lived a different life—a devastating realization that would do her no good.

"I almost forgot." Vardit reached into her pocket and pulled out a copper ring. "Prince Antipartis found this in your sack. He asked me to give it to you and tell you to put it back on."

"I don't want it."

"He anticipated that you would argue." Vardit smiled as she slid the ring onto Deborah's finger. "He said to remind you that there's always a shortcut, but you need to survive and keep going until it shows up on your path."

Deborah understood, but Kassite's kind words of encouragement gave her no hope. Yahweh had shortened the way already, though not to her True Calling, but into Seesya's hands—a shortcut to her final demise. She hung her head, tears flowing again.

"Here, drink some water." Vardit held forth a waterskin. "What shortcut was he talking about?"

"It's something I heard along the way." Deborah took a sip. "When you pursue your True Calling, God provides the shortcuts."

Vardit glanced up at the sky. "I hope Yahweh knows it, too."

"Do you have a True Calling?"

"Me? I'm a wife." The older woman sighed. "I bore my husband's children and now help his younger wives, who are like sisters to me. I make sure the slaves get the meals ready and the clothes mended. And when Seesya finally matures and gains wisdom and patience like his father, I'll take pride in his achievements, because I've suffered through his growing pains."

What Vardit described didn't sound like one's True Calling, especially the part about Seesya, who would never grow wise or patient, Deborah was certain. Hearing the sadness in Vardit's voice, Deborah didn't say anything more.

"After your escape," Vardit said, "and the terrible flogging I received, Obadiah of Levi told me something about the future, which comforted me a great deal."

Deborah watched her, waiting.

Vardit glanced at the guards and lowered her voice. "The priest said that, after death, sinners go to a place of fire and torture, but the righteous go to a place as wonderful as the Garden of Eden. That's where I hope to go."

"A place like the Garden of Eden?" Deborah closed her eyes and imagined it. Could this be a person's True Calling—to win God's approval by living righteously in order to be rewarded after death? It was a tempting idea. Life was too painful and unfair. How pleasing it would be to arrive at a place where God made everything perfect, where He walked among the trees and greeted you. But was she righteous enough to be among those chosen to go there after death? Not only was she a rebellious wife, who had struck her husband and escaped her marriage, but she had also lied repeatedly to people during her quest to find the Elixirist, violated the Sabbath many times, pretended to be a man while carrying weapons, and participated in defrauding Judge Zifron—a game, a show, a fake!

"The pain should ease up soon," Vardit said. "Try to rest. It'll be all over tomorrow."

"What happens tomorrow?"

"A trial. Seesya sought his father's permission to kill you, as any husband may do to a rebellious wife, but the Edomite prince complained that he'd paid you for your services in advance and deserved compensation if Seesya killed you." Vardit adjusted her robe, making sure it covered her lower legs down to her sandals. "They searched your sack and found only a few coins, and my husband doesn't like to part with his money, so there will be a trial in the morning. The prince can't claim compensation if you've been convicted and executed by the townspeople according to the law."

"Seesya should be on trial," Deborah said. "Not me."

"Poor girl." Vardit caressed her head. "All the beautiful hair we dyed black is gone. What a shame."

"I didn't want to hurt him, only to save myself. He's the murderer, not me."

"It will be easier if you accept your fate." Vardit's voice broke. "Soon, your suffering will be over."

"I don't want to die."

"A quick death is better than a painful life." Vardit gestured at Tamar's bones. "Your sister is waiting for you in the Garden of Eden, together with your parents."

The older woman left, and Deborah lay back on the ground with her eyes closed, shutting out the harsh world around her.

When the sun went down, the soldiers started a small fire. They loosened the rope on her wrists and gave her a piece of bread and some water. After eating, she went behind the tree and relieved herself.

Curled up on the ground, Deborah tried to sleep, but her wounds hurt badly and thoughts of the impending trial assaulted her mind with images of stones hitting Tamar's bloodied head. She began to shake, which in turn caused her to become angry. Where had all her strength gone? Her resilience? Her masculine posture and male character? She had made it two-thirds of the way with determination, hard labor, and lonely suffering, accelerated by the first and second doses of the Male Elixir. And yet, despite coming so close to manhood, here she was, trembling like a little girl. It reminded her of the Edomite proverb Sallan had once quoted: "The higher the rise, the steeper the fall." But she didn't want to fall, didn't want to let her fear take control, didn't want to go back to the way she had once been, subjugated and helpless.

The pain grew progressively worse. Her whole back was on fire, and she bit her lips to avoid crying out loud. Why had Yahweh forsaken her like this? Was this her punishment for all the sins she had committed?

Deborah turned her head to look up at the night sky, but Yahweh didn't answer.

Thinking simultaneously of Yahweh and pain, Deborah remembered Miriam, the leader of the lepers who had sheltered her in Shiloh, saved her from capture by Seesya's soldiers, and helped her reach Aphek.

Miriam had explained why the lepers were missing limbs: "It's the worst aspect of our curse. We lose the ability to feel pain. Mice chew our fingers and toes, fire burns our feet and hands, and boiling water peels our skin away—all before we notice anything. Pain is the real gift from Yahweh, for without pain, there is no life. You should thank Him for this gift, for your ability to feel pain."

And with that memory, Deborah began to feel better, because she realized that God wasn't punishing her. He was rewarding her with pain, both physical and emotional, by subjecting her to flogging right under her sister's remains. This realization changed everything. All this agony wasn't a punishment, but a divine gift that tested her physical strength and mental resilience. God had given her a challenge whose harshness matched the greatness of her True Calling. As Miriam had said, she should welcome the pain as a gift from God. Had it not been the same with the terrible work in the tannery—stomping in urine and feces up to her knees, feet bleeding, blisters festering, lonely amidst a hundred Philistine slaves—which ultimately made her stronger? Yes, this new torment would make her even stronger!

The shaking diminished, her tears dried up, and Deborah fell asleep.

Long before sunset, traffic on the road became busy, waking her up. News of the trial must have spread through the region, and people traveled during the night to attend the event. They stopped by the Weeping Tree and held up their torches to look at her. Some yelled insults, others tossed rotting vegetables, and a couple of men pulled down their undergarments and urinated in her direction, which made the soldiers laugh.

21

The girls came early to the stoning. They emerged one by one from the gates of Emanuel, which opened at sunrise, but in a break from tradition, they did not spread out across the barren hillside to collect rocks. The sentries watched curiously as the girls walked up the road to the Weeping Tree and put down offerings—a piece of fruit, a chunk of date-honey, or a flower from a roadside bush. Deborah thanked each of the girls, who smiled shyly and went to collect stones.

The pile of stones grew until one of the sentries whistled, and the girls gathered back to the gate area. They sat in a circle around the Pit of Shame and waited.

Vardit came over a little later. She saw the pile of gifts and shook her head.

Deborah raised her red robe to expose her back. Vardit applied a fresh layer of Kassite's oily medicine on the wounds.

"Thank you," Deborah said. "Do you know why they brought me gifts?"

"Because they hear the lies." Vardit pulled down the red robe, covering Deborah's back. "Their ignorant, ungrateful mothers whisper lies about my son!"

The words gave Deborah home. The people of Emanuel knew that Seesya was evil, which was the reason she had tried to escape from him. Would they stand by and allow her unjust stoning to go through?

"Don't fool yourself," Vardit said. "No one will speak up for you. If not for Seesya and the soldiers he commands, Emanuel and all the homesteads around it would be easy prey to the Manasseh tribesmen or the Canaanites." Vardit handed her a clay bottle. "Sallan sent this to you. He said it would give you strength as it has done for you in the past."

The Reinforcing Liquid!

Deborah was filled with gratitude. When Sallan had given her a cup of the Reinforcing Liquid to drink on the night she escaped Emanuel, he had said, "Your heart must not resist or doubt the magic of your strength, but allow it to grow and make you mightier than the challenges facing you and taller than the barriers on your path." His words had come true as she went on to overcome impassable challenges and broke through impregnable barriers on her quest to find Kassite and convince him to help her. The Reinforcing Liquid had worked then, and it would reinforce her again today. She unplugged the bottle and drank its contents until the last drop.

Vardit took back the empty bottle. "What was it?"

"The Reinforcing Liquid."

"From the tub in the basket factory?" Vardit twisted her face. "That's disgusting."

"Quiet," one of the soldiers yelled. "Go home, woman!"

Deborah turned to face him. "How dare you speak like that to the wife of Judge Zifron?"

The soldier looked at her in disbelief and raised his spear as a club, threatening to strike.

"Untie this," Deborah said, raising her bound wrists. "Then you can try to hit me, and see what happens."

The soldier turned to his friends, and they all laughed.

"Pray to Yahweh," Deborah said as Vardit walked away. "Pray that He will save me."

The whole area near the gates filled with people, attracted not only by another spectacle involving the family of the town's ruler, but also by the whispered stories about a young wife who might be a boy. Hundreds of men, women, and children spread straw mats and settled down, eating and chatting in eager anticipation. In the fairgrounds, vendors and shoppers cut quick deals for jugs of wine and baskets of food to enjoy while waiting for the trial. Beggars worked the crowd, taking advantage of people's generosity, fueled by the mix of excitement and gratitude for being a spectator and not the one to die by the heavy hand of Judge Zifron's justice.

The sun had reached a third of the way up in the sky when Obadiah of Levi emerged from the gates in his white robe and bejeweled breastplate. The blue strings attached to the lower fringe of his robe swayed back and forth as he walked. Leaning on his oak staff, he gazed left and right in amazement at the size of the crowd. A dense mass of people covered the hillside and the open area between the road and the fairgrounds. Even the town wall had become a perch for spectators, who sat shoulder to shoulder, their legs dangling over the side.

The priest looked up the road toward the Weeping Tree. Despite the distance, Deborah could see the sadness on his face. After a long moment, he raised the ram's horn to his lips and blew. She remembered the same sound at the beginning of Tamar's trial—low and scratchy like an angry growl that went on and on until the spectators quieted down and no one moved except for the scavenger birds that circled above.

The seven elders appeared in their white Sabbath robes and solemn faces and sat on their bench near the gates.

Obadiah blew the horn in a series of sharp bleats, and the audience stood up.

Soldiers on foot marched out of the gates, followed by Judge Zifron on his horse, carrying the banner of the tribe of Ephraim on a pole. The aging sovereign wore no hat, and his shaven cheeks stood out in their whiteness. His young sons trailed him on ponies, starting with Babatorr, who seemed too big for his mount and too nervous for the occasion.

The soldiers grabbed the reins of Judge Zifron's horse before it had a chance to rear up in apprehension of the crowd. The judge handed over the banner and dismounted with some difficulty. He climbed the steps onto an elevated platform. His young sons sat at the foot of the platform.

A soldier brought the effigy of Mott, the Canaanite god of death, and Judge Zifron held it up. The crowd muttered at the sight of the dreaded, human-like black figure with gaping wolf jaws, holding the scepter of bereavement in one hand and the scepter of widowhood in the other. The judge placed Mott on the platform by his chair and sat down.

Seesya emerged from the gates on his white stallion at a fast trot, followed by a dozen mounted soldiers. He also held a pole, but rather than a banner, it brandished the golden effigy of Ra, the Canaanite sun god, which had a man's body and a hawk's head, crowned with a solar disk that had a serpent coiled around it. Seesya rode up to the platform, dismounted with a quick jump directly onto the platform, and grinned at the scattered applause, his scar burning red across his face from the left cheek to the right chin. He wore his leather armor and the sword with the silver hilt, but no helmet, spear, or shield. He raised the pole with the effigy of Ra, and when the crowd didn't respond, stuck the pole between the planks of the platform, where it remained upright beside him. The soldiers, meanwhile, rode on to the Weeping Tree and joined the three who were guarding Deborah.

Obadiah climbed the platform and stood at the opposite end from the judge and his son.

A trumpet sounded, and Kassite emerged from the gates on his horse. His wide-brimmed white hat and long leather coat looked worthy of a prince. Behind him came the eight Edomite men in leather armor and helmets, mounted on their horses, their backs straight and their faces stony. They carried all their weapons, and their horses were loaded with supplies for the road to Edom as they had been the previous morning. Deborah wondered about Sallan and his boy-servants, as well as her own horse, Soosie.

The judge clicked his fingers at Babatorr, who stood up and announced in a thin voice, "Our honored guest, Prince Antipartis of Edom."

The audience murmured, probably wondering why an Edomite prince was attending the trial.

Kassite climbed down from his horse and sat in a chair that had been set up for him next to the platform. The Edomite men dismounted, pulled the horses aside, and stood behind Kassite.

Judge Zifron clapped a few times to quiet down the crowd and yelled, "Bring forth the accused!"

The spectators turned to look at Deborah.

One of the soldiers untied the rope from her wrists and ankles. She stood up, fixed the hood of the red robe over her head, pulled back her shoulders, and marched down the road toward the platform. Her wounds hurt badly, and she felt countless eyes staring at her, but there was no fear in her heart, banished by Sallan's Reinforcing Liquid and by the knowledge that this whole trial was a gift from Yahweh, a challenge and a test that she was determined to pass. The horses' shoes rapped the road behind her, and she imagined that the soldiers were following her not as jailers but as an honor guard.

Reaching the platform, she turned to face it and looked straight at Seesya, who grinned at her, cleared his throat, and spat.

Judge Zifron held up his hand. "Who among you wishes to accuse this woman?"

"I accuse her." Seesya spoke loudly, his voice reaching the farthest members of the audience. "First, while she was betrothed to be my wife, she ran away from here and conspired with a group of Moabite marauders to murder me on the road to Shiloh, which they tried to do, killing six of my soldiers. Second," he counted on his fingers, "on the night of our marriage, after I possessed her in bed as my lawful wife, she hit me several times with rocks upon my head to kill me. Third, she spilled my blood, even though Yahweh made me in His image."

The audience burst out laughing. Even the elders sniggered.

"Go on," Judge Zifron said.

"Number four," Seesya said, "she rebelled against me, ran away, and came back here under masquerade, dressed up as a man and carrying men's weapons, and when I recognized her, she tried to kill me again— this time with a sword!"

All the men in the audience booed.

"That's right," Seesya yelled. "She took up arms as a soldier!"

Deborah wished she had her sling right now, fitted with a fist-sized rock in the pouch, swinging from her hand, ready to go.

Clapping energetically, the judge managed to restore calm. "Let us hear the law!"

"Hear! Hear! Hear!" Obadiah put aside his staff and pulled several parchment scrolls from under his white robe. "This is the law of Yahweh, our God, King of the world!" He glanced at the effigy of Mott, which stood by the judge's boots, and the effigy of Ra, mounted on the pole beside Seesya. "Our one and only God, Yahweh, who gave the law to Moses on Mount Sinai, starting with the first commandment: "Do not take other gods over me!"

Judge Zifron grunted, but said nothing.

The priest unrolled a parchment and read aloud: "A person who conspires against another, to murder a man by trickery, death shall be the punishment, even if you must pull the accused from my altar to be executed."

Putting this one aside, Obadiah unrolled another parchment and read from it. "A person who hits a man to kill him shall be executed and die for such sin."

From a third parchment, he read: "A person who spills the blood of a man, the attacker's blood shall be spilled, too, for I created man in my own image."

"That's it," Seesya yelled. "He's talking about me!"

The crowd laughed.

Obadiah shook his head and read aloud from a fourth parchment: "Men's trappings shall not be taken up by a woman, and a man shall not wear a woman's dress, for Yahweh loathes such abomination."

The priest rolled up the parchments. "This is the law of our God, Yahweh, the one and only God of the Hebrews."

Mutterings flared up among the crowd. The rumors were apparently true—not only had the priest read four different laws, each carrying capital punishment, but the girl had engaged in that rare and repulsive transgression of wearing men's clothes and worse, had taken up weapons, which were the sole prerogative of men.

Obadiah pounded his staff until quiet was restored.

"We heard the accusations and the law," Judge Zifron said. "What is the evidence?"

Seesya pushed back his hair on both sides, exposing his ears, which were still bruised and scarred. "That's what she did on our wedding night."

The audience groaned, but Deborah was pleased. If the ears looked like this after so many weeks of healing, the initial damage must have been severe.

Seesya lowered his collar and lifted the hair on the back of his head, showing the fresh cut in the back of his neck. "That's from the sword she pointed at me yesterday."

Angry calls for punishment came from the men in the crowd.

"She was wearing a man's armor and boots." He jumped down from the platform, went to Deborah, and pulled down her hood. "Look at her hair, shaved as a man, too."

Deborah faced him. He was taller, but the difference between them was smaller than she'd remembered. Rather than cower like a girl or look down at the ground, she stood erect and stared at him as a man would face his equal. Seesya's eyes were dark—not the glistening, intelligent spark of Barac's eyes, or the rich, warm glow of Zariz's eyes, but the cold, arrogant black eyes of a man without a heart. A tide of rage swelled inside her. Her fists clenched, and she took a step toward him.

Seesya stepped back and yelled, "There you have it—she's ready to attack her husband again!"

A collective groan came from the crowd.

"If you needed more evidence, you have it now." Jogging over to the pile of stones, Seesya picked one up. "My wife is guilty of each of the four sins, for which the punishment is death!"

The men in the audience cheered.

Pounding his staff, Obadiah called for order.

Judge Zifron waited until they calmed down. "This matter is clear," he said. "We heard the accusations. We learned Yahweh's laws. And we saw the evidence. Let the elders of the town pronounce her guilt, and I will declare her punishment." He pointed at the Pit of Shame.

The elders looked at each other, hesitating.

"The law," Obadiah said, "allows the accused to present a defense to the accusations and explain away the evidence."

Judge Zifron turned to the priest. "The accused is a woman, in case you haven't noticed."

The audience laughed.

Obadiah waited for silence and said, "In every trial under the laws of Yahweh, the accused deserves justice, which includes an opportunity for defense against the accusations."

The judge banged his hands on the armrests. "Fine. Her husband will speak in her defense."

"That won't do," the priest said. "Her husband is the accuser."

"How about her father?"

Obadiah sighed. "She has no father, as you know."

"Is that right? I must have forgotten." Judge Zifron chuckled. "Surely you don't suggest that we allow a woman to speak here?"

"Why not?" Deborah stepped forward. "I can speak for myself."

The men in the audience booed.

Obadiah pounded his staff. "A woman may not address a court."

"Exactly," Judge Zifron said, exchanging smiles with Seesya. "That's why we're ready for the elders' judgment."

"Not so fast," Obadiah said. "Someone else could speak for her."

The judge shrugged. "If you can find such a gullible volunteer."

"Hear! Hear! Hear!" The priest raised his voice, addressing the whole crowd. "Is there a man here willing to speak for the accused?"

The men booed even louder. Someone threw a half-eaten apple, hitting Deborah's back, making the wounds flare up painfully.

Pounding his staff, the priest yelled, "Silence! Silence! Silence!"

The crowd continued to boo, and Judge Zifron shook his head, amused.

When they finally quieted down, Obadiah was red-faced and hoarse. "This is a trial under the laws of our God! The accused deserves a defense! Is there not even one man among you who will speak for her?"

No one volunteered.

"Enough with the talking." Seesya climbed onto the pile of stones and opened his arms wide. "Would you let your wife conspire against you? Strike you? Try to kill you?"

"Hell, no," a man yelled from the top of the wall, winning applause and laughter.

"Death!" Seesya picked up the stone. "Death!"

Many men in the audience raised their fists and chanted, "Death! Death! Death!"

Deborah glanced at Kassite, but he was sitting calmly in the armchair, observing it all with a faint smile. She looked around at the hundreds of angry men yelling, "Death! Death! Death!" Their hate was shocking, and the realization hit her that this trial might end in her death!

Could she get away?

The horses were tied behind Kassite and the Edomite men. She could make a run for it, jump on a horse, and ride, but there were people everywhere, even on the road. She would have to trample them, cause injuries, or even worse, and then get through Seesya's soldiers, who sat on their horses by the road halfway up to the Weeping Tree.

Obadiah pounded the platform, but no one could hear it over the noise of the crowd, which kept chanting, "Death! Death! Death!"

From the corner of her eye, Deborah saw Seesya do something, and as she turned to look, his arm completed the pitch, and the stone he had held was flying at her. She dodged instinctively, but there wasn't enough time to get completely out of the way, and the stone hit her shoulder. She lost her balance, fell down, and rolled on the ground, which caused her wounds to hurt badly. She cried out in pain, rising on all fours.

Around her, the men cheered.

The stone that had hit her was lying in the dust within reach. She picked it up, rose to her feet, and turned toward Seesya. He was still on top of the pile of stones, fists in the air, basking in the adoration of the crowd.

Deborah put a foot forward to gain balance, aimed carefully, and threw the stone.

It hit Seesya exactly where she intended.

His hands dropped to his crotch, his expression went from glee to horror, and he uttered a high-pitched wail. Bending over, he rolled down from the pile of stones and lay on the ground, moaning.

The audience exploded with laughter—men, women, children, soldiers, Kassite and his Edomite entourage. Even Judge Zifron, his younger sons, and Obadiah couldn't hold it back and laughed.

Two of the soldiers helped Seesya up to the platform, and someone brought a chair for him, placing it next to Judge Zifron. Seesya's face was pale, and he kept his eyes on Deborah, staring at her with naked hatred.

When the laughter quieted down, Kassite rose from his chair.

"With your permission, Judge Zifron," he said, "I would like to speak in defense of my soldier Borah, who is accused here."

His slow, deliberate manner of speaking, and the foreign accent with which he pronounced the Hebrew words, drew the crowd's full attention.

"Thank you, Prince Antipartis," Judge Zifron said, "but I wouldn't dream of burdening my guest with this unpleasant task."

"Not at all," Kassite said, smiling. "It is the unpleasantness of the day's heat and needless delay that I wish to save us all from enduring. The facts seem clear enough to proceed quickly, once a brief defense is presented."

"I'd very much like to hear it," the judge said. "However, our law allows only Hebrew men to speak during a trial."

Kassite opened his arms, feigning shock. "Is it possible that your law would grant the privilege of speaking at a trial to any Hebrew peasant, yet shut your ears to the wisdom of a prince who has spoken in many affairs of law, commerce, and diplomacy, and has addressed many estimable tribunals?"

"I wish it were possible, but that's the law, as our priest will confirm."

Judge Zifron turned to Obadiah of Levi.

"The law is clear," Obadiah said. "Only a Hebrew man may give testimony as a witness at trial, but there's no prohibition against allowing an honorable guest to speak in defense of the accused, as long as it's not testimony."

The judge gave him a hostile stare. "If that's the case," he said, "then we're honored to hear Prince Antipartis."

Deborah watched this exchange anxiously, and when it was resolved, she could have cheered. In allowing Kassite to speak, the judge had unwittingly opened the door to a whole set of crafty maneuvers. Kassite's brilliant performance had saved Sallan's life and earned him freedom against all odds. Now it was her life that hung in the balance, and the Elixirist himself had taken on her defense. Her hopes revived, she observed him with rapt attention.

Kassite took a few steps, placing himself before the center of the platform. "To speak competently for the accused," he said, "I would like to ask a few questions of the only witness against the accused."

"What questions?" Seesya's voice came off scratchy and high. "The evidence is clear, and a moment ago she tried to kill me again—didn't you see that?"

The audience laughed.

"If I may point out," Kassite said, "she only tossed back the stone you threw at her. Being a good wife, she must have realized that you needed it to try a second time."

Again, the audience laughed, which infuriated Seesya.

"She's my wife." Seesya raised a clenched fist. "Are you arguing that a wife should be allowed to return her husband's discipline? Yell back at him? Flog him in retaliation? Cast stones at him?"

Whatever support Seesya expected to win from the crowd, his words were greeted with only scattered approvals.

"I'm her husband!" Seesya shouted. "By law, I speak for her, and if I say she did something, it's as if she herself confessed her crime!"

"Of course." Kassite bowed. "There is no question that your position as the master of your wife in every respect gives you complete control over her—under normal circumstances, that is. But since she is not only your wife, but also my hired soldier, please indulge us by answering a few simple questions."

Seesya turned to his father.

"What's the purpose of this?" Judge Zifron rubbed his hands. "My son has testified to everything he knows, and the evidence is clear that she's guilty."

"Yes, it appears so," Kassite said. "But when a life is in the balance, even a woman's life, which is of little importance, the court surely wishes to administer justice in fairness before all these good people." He gestured at the crowd. "The court does not want the people to doubt its objectivity and evenhandedness in taking the life of this woman—a girl, really, and one who only a year ago was orphaned when her parents were murdered on their homestead by unknown assailants."

The crowd voiced its agreement. Like Deborah's late parents, many of the spectators lived on isolated homesteads.

"The questions you ask," the judge said, "should not be disrespectful to my son."

"Nothing of the sort," Kassite said. "My only wish is to assist the court with a few clarifications in order to substantiate the evidence."

Judge Zifron hesitated. "Fine," he finally said. "A few questions."

At that moment, Sallan appeared through the open gates, walking slowly with his two boy-servants, followed by the two horses Kassite had bought the day before, as well as Soosie. The sight of her horse made Deborah smile, remembering how he had rushed at Seesya and knocked him down by the gate the previous day. Despite his age and weathered appearance, Soosie was a special horse, and she hoped to ride him again before the day was over.

Everyone watched Sallan. In his good hand, he carried a jug with an upturned goblet on its neck. His other hand was heavily bandaged. He gave the jug to Kassite before walking over to join the Edomite men, who made room for him. His two servants, one of them bandaged around the head, tied the horses next to the others.

Kassite removed the goblet from the jug and placed both items on the edge of the platform. To Deborah, the goblet seemed identical to the one from which she had drunk the first two doses of the Male Elixir.

"Please excuse my indulgence," Kassite said. "In my old age, the mind dries up unless it is irrigated with a sprinkle of wine once in a while."

The judge smiled. "Enjoy, my friend."

Filling the goblet, Kassite raised it. "To life!"

He swiveled, toasting the crowd, which replied with clapping, and brought the goblet to his lips, tilting it. Deborah, who stood near him, could see that he drank none of the wine.

"In this land," Seesya said, "we say that a man who drinks alone, dies alone."

Kassite poured more wine, causing some to spill, reached up toward the platform, and offered Seesya the goblet.

Seesya leaned forward in his chair, took the goblet, and gulped it down until it was empty. He smacked his lips and tossed the empty goblet, which landed in the dirt by Deborah's feet.

Kassite ignored the goblet and placed the jug on the edge of the platform. "Did you like my wine?"

"Hated it," Seesya said. "Worst wine I ever tasted."

Opening his arms wide in exaggerated surprise, Kassite said, "The worst ever?"

"Yes." Seesya cleared his throat and spat on the platform. "Calling it wine is an insult to all spirits."

Finally, he was winning laughter from the crowd, which fueled his confidence. "It's so bad," he yelled, "that I'm about to puke—"

"That's enough," his father said. "You're insulting our guest."

"Not at all," Kassite said. "In fact, your son is being very helpful to me."

An awkward silence greeted his statement, which made no sense.

"You see, I only drink good wine." Kassite raised the jug in the air, showing it around. "However, there's more than good wine here."

Again, there was silence, and Seesya's grin began to fade.

"My studies," Kassite continued, "covered not only commerce and medicine, but also the art of mixing powerful potions. This wine, for example, is mixed with a tasteless addition that we, in Edom, call the Truth Elixir. Once a witness drinks it, his testimony shall always be truthful."

Seesya became visibly pale. "What did you give me?"

"No harm will come to you," Kassite said pleasantly. "Unless you lie, in which case, the Truth Elixir will ignite a fire inside you."

"What?" Seesya lurched to the edge of the platform, his hand on the hilt of his sword. "I'm going to—"

"You better sit down," Kassite said. "Excitement or physical movement will have the same ruinous effect as a lie. You probably feel already a certain burning in your palate and stomach due to the lie you told about hating my wine. Do you feel the burning? Do you?"

Seesya clutched his chest and dropped back in his chair.

"Let me ask you again, then. How did you like my wine?"

"Hated it!" Seesya folded his arms around his chest and moaned in pain.

"Prince Antipartis!" Judge Zifron got up. "What have you done to my son?"

"If he calms down and tells the truth," Kassite said, "he will be fine."

The judge beckoned the soldiers, who were gathered near the Weeping Tree. They mounted their horses and started down the road toward the platform.

"I wouldn't do that," Kassite said. "The last thing your son needs now is excitement."

Raising his hand to stop the soldiers, Judge Zifron glared down, his face red with anger. "Give him something to fix it, or by all the gods of Canaan, I will have you cut down this moment!"

"There is nothing to give him," Kassite said. "The only antidote is to tell the truth. As long as the witness answers honestly, no harm shall come to him." Kassite stepped closer to face Seesya from the foot of the platform. "My first question is—"

"I won't answer any questions," Seesya yelled.

"That would be unwise," Kassite said. "The Truth Elixir reacts the same way to lies, failures to respond, and attempts to leave. It is cleverer than you, my young friend. Now, sit back and answer my questions. Are you the son of Judge Zifron?"

Seesya moaned harder, bending until his chest rested on his knees.

Judge Zifron put a hand on his shoulder. "Son, answer the question."

"Are you," Kassite repeated, "the son of Judge Zifron? Yes or no?"

"Yes!"

"Very good. The pain should ease now. Next question: Is your mother's name Vardit?"

Seesya stopped moaning but remained bent over. "She's my mother."

"Yes or no."

"Yes!"

"Is the sky blue?" Kassite winked at the crowd, winning laughter. "Is it?"

Seesya glanced up. "Yes."

Deborah was amazed at this turn of events. She realized that Kassite had planned it beforehand, arranging for Sallan to bring the jug at the right moment to set the trap for Seesya. The potency of the Truth Elixir made her rejoice, for it meant that his Male Elixir was similarly potent, and she was closer to manhood than she had expected—if she survived this trial. She glanced at the Pit of Shame and shuddered. Would Kassite know what questions to ask? She had told him her story when she first arrived at the tannery, but it had been a long and eventful time since then. Did he remember the details?

"Excellent," Kassite said. "Do you know the accused?"

"Yes." Seesya glanced at Deborah, his eyes feverish with hate.

"Is her name Deborah, daughter of Harutz?"

"Yes."

"Did you know her sister?"

"Yes."

"Was her name Tamar?"

"Yes." Seesya's eyes turned toward the Weeping Tree up the road.

Kassite followed his gaze. "Are those her bones, hanging from the tree over there?"

"Yes. Those are the whore's bones."

"Answer only yes or no. Otherwise, the Truth Elixir may cause irreparable damage. Do you feel it burning inside you right now?"

Seesya rubbed his stomach and grimaced. "Yes."

The crowd murmured as people shared the story of Tamar's trial and stoning.

"Is it raining now?"

"No."

"Very good. Was Tamar betrothed to you with a ring?"

"Yes."

"That's irrelevant," Judge Zifron said. "What happened to that whore isn't related to this trial. Finish up before my son is harmed, or you will be harmed worse yet."

Kassite bowed. "I am almost done, but please refrain from interrupting if you wish your son to live through the next half hour."

Judge Zifron opened his mouth to respond, but sat back, saying nothing.

"Next question," Kassite said. "Was Tamar fifteen when you married her?"

"Yes."

"Did she have orange hair?"

"Yes."

"Did she stand trial here?"

"Yes."

"Is this town named Emanuel?"

"Yes."

"Did you testify against Tamar?"

"Yes."

"Did you say that she didn't bleed after you possessed her in your bed on your wedding night?"

"Yes."

"Was she convicted as a whore based on your testimony?"

"Yes."

"Was she stoned to death here?" Kassite pointed at the Pit of Shame.

"Yes."

"Do you live in your father's house?"

"Yes."

"Back to the time of your wedding day. Was Tamar taken on a wedding procession?"

"Yes."

"Did she come to your bed for the first time that night?"

Seesya turned to his father. "Make him stop."

"Answer yes or no," Kassite said, his tone sharper, "or you will burn from within. Did Tamar come to your bed that night for the first time?"

"Yes!"

"Did you possess Tamar in your bed as her husband?"

Seesya beat his chest as if trying to subdue it.

"I asked you a question," Kassite said. "Did you possess Tamar in bed?"

"Of course!" Seesya bent forward, groaning. "I was her husband!"

"Do you want to burn from the inside?"

"No!" Shoving a finger in his throat, Seesya tried to vomit, but couldn't.

"Do you want to die today?"

"No!" Seesya fell to his knees, folded in pain. "No!"

Judge Zifron pulled himself up again. "Prince Antipartis! I demand that you—"

Kassite ignored him and addressed Seesya, "Answer truthfully. Did you possess Tamar in bed? Yes or no?"

"No! I didn't!"

The crowd rose as one and roared in shock, and the judge dropped back in his chair, the redness draining away from his face.

Deborah only smiled. She had already known Tamar's innocence, but now the whole world heard Seesya admit that he had lied in order to have Tamar convicted and executed.

On the platform, Judge Zifron covered his face with his hands while Seesya leaned forward and swayed back and forth, moaning in pain.

Kassite raised a hand to quiet the crowd. "Have you ever possessed Tamar—on your wedding night, or on any other night?"

Seesya shook his head.

"Answer!"

"No."

"Have you ever become Tamar's husband, then? Yes or no?"

"No."

The crowd again groaned, and several men cursed at Seesya.

Not waiting for silence, Kassite leaned forward against the edge of the platform and asked, "Did you take the ring from Tamar and put it on the finger of the accused?"

"Yes."

"And when she ran away, you found her in Shiloh and married her, yes?"

"Yes."

Members of the crowd hushed their neighbors, trying to hear.

"And did you possess her as a husband in your bed?"

Seesya mumbled something.

"Louder! Did you possess her as a husband in your bed?"

"Not yet."

"She managed to stain the bedcloth with blood so that you couldn't accuse her of whoring, correct?"

Seesya sat back, then forward again, clutching his chest. "Yes."

"On your wedding night in Shiloh, later in your mother's room, did you try to kill your bride?"

"Yes," he yelled. "I tried to kill her, because she's a witch like her sister and mother!"

The roar of the crowd was beyond control. Men flung pieces of food and trash. The soldiers rode over and took positions around the platform.

Kassite raised his arms and turned around, asking for silence. When it finally came, he turned back to face Judge Zifron. "The evidence is now clear," he said. "This young man lied about his first wife, Tamar. His false testimony convinced the elders that she had whored with another man, and she was stoned here—an innocent girl. Then he betrothed the accused to himself with the same ring." Kassite held up Deborah's arm so that everyone could see the ring on her finger. "And he planned to do to her what he had done to her older sister. When that scheme failed to work, he went to her room to kill her."

Kassite paused, letting the words sink in. "All this he has just admitted. Now, let me fill you in on what the accused had to do. She ran away to save herself from this man, and when he caught her and tried to kill her, she hit him hard enough to escape again. To evade capture, she had to pretend to be a man and carry weapons. Are we going to fault her for doing what was absolutely necessary to save her life from ending at the hands of this murderer?"

Many in the audience yelled, "No! No! No!"

"I submit to the elders of this town that the accused, Deborah, daughter of Harutz of Ephraim, should be declared innocent and set free."

On the platform, Seesya sat with his head down, ignoring the soldiers who milled about on their horses glancing at him, waiting for orders.

Judge Zifron looked across the way at the elders and his voice shook when he spoke.

"You may decide the judgment now."

The elders conferred in hushed voices, glancing at the judge. Clearly, they were too nervous to make a decision even with the irrefutable confession of Seesya.

The crowd shouted, "Innocent! Innocent! Innocent!"

The oldest elder addressed the judge. "We require more guidance."

The crowd booed, and Obadiah pounded the platform with his staff.

"You may decide," Judge Zifron said, "according to the evidence presented."

With permission to do their job without fear, the elders conferred quickly and announced the judgment. "The accused is not guilty. She may be released from the custody of the soldiers into the custody of the man who betrothed her, so that he may possess her in his bed and consummate the marriage."

The crowd roared in protest, but Seesya looked up and grinned.

Kassite raised his hand to silence them and addressed Judge Zifron. "Surely you would not sustain such an unjust judgment."

"The trial is over," Judge Zifron said.

Deborah stepped forward and held her hand up to Seesya on the platform. "Pull off this ring and release me," she demanded. "Do the right thing, for once in your life."

"Never!" He slapped her hand away. "You are betrothed to me, and I will possess you!"

Deborah turned to the elders. "I accuse this man, Seesya, son of Zifron, of murdering my sister, Tamar, by falsely accusing her—"

"Be quiet," Judge Zifron said. "A woman cannot make accusations against a man."

Again, the crowd yelled in protest, followed by a shower of food items.

"You all heard the priest," Deborah yelled. "He recited the law: 'A person who conspires against another, to murder a man by trickery, death shall be the punishment.' That's exactly what Seesya did to my sister!"

"Ha!" Seesya spat in her direction. "You remember the words like a parrot, but you're too stupid to understand them. The law says, 'To murder a man.' A man. Not a woman, a goat, a sheep, a chicken, or a pig,"

When she turned back to Obadiah, he nodded sadly. "It's true," he said. "There is no murder under Yahweh's law when the deceased is a woman."

Seesya rose from his chair, grabbed the pole bearing Ra, and held it up victoriously. "Let's go, girl. We have some business to conduct in my bed."

Deborah saw the soldiers ride toward her. She turned and ran toward the Edomite men, determined to jump on Soosie and try to escape, even if she died in the process. But the soldiers sped up and blocked her way with their horses, encircling her. One of them threw a rope with a noose, slipped it over her head, and jerked on it, tightening the noose around her neck.

She was immobilized.

Seesya laughed, and the crowd groaned.

"I accuse him," a thin voice yelled. "I make an accusation!"

Everyone looked around to find where the voice had come from.

Babatorr stepped forward from where he and his younger brothers were sitting near the platform. "I saw Seesya murder a Hebrew man!"

The crowd sighed collectively.

Judge Zifron got up from his large chair, tripped over the effigy of Mott, and fell.

Ignoring his father, Seesya threw aside the pole with Ra's golden effigy, jumped off the platform, and rushed at Babatorr, who ran around the platform quickly, then up the steps, where he stood behind the priest.

Obadiah of Levi pounded his staff several times, but the noise was too great. He raised the ram's horn and blew. The sound had the desired effect, and everyone quieted down. He lowered the ram's horn.

"An accusation has been made," the priest announced. "The law requires that a trial take place."

Seesya got back on the platform, grabbed his younger brother by the neck, and led him to their father.

Judge Zifron got up with help from the soldiers and glared at Babatorr. "What's the meaning of this?"

Pressed against the side of a sweaty horse with a tight noose around her neck, Deborah held her breath to hear the answer.

"Forgive me, Father," Babatorr said, his voice shaking yet defiant. "I should have told you right away. Last year, I rode with Seesya to see a Hebrew man about buying his homestead for a hundred silver shekels, and when—"

"Shut up!" Seesya pushed him. "Not another word!"

Babatorr almost fell, but recovered his balance.

Seesya turned to his father. "Tell him to stop talking!"

Judge Zifron looked at Babatorr at length. "Go on, Son. Tell us what happened."

The crowd went completely silent.

"We found them," Babatorr said. "The man and his wife were working in the field. Seesya offered him money, but he refused, saying the land it had been his forefathers' homestead since the time Joshua divided the land among the tribes. Seesya threatened to kill him, but the man continued to refuse, so Seesya ran his sword through the man's chest."

A growl came from the crowd, but the judge raised his hand, and they quieted down.

"The wife defended herself with a scythe, slashing Seesya's face." Babatorr pointed at his brother's face. "She gave him that scar, and he cut her throat."

Another growl came from the mass of spectators, louder this time. Many of them were small farmers from all over the Samariah Hills, working hard to draw sustenance from their parched family homesteads, which they had inherited from their forefathers. What Babatorr had just described could have happened to each one of them.

"It's a lie." Seesya waved in dismissal. "A stupid boy's imagination."

Obadiah broke the silence with three poundings of his oak staff on the wooden platform. "Do you know the name of the Hebrew man your brother killed?"

"Yes, I do," Babatorr said. "The man's name was Harutz of Ephraim, owner of Palm Homestead, and as he died, he cried his wife's name: Raquellah!"

This time, the silence was broken by Deborah's heart-wrenching scream.

22

Seesya was quick to realize that it was time for action. He put two fingers in his mouth and whistled. His white stallion sprinted with quickness that defied its size and came to the platform, where Seesya leaped into the saddle. The soldiers rode up to join him, leaving Deborah to stand alone, the noose still around her neck, the rest of the rope loose on the ground. Her knees gave way and she collapsed, her eyes blind with tears, her mind burning with Babatorr's description of her parents' murder.

As Seesya and his soldiers started to ride away, the spectators swarmed the road and started hopping in the air, waving their arms, and shouting frightfully. The spooked horses stopped and reared up, pawing the air with their front hooves. More men ran over. Within a moment, the mob pulled the soldiers down from their horses and took their weapons. Only Seesya remained mounted. He drew his sword and swung it left and right to keep people away.

Obadiah blew the horn at length, until calm was restored.

"Son!" Judge Zifron stood at the edge of the platform. "That's enough!"

Encircled by a dense ring of angry men, Seesya hesitated. He turned his horse around, his sword held high.

"Come back here," the judge said, "and face justice like a man."

The ring of men around Seesya grew tighter, closing in on him.

He lowered his sword.

The ring shifted to let him pass, and he jumped off the saddle onto the platform.

Glaring at Babatorr, Seesya sheathed his sword, dropped in his chair, and lounged back with feigned carelessness, his legs stretched before him.

The judge sat back down, and Babatorr stood next to the priest.

Obadiah pounded his oak staff. "The law of Yahweh has already been read here today. A person who murders another man shall be killed for his sin."

"The accused," Judge Zifron said, "will now respond to the accusations."

"It wasn't murder," Seesya said. "The man insulted me by refusing a reasonable offer, and he paid with his life. No one insults a son of Zifron and lives to mock us again."

A deep grumble came from the crowd.

Judge Zifron looked around, rubbing his hands nervously. He was without soldiers and would be unable to get behind the gates quickly enough to lock up the town.

Meanwhile, Kassite and the Edomite men collected Deborah from the ground, removed the noose from her neck, and carried her to their corner. Sallan was ready with a waterskin and a wet cloth to wipe her face.

Turning to his son, Judge Zifron said, "Harutz attacked you, yes?"

"No." Seesya threw his head back, shaking his black hair. "The man's rudeness was enough reason to cut him down."

"Did he hold a weapon, or perhaps an implement that could be used as a weapon?"

"Father, we don't need an excuse to discipline our subjects." Seesya crossed one leg on top of the other and raised his voice to be heard across the whole area. "Listen to me, all of you ignorant peasants. The house of Zifron rules these hills. We are the law, and if we want to buy your land, you'll sell it to us, or die like Harutz of Ephraim at Palm Homestead!"

"Son!" His voice low and urgent, Judge Zifron leaned over. "Stop it! They'll lynch us!"

Seesya looked at him with a crooked smirk, cut across by the red scar. "You're acting like a frightened old woman."

The judge was too stunned to respond.

Seesya got up, his hand on the silver hilt of his sword. "Go home," he yelled to the crowd. "All of you! The show is over!"

The crowd was silent, uncertain. They knew the force of their ruler and the ferocity of his soldiers.

Deborah broke the silence. "Justice!"

Everyone turned to look at her.

"Justice," she called out loud. "We deserve justice!"

The silence lingered. No one answered her call.

She filled her lungs and yelled, "Justice! Justice! Justice!"

A few solitary voices sounded. "Justice!"

With the Edomite men's help, Deborah stepped forward, chanting with a growing number of voices, "Justice! Justice! Justice!"

Seesya unsheathed his sword and raised it overhead. "Go home, you fools!"

"Justice! Justice! Justice!" A horde of men advanced on the platform, picking up stones and sticks. "Justice! Justice! Justice!"

Judge Zifron got up. "Give me your sword, quick!"

"Justice! Justice! Justice!"

Seeing the huge crowd closing in, Seesya realized that his gamble was turning into a fatal miscalculation. He handed the sword to his father, who passed it to Babatorr.

"Justice! Justice! Justice!"

"I agree," Judge Zifron shouted. "You shall have justice!"

Deborah wouldn't stop shouting, joined by hundreds of other voices, "Justice! Justice! Justice! Justice! Justice! Justice!"

As if waking up from a stupor, Obadiah blew the ram's horn until its sound caused the crowd to calm down. Deborah stopped chanting, but the men and women around her remained electrified, ready to resume chanting at the first sign of trouble.

The judge turned to the elders, who were sitting pale-faced on their bench across the way. "Elders of Emanuel," he said. "You heard the evidence against the accused on the charge of murder and his unrepentant admission. Pronounce your verdict of guilty or innocent based on the evidence and with justice alone as your guide."

The elders put their heads close together and consulted briefly.

The oldest one rose to his feet. "We have reached our verdict," he said tremulously. "Guilty."

Applause broke out across the hillside, all along the road, and at the top of the town's walls. Deborah raised her right fist and cheered, "Justice! Justice! Justice!"

When the crowd had quieted down, Judge Zifron said, "The accused has been found guilty by the elders of this town of murdering another Hebrew man. The punishment under the law is but one: a murderer must be stoned to death."

Seesya appeared dazed by his quick downfall and didn't resist as two men took him by the arms and led him down from the platform. Obadiah followed. They went around the platform, past the pile of stones, through the circle of girls, and reached the Pit of Shame.

Seesya looked over his shoulder and cried, "Father, help me!"

Judge Zifron looked on, his face pale, his lips pressed tightly together as his son's pitiful voice made the crowd laugh. Deborah, however, didn't laugh. Even in this pathetic state, Seesya was pure evil. She remembered their wedding night, his failure to possess her in bed and his admission that the same had happened with Tamar, whom he'd then accused falsely of not being a virgin. When Deborah had asked him, "Don't you fear Yahweh?" he'd grinned and answered, "Why should I? Yahweh loves me. All the gods love me. Otherwise, why would they give me power, wealth, and the future of a king?" Watching him now, a convicted murderer about to receive his due punishment, Deborah felt no relief or satisfaction. As much as she longed to see him stoned to death, her heart told her that he was too conniving, too elusive, and too resourceful—that the evil force in him was too great to be pinned down and killed with stones.

The soldiers made Seesya stand at the edge of the Pit of Shame.

"Repent now," Obadiah said. "Ask Yahweh's forgiveness, for you have sinned."

"Father! Save me!"

"Repent," the priest said, "and God will forgive you."

"Shut up, old man!" Seesya tried to get out of the soldiers' grip. "Let me go!"

The crowd laughed harder.

Obadiah turned and walked away from the Pit of Shame. His gaze briefly met Deborah's, and he nodded. She understood. They both remembered Tamar's dying words: "Seesya, son of Zifron, I curse you that you will suffer the same fate as I suffer today!"

The soldiers lowered Seesya, legs first, into the tight hole until only his head and shoulders showed above ground level. A puff of wind blew at his hair, fanning it like a black cloud over his pale face.

On the platform, Judge Zifron picked up the effigy of Mott and held it to his chest with its face toward the Pit of Shame.

Babatorr went over to the pile of stones and selected one. As the accuser, he would have to cast the first stone. The elders lined up behind him. Other men from Emanuel joined the line.

Back at his spot next to the judge, Obadiah pounded his staff three times. "The condemned may plead for a pardon now."

The crowd's booing grew as loud as the rumbling of a thunderstorm. At the Pit of Shame, Seesya's face stuck out above the ground, his eyes wide and his mouth open.

The priest raised his hand to silence the crowd.

"Father," Seesya yelled, his voice screeching. "Have mercy. Pardon me, Father!"

Countless eyes focused on Judge Zifron. He could either grant his son a pardon by putting down the effigy of Mott, or refuse a pardon by raising Mott high, its face remaining toward the condemned.

For a long moment, Judge Zifron stood motionless. He looked around at the spectators, then down at his feet, clearly contemplating putting down Mott to pardon his son.

Deborah raised a clenched fist, took a deep breath, and shouted, "Justice!"

The crowd immediately answered her call with chanting, "Justice! Justice! Justice!"

Judge Zifron glanced at the sky, now appearing to contemplate raising Mott up to deny a pardon.

This hopeful sign energized the crowd, which chanted on and on, "Justice! Justice! Justice!"

Having run out of strength to yell, Deborah kept pumping her clenched fist in the air at the pace of the crowd's chanting.

With a deep sigh, Judge Zifron pulled Mott away from his chest, held the effigy in front of him, and began to raise it.

"No!" A woman's scream, filled with desperation, made the judge pause. "No!"

Vardit appeared from behind the platform, ran to the Pit of Shame, and stood in front of Seesya to shield him from the stones. She raised one hand and brandished a figurine. It was a very small statue of a naked woman with long hair, her arms folded under her breasts, which were full and healthy. Below the hips, the shape blended into a pillar, with the base flaring out like a dish. It was the Womanhood Charm, Deborah remembered, and the people close enough to recognize it began to spread the word to the rest of the crowd, which quieted down.

"In the name of Yahweh," Vardit pleaded, "I beg of you, don't kill my boy!"

The crowd's murmuring grew louder, and Judge Zifron looked around, frozen with indecision.

Falling to her knees, Vardit turned to Deborah, and cried, "You're like a daughter to me. Have mercy. Forgive him, and God will forgive your sins, too."

Deborah approached the platform and faced the judge. She raised her hand, unclenching her fist, and showed the ring, which glistened in the sun.

The murmuring died down, and all eyes focused on the ring.

"Tell your son to release me," Deborah said.

Judge Zifron turned to the Pit of Shame.

Seesya shook his head.

"Fine," Deborah said. "His death will end my betrothal."

Still on her knees, Vardit turned and faced the Pit of Shame, "My son," she cried, "soften your heart! Release this girl!"

Voices in the crowd yelled, "Release! Release! Release!"

On the platform, Judge Zifron moved Mott to his left arm, hugging it, and pointed at Seesya. "I order you," he said. "Release the girl!"

Vardit dropped forward and prostrated herself on the ground, sobbing uncontrollably.

This time, Seesya didn't shake his head.

Deborah walked over, passed by the weeping Vardit, and held out her hand to Seesya.

From the depth of the Pit of Shame, Seesya looked up at Deborah. In his dark eyes, for the first time, she saw something other than coldness and glee. It wasn't exactly fear or regret, but a glint of human understanding. He struggled to get one of his arms out of the tight hole and reached up to pull the ring off her finger. The touch of his hand made Deborah shudder in revulsion, but she didn't step back. It wasn't only about recovering her freedom from a forced betrothal to a cruel husband. To watch him pull off the ring and release her in front of all these people would be a great victory over this evil young man, who had murdered those she loved.

His hand shook, and the ring was tight.

"Pull harder," she said. "Put your heart into it, if you have a heart."

Seesya's face twisted into a grin, or a grimace, it was hard to tell. "It's not over," he said, his eyes cold again. "You belong to me."

"I belong to no one." She put her ring finger in her mouth, moistening it, and thrust her hand back at him. "Pull!"

He grasped the ring carefully between a finger and a thumb and managed to get it off her finger. Raising the ring to his right eye, he peered at her through it and said, "Until next time, girl."

Deborah cleared her throat and spat in his face. She turned her back to him, raised her hand, now without the ring, and waved it at the crowd, which broke into cheers.

Clenching her fist, Deborah yelled. "Justice!"

The crowd roared back, "Justice! Justice! Justice!"

Seesya tried to climb out of the Pit of Shame, but the soldiers, glancing around fearfully, pushed him back in.

At the pile of stones, Babatorr got ready to throw the first one.

"No! No! No!" Vardit leaped to her feet, screaming, "You'll have to kill me first!"

The crowd continued to chant, but with less enthusiasm.

"Will you kill an innocent woman?" She held the Womanhood Charm up front as a tiny shield. "Will you kill a mother for her boy's sins?"

The chanting died down.

"People of Emanuel," Judge Zifron said. "Listen to the cry of a desperate mother."

"Justice!" Deborah raised her fist. She knew the judge would find a way to spare his son's life, but wanted to make sure he would impose an adequate substitute punishment. "Give us justice! Justice!"

Many voices joined her, but no longer the whole crowd.

"I'm your leader," the judge said. "Your protector and humble servant. This poor woman is my oldest wife, and the condemned is her firstborn, her little boy, her flesh and blood."

Vardit was on her knees now, sobbing uncontrollably.

"He is my firstborn, too," Judge Zifron continued. "My heir and namesake. How can I let him die like this?"

A few voices protested, but most of the crowd remained quiet.

"You also have sons." The judge looked around, seeking their sympathy. "We all try to be good fathers, good teachers. My son erred terribly, and his errors are my fault. The burden of leadership is heavy, full of worries, responsibilities, and risks. We have many enemies, near and far. Not only the mighty Canaanites, but also the Ammonites and Moabites in the east, the Hittites and Assyrians in the far north, the Philistines and other sea people in the west, the Egyptians and desert nomads in the south—they all desire our land, crave our women, and dream of our enslavement. Even our fellow Hebrew tribes—Judah, Benjamin, and Simeon in the south, Dan in the west, and the greedy Manasseh in the north—are always ready to pounce, steal our wheat, and take our daughters."

Many men in the crowd shouted in agreement, cursing the neighboring tribes.

"I'm growing too old to carry alone the burden of your safety and survival." Judge Zifron sighed loudly. "It's you and your families that I had in mind when I taught my son to be aggressive, to fight hard, and to have no mercy, because I knew that he would have to lead our soldiers in battle to protect this town of Emanuel, to defend the Samariah Hills, and to preserve the tribe of Ephraim."

It was a clever argument, and Deborah could see that the people were buying it. She wanted to yell for justice again, but Kassite put a finger across his lips.

"This trial," Judge Zifron said, "taught my son the importance of humility, which I, being preoccupied with my duties to the people of Ephraim, have failed to teach him. Today my son will learn a painful lesson through his punishment. It will be painful for me, as well, but it's a worthy lesson that will stay with him when he returns to serve you in defending this land from our vicious enemies."

Turning to the Pit of Shame, the judge declared, "Seesya, son of Zifron, I sentence you to fifty lashes of the knotted whip."

And with that, the judge put down the effigy of Mott, sparing Seesya's life.

Her anger was boiling, but Deborah knew that there was nothing she could do to change what Judge Zifron had cleverly achieved. His words, together with the harsh punishment he had imposed on Seesya, satisfied the crowd. With the heat of the day reaching full blast, even the angriest spectators had calmed down. She stood between Kassite and Sallan and watched the soldiers take Seesya up the road to the Weeping Tree, strip his top leather armor, and tie his wrists to a high branch. At the same time, a few men cut down Tamar's bones and collected them in a sack, which they brought over to Obadiah of Levi.

Babatorr held the knotted whip and prepared to administer the first strike. He hesitated. Seesya glanced over his shoulder and said something. Raising his arm, Babatorr landed the whip on the exposed back. It made no sound.

A grumble of dissatisfaction came from the crowd.

On the platform, Judge Zifron yelled, "Don't stroke him. Strike him!"

Babatorr raised the whip again and struck, producing a noise like that of a hand slapping a horse's behind. Seesya groaned, but the skin on his back remained intact. Next came the oldest of the elders, who barely managed to hold up the whip. He moved it across Seesya's back gently, like a paintbrush. The other elders seemed almost as weak, but behind them, a line of men was forming, ready and eager, each likely bearing a grudge over some wrong Seesya had inflicted in the past.

Meanwhile, Judge Zifron picked up the effigy of Mott and stepped down from the platform. He hurried to the gates with his young sons and disappeared inside Emanuel.

Deborah felt an overwhelming sadness. Her parents had been murdered, cut down for no reason other than Judge Zifron's greed and his son's unbridled violence. The flogging did nothing to ease her grief.

The red robe stuck to the wounds on her back, and the pain was spiking again with each movement.

Obadiah of Levi came down from the platform and stopped at the spot where the effigy of Ra lay in the dust. Using the butt of his oak staff, the priest shattered the Canaanite sun god, leaving it in small pieces. Satisfied, he turned to head for the gates, but paused when he saw Deborah.

"This isn't justice," she said, glancing at the sack of bones in Obadiah's hand. "He murdered my parents, Tamar, and Barac, son of Abinoam, as well as many other victims he has slaughtered. Flogging isn't punishment enough."

Sallan and Kassite nodded in agreement.

The crowd noticed the priest speaking with Deborah, and everyone paused. At the Weeping Tree, an elder standing with the whip over Seesya paused and turned to watch the unusual sight of the white-robed priest speaking with the young woman in the red robe of the condemned and impure, her shaved head bare under the blazing son.

"He deserves to be stoned to death," she said.

"Your courage inspired the people," the priest said. "They answered your call for justice, and they will resist him from now on."

"Will you resist him?"

Obadiah touched his breastplate. "Faith frequently falters under fear."

"Frequently, or always?"

"Not always. I've seen men die for their faith."

"Were any of them priests?"

He sighed. "To judge others, one should be without sins. Are you free of sins?"

Her face flushed. "I only ask for justice."

Obadiah tilted his head at the Weeping Tree. "You're free of his betrothal now, but not of his hate. I suggest that you travel far away before he recovers."

"I'm not afraid of him," Deborah said. "I'll go to Palm Homestead and work the land."

"Without a husband, you're nothing. By law, only men may possess land. If a man dies with no son but a daughter, the local judge will hold the land in trust until the daughter marries and her husband becomes owner of the land, provided that he is from the same tribe."

"But Judge Zifron is the one who tried to steal it from us. Who will protect Palm Homestead while I'm away?"

"It's land," Obadiah said. "They cannot hurt it, but they can hurt you. And after today, Seesya will seek to murder you with no witnesses. Your only choice is to go away with your master, if he is willing."

"Of course," Kassite said.

"You're safe with the prince," Obadiah said. "The judge will not allow Seesya to pursue a foreign dignitary and a business partner. Stay with them for a while, and then find a Hebrew man to marry—but make sure he is not of another tribe, or he will not be allowed to own land in Ephraim's territory, just as a man from Ephraim may not own land in

Judah, or Manasseh, and so on. Do you understand?"

Deborah nodded.

"Good," Obadiah said. "When you come back with a husband, Palm Homestead will still be here, and your husband will become the rightful owner, entitled under Yahweh's law to work the land, hire workers, and defend his land by force, if necessary. The people will not allow Seesya to deprive a rightful owner of his land."

She had no intention of giving herself away to a husband, Hebrew or not, but telling the priest that she intended to come back as a man would, at best, make him laugh.

"Guard my land," she said. "Don't let your faith falter under fear."

Sallan and Kassite mounted their horses, and the other Edomite men did the same.

Deborah paused before mounting Soosie. "Will you give my sister a proper burial?"

He nodded. "May I bless you?"

Deborah bowed her head.

Obadiah held his hands over her head, the four fingers in each hand spread in two pairs. "May Yahweh bless you and protect you. May He show you kindness and grace. May He illuminate your path and grant you peace."

Back on her horse after a day and a half of humiliation, pain, and mortal danger, Deborah filled her lungs with air and exhaled with a sigh that carried both anguish and relief. She had survived, but she had to leave the Samariah Hills and abandon Palm Homestead in the hands of Judge Zifron. She knew that Obadiah was right—who better to know the law than a priest? But following his advice broke her heart.

Leaning forward, she rubbed Soosie's neck on both sides and whispered into his ear, "We'll be back."

The horse rocked its head up and down.

They began to advance, but Deborah felt a tugging at her robe.

"Please forgive me." Vardit was walking beside the horse, her cheeks wet with tears. "I beg you, forgive me!"

Conscious of the silent crowd watching them, Deborah pulled on the reins to stop Soosie and bent down, speaking softly, "There's nothing for me to forgive. It wasn't your fault."

"It was all my fault." Vardit wept. "I pushed you to submit, to obey, to be a good wife to my son. I didn't know that he'd killed your parents, that he hated you and Tamar because you looked like your mother, who gave him the scar. I should have helped you run away from the start. Oh, I'm such a stupid woman!"

Deborah held Vardit's hand. "You're not stupid, only goodhearted and kind, which is why you didn't realize the depth of Seesya's hatred."

Vardit glanced at the Weeping Tree. "I'm his mother, and his life is my life. I had to save him. Do you understand?"

"I forgive you." Deborah squeezed her hand. "With all my heart."

"Thank you." Vardit wiped her tears. "God bless you. Travel safely with these Edomites, find a place far away, marry a good husband, and have a good life."

It wasn't the plan Deborah had in mind, but she let go of Vardit's hand and urged Soosie forward, following Kassite and Sallan.

The last of the elders delivered his perfunctory lashing and stepped aside for the other men of Emanuel to mete out the punishment. When the first real strike landed on his back, Seesya screamed in pain, the knotted straps of leather leaving red lines on his skin. The next was even harder, making a sharp, popping sound and leaving deep lacerations. Seesya wailed.

As the Edomite men and Deborah trotted away from the gates of Emanuel, the dense crowd over the hillside, on top of the wall, and along the road began to clap, slowly at first, then faster and louder. Kassite slowed his horse down and beckoned Deborah to take the lead. She hesitated, conscious of her stained red robe, soiled with dirt and blood from a night under the Weeping Tree. But the clapping intensified, and she relented.

Advancing to the front, Deborah pulled her shoulders back, held her head high, and let go of the reins. Raising her right hand with a clenched fist, she rode past the Weeping Tree, where Seesya shouted in pain at each strike of the knotted whip. With the roar of clapping behind her, Deborah pressed her heels inward, and Soosie broke into a gallop. The Edomite men followed her close behind, quaking the ground with their horses' hooves. In leather armor and helmets, with their swords, spears, and shields, they were no longer her fellow tannery slaves, but her honor guard.

23

The road south was empty as all the spectators stayed to watch Judge Zifron's hated son being flogged like a common criminal. Deborah slowed to a steady trot, riding abreast with Kassite and Sallan. The land was parched and dusty, the hills rising on the left side of the road. At this pace, they would reach Bethel in the evening.

Sallan asked, "How are you feeling?"

"Numb with agony," Deborah said. "I can't stop thinking of my parents, how Seesya slaughtered them without a second thought, as if it were his right to take away another person's life on a whim."

"It is the ultimate injustice," Kassite said. "To murder and then inherit from the victims."

"I don't understand," Deborah said. "How could Yahweh allow it?"

Her question remained unanswered, and they rode on for a long while in silence. The sun beat down on them, the heat of the day getting worse. Deborah pulled the robe up to her hips and tried to shake it loose from her wounds.

Sallan brought his horse closer, fanned her with a piece of cloth, and asked, "How's your back?"

"It hurts," she said, "but not as badly as Seesya's back feels right now."

They chuckled.

"Thank you," she said, "for sending me the Reinforcing Liquid with Vardit. It gave me strength when I needed it most."

Sallan and Kassite exchanged a cryptic look, and Sallan said, "No potion can inject courage into a coward's heart. You're blessed with strength, which is always within you, even when it needs a little encouragement."

"All potions," Kassite said, "are mere accelerants, nothing more, nothing less."

She looked at Kassite to make sure he could hear her. "Thank you, Master, for saving my life at the trial."

Kassite smiled. "You saved my life first by forcing me to choose freedom and liberate my only true friend in this world."

Sallan nodded, also smiling.

"Even today," Kassite continued, "at the trial, I could not have done anything for you if not for the useful information you gave me back at the tannery. And even with Seesya's confession, it was the powerful impact you had on the crowd that really tipped the scales. They sensed the force of your spirit and recognized that you were righteous."

"It's true, Deborah," Sallan said. "The people started off hating you, but in the end, they sided with you completely and joined your call for justice. Judge Zifron was lucky that you're a girl, because if you were a man, the people would have deposed him and made you their judge."

"If I were a man, the trial wouldn't have happened in the first place." She looked at Kassite. "Speaking of that, do you think I'm ready?"

He tilted his head in contemplation. "I am not sure."

"Why?"

"It worries me that you occasionally become too emotional. I have seen you come very near to losing your composure several times."

"When?"

"Back at Judge Zifron's house, for example, during the negotiations over Sallan's release. Your anxious actions came close to exposing us."

"But I was right about it!"

"Please." Kassite stopped her with a hand. "No need to become defensive or argumentative, both of which are also typical of the female character. We view this process of transformation very seriously—not only for your well-being, but also because we are meddling in nature itself and its divine order of pairing males with females."

Having expected ambivalence, Deborah was stunned by his rejection of her readiness and by his implication that she was fundamentally unsuited for the goal she was pursuing. Was this it? A turning point? The Elixirist himself sentencing her to life in a woman's body?

"These challenges are at the core," he said. "At the same time, it is obvious that you have made great strides both physically and mentally."

"True," Sallan said.

"Mutating across gender lines," Kassite continued, "requires much more than muscles and attitude."

"A lot more," Sallan said. "There are fundamental differences between men and women."

Deborah looked from one to the other, taking in what they said, trying to remain calm rather than defensive or argumentative.

They rode in silence for some time.

"I assume you remember," Kassite said, "what I explained back at the tannery about the differences between men and women."

"I remember," Deborah said. "A man's character is proactive, even-tempered, adventurous, and logical, in contrast to a woman's passive, temperamental, small-minded, and anxious character."

"Well put," Sallan said.

"Most women might fit this description." Deborah kept her voice even. "You two have known me long enough to realize that I'm not passive, temperamental, small-minded—"

"You're clearly anxious," Sallan said.

"Which is understandable." Kassite sighed. "I do not wish to upset you, but we must consider the issue of fundamental compatibility. Perhaps your character, deep down, remains quite feminine."

Deborah struggled to control her anger. "I respectfully disagree."

"No need to argue now," Sallan said, his tone conciliatory. "We have plenty of time until we make the final decision."

Deborah looked at him. "We do?"

"Yes," Kassite said. "To prepare the third dose of the Male Elixir, we need several ingredients that are available only in Edom."

"In Bozra, our great city," Sallan said. "Those are rare and precious ingredients."

Deborah stared at Kassite with rising resentment. "Why didn't you mention that before?"

"I did not expect you to survive the first phase, let alone the second. What was the point of telling you about the third dose when I was certain you would not even require the second dose?"

"For a girl," Sallan said, "your determination and fortitude are exceptional."

The compliments were nice, but Deborah felt cheated. "The Edomite women had no trouble turning into men. Were they all exceptionally determined? Were they not passive, temperamental, small-minded, or anxious?"

The two men looked at each other and quickly averted their eyes, as if they were afraid to make each other laugh.

"You are very sharp," Kassite said.

Sallan shook his head, chuckling. "I almost forgot what an eager debater you are."

"To answer your question," Kassite said, "the women in Edom were exceptionally determined, not by character, the way you are, but by temporary circumstances. With the Edomite kingdom facing an Egyptian army that had already killed most of their men in battle, our women did not face a choice between womanhood and transforming into men. They faced a choice between womanhood and death."

"For me," Deborah said, "womanhood is death."

Her words came out sharply. Soosie slowed down, his head turned to glance at her. She patted his neck to reassure him.

The rest of the group caught up.

"Do you have my armor and weapons?" she asked.

Antippet rummaged around in his saddlebags and handed her a large bundle. She rode off the road and dismounted behind a cluster of boulders, which sheltered her from sight. She pulled off the red robe and put on the armor, bending over to tighten the straps over her shoulders. Next came the helmet, boots, and the belt with the sheathed short sword and the sling. The chest and back pieces of the armor pressed on her wounds, but she ignored the pain. She bundled up the robe and buried it under a few rocks where no one would find it.

Back on her horse under the hot sun, Deborah was sweating. Soosie took off at a fast gallop, and the wind cooled her body and soothed her anger. She felt strong and confident, not "passive, temperamental, small-minded, and anxious." It was only a matter of time until she could prove to Kassite that her character was adequately "proactive, even-tempered, adventurous, and logical." There was no other choice for her but to keep going.

After a while, another question occurred to Deborah, and she slowed down to let Kassite and Sallan catch up.

"If all potions and elixirs are mere accelerants," she said, raising her voice over the noise of the horses, "how does the Truth Elixir work?"

"Excellent question," Sallan said. "It works because, deep down, even the worst liar wants to tell the truth."

"Deep down," Deborah said, "even I know that's nonsense. Seesya had no wish to tell the truth. Zero!"

Neither of them responded, and they slowed down, falling behind.

Glancing over her shoulder, she saw them laughing.

"What's so funny?" she asked. "I want to know how it works."

They laughed harder, and Kassite managed to say, "Hot pepper," choking on the words as his laughter exploded again, causing Sallan to holler as well, throwing his head back. Behind them, the rest of the Edomite group looked at each other, smiling, unsure why the two old men were laughing.

"It was a trick," she said. "You put hot pepper in the wine and made Seesya think that the sense of burning was caused by his lies."

Still laughing too hard to speak, Sallan pointed at her and nodded.

As she reflected on it, Deborah realized how easy it had been. Kassite knew Seesya's character well enough to expect him to grab the goblet and gulp the wine, before noticing its unusual kick. Then Kassite quickly introduced the story about the Truth Elixir, and from that point on, Seesya attributed his burning palate and the heat in his stomach not to pepper and strong wine, but to his lies. The fear and panic only made him more certain that his innards were burning from the mysterious Truth Elixir. It was a brilliant trick, but so much could have gone wrong!

Again her feelings were too mixed for comfort. She sped up, pushing Soosie harder, away from the group. Kassite had taken a risky gamble. A failure would have cost her everything—the hope to recover Palm Homestead and fulfill her father's vision, even her life. But Kassite, with Sallan's help, had prevailed at the trial, and here she was, free to pursue her True Calling.

Up ahead, a great distance away, she saw a puff of dust above the road. At first, she couldn't tell whether it was moving toward them, or in the same direction. Gradually growing larger and clearer, she saw a single rider. A little later, a man on a donkey came into view. The donkey walked very slowly, its head slumped down almost to the ground. Closer yet, she saw the rider lower the hood of his brown travel robe.

Deborah recognized him. Ramrod was the nephew of Miriam, the leper woman who had saved her in Shiloh. If not for Miriam and her group of lepers, Deborah would never have made it to Aphek and the tannery. Directing Soosie to stop across the way, blocking the donkey, Deborah looked down from the horse as the rider came up close.

The donkey stopped, and Ramrod looked up. His narrow face and sharp features were tense with apprehension.

"Shalom," she said.

He blinked, and his dark eyes widened. "Deborah? Is that you?"

She took off her helmet and rubbed her smooth scalp.

"What happened to you?" he asked.

"It's a long story." She jumped down from the horse. "Where are Miriam and the others?"

He got off the donkey, which wandered to the side of the road and nibbled at dry weeds. "They're still at the Sea of Salt. You told them to go there, remember?"

Deborah nodded. "What about you?"

Ramrod crinkled his face. "I hated the place. It's as hot as an oven, even inside the caves, and the village at Ein Gedi is tiny and poor. Miriam made everyone do what you told her—smear oil and garlic paste all over and dip in the Sea of Salt. In fact, you can't really dip in it. You float on it, like a piece of meat in a pot of hot soup. It was terrible, a place of death, but Miriam wouldn't leave. She believed in your vision."

"Are you sure she's still there?"

"Yes, if she's alive."

Doubts filled Deborah. Had she been wrong to send Miriam and the other lepers to the Sea of Salt based on a single dream whose meaning she could only guess?

"How did you make it out of there?"

"It wasn't easy," he said. "I walked for three days in the direction of Jericho and caught a ride with a caravan heading to Jerusalem. From there I walked to Bethel. But it was worth it. I live among normal people now."

"What if they find out about your curse?"

"It's going away." He raised his forefinger, the only part of him that had been infected with leprosy. "See?"

Deborah looked closely. The finger was still darker than his other fingers, but not as black as it had been.

"Miriam allowed me to go," Ramrod said. "She wanted me to live on even if they all perished there."

"I'm to blame," Deborah said. "Sending them to the Sea of Salt was a foolish mistake."

Ramrod shrugged.

"Where do you live now?"

"My late father's relatives own a small homestead near Bethel at the edge of the territory of Ephraim. The next homestead belongs to a family from the tribe of Benjamin. My relatives are old, and their children died of the red fever. I work in the fields and take care of the animals. When they die, I'll inherit the land." He blushed. "And one day, God willing, I'll find a wife and have a son to continue my name."

The rest of the group caught up. Kassite and Sallan climbed down from their horses.

"This is Ramrod of Ephraim," Deborah said. "His aunt, Miriam, helped me hide from Seesya after he tried to kill me in Shiloh."

"That's commendable," Sallan said, "but what are you doing here alone?"

"Looking for Deborah."

"For me?" She was stunned. "Here? How did you know I'd be on this road?"

"I didn't," Ramrod said. "I thought you'd still be in Emanuel."

"Tell us the whole story," Sallan said.

"My relatives sent me to sell a few sacks of barley in the market at Bethel yesterday. In the evening, a group of soldiers from the land of Manasseh came and walked among the stalls, asking everyone about an Edomite slave from Aphek who had helped two hundred Philistine slaves escape from a tannery that he was managing. They said that he rode away with a small group of slaves. I remembered Deborah telling Miriam that she was seeking a slave who ran a tannery for his owner in Aphek."

"That's true," she said. "I didn't know you were listening."

Ramrod looked at Kassite. "The soldiers were looking for a tall Edomite slave with white hair and a noble stature."

Sallan sighed. "I've always wanted to be tall. It's impossible to appear noble when you're short like me."

"And hairy," Kassite said, and they laughed.

Deborah couldn't believe they were laughing again. "Didn't you hear what Ramrod said? The goat blood didn't fool Orran—he knows you're alive!"

"It was only a delaying tactic," Kassite said. "I did not expect Orran to really believe that my workers turned against me, or that they came up with a perfect escape plan without me."

"His soldiers are coming for us!"

"Unlikely," Sallan said. "They expect Kassite to travel south from Bethel along the main trade route through Gibeon, Ramah, Jerusalem, Hebron, and Beersheba, before heading southeast to Edom. They have no reason to go north."

"They do," Ramrod said. "A merchant came from Emanuel last night and told everyone in Bethel about a scandal involving the rebellious wife of Seesya, son of Judge Zifron, who pretended to be a boy and hired herself out as a soldier to an Edomite prince. The merchant said the wife would stand trial this morning and be stoned to death. I immediately knew it was you and decided to go to Emanuel and try to help you. Meanwhile, I heard the soldiers from Aphek question the merchant, who described the Edomite prince as very tall, with a slight limp, white hair, and noble stature. They cheered and yelled, "That's him!" It was the middle of the night when I left, but my donkey is old and often refuses to keep going. They left in the morning, but with their good horses, they'll be here soon."

"That changes everything," Sallan said.

"It does." Kassite sheltered his eyes and gazed in the direction of Bethel. "We must get off this road immediately."

They mounted their horses, and Kassite started up a dry streambed between two hills, followed by the other Edomite men.

Deborah settled in the saddle, but held Soosie back. "How many soldiers?"

"Five," Ramrod said. "They had good horses."

"What kind of weapons?"

"Nothing special. Spears, swords, and shields."

"Thank you," she said. "You are brave and honorable. May Yahweh reward you by granting all your wishes."

"My wishes involve you." He blushed again. "I'd like you to come with me to Bethel."

Deborah wanted to explain to him why his wishes could never be fulfilled, but there was no time, and she had a feeling he wouldn't believe in the power of the Male Elixir.

"I have to go." She shook the reins, urging Soosie forward.

"You don't need to go with the Edomites." Ramrod walked beside her horse. "You're not a slave. The soldiers aren't after you."

"My enemy is much worse than Orran's soldiers."

"The son of Judge Zifron?"

She nodded.

Ramrod followed her up the dry stream. "We have a small homestead, far into the hills, and a small spring. You'll be safe with us, and you won't starve."

"One day," she said, "I'll tell you why I can never be a good wife."

He reached up and touched her forearm. "I can be good for both of us."

"Find a kind and happy woman who wants to bear you sons and daughters." Deborah urged Soosie forward. "And treat her well."

"Pray for me," Ramrod called after her. "For us!"

Deborah looked over her shoulder and waved.

24

They rode into the barren hills until the main road was far behind and the sun was halfway down to the western horizon. The armor rubbed against Deborah's wounds, worsening the pain. The horses were tired and thirsty, and a few hooves were bleeding from the rocky terrain. Soosie showed his age with an occasional wobbly step. Deborah scratched his neck and whispered words of encouragement.

Sallan pointed to a level spot, and they stopped for the night. The Edomite men gave the horses water and tended to their hooves. Deborah took the saddle off Soosie and untied her sack. Inside it, she found Vardit's old travel robe, which had been in the sack since the night of her escape from Shiloh. Deborah walked around the curve of the hill until she was out of sight, took off the armor, and put on the travel robe. When she came back, Kassite took out a jar of his medicinal paste and applied it to her back, as well as to Sallan's injured hand and the boy-servant's ears.

Deborah collected twigs and dry weeds, took her father's fire-starters from her sack, and started a small fire next to a boulder.

Sallan drew a map with a stick in the sand, just as Zariz had once done. Deborah recognized the Samariah Hills, with the watershed line along the peaks and the Jordan River running parallel to it in the valley, passing Jericho at the bottom, where it entered the Sea of Salt.

Sallan indicated with the stick. "This is the main trade route through Bethel, Jerusalem, Hebron, and Beersheba, where merchant caravans enjoy a sort of immunity, and the tribesmen of Judah punish robbers harshly. Unfortunately, that's where Orran's soldiers will be looking for us once they learn what happened in Emanuel. They'll ride south at high speed with swords at the ready, perhaps with some help from Zifron."

"You mean Seesya?" Deborah's voice quivered, and she cringed with embarrassment.

"Not him. That swaggering brute will be lying down on his belly and moaning for a week."

She didn't share Sallan's optimism. Seesya's enthusiasm for violent expeditions should not be underestimated.

"Judge Zifron," Sallan said, "will provide reinforcement for Orran's soldiers, maybe ten of his own soldiers, to help in the search."

"Why would he bother?"

"Because he'll be furious to learn that he was tricked by an Edomite slave, who pretended to be a prince, into releasing his own Edomite slave, who made him lots of money."

"But you gave them the formula for the Reinforcing Liquid," Deborah said.

"We humiliated him," Kassite said. "We made him sentence his own son to flogging."

"He might not be so upset about that," Sallan said. "That son was getting too arrogant. He needed a good beating. The real reason to hunt us down is you."

Deborah was surprised. "Why me?"

"Palm Homestead represents a fortune for the house of Zifron. They can't afford the risk of you coming back with a husband to claim your father's inheritance. And if Kassite isn't a real Edomite prince, then you're no longer the soldier Borah, protected by a prince, but a fugitive girl who can be cut down in the middle of nowhere, never to be seen or heard from again. That's what Zifron's soldiers will do as soon as they catch us."

"That is a fair analysis of our situation," Kassite said. He bent over, his hands on his knees, and examined the map in the sand. "The main trade route is where the soldiers will chase us—down to the Negev Desert and the land of Simeon, if they have to."

The mention of the Simeon tribe gave Deborah a pang of sorrow, thinking of Barac and his father, Abinoam, who had been heading there on the night of Tamar's stoning.

"We are here." Sallan pointed with the stick. "We'll continue up the Samariah Hills, over the watershed line, down to the Jordan Valley, and then south along the west bank of the Jordan River through the land of Benjamin to Jericho. It's a bustling Hebrew city, and we'll be able to buy food and wine there. From Jericho, we have two options, either of them about a week's ride to the northern border of Edom. One is to take the road along the western shore of the Sea of Salt, which is part of the land of Judah, but sparsely inhabited. Or we can cross to the east bank of the Jordan River and ride south along the eastern shore of the Sea of Salt, which is controlled by the Hebrew tribes of Gad and Reuben and, further south, by the nation of Moab."

The mention of Moab quickened Deborah's breath as she thought of Zariz. She cleared her throat. "I'd like to see Moab one day."

Sallan shook his head. "Moabites don't like Hebrews."

"Hebrews?" Deborah smiled. "I'm Borah, an Edomite soldier."

"Much of Moab is roamed by marauders," Kassite said. "We lost our freedom there eighteen years ago."

"It's better now," Sallan said. "Travelers say that the Moabite king has raised an army to enforce his law across the land."

Kassite looked at the map. "The western shore would be safer. Marauders rarely prowl that area."

"Why?" Deborah asked.

"There are no travelers to rob," Sallan said. "The caravans don't take that road because there are no towns for resting and trading. The steep Judean Mountains, which rise up near the water's edge, make cultivation almost impossible. The only settlement I've heard of is at Ein Gedi, and it's very small."

She thought of Miriam and the other lepers, living in a cave, suffering in the heat, smearing themselves with olive oil and garlic, struggling to wash in the thick water of the Sea of Salt—all because of a strange dream Deborah had had while traveling with them.

"I have one concern," Sallan said. "Our pursuers might figure out that we're likely to take the road along the western shore of the Sea of Salt and send a small contingency to look for us there."

"It is logical," Kassite said. "Perhaps we should take the risk of traveling east through Moab, but away from the Sea of Salt. Surely Orran's soldiers would not go that far."

Deborah looked at the map in the sand. "How would we cross over to the east bank of the Jordan River?"

Sallan pointed with the stick. "There's a raft in Jericho that ferries people across when the river isn't too high. People say it's not a sturdy raft, even at the best of times. We might lose some of our horses."

"We might lose more than horses in Moab," Kassite said.

Sallan looked away, his face to the setting sun, his eyes creased. Kassite sighed, shifted his hat, and fixed his hair over the missing ears. Deborah knew they were thinking of what had happened to them eighteen years earlier. She wanted to comfort them but stopped herself, worried that Kassite might view it as yet another manifestation of feminine weakness.

After a modest meal, they put out the fire and went to sleep. Deborah stood watch first and woke up Patrees for the second watch. She used her blanket for cover and her sack for a pillow, but the hard ground, her lacerated back, and intense thoughts kept her awake. The dilemma they faced was about topography and enemies, and as hard as she tried to figure out which path would be less perilous, the more confusing it became.

The distant howling of a lone coyote reminded her of the tiger tail, which changed her perspective about the road ahead. The facts were clear, the risks and dangers each route presented, but their strategy should be based not on which route was less risky, but on which route offered an opportunity to eliminate the risk. Crossing the Jordan River meant traveling south through the land of Moab, where Kassite and Sallan feared an attack by any number of Moabite marauders. Traveling around the Sea of Salt through Ein Gedi presented only one risk: a group of soldiers sent to hunt them down—a serious risk, for sure, but one that could be confronted by setting an ambush for their pursuers. Once that single risk was eliminated, their path to Edom would be safe. Another benefit to taking that route would be an opportunity to find Miriam, beg her forgiveness, and tell her to take the group of lepers back to the Samariah Hills.

At sunrise, Deborah woke up the men, except for Sallan and Kassite, who continued to sleep. She told Sallan's boy-servants to prepare food and give the horses water, and instructed the other men to put on their armor and line up.

Antippet, Patrees, and the other Edomite men were reluctant to follow her instruction, exchanging doubtful glances. It was understandable. They had seen Seesya pull off the armor from the young man they knew as Borah, expose her undeniably female breasts, and flog her under the tree. Deborah recalled what Zariz had once said: "You must pretend to be confident, or the horse will not respect you." Applying this advice, she pretended not to notice their recalcitrance and divided them into two groups of four men each, placing Antippet and Patrees in charge of each group. None of them dared to disobey her outright, having seen how Kassite had fought for her life at the trial and continued to treat her with affection and respect.

She showed them how to erect stone columns as targets for practice shooting with the slings. Every few rounds, she made them move further back and change position, shooting upward or downward, to the left or to the right. The arid, rocky hills provided plenty of stones, the men's competitive instinct drove them to try harder, and the applause won for hitting difficult targets raised everyone's spirits.

By the time the sun cleared the hilltops, their stones were flying over a hundred steps away, hitting the targets at least once in every five shots. Next, they worked on throwing spears at clusters of dry shrubs, where the tips wouldn't break on impact. It gave the men a feel for weight and direction when throwing a spear, though their accuracy remained poor. Lastly, the two groups engaged in face-to-face combat, using the spears as clubs. There were many laughs and a few bruises, but Deborah didn't mind. She knew they would never turn into real soldiers without professional training, but at least they'd acquired a basic level of confidence with their weapons. She hoped it would be enough to surprise and chase away a handful of Orran's soldiers.

Sallan and Kassite came over to watch. Deborah joined them.

"They're not so good with the spears," Sallan said.

"Not good?" Kassite sighed. "They are outright terrible."

Deborah wiped the sweat from her brow. "The slings are our only hope." She cupped her mouth and yelled. "Back to slingshots. One hundred and twenty steps from the targets."

The men spread out and climbed higher on the hillside.

Deborah, Kassite, and Sallan watched. The hit rate dropped to about one in ten, but those hits were deadly, knocking down the columns of stones.

"Not bad," Sallan said, glancing at Kassite, who nodded.

Cupping her mouth again, Deborah yelled, "Collect a bunch of stones—twenty stones each—and shoot faster, one stone after another!"

The men spread out to find stones that would fit in the pouches of their slings.

"We should get going soon," Kassite said.

"We'll reach Jericho tonight," Sallan said, "cross the Jordan River tomorrow, and head south toward Moab."

"That's a passive strategy," Deborah said. "I think we should confront the enemies we know rather than become a target for unknown marauders in Moab."

They looked at her, surprised.

Deborah waved at the group of Edomite men, whose slings released one shot after another. "There are enough of us to set an ambush and take on a small group of soldiers by surprise. We can do it, and when they run away, we'll be safe."

"Look at you!" Sallan chuckled. "Two doses of the Male Elixir, and you're so full of piss that you'd take on the whole Hebrew army if it came after you."

Deborah blushed. "There's no such thing as a Hebrew army. Each tribe is independent, living on its own land and protecting its own people."

"And fighting each other," Kassite said.

They watched the men practice with their slings for a while. If there was improvement, it was hard to measure.

"They're good men," Sallan said, "but they're no fighters."

"It's a matter of chances," Deborah said. "Going through Moab carries a high risk of a marauder ambush, which we're unlikely to survive. Aren't we better off setting our own ambush for Orran's few soldiers, who may not be coming at all?"

Sallan sat on a large rock, looking up at her. "Go ahead, tell us your strategy."

"We'll take the western road from Jericho around the Sea of Salt and set an ambush." She picked up a twig and drew a crude map in the sand. "We'll pick an isolated spot about halfway down the road, a place that gives us the advantage of complete surprise. We'll collect stones for the slings, hide well, and wait for Orran's soldiers."

"For how long?"

"Three days at the most. If they don't show up, we can safely assume they're not coming and continue on our way to Edom."

Kassite pointed at the Edomite slaves on the hillside, who were scouting for stones and teasing each other at the same time. "With these clowns you propose to fight trained soldiers?"

Deborah shrugged. "Would you rather rely on them to fight off a surprise marauder attack?"

"Perhaps she's right," Sallan said. "We can't run forever. That young man Ramrod said there were only five soldiers looking for us in Bethel. Even if Judge Zifron sends another ten, most of the soldiers will search for us on the main trade route. We'll face no more than a handful of soldiers, and the element of surprise could tip the scale."

"Ein Gedi." She pointed at a spot about a third of the way around the western shore of the Sea of Salt. "It means Goat-Kid Spring in Hebrew. The name implies that the spring supports a population of wild goats, so there must be a nice stream running across the narrow strip of land between the foot of the Judean Mountains and the Sea of Salt."

"That is likely," Kassite said. "But it could be dry, too."

"We'll set up an ambush near the stream, where there must be some bushes and rocks to hide behind. When the soldiers come—if they come—we'll let them cross the stream and attack them from three directions. Caught in a crossfire of stones flying at them from our slings, with the sea on the left and the cliffs on the right, they'll panic and run back toward Jericho."

Sallan and Kassite looked at each other.

"A logical plan," Kassite said.

"And proactive, as well." Sallan smiled.

Deborah nodded, keeping a calm expression, although inside she was bursting with pride, having pushed for a plan that would entail a deadly confrontation in the most isolated place imaginable.

The men on the hillside were slacking off, obviously getting tired.

She cupped her mouth and shouted, "Another round—shoot quickly, one stone after the other, but aim well!"

The men's slings began to rotate, stones flying in rapid succession. The hit rate seemed better, and when they were done, all the targets were down.

"Very good," she yelled. "Collect stones for another round."

While they did, she brought Soosie over, tied a spear vertically to the side of the saddle, and tied a leather helmet on top. Leading the horse by the reins, she started running. Soosie was hesitant at first, or maybe his muscles were stiff from the previous day's hike up the hills, but soon he relented and began trotting after Deborah.

"Aim at the helmet," she yelled to the men, who were lined up about a hundred steps away on the hillside. "Don't hit me or my horse!"

They began shooting. The stones flew overhead, pounding the ground nearby until one of the stones knocked off the helmet. It was Antippet's shot, and everyone cheered him.

Deborah repeated the exercise several times, and the men improved their timing and angles. Eventually, a stone struck Soosie. He neighed, pulled away from her, and ran back to camp.

The men gathered, talking excitedly, their faces glistening with sweat. Kassite made the customary offering of food to Qoz, recited a prayer, and invited everyone to eat. They finished quickly, packed up the horses, and continued up the Samariah Hills.

It took the rest of the day to go over the watershed line and descend the eastern slopes, bypassing isolated homesteads that struggled to cultivate the rocky hills. The Jordan Valley, on the other hand, was level and fertile, dotted with flourishing homesteads that enjoyed the endless supply of river water. Further east, the Gilead Mountains shot up to great heights—dark, imposing, and seemingly close enough to stretch her arm out and touch them.

Further south along the foothills, they stayed away from the main road, which ran near the river. When night came, they set up camp across the valley from Jericho, which lit up with torches and cooking fires. Whiffs of roasting meat and sounds of playing music drifted over to their camp. Kassite and Sallan sat by a small fire, conversing quietly. Sallan's servants went to sleep, pressed against each other under a blanket. The other men finished taking care of the horses and gathered on a heap of rocks near the camp, chewing on carobs and gazing at the city. Deborah asked Patrees to stand watch and went to sleep.

During the night, Deborah woke up and noticed that the men were gone. She peered into the darkness in the direction of the city, where the music and singing continued, but there was no sign of the men. She was about to wake Sallan and Kassite up, but decided not to, reluctant to make them think that she was anxious.

Checking on the horses, Deborah found that none was missing. She patted Soosie. "You'll have to stand watch," she said. "I'm too tired to stay up."

Soosie licked her face.

Deborah laughed, ruffling the plume of hair between his ears. "I wonder if you really understand what I'm saying."

Soosie's head went up and down, and she laughed again and kissed his nose. "Good night," she said. "Wake me up if bad people or nasty animals come by."

When she woke up, the sun had already cleared the Gilead Mountains in the east, and the Edomite men were still missing. Sallan's servants were up, and a pot of water was boiling on a small fire. The view was magnificent, with Jericho sitting in the lap of a green valley, surrounded by thousands of palm trees. A wispy fog lay over the valley like a translucent silver blanket. To the right she could see the northern edge of the Sea of Salt and, beyond it, a sharp peak above the surrounding mountains. Remembering the stories her father had told her, Deborah guessed it was Mount Nebo, where Moses had climbed to see the land of Canaan, which he would never enter.

When Sallan and Kassite woke up, she told them about the men's disappearance.

"They'll be back," Sallan said. "Drunk and blissful, but no damage that sleep won't fix."

"It will delay us a whole day," Kassite said.

He took out the jar of olive paste and applied some to Deborah's wounds, which had been healing rapidly, as well as Sallan's hand and the boy's ears, which he wrapped with clean rags.

The men started coming back in the afternoon. They appeared one by one, intoxicated and unkempt, sporting foolish grins and bruises from scuffles they had already forgotten, and went to sleep.

Sallan and Kassite rode into Jericho in the afternoon. They returned later with sacks of fruit, dried meat, and jugs of wine, as well as several full waterskins.

After dark, with everyone already asleep, Deborah sat on a rock and watched Jericho's many lights, blinking in the night like fireflies. When she could no longer keep her eyes open, she woke Antippet up and told him to stand watch.

25

They were flying again, Barac's arm around her, just as it had been before the giant black crow poked its beak into her back. The pain was much duller now, the crow was gone, and the sun was shining again. They flew in a circle over Jericho. From above, the countless canopies of palm trees looked like green flowers in full bloom. She pointed at their campsite, a cluster of sleeping men and horses near the foothills. Barac smiled, his teeth glistening against his dark skin, his black curls fluttering in the wind.

The eagle turned south and flew along the Jordan River, and then bore right to follow the white-encrusted western shore of the Sea of Salt. The arid cliffs of the Judean Mountain towered on the right. Up ahead, a green patch appeared on the shore. As they flew closer, she could see a stream flowing from the foot of the cliffs on the right, across a narrow strip of land, to the opaque water of the Sea of Salt on the left. Wild goats and antelopes grazed on a patch of grass near the stream. She guessed it was Ein Gedi and leaned forward to direct the eagle to fly lower. She wanted to check out the best spot for an ambush and search for the cave where Miriam and her fellow lepers might be staying, but before reaching Ein Gedi, the eagle banked to the left, swerved over the Sea of Salt, and headed back north toward Jericho. Deborah leaned on the eagle's neck to force a turn back toward Ein Gedi, but the eagle continued flying north. As they passed Jericho, the eagle swerved again, dove toward their campsite at the edge of the valley, and flipped over, tossing the two of them off. She tried to hold on to Barac, but he wasn't there anymore, and she plummeted through the air, her stomach rising to her throat. The campsite below grew larger, but everyone kept sleeping soundly, except for her spot, where her blanket was crumpled. A second before she hit the ground, Deborah shut her eyes tightly, expecting a terrible blast of pain, but there was no pain, only a sudden silence as the rushing wind vanished. She opened her eyes and found the blanket covering her, the sack resting under her head, and the sun rising on a new day.

Deborah sat up and searched the sky for the eagle and Barac, while her mind sluggishly comprehended that what she had experienced was yet another dream. What did it mean? Was it a preview of the road ahead, preparing her for a safe journey, or a warning not to go to Ein Gedi? Did the eagle know the future, or was it a creation of her mind? And why was Barac on the eagle? Did she bring him into her dream because she was still a foolish girl inside, as Kassite had suggested? No! Barac was there to test her resolve, and she was determined to pass this test and any other test put to her by anyone—the eagle, Kassite, or Sallan. Even if Barac somehow returned from the dead and showed up in this camp right now, she would greet him warmly, but send him away!

Angry with herself, Deborah got up, put on her boots, and clapped her hands at the sleeping Edomite men. "Get up! Time to go!"

They packed up and rode off quickly to beat the heat, following the base of the Samariah Hills to avoid Jericho and the many homesteads along the Jordan River. The Sea of Salt appeared ahead before noon, and as they approached the shore, they found the road. Deep holes, patches of sand, and flood-swept sections told of little use. Bent over to hide her face from the oppressive sun, Deborah grew even more remorseful over telling the lepers to go to Ein Gedi after they had saved her life in Shiloh and provided her safe passage to Aphek.

The group reached the foothills of the Judean Mountains in the midafternoon and rested in the shade of the towering cliffs. The road veered south, and they followed it in the narrowing strip of level ground between the cliffs on the right and the white-encrusted shore on the left, which she remembered from her dream. The flat water of the Sea of Salt stretched all the way to the Moab Mountains on the opposite side. The scorching heat weighed down on the men and the horses, whose hooves stirred up a cloud of dust that traveled with them.

By early evening, they reached a dry stream that intersected the road with a deep, rocky depression. Beside the road was a pile of charcoal and a few bones from a roasted animal, as well as date pits, apple cores, and lemons skins. The trash seemed recent, not more than a day or two old. Deborah wondered whether Orran's soldiers had camped here and were now somewhere ahead already, searching for Kassite along the road south. Could they have gotten here so quickly? And if they had, would they come back the same way, or turn west after reaching the border of Edom and ride to Beersheba and north along the main trade route? It was impossible to guess. She would have to plan the ambush to work in either direction and set up lookouts high on the cliffs to watch for the soldiers.

The heat left them with little appetite, and the evening meal consisted of dry fruit, cheese, and water with lemon. Kassite again applied his medicinal paste to Deborah's back, which wasn't hurting any longer, and treated Sallan's hand and the boy-servant's ears, which had finally stopped bleeding.

Deborah took first watch and instructed Antippet, Patrees, and the others about the rest of the night. Everyone went to sleep. She gazed at the stars, which seemed hazy in the dark sky. The night was completely quiet, not a bird chirping or a coyote howling. She hoped the eagle would stay away, too.

When her watch was over, she slept without dreams.

Waking up at dawn, Deborah got everyone going. She was eager to find Miriam and apologize for sending her and the other lepers to this terrible, furnace-like place.

The day grew very hot almost from the start. The horses paced slowly, and the men were quiet. Deborah took the lead, setting a steady pace. Her imagination conjured various possibilities about the way Ein Gedi would look and how the topography would provide hiding places for each of the Edomite men for the ambush.

Sallan brought his horse in line with Soosie. "For me," he said, "this heat feels like home. How are you managing?"

Deborah fanned her face with her hand. "It's like an oven."

"Don't worry. We'll reach Ein Gedi before nightfall, wash up in the cool spring, and rest."

"It sounds too good to be true."

"We must prepare, though. Our pursuers might be upon us in a day or two."

"I'll make sure we're ready." She spoke with more confidence than she felt.

"What's your plan?"

Deborah was simultaneously flattered and intimidated by his assumption that she had a plan. She had neither the experience nor the skills to lead a fight like this. Was Sallan testing her? Her answer must be proactive, even-tempered, and logical.

"As soon as we arrive," Deborah said, "I'll look around, see what's possible, and discuss it with you and Kassite."

"What will you look for?"

She kept her voice calm. "I'll need hiding places for the men—bushes, boulders, or depressions in the ground where they'll wait until the right time to attack. If such hiding places aren't available, we'll dig holes big enough to hide in."

"Then what?"

"I'll send two men to climb up to high vantage points to watch the road in both directions. Orran's soldiers might show up within hours, a day, or even longer. It doesn't matter. While we wait, I'll continue to practice with the men, shooting targets with the slings and getting used to the spears—although I hope the slings will end the confrontation quickly and chase the soldiers away."

"Scattering them would win the battle," Sallan said, "but not the war. What if they regroup and come back to fight?"

"That's possible. We'll have to prepare—"

"Do you realize they're trained soldiers?" His voice trembled, and he took a deep breath. "Our only advantage is the initial surprise. Once that's over, we're nothing but sheep for the slaughter!"

Deborah was taken aback by his overt anxiety, in contrast to the masculine, even-tempered logic she was striving for. What more could she do? A memory came to her of the day she had hit a boulder across the river with the sling by imagining that the boulder was the head of the condescending tall boy. Kassite had guessed it and said, "When circumstances force a choice between getting killed and becoming a killer, most men fall apart, beg for their lives, or start weeping like children, whereas the truly brave harden up with firm resolve, total focus, and icy determination to kill."

"Scattering them," Sallan repeated, "will not be enough. They'll come back and kill us!"

Deborah wanted to answer him and satisfy his doubts, but words wouldn't come to her. Had Kassite been right that she belonged in the truly brave category—that she could summon the icy determination to kill? At the time, she had disagreed with him. Shooting her sling at a target while imagining it to be her opponent wasn't the same as actually killing a living, breathing man in violation of Yahweh's sixth commandment. There was no way she could do such a thing.

"They won't come back," she said. "We'll scare them so badly that they'll run off and keep running all the way back to the land of Manasseh without stopping."

Sallan sighed and slowed down his horse to rejoin Kassite.

Alone in the lead, Deborah heard them talking behind her, but couldn't make out the words. Was Sallan telling Kassite that she was a naive girl who was about to lead them to their demise?

They stopped only once, to rest under a solitary, half-dead tree. Their waterskins were nearly empty. There were no other travelers on the road, only a few remnants of food and the occasional mound of horse manure.

Riding through the afternoon tested the horses' resilience, and they were nearly drained by the extreme heat when Ein Gedi appeared in the distance—a solitary patch of greenery in an otherwise desolate coastline. Drawing closer, they saw a few trees and a couple of date palms, as well as bushes that lined a stream from the foot of the cliffs across the strip of level ground to the edge of the flat sea.

Revived by the sight of their destination, Deborah sat straight, as high as she could, to see over Soosie's head, but could spot no shacks or tents.

They came upon a tree laden with ripe plums. Patrees got off his horse, pulled a plum off a branch, and bit into it. Red juice dripped down his chin. He grinned and took another bite. The others followed his example, tearing off fruit and gobbling it. Patrees picked a few for Kassite, Sallan, and Deborah, who remained on their horses.

Leaving the others behind, Deborah approached the stream while chewing on the plum. The fleshy fruit was warm after a day in the sun, but it was sweet, juicy, and wonderful.

The creek was about ten steps wide and knee-deep in the middle. The bottom was visible in the clear water, strewn with stones, made round and smooth by the constant flow. She dismounted Soosie and let him drink.

Kneeling beside the horse, Deborah scooped water into her hands. It was cold and fresh. She drank some and splashed her face, which felt wonderful. She took off the leather helmet, filled it with water, and put it back on. The sudden coldness shocked her, and she laughed. Soosie raised his head from the water, turned to her, and licked her cheek.

Deborah reached into the water and picked up a stone. It looked like a large chicken egg. She fitted it in the pouch of her sling. It was perfect. She turned back, rotated the sling, and let the stone fly. It hit the trunk of the plum tree and startled the Edomite men, who by now had had their fill of the plums and were tossing pits at each other.

She beckoned them over and showed them the stones. "Start collecting a stockpile of stones. Make sure they're the correct size for your slings."

They didn't argue, but the sight of running water was too much for them. They pulled off their belts, armor and boots and dropped into the stream, lying flat on their backs in the shallow water, hooting and splashing like little boys.

Sallan and Kassite also dismounted and began to strip.

Getting back on Soosie, Deborah crossed the line of bushes to the other side of the creek. Out in the open, she could see that the stream flowed out of a canyon, which cut through the steep face of the cliffs into the Judean Mountains. Several lean-to wooden shacks were built on a ledge along the side of the canyon. Clothes had been hung to dry on lines near the shacks, several goats and sheep milled about in crude enclosures, and a stone oven emitted a thin column of smoke. The dwellers probably stayed indoors because of the heat, but she wondered why they didn't come out to greet the men bathing in the stream so noisily.

South of the stream, the ground was divided into small squares, tilled, and planted with vegetables and barley. Beyond the cultivated area, the road continued south along the shore. Deborah wished they could ride on, rather than dig in for a confrontation with trained soldiers, but that wasn't a safe option, not yet.

Soosie neighed and turned around to go back to the stream.

"We'll go back to the water soon." She pulled the reins to bring him back around. "I want to find Miriam."

Further down from the mouth of the canyon, Deborah noticed a cave in the face of the cliff, about two stories above the ground. She didn't see a stepladder or a rope for climbing and assumed it couldn't be the cave where the lepers resided. But then she saw something move in the dark cave. Was it a bird, or an animal? Shielding her eyes from the sun, Deborah squinted, trying to see better, but the interior of the cave was completely dark.

Behind her, the Edomite men hollered and splashed, and even Sallan could be heard laughing.

Deborah urged Soosie toward the cave. The horse took a few steps and stopped, refusing to go further. They were still fifty or sixty steps away. She leaned forward and patted his neck.

"You'll get more water soon," she said, tapping her heels inward to get him moving again. "Go on."

Soosie whinnied.

A woman appeared in the mouth of the cave. She was dressed in black from head to toe, her face was covered, and her hands were swaddled in rags.

Deborah waved. "Miriam? Is that you?"

The woman pulled the sheer cloth from her face.

Flooded with relief, Deborah recognized her. Miriam was alive!

"It's me." Deborah pulled off her helmet. "I'm sorry about telling you to come here."

Miriam waved her hand as if she meant to shoo Deborah away.

Deborah waved back. "I'm so happy that I found—"

"Run away," Miriam shouted. "Run, Deborah! Run!"

A pale face, framed by black hair, emerged from the darkness of the cave behind Miriam, and a second later the point of a sword came out her chest, followed by a jet of blood. Miriam fell forward, dropping to the ground below, and landed face down, the sword hilt protruding from her back, shining like polished silver.

The pale face came into the sunlight. It was Seesya, bare-chested and grinning.

His appearance paralyzed Deborah. It was impossible. He was in Emanuel, bedridden after fifty lashes. He couldn't be here. Was she dreaming?

"Hello, wife," he yelled. "And goodbye, wife!"

The spear in his right hand was made of dark wood and fixed with a sharp flinthead. He leaned back, half-turning his shoulders, and hurled the spear at her. It flew in a perfect arc, its pointy head swiveling like a screw. She knew without a doubt that his aim was true and that the breath she was taking now would be her last, cut short by the spear that was about to strike her chest, pierce her heart, and kill her. There was nothing she could do. In that slow-moving instant, Deborah resigned herself to this devastating reversal of fortune, the end of her life, and the silencing of her True Calling—she would never deliver Yahweh's message to the Hebrews at Palm Homestead. She saw the faces of her parents, of Tamar, Barac, and Zariz, whose soft brown eyes squinted with a smile.

Soosie's head jerked down and up, and he reared up on his hind legs just as the spear completed its flight. It hit Soosie's chest with the hollow sound of a stone pounding on wood, and she felt the horse jolt under her, suspended on his hind legs for a moment longer before he came down heavily on all fours.

Up in the mouth of the cave, Seesya cursed while several soldiers appeared next to him. A cluster of new spears shot out toward her. She felt Soosie writhing under her as animals did while dying, but rather than collapsing, he neighed in an almost human voice of sorrow and anger, and rose again on his hind legs. The cluster of spears hit Soosie's chest with quick succession of thumping sounds, except for one spear that went clear through his neck, slightly off center, the pointy flinthead popping out through the patchy fur on his nape, halfway between the saddle horn and the fluff of hair on Soosie's head, and came within a finger of Deborah's chest.

With a final agonized neigh, Soosie fell over to the left. Deborah would have been crushed under his weight, but she leaped off and rolled on the ground.

When she raised her head and looked, Seesya was sliding down from the cave. Deborah wanted to run but knew he would be faster, and when he caught up with her, she would have no chance against him in a sword fight, having never engaged in one before. Her spear was stuck under Soosie. She pulled on it with both hands, but it wouldn't come out.

Seesya reached the ground, drew his sword out of Miriam's back, and started running toward Deborah.

She pulled the sling from her belt and searched the ground for a stone.

The soldiers in the mouth of the cave began to climb down, one at a time.

Her hand closed on a stone. She turned toward the stream and yelled, "Attack! Get your slings!"

Seesya sprinted toward her, already a third of the way over, his boots hitting the ground hard.

She fitted the stone in the pouch and let it hang down.

Halfway over, Seesya's dark eyes focused on her, his bare chest white in the sun, he raised the red-stained blade above his head.

Deborah swung the sling slightly back and forth, weighing the stone while realizing with a jolt of fear that a miss would mean her death.

Focus!

Two thirds of the way over, his lips twisted in a satisfied grin.

He killed Father! And Mother!

Seesya's sword rose high, angled slightly, ready to come down and chop off her head.

And Tamar!

Ten steps away, his teeth shone in the sun.

Murderer!

She rotated the sling once and let the stone fly. It hit Seesya in the chin, producing a sound like a breaking twig. His head cocked backward, followed by his upper body, whereas his legs continued running, causing him to flip and land on his back, right by her feet.

The soldiers slid down from the cave, one after the other. One of them tripped on Miriam's body and fell, causing another one to fall as well.

"Patrees! Antippet!" Deborah glanced back, shouting at the top of her voice. "It's an attack! Get ready!"

The shouting and splashing had stopped, but there was no response.

The first two soldiers were already running at her while drawing their swords. She didn't run, but stared at Seesya to see if he was moving, but he remained where he had fallen, his sword resting on the ground by his side.

The soldiers slowed down, realizing their leader was down.

She counted six soldiers. They had already used their spears, and their horses were out of sight. Assessing the distance, she saw a chance to get across the stream before they caught up with her.

Deborah turned and ran. "Shoot your slings," she yelled. "Shoot!"

Nothing happened. Where were the Edomite men?

"Shoot! Shoot!"

She kept running and glanced over her shoulder. The soldiers were chasing her at full speed, faster than she had expected.

The bushes lining the stream were fifteen or twenty steps away. Could she get there before one of the soldiers slashed her with his sword?

Deborah inhaled and shouted, "Shoot them! Now!"

One of the soldiers got ahead of the others, and as she glanced back, he leaned forward to close the distance, raised his sword, and swung it at her. She dodged the blade and fell down, colliding with the hard ground. He tripped on her, but regained his balance and came at her, his sword clasped with both hands, the blade pointing down, and drove it at her belly.

Rolling aside, Deborah felt the blade nick her arm as it stabbed into the ground. The soldier cursed, pulled the sword out, and swung it high, stepping after her, ready to chop down on her.

A stone hit him in the leg. He shouted in pain and stumbled.

Deborah used the delay to crawl away on all fours. "Aim at the chest," she shouted. "Shoot!"

Finally, the stones began to fly over her while she kept crawling to the bushes. She heard the familiar whacks of stones hitting targets, the soldiers yelling in pain.

Once through the bushes, she rolled into the water, shocked by the coldness. The Edomite men stood shoulder to shoulder in the water. They picked stones from the bottom, fitted them in the pouches, rotated the slings, and shot the stones on after the other. They were doing exactly what she had trained them to do. Deborah felt a surge of pride. She got up, found a spot next to Patrees, and grabbed a stone from the bottom of the stream. Preparing to shoot, she glanced back quickly, worried about Kassite and Sallan.

The two old men were on their horses, sprinting away from Ein Gedi, heading back north.

Next to her, Patrees yelled a warning.

She turned back and saw one of the soldiers burst through the line of waist-high bushes, his sword high. There was no time to use the sling. She hurled the stone by hand at his face. He raised his left arm, deflecting the stone, but his momentary distraction gave her an opening to draw her short sword. She bent over to dodge his sword while aiming the tip of hers at a patch of skin right below his chest armor. She paused, unable to make her hand push forward to stab him, but as he splashed into the water toward her, the tip of her sword entered his gut. He screamed and slashed sideways with his own sword, the blade barely missing her bent back. They collided, twisted around, and fell together into the water, she on top of him, her weight pushing her sword deeper into his stomach.

He was a young man with a full beard, and his eyes stared up at her from underwater, wide with surprise. Deborah looked down at him, stunned by what had just happened. His lips moved, blood drifting from his gaping mouth like red smoke, trailing downstream. He was trying to say something, a word, which he repeated twice, three times, until she understood and yelled it out loud:

"Yahweh!"

His lips stopped moving, and guilt overwhelmed Deborah.

Do not kill!

She let go of the hilt of her short sword, which was lodged in the soldier's gut up to the crossguard, and began to rise. The soldier's hands burst out of the water, grabbed her throat, and squeezed hard. She tried to pull away, but his hands were big and strong, pressing her thin neck like a vice. He glared at her with hateful determination from underwater.

Deborah couldn't breathe, and her vision blurred. Through the foggy terror of approaching death, she saw a glint of satisfaction in the soldier's eyes, which ignited an explosion of rage inside her, for even as he was dying, this young man rejoiced at doing Seesya's bidding—killing her so that Judge Zifron could complete his theft of Palm Homestead!

Drawing on her last reserve of strength, she harnessed her rage to make her arm move, and it did, as if by its own will. Her hand clasped the hilt of her short sword, pulled it from his gut, tilted the blade between his chest and hers, and drove it up into his chin under the bushy beard. The point of the blade slipped in easily, and she drove it in all the way until it could go no further.

Looking down at the soldier's face underwater, Deborah saw the steel glisten in the back of his open mouth, followed by a thick surge of blood. His legs thrashed wildly in the water one last time and stopped, but his fingers remained tight on her neck. She felt the world closing in and knew that if she fainted, her face would drop into the water, and she would drown. Letting go of the hilt of her sword, she grasped at his fingers with her wet, trembling hands and peeled them off her neck one by one until, suddenly, her chest expanded and air filled her lungs.

She sat in the bloody water next to the dead soldier, panting and dazed. The rest of the world slowly reappeared around her. Antippet was a few steps away, groping in the water for a stone. The others were busy shooting their slings or picking up stones.

Another soldier burst through the bushes, his sword up, ready to swing at Antippet, who rose with a stone in his hand and froze at the sight of death coming at him. Without thinking, Deborah leaped at the soldier's legs, which were shielded in leather armor.

The soldier fell on top of her, pushing her into the water. She managed to get out from under him, but his boot kicked her in the head, stunning her. She clawed at the bottom of the stream, gained a bit of distance, and poked her head out for air. The soldier was still kicking frantically. He was in the water facedown while Antippet knelt on his back and hammered his head with a stone repeatedly in a frenzy of violent terror. The soldier's helmet came off, and with each blow the bloody depression in the back of his head grew deeper.

Yet another soldier appeared in the line of bushes, but a stone from one of the men hit him in the face, knocking out his teeth. He screamed, dropped his sword, and turned around, running away with his hands on his face.

Antippet stopped hammering the dead soldier's head and stood up. He fitted the bloodied stone into his sling pouch, rotated, and let it fly. The stone hit the escaping soldier in the upper back. He went down and didn't move.

Looking over the bushes, Deborah saw only one more soldier coming at them. He must have been the last to exit the cave, and was now alone in the open area. He slowed down, looked at his fallen comrades, and stopped. Dropping his sword, he raised his hands in surrender.

Patrees and two others shot their slings at him. One stone hit his stomach, and he stumbled back, but caught his balance and turned to run.

"Let him go," Deborah said.

Patrees found another stone, fitted it in his sling and shot it. The stone flew in a long arc and hit the soldier in the leg, causing him to fall. The Edomite men dropped their slings and sprinted, shouting in rage.

Deborah could barely move. "Leave him alone," she said, her voice too weak to be heard.

As the soldier was getting up, they attacked. He screamed while they pounded him with their fists.

"Leave him," Deborah said, louder now.

They kept hitting the soldier, and Patrees picked up a large rock, lifting it high.

"Patrees!" She cupped her mouth and yelled. "Stop!"

They paused and turned in her direction.

Patrees kept the rock high, ready to drop it on the soldier's head.

"Bring him here!"

They hesitated.

"Bring him to me! Now!"

Patrees dropped the rock. They dragged the soldier over. He fell to his knees at the edge of the stream, facing Deborah.

She stood in the water, barely able to keep upright. "What's your name?"

"Mishneh of Ephraim," he said, his voice trembling. "In the name of Yahweh, don't let these Edomites kill me! Please, have mercy!"

"Didn't you come here to kill me?"

There was nothing he could say to that. With a desperate moan, he bowed to her, pressing his forehead to the ground.

Patrees picked up a sword and aimed it at Mishneh's back.

Deborah put up her hand, and Patrees paused.

The soldier looked at her, his eyes wet with tears.

"Do you know my name?" she asked.

"Everyone knows you," he said. "You are Deborah, the girl who called for justice."

"Go back to Emanuel," she said. "Tell the people that Seesya ambushed me and my companions, that he attacked us from a cave without provocation, and that he killed an innocent leper woman, Miriam, who was more righteous than the highest priest. Tell the people that we killed Seesya and his soldiers because we had no choice. Tell them that I spared your life because I believe in justice."

He nodded quickly and wiped the blood and dirt from his face with a shaking hand.

"Swear to me, Mishneh of Ephraim, that you will tell the truth to the people of Emanuel."

"I swear it. I will tell them the truth."

"Go in peace." She gestured in the direction of Jericho. "And give offering to Yahweh for sparing your life."

Still unconvinced of his good luck, he got up and stepped into the stream, walking backward. "Thank you. May God bless you with a long life."

Deborah turned slowly, watching him.

Halfway across the stream, he stumbled on the body of the young soldier she had killed. Her sword remained stuck in his bearded chin.

Pointing at the body, she asked, "What's his name?"

"Hashkem." Mishneh recovered his balance and continued moving backward. "His name is Hashkem of Ephraim."

Deborah nodded, heavy with sadness. Unlike Seesya, who had chosen to come here and murder them, the soldiers had no choice but to obey their master. Knowing the name of the man she had killed would enable her to pray for Yahweh's forgiveness.

Out of the stream, near the plum tree, Mishneh turned and walked faster.

"Don't break your oath," she called after him. "Tell them what happened here."

"I will," he yelled, now running away. "I'll tell them that Deborah is brave, just, and merciful!"

When Seesya's only surviving soldier was gone, Deborah took a deep breath and exhaled with a sigh, feeling weak and nauseated. She stood in the middle of the stream, the water up to her knees running red with blood from the dead soldiers. Steeling herself, she gripped the hilt of her sword, looked away, and pulled. It wouldn't come out, instead causing Hashkem's body to move underwater toward her. She would have given up, if not for the Edomite men watching her. She gripped the hilt with both hands, placed her boot on the dead soldier's face, and yanked the sword out. She rinsed the blood off the blade and sheathed the sword on her hip.

Stepping out of the water, she bent over and vomited.

What came out of her mouth was dark red, with pieces that looked like congealed blood. It resembled the stuff that had poured out of Judge Zifron's young wife, Mazal, before her baby was born dead.

Deborah noticed that the whole front of her leather armor was red. Had she been stabbed by one of the soldiers? There was no pain yet, but a sense of doom came over her, accompanied by a fog of lethargy. Struggling not to faint, she took a few steps upstream, where the water was clear, dropped to her knees, and untied the straps over her shoulders that held together the chest and back sections of the armor. She splashed water on her bare chest and belly to clear off the blood and find the wound.

The front of her body was clean and whole. Not trusting her eyes, she ran her hands over her breasts, ribs, and stomach. There were bruises, but no wounds.

She splashed water on her back and looked over her shoulder and down, searching her back, feeling it with her hands. Other than the fresh scabs over the lacerations from the flogging, she found no injuries or fresh bleeding.

The only open cut was on her upper arm, and it wasn't deep.

The red vomit, Deborah realized, consisted of the plum she had eaten just before the attack, and the blood on her chest had belonged to the dead soldiers.

She stood up, dizzy with relief, letting the water drip down from her body.

The Edomite men were standing at the water's edge, their eyes glued to her breasts.

Deborah turned away, showing them her back, and struggled to put on the front and back sections of the armor. Normally, she would dress in private behind a rock or a bush. She would crouch and lean forward to get the back section to rest flat on her back, and press up the chest section with her knees while tying the straps over her shoulders. With the men standing behind her, lust burning in their eyes, she didn't dare to crouch or bend forward.

No one moved, and the only sound was the rushing water of the stream. Deborah sensed that the men, charged up by the ecstasy of fighting and the euphoria of surviving, were kept back by mere remnants of self-restraint, which could evaporate as soon as they noticed that

Kassite and Sallan were gone. She had to take control, but how?

She recalled Zariz's advice: "You must pretend to be confident, or the horse will not respect you."

"Don't just stand there," she snapped with as much disdain as she could muster. "Help me secure this damn armor!"

There was no response from the men.

Deborah held her breath.

The water splashed as someone walked into the stream behind her. She prepared to draw her sword, but felt the armor being lifted up to cover her back. It was Patrees, soon joined by Antippet. While she pressed the front armor to her chest, they quickly tied the straps over her shoulders.

"That's better," she said, turning to face them. "Patrees, take another man and ride north." She pointed up the road. "Don't hurt the Hebrew soldier—I gave him my word. In fact, take him a waterskin, some bread, and his sword so that he can survive on the road. Then catch up with Master and his old friend and bring them back."

She turned to Antippet. "You will take the rest of the men, collect the bodies, put them together in a ditch, and pile rocks over them. Otherwise, they'll attract wild animals from the desert tonight."

The men obeyed her.

Deborah crossed the stream back toward the open area. Above, scavenger birds began circling. She was shocked by how quickly they knew to come here, but there was a measure of justice in their arrival. Seesya had ordered Tamar's body to be strung up on the Weeping Tree, where the birds had picked at her until only bones remained. Now the birds had come to feed on his body. Gazing up at them, Deborah felt neither glee nor satisfaction. It was true that she had pleaded with Yahweh for Seesya's demise, but she'd never expected God to cause her to commit the sin of killing him.

The Edomite men dragged the soldiers' corpses across the open area. Soosie lay in the middle, at the spot where he had fallen. He seemed larger in death than in life. She knew that others might not believe it, but in her heart there was no doubt that her old horse had intentionally sacrificed himself to save her—not once but twice! Deborah felt tears well up. It seemed that everyone she loved had to die, and Seesya's hand was in every one of those deaths. Well, no more! The evil son of Zifron got his due punishment, and she hoped Yahweh would make him suffer in the afterlife!

Expecting to see Seesya's body a short distance beyond Soosie's corpse, Deborah was startled to find the spot vacant. Seesya's bloody sword remained on the ground where he'd dropped it, but his body was gone. Had the Edomite men dragged his body away already? She noticed dark stains of blood in the light-brown dirt and followed the trail of blood all the way to the white-encrusted shore.

The surface of the Sea of Salt had been completely flat before, but now it was lapping lazily, disturbed from its normal placidity. About two hundred steps away, Seesya lounged in the water on his back, rowing with his hands. His white feet showed above the water, and between them, his face was looking back at her.

He paused for a moment, placed a hand under his bloody jaw and pantomimed cutting his throat.

Already shocked that he was alive, Deborah was stunned by his audacity in making a promise to kill her. Had he not done enough evil today, killing Miriam and Soosie?

Seesya repeated the gesture, slicing sideways with his hand across his throat.

Overcome with explosive rage, Deborah shouted, "You won't kill anymore! Never!"

Pulling her sling from her belt, she found a stone, and fitted it into the pouch. She focused her gaze on Seesya's bobbing head, rotated the sling twice for high speed, and let the stone fly.

It hit the water about three-quarters of the way to him.

Seesya kept rowing with his hands, gaining distance.

Deborah realized he was well beyond the reach of her sling. Drawing her sword, she rushed into the water.

At first, the sea was shallow. It was also hot and thick, like soup. The dense water made her legs sluggish, and when it reached above her hips, the unexpected buoyancy caught her. She tried to keep her feet on the bottom, but it was too late. The water lifted her, and she rolled over sideways.

The cut on her arm and the wounds on her back burned as if touched by fire. She let go of her sword and splashed with her hands, trying to stand straight again. The salty water got in her eyes, which flared up with terrible burning. She beat the water with her arms, trying to get back to shore, and the splashing threw more water at her face. She swallowed some, her throat constricted, and she convulsed with coughing.

Through her agony came the realization that this might be the end, all because Seesya had managed to trick her into the Sea of Salt and would now have the satisfaction of watching her drown in waist-high water. Determined not to give him this pleasure, Deborah forced herself to stop moving and pressed her hands to her burning eyes. With agonizing slowness, her body floated to the surface. She lounged on her back the way she had seen Seesya do and opened her eyes slightly to see where the shore was. Crying in pain, she paddled slowly with her hands until she felt the ground against the small of her back. Closing her eyes again, she groped for balance, rising to her feet.

The sound of Seesya's laughter traveled over the water.

"Here, I'll help you." It was Antippet's voice. He supported her onto the shore. "Wait here one moment," he said.

He came back and poured fresh water over her head. Deborah lifted her face toward the sky and let the water run over her eyes, clearing the salt. Her still eyes hurt badly, but Antippet was ready with another waterskin, pouring it gently onto each eye.

Laughter came from the water, where Seesya was watching from a safe distance.

Deborah stood at the edge of the Sea of Salt and shouted, "I hate you!"

He laughed.

"I hate you for killing my parents! And my sister!"

He laughed louder.

She wept, her parched throat burning. "I hate you for killing Miriam!"

He hooted, raising both arms in victory.

She stepped into the water, driven by desperate rage. "And Barac!"

Antippet held her back.

"I hate you ... for killing ... everyone I loved."

She ran out of air, her voice barely audible.

"I hate you ... for making me kill."

26

Seesya became a dark stain in the middle of the Sea of Salt. Deborah emptied the water from her boots and put them back on. When she looked up again, he had faded away.

Her body ached as she walked slowly to the spot where Seesya had been hit by the stone from her sling. His sword lay on the ground. It was almost double the length of her sword, which would forever remain submerged in the Sea of Salt, a silent witness to her momentary surrender to absolute, mind-numbing hate.

Seesya's sword was stained with Miriam's dry blood. Deborah shuddered, averting her eyes, but her gaze was drawn back to this unusual blade. It was exceptionally smooth, with both edges sharpened flawlessly, and ended in a perfect point that would easily penetrate leather armor. The whole hilt, comprising the crossguard, the grip, and the round pommel at the back end, was silver-plated. The crossguard, which separated the blade from the grip, was decorated with tiny blood-red gemstones. The grip was cast with little bumps to improve one's grasp. The pommel—a disc attached at the end of the grip to prevent the sword from slipping out of one's hand—was decorated with a black stone about the size of a man's eye. It made sense to Deborah that the butt of Seesya's sword would be adorned with a stone as black as the evil spirit that drove him to violence and murder.

The silver hilt gleamed, and she reached down to hold it, but paused. Yahweh had commanded, "Do not steal!" On the other hand, Seesya had probably taken it from one of his victims, killing the unlucky owner with his own sword.

Using both hands, Deborah gripped Seesya's sword by the silver hilt and picked it up. It was much heavier than her lost sword. She swung it left and right, which almost caused her to fall over, and realized she would have to grow stronger and practice her swordsmanship a great deal more before this magnificent sword would be truly hers.

At the foot of the cliffs, under the cave, she found the group of lepers standing around Miriam's body. They looked at the sword she was carrying and shifted nervously. Their faces were veiled, except for one.

Deborah stared at the small and wiry young man, who could not possibly be standing here in Ein Gedi. "Ramrod?"

"Shalom, Deborah." His thin face broke out in a smile. "I knew you'd beat him. I knew it!"

"How can you be here?" Deborah's voice sounded odd to her, raspy and distant. "We saw you on the road to Emanuel only three days ago."

"Seesya forced me to come with him."

The comprehension hit her hard. "That's how he knew to come here—you told him!"

Ramrod's face wore the expression of a frightened child. "He was going to hurt me badly."

Deborah recalled what Seesya had said: "Pain is the best extractor of information." She shut her eyes, trying to comprehend this new development.

"I tried to remain silent," Ramrod said, "I really did. I wouldn't answer his question. I refused. He laughed at me and took out knives and said he'd cut my fingers one by one and go on to my toes and my ears and keep cutting until I spoke. I had no choice. Who could keep quiet when such a horrible man, the son of a powerful judge, who can do anything he wants—"

Deborah hushed him with a raised hand. "Why did he question you, of all people? How did he know that you had information about us?"

"After you left me on the road, my donkey wouldn't move, and Orran's soldiers showed up. I ran into the hills, but they chased me, because their leader recognized me from the night before in Bethel, where I'd asked them questions about the escaped slaves they were chasing."

She saw the guilt on his face and knew he was telling the truth. Orran's soldiers must have seen the same guilty expression and known that he harbored useful information. "They took you to Emanuel?"

"Yes, and then Seesya interrogated me. What could I do?"

"You could have kept your mouth shut."

Ramrod stepped closer to her, his hands pressed together, pleading.

"Forgive me, Deborah. I tried to delay, give you time to get here before us, but Seesya was like a madman, terrifying! He showed me ears he'd cut off some boy the day before. Do you know what he said to me?" Ramrod was on the verge of crying. "I'm starting a collection!"

"Of ears?"

"Of body parts!"

"He's more evil than I imagined," Deborah said. "But I'm wondering—why did he come with only six soldiers?"

"His father forbade him to go at all."

"Judge Zifron told him not to follow us?"

"I heard it myself," Ramrod said.

"And Seesya went anyway?"

"He went completely mad when he heard that the prince was a fake. Also, the pain from the flogging was so bad, he couldn't even put on a shirt, or fall asleep. He knew that Orran's soldiers were going to leave the next morning, but he didn't wait for them. In the middle of the night, he took a few soldiers and snuck away. We rode south to Bethel and Jerusalem, down the hills to the Jordan Valley near Jericho, and then here, to Ein Gedi. The whole way, my hands were tied." Ramrod held his wrists together to demonstrate. "We rode nonstop, because he wanted to get here before you did."

"To set an ambush." She chuckled sadly. "I had the same plan, though I didn't intend to kill anyone, only chase away a few of Orran's soldiers so that we could continue on our way to Edom safely."

Ramrod glanced up at the cliff. "He made us sit in the back of the cave, except for Miriam. She was supposed to draw you and the others close to the cave, and then Seesya and his soldiers were going to throw their spears and kill you and the Edomite slaves. He wanted to catch the two old men alive. Apparently, Orran of Manasseh is willing to pay for the return of his old slave, and as for the other one—the slave who used to manage Judge Zifron's basket factory—Seesya wanted to take him back to Emanuel in order to win his father's forgiveness. But then you approached the cave by yourself and—"

"I know what happened then." Deborah looked at Miriam's body and sighed. "She warned me, even though she knew he would kill her."

"My aunt was a brave woman." Ramrod knelt by the body, his voice breaking. "She took care of me since I was a baby, and I ended up causing her death."

"It was my fault," Deborah said. "I sent her here based on a dream, caused her unnecessary suffering, and by coming here to correct my error, I brought about her death."

Ramrod and the lepers watched Deborah in silence while she struggled not to cry.

"May Yahweh forgive me," she finally said. "It's too late for Miriam, but the rest of you can go back. In the morning, Ramrod will prepare for the journey and lead you back to your cave in the Samariah Hills."

The lepers put their heads together and spoke quietly to each other.

"They want to stay," Ramrod said.

Deborah thought she hadn't heard him right. "What?"

"Since they arrived and began following your prescription of garlic, olive oil, and washing in the water of the Sea of Salt, the curse has stopped. It's not progressing any more, and some of them have started to feel pain where before they felt nothing."

The lepers nodded.

Deborah looked at them, wishing she could see their faces. "Are you sure?"

"It's true," a man said in a croaky voice from behind his sheer veil. "Your dream was true."

They bowed to her, murmuring thanks.

"Don't bow to me," Deborah said, stunned by the news. "Give thanks to Yahweh, the one true God. He alone is helping you."

Examining his hand, Ramrod said, "The few weeks I spent here before I left, complaining about the heat, garlic paste, and olive oil, actually helped my finger to heal."

"That's good," she said. "They need you to stay here and take care of them, as Miriam had done until she died."

Ramrod seemed ready to protest, but Deborah gave him a stern glance, and he said nothing.

A meek whine came from above. Everyone looked up at the mouth of the cave. The sound repeated, and the lepers turned to Ramrod. He climbed up to the cave, disappeared inside, and reappeared with a cloth sack. Back on the ground, he untied the string bound the sack, and Miriam's black-and-white cat came out. It went to Deborah and rubbed against her leg. She picked up the cat, held it to her chest, and scratched its head, which was divided down the middle between white and black. She remembered seeing this cat for the first time back in Shiloh and thinking that its colors were like the good and evil spirits, always competing to dominate men's hearts.

The lepers buried Miriam under the plum tree. The inhabitants of Ein Gedi, about thirty men, women, and children, came out of their shacks, where they had stayed out of sight under Seesya's orders, and stood at a distance, watching the burial. In this harsh place on the shores of a lifeless sea, the two groups had managed to live peacefully side-by-side and share what little food could be grown.

After the burial, a few of the local men chased away the scavenger birds from Soosie's corpse and dragged it toward their shacks at the mouth of the canyon. Deborah ran over and blocked their way.

"This is my horse," she said.

None of them responded.

"He saved my life."

Still, they said nothing. Their eyes were drawn to Seesya's sword in her hand. They were scrawny and carried no weapons. She heard noises behind her and turned to see the women and children standing near the shacks, watching the standoff with large, sad eyes.

Deborah moved aside. "After you take the meat," she said, "bury what's left."

She watched them drag the dead horse the rest of the way to their shacks. Her grief was lessened by the thought that, with this rare gift of meat, their children would have a better chance to survive. It was an honorable way for her good horse to end his existence.

Ramrod was waiting for her at the entry to the canyon. "You need a new horse," he said. "Come with me."

Seesya's soldiers had tied their horses to a tree a few hundred steps up the canyon. Deborah approached Seesya's white stallion. It was fitted with a leather saddle, a good waterskin, and a bridle with ornate silver fasteners. Seesya's belt, with the attached leather scabbard for the sword, rested on a rock near the horse. Deborah strapped on the belt, adjusting it for her narrow waist, and sheathed the sword in the scabbard. It hung against her hip, the point reaching down to her shin, but when she pushed the hilt forward, the sword hung in an angle and didn't interfere with her walking.

A short pole was attached to the saddle, topped with the golden effigy of Ra, the Canaanite sun god, whose man's body and hawk's head was topped with a solar disk and a coiled serpent. Seesya must have had several of these effigies made for him. Deborah removed the pole from the saddle, threw it on the ground, and stomped on Ra the way Obadiah of Ephraim had done back in Emanuel. The stallion neighed and pawed the ground.

Ramrod handed her a plum, and she held it out until Seesya's horse calmed down and ate it from her hand. She rubbed the stallion's neck for a few minutes, untied its reins, and walked it down the canyon.

When Antippet saw Deborah with Seesya's great white stallion, he clapped. Deborah, however, felt no joy. Knowing Seesya's vigor, physical strength, and unreserved viciousness, she had no doubt that he would survive. The Sea of Salt sustained no snakes or crocodiles, and its buoyancy prevented drowning. The only deadly force was the sun, but by tomorrow morning Seesya would reach the opposite shore and find shelter. She had no doubt that he would survive. He was evil, and evil men didn't die as easily as good men did.

In the coming days though, he would have to walk in the harsh desert alone and half-naked, his back lacerated and his jaw broken, while she would ride his stallion to Edom, his bejeweled silver sword strapped to her hip. There was sweet revenge in all of this, Deborah thought, and gave the horse another plum, winning a grateful snort.

The Edomite men made camp near the stream and cooked a pot of soup with barley and vegetables. Deborah set up a watch rotation and instructed the men to patrol the shore with a torch in case Seesya came back.

After the meal, she stood for a while on the shore, looking out at the Sea of Salt, which was dark and flat. Across the sea, the last rays of the sun touched the peaks of the Moab Mountains. She thought of Zariz with his deadly bow and arrows, roaming the trade routes with his father. In a few months, they would return home to Dibon, the largest city in Moab, for the winter. Zariz would be older, his juvenile hint of a beard fuller, his stature taller and more muscular. When would he be ready for a wife to accompany him on the road, visiting different tribes and kingdoms, seeing strange places, meeting fascinating people? She would be a lucky girl, Zariz's wife, not only for the life of adventurous travels that awaited her, but also because Zariz's heart was both kind and brave, a combination Deborah had yet to see in any other man—except, perhaps, Barac, son of Abinoam.

She imagined Zariz's surprise if she showed up this winter in Dibon. His father wouldn't be too happy. He had disapproved of their friendship, quoting an old Moabite saying: "Beware of the Hebrews, for their tongue is oily and their sword is invisible." Later, at the gates of Shiloh, when she'd said, "Better check your chest, make sure I didn't filch your heart," Zariz answered, "It's too late," and promised, "I'll see you in my dreams." Was it a true, that she would exist only in his dreams, that they would never see each other again in person?

It didn't matter. By winter, she would convince Kassite that she was ready, ingest the third dose of the Male Elixir, and leave Edom, heading back to Emanuel as a young man, ready to fight for Palm Homestead.

When she lay down to sleep, the day's events replayed in her mind. She shuddered at the memory of shoving the sword into the young soldier's chin, the steel blade glistening at the back of his open mouth, piercing his brain. She had taken a life—the life of a man created in God's image. Deborah prayed quietly to Yahweh to forgive Hashkem for his sins and forgive her the sin of killing him.

Sleep continued to evade her. Deborah imagined that she wasn't in this desolate, harsh, and lonely place, but at the small house in Palm Homestead, snuggling under a warm blanket, a fire burning in the stove, a soft breeze rustling in the thatched roof, Tamar and their parents sleeping nearby. The memory made her smile as she fell asleep.

Sometime during the night, Deborah woke up and saw Patrees helping Sallan and Kassite dismount their horses. She didn't rise to greet them, but turned away and closed her eyes. It was good to know that they were back safely. Without them, the journey to Edom would not be possible, depriving her of the third dose and all that it entailed. At the same time, her feelings for the two men had suffered a painful blow. They had run away at the moment of the attack, when everything hung in the balance. She couldn't reconcile such a cowardly act of selfishness and betrayal with their wisdom, which she had grown to admire, or their calm tenacity, which she had aspired to imitate. The sight of their backs, galloping away as fast as their horses would go, would be hard to forget.

27

Deborah stood on the shore, looking out at the Sea of Salt and the great mountains across. A small dot appeared above the water, growing as it approached until she recognized a white head over a dark, wide wingspan. The eagle descended in graceful silence and landed before her, clenching the crusty dry salt with hooked talons that were larger than her feet. The giant wings folded in, and the yellow eyes glowed with an intense radiance that reminded her of the sun, but rather than heat, they burned with acute intelligence.

The eagle reclined one shoulder, and Deborah climbed onto its back. She tightened the chinstrap of her leather helmet, slipped her fingers into the white feathers on its neck, and held on as the wings spread and flapped mightily.

Gaining altitude, they flew by the dark mouth of the cave and above the tilled squares of barley and vegetables, past the sleeping Edomite men near the stream, and over Miriam's fresh grave. Leaving Ein Gedi behind, they veered east and soared over the placid expanse of the Sea of Salt. To her left, in the distance, Deborah saw Jericho among countless palm trees.

The cliffs of the Moab Mountains came up fast. The eagle flapped its wings a few times to gain height, and they passed over the jagged peaks. Down the eastern face of the mountains, they flew over barren land for a great distance and passed over another mountain range. A lush valley appeared below, with laden fruit trees, golden wheat fields, and green pastures.

The eagle circled over a large house. It was rectangular, with a flat roof and no courtyard. Against the side of the house, a corral held livestock. A young man pitchforked bundles of straw over a fence into a corral teeming with livestock.

The eagle landed about fifty steps away from the corral. Deborah hopped off and stood on solid ground. The young man turned. It was Zariz, and as she had expected, he was taller and more muscular, but his face remained mostly smooth. His large eyes were exactly as she remembered—soft, brown, and warm.

"Zariz!" She ran to him, her arms open for an embrace. "It's me!"

He recognized her voice and sprinted in her direction, but stopped halfway.

She kept going, longing to hold him in her arms.

He held up the pitchfork. "Stay away!"

"But it's me!" She slowed down. "Deborah!"

"What happened to you?"

"What do you mean?"

"Your face—it's hideous!"

She touched her cheek and felt stubble. In disbelief, she noticed tufts of reddish hair on the back of her hands. She pulled up her sleeves and found fuzz growing on her forearms.

When she looked up, Zariz was running to the house, shouting Moabite words. Family members rushed out of the house and advanced in her direction. She recognized Abu Zariz in his multicolored coat and young Orpah in her blue dress among the group of men and women, who shouted and waved their fists. Orpah picked up a clump of dry animal dung and hurled it at Deborah. It would have hit her in the face, but she dodged, and it hit her shoulder—not hard, but gently, almost like a caress.

Deborah woke up to find Antippet touching her shoulder. The sun was up. He handed her a chunk of bread and a cup of goat milk, pointing at the shacks to indicate where it came from. She nodded and turned away from him while tears filled her eyes. The dream had felt real, from the joy of seeing Zariz and the overpowering urge to hug him, to the piercing insult of his revulsion, and the crushing disappointment of his rejection. She told herself it had been only a dream, but the pain she felt was real, and the meaning of the dream was clear: if they ever saw each other again, it would not go well.

After eating and washing her face in the stream, Deborah fed a fresh plum to her new horse. He chewed as she led him into the stream for a thorough scrubbing from head to toe until she felt certain that all traces of Seesya were gone.

The Edomite men kept glancing in her direction, and she cringed at the memory of them standing by the stream the day before, ogling her bare chest, their eyes burning with naked lust. She was puzzled by it. What did they see in her puny breasts, which were nothing like the ripe pomegranates of childbearing women?

She took the horse for a ride up the canyon. They passed by the line of shacks, where the locals had resumed working with knives and axes on Soosie's corpse.

Seesya's stallion was strong and full of energy, his trot was eager as if he'd rather run than walk. Despite the time he had spent serving an evil master, his temper seemed agreeable as he obeyed all her commands. She decided to name him Rogez, the Hebrew word for "rage," to remind herself always of Kassite's advice: "Rage is like a mighty stallion, an explosive force of nature. If you fail to tame it, the result could be deadly, but if you harness it wisely, it will carry you over the highest peaks, trample your enemies to oblivion, and deliver you through the toughest battles, all the way to the ultimate victory your heart desires."

The canyon ended in a large pond fed by a waterfall that jetted out of the face of the rocks. It was the spring that gave Ein Gedi the first part of its name, and as if to confirm the second part, a family of wild goats was drinking from the pond.

Deborah let Rogez drink. She scooped up some water for herself. It was cold and fresh.

Arriving back at the camp, she found the Edomite men packing up and getting the horses ready for the road. She didn't greet Sallan and Kassite.

Rogez shifted impatiently, eager to go, while Deborah tied her spear and shield to the sides of the saddle, along with her sack and waterskin. Seesya's sword was sheathed on her belt beside the sling.

When everyone was mounted, Deborah took the lead.

Ramrod and the lepers stood by the cliff under the mouth of the cave. Deborah paused by the dry blood on the ground, where Miriam's body had fallen. The black-and-white cat sat beside the bloody spot, its tail coiling like a restless snake.

Turning Rogez around, Deborah faced the Edomite men and waited until everyone gathered, including Sallan and Kassite.

"I want you to look and remember." She pointed at the ground. "This blood came from a leper woman. She knew that yelling a warning would cause her death, but she did it anyway. Her name was Miriam. Her body was deformed by the curse, but her heart was whole and beautiful. She was courageous and faithful—the two rare qualities that together enable a person to make such an honorable sacrifice as Miriam made yesterday."

Sallan and Kassite blushed and looked away.

"For the rest of your days," Deborah said, "you should remember that a leper woman named Miriam gave her life to save yours."

Making Rogez step back, Deborah watched them pass by Miriam's blood and bow their heads.

Sallan stopped next to Deborah. "Miriam was a brave woman," he said. "But you are the one who saved everyone yesterday. You acted with courage beyond—"

"How do you know?" Deborah pulled on Rogez's reins, and he turned sharply, startling Sallan's horse. "You didn't see what happened here. You ran away."

"But if not for you—"

"Do you want to know who, besides Miriam, saved everyone here?" Deborah turned toward the canyon. "Follow me!"

Sallan and Kassite rode behind her. She led them up to the shacks and stopped by the group of men, who were busy carving the meat off Soosie's hind legs. The rest of his body had been reduced to bones, except for the head, which they had not touched. The odor was sharp, and birds picked at the pile of intestines and skin the men had discarded.

"Look at my dead horse!" Deborah circled it. "That's who really saved us!"

Sallan and Kassite covered their noses and mouths as they came closer, their horses snorting, reluctant to approach.

"When Miriam yelled to warn me, Seesya ran his sword through her and hurled his spear at me." Deborah pointed at the cluster of spears protruding from Soosie's chest bone. "My horse stood up to take it in my place. Then the other soldiers threw their spears, and my horse did it again!"

The locals stopped butchering the dead horse and stood aside with their bloody hands and knives.

"The result of the battle was determined the moment my horse reared up and the soldiers used up their spears. After that, they had to climb down from the cave and run across the open area with their swords under a shower of slingshots from a stream full of perfect stones. That's what really happened while you were running away!"

Sallan and Kassite looked down in shame.

"My poor old horse," she said, pointing at Soosie's corpse, "had more courage in his heart than the two of you together."

Leaving Ein Gedi on the road south, the land became barren again. Deborah rode up front alone. By midday, the heat was unbearable. She veered off the road and led the group to a shaded spot at the base of the cliffs. They rested until the sun went far to the west and the Judean Mountains cast a wide shade over the road along the shore.

They reached a small oasis in the evening. A clan of nomads had set up tents and a corral made of ropes and tumbleweed for their sheep and goats. Sallan went over and spoke with their elder. Their conversation went well, and they parted with a hug as old friends.

"Everything is fine," Sallan said when he came back. "They won't bother us."

Deborah found a spot with soft sand and thorny bushes on three sides. She set down her sack and gave Rogez food and water. She noticed the Edomite men glancing at her while setting up camp. Rather than look away, she made sure to catch the eyes of each one who looked at her and glare back at him. Meanwhile, she pulled over more dry shrubs and thorns to thicken the barrier around her spot.

"You'll have to stay alert." She rubbed Rogez's neck. "Make noise if someone comes near me."

After nightfall, Sallan brought over bread and cheese and sat down on the ground near her.

"I'm not trying to excuse our flight," he said. "Running away was cowardly, but Kassite and I, we are strong only with words, in dealing with people who are willing to speak, to discuss, to be influenced—"

"To be manipulated, you mean."

"Oh, you're truly angry with us." He took a deep breath and sighed. "Please understand. We're old men who have never held a sword. For us, the fear of being enslaved again is worse than death."

"They're not soldiers either," Deborah said, gesturing at the Edomite men. "They're tannery slaves dressed up in costumes, but they stood up and fought as best they could."

Sallan doodled in the sand with his finger. "They showed courage, I agree. I wish Kassite and I had such fortitude, but we are frail and weary after a life of misfortune and servitude. At the moment of being attacked by violent men like the son of Zifron and his thugs, one doesn't know what to do."

"He knows." Deborah glanced at Kassite, who was lying down already, his white hat covering his face. "He once told me an something." She imitated Kassite's slow, deliberate manner of speech. "Winning one battle does not ensure a lasting freedom. You have to win every battle, again and again, for as long as you wish to remain free."

"You have a remarkable memory," Sallan said. "One should say nothing to you, or expect to have his words come back and slap him in the face."

"Not if you behave the way you advise others to. For example, I remember you telling me this: 'Banish your fear and embrace your strength.' And this: 'A shackled man who desires freedom expects to pay a heavy price.' Do you remember saying these things?"

"Kothar-wa-Khasis!" Sallan raised his hands at the dark sky. "Have mercy on me!"

"Why do you look to the sky? Isn't your god packed away safely in your sack?"

"You're too smart for my old mind and too angry for my old heart." He held his hands together under his chin. "Please, will you forgive us?"

"Both of you?"

"There's much you don't know about my dear friend. Kassite struggles with more demons than any of us." The small fire was reflected in Sallan's eyes, which were moist. "Find it in your heart to forgive both of us."

"Why do you care whether I forgive you or not? Why does anyone care about my forgiveness? I'm just an orphan Hebrew girl with no property or family."

"Oh, you're much more than that."

"What am I?"

"You're wise and brave, yet completely blind to your own exceptional qualities." Sallan sighed. "Don't you realize how special you are?"

"Ha!" Deborah clenched her hand on a fistful of sand and tossed it at the wall of thorns she had erected. "I'm nothing but a foolish girl with big dreams. Didn't you see what happened in Ein Gedi? I fell right into Seesya's trap, got my beloved horse killed, and was lucky to survive at all."

"That's not what happened."

"Once again, you claim to know what happened?" Deborah knew she was being rude in the extreme, but her anger forced the words out of her mouth. "Do you have eyes in the back of your head?"

"That's not a bad idea." Sallan smiled. "But in the meantime, I have the next best thing, which is information from those who did see what happened. Yes, you fell into an ambush, but that happens to the best military leaders all the time. No one can predict all the possibilities, and everyone makes assumptions, some of which turn out to be wrong. A wise leader doesn't dwell on mistakes remorsefully, but reflects and learns from those mistakes in order to do better next time. The painful lesson you learned in Ein Gedi will help you set a better ambush for your enemies in the future."

"Or fall into another one of theirs."

"It might happen, and if it does, you'll learn another important lesson. That's the life of a leader."

His words sounded strange to Deborah, as if he were speaking of someone else, not her. A leader? She wasn't a leader.

"We have a dangerous road ahead of us," Sallan said. "I'm not sure what to expect when we reach Bozra." He pressed a hand to his chest. "My heart is filled with hope, but in my country, unlike yours, there is a king who rules over all the people with unlimited power. And a young king might use his power unwisely—and harshly."

"I thought you found out about the king—"

"Word of mouth travels at slobber's pace." Sallan chuckled. "Merchants carry last year's news. Whatever happens, we'll need you to be confident and clear-minded, which means you must think of what happened in Ein Gedi as a victory, not a failure. Results speak for themselves. What counts is that you survived the ambush."

"Saved by a horse!"

"Exactly," Sallan said. "Your horse sacrificed his life for you, and it wasn't an accident. He did it again when the other spears flew. My horse would never do that for me, and none of the other horses would do it for their masters. Do you know why?"

Deborah shook her head.

"Because you bonded with that old horse in a short time to an extent greater than anyone I've ever seen. And even at that moment of shock and grief, you landed on your feet and remained composed while your sworn enemy, a man twice your size and a hundred times your fighting skill, was rushing at you with his sword drawn. You didn't run away as any other person would, but found a stone for your sling, primed it, and knocked him down with a perfect shot, and not a second to spare."

"I had to. There was no chance I could outrun Seesya."

"That's logical thinking, which means you remained calm and observant at a moment of disaster that would have caused others to run away screaming in terror. And after you knocked down Seesya, when his soldiers rushed to attack, you managed to inspire a bunch of former slaves to stand and fight, even though they were terrified and ready to flee."

"I don't deserve any praise," she said. "I killed a man—a young Hebrew soldier, who was there only because of his duty, whereas I was there because of my foolish error."

"It's irrelevant why each of you arrived at Ein Gedi. It was a deadly confrontation, and you won."

"Yahweh commanded us: 'Do not kill!' And I did."

Sallan shook his head and sighed. "You achieved the unthinkable—turned a deadly ambush into a victory. If your god is a true god, as you believe, then He must have helped you win this victory. He wanted you to win, because you're special, and you should accept it."

Deborah tried to find flaws in his description of the events. Was she special? In her heart, she knew he was right. Her father had foreseen it even before she was born, dreaming that she would one day deliver Yahweh's message to the Hebrews.

"That's why," Sallan continued, "we beg for your forgiveness—not only for our cowardice at Ein Gedi, but for our absolute selfishness in all our dealings with you."

"Selfishness?"

"It's a harsh term, I admit." Sallan shrugged. "But it fits. You see, I noticed you in the basket factory, recognized that you're unlike the others, and saw an opportunity. It goes to show you that being gifted with unique capabilities is both a blessing and a curse. A blessing because you can achieve extraordinary goals, and a curse because others might try to use you to achieve their goals."

"Is that what you did?"

"Yes. On the morning of your sister's execution, I told your friend Barac the story of the Elixirist in the hope that he would tell it to you, which he did. From that day on, my efforts—and Kassite's, later on—have been focused on using you to unshackle ourselves from slavery and get back home to Edom, even when it required causing you to risk your life repeatedly. For all that, we ask for your forgiveness."

The disclosure left Deborah bewildered more than angry. It didn't matter. Had she stayed in Emanuel to become Seesya's wife, he would have gotten her executed too. Whatever selfishness had driven Sallan and Kassite, Deborah was driven by her own selfish goal of transformation, unshackling her own version of slavery—womanhood!

"I forgive both of you," she said, "on the condition that you tell me about Kassite's demons."

For a long moment, Sallan looked toward Kassite. "Ah, it's very complicated. He'll have to tell you—when he can speak again."

Deborah realized she hadn't heard Kassite say a single word since before the battle in Ein Gedi.

"The shock of the attack," Sallan said, getting up, "has rendered him mute. Please pray to your Yahweh for Kassite."

Deborah watched him limp away, illuminated by the glow from the fire. He spread his blanket and lay down next to Kassite. She wondered how shock could take away a grown man's ability to speak—especially as great a man as the Elixirist. Sallan had said, "The fear of being enslaved again is worse than death." She thought about their amputated feet and mutilated ears, and the eighteen years each had spent in slavery—more years than she had been alive. Their escape from Ein Gedi had been an act of cowardice, but did she have the right to judge them?

Lying down on her back, her fingers interwoven behind her head, Deborah looked up at the sky. It had a faint blue hue and countless glistening stars.

28

They spent the next day on the road hugging the southwest shore of the Sea of Salt and made camp near the Zered River, which was a river in name only, its flow down to a mere trickle.

Before sunset, all the men stripped down and went into the sea. They floated on their backs, their feet poking out of the water. Deborah waited until darkness had settled, pulled the tiger tail from her sack and walked along the shoreline a good distance away from camp. She stripped down, placed the tiger tail on top of her clothes, and went in.

Unlike her traumatic near-drowning experience in Ein Gedi, this time she moved slowly, careful not to splash. It felt odd to relax and lounge back in the warm water, which supported her weight like a hammock. The wounds on her back and arm burned sharply at first, but not for long. She thought of the lepers and their insistence that the regimen of olive oil, garlic paste, and a daily dip in the Sea of Salt had countered the curse of leprosy. Seeing how quickly her own wounds were healing since her misguided plunge into the Dead Sea the previous day, Deborah began to believe them.

She moved her hands slowly in the water and thought about the eagle. The last dream had granted her foolish desire to see Zariz again, only to have him reject her and rouse his whole family against her.

Reflecting on the hurtful dream now, she was forced to think of how life would be the day after drinking the third dose of the Male Elixir. The physical manifestations of becoming a young man—the start of a beard, the hair on her arms—made her uncomfortable. Was her own mind trying to sabotage her efforts, sow doubts, and derail her from the path of her True Calling by conjuring up the eagle and the visit to Moab? On the other hand, hadn't the eagle warned her during an earlier dream about the danger awaiting her in Ein Gedi, when it refused to fly there despite her efforts to redirect it? That warning had turned out to be truly prophetic! And earlier yet, in the tannery, hadn't the eagle tried to warn her about returning to Emanuel by flying into a cold, dark cloud—as dark as the eventual capture by Seesya, the flogging, and the trial?

The validation of the dreams by subsequent events contradicted the possibility that they were mere products of her sleeping mind and fertile imagination. Deborah longed to believe that the eagle was a messenger sent by Yahweh to warn her about the future—not explicitly, but with implied clues that honed her ability to interpret dreams. And how should she interpret the most recent dream? Was it a warning against her continued desire to see Zariz again, or a warning that her efforts to transform from a girl to a boy were doomed to failure, disappointment, and self-loathing?

Deborah remembered her father's stories about Joseph, father of Ephraim and Manasseh, whose gift for interpreting dreams had been both a curse and a blessing for him and his brothers. If Joseph's gift had somehow passed down through the generations to his descendants, it had skipped her, for she had great difficulty interpreting her dreams.

She bobbled in the thick, warm water, realizing how alone she was in the world. Other than the golden glow of the small campfire—a lone beacon of human presence—she was surrounded by darkness, softened only by a partial moon and the speckling canopy of stars. Was this the way an unborn baby felt, cocooned inside a mother's womb? She recalled Obadiah of Levi's blessing on the night she left Emanuel on her quest to find the Elixirist, concluding with: "May He illuminate your path and grant you peace." How else could she have survived along the perilous path since the priest had given her the blessing? Who else but Yahweh could have granted her peace despite all that had happened to her on the way to Shiloh and at Shatz's house, on the way to Aphek and at the tannery, on the way back to Emanuel and at the trial, on the way to Ein Gedi and at the deadly ambush, and to this magical place, floating in a warm, soothing sea, ensconced in complete peace?

When she returned to the campsite, everyone was asleep. No one stood watch, but Rogez snorted and turned to her. Deborah lay down next to the horse, wrapped herself in her blanket, tucked her sack under her head, and fell asleep.

It seemed as if only a moment had passed when she sat up with a fright, panting hard. Dawn illuminated the sky in the east, and Rogez stood nearby, looking at her. She was dreaming of the young soldier, Hashkem, mouthing Yahweh's name underwater as his hands burst from the water and grabbed her throat, refusing to let go even after she shoved the sword into his chin and saw the steel blade glisten in the back of his open mouth, followed by an explosion of blood. Awakened by the desperate agony of suffocation, Deborah touched her throat, expecting to find it wet from Hashkem's hands.

Leaving the Sea of Salt behind, the group began the journey south while the air was still cool. As the day heated up, the road at times disappeared, blurred by shifting sands, only to reappear further south. At midday, finding no shelter, they tied blankets to the horses' saddles and sat underneath in the shade.

In the afternoon, when the heat subsided, they set off again. The road gradually improved as the land hardened and became hilly. They kept going until evening and reached a small town. There were no defensive walls or guards, and many of the houses lay in ruins, some blackened by fire. Merchant caravans had set up camps among the trees on the side of the hill along a running stream.

"Three worlds meet here," Sallan declared as he stopped his horse at the edge of town, where several roads intersected. He pointed left at the road stretching across the valley and into the mountains. "East is the road to Arabia, Persia, and the exotic lands beyond." He turned to the road heading down the wide valley. "South is the road to Bozra, our capital, where the kings of Edom have reigned since Esau lost his birthright to his younger brother Jacob and left Canaan. And there," he turned right and pointed to the west, "is the road to Beersheba in the land of the Hebrew tribe of Judah. From there, caravans may turn either south to Egypt to trade with the pharaohs, east to Gaza to bargain with the Philistines, or north to barter with the Hebrew other tribes, the Canaanites, and further on, the great kingdoms of the north."

Deborah imagined reaching all those distant lands and trading in their exotic spices and goods—not as Zariz's wife, but in her own right, once she became a man, leading her own caravan and enjoying a life filled with adventure, awe, and wonder.

"Tomorrow," Sallan said, "we continue south to Bozra. May the gods be with us."

They chose a campsite a good distance away from the noise and smoke of the caravans. Deborah took a spot amidst a cluster of bushes that provided natural protection. The tree overhead was as wide and as tall as a two-story house. She had never seen this type of tree in the Samariah Hills, or even in Aphek, where many different trees grew to maturity with the abundance of water and sun, but there was something familiar about this tree. Had she seen it in her dreams? She couldn't remember.

Sallan went to buy food while Kassite sat with his back against the tree trunk and covered his face with his hat. It saddened Deborah to see him—Master at the tannery, Prince Antipartis in Emanuel, and the mythical Elixirist of Edom—so dispirited and withdrawn.

The men brought water from a stream at the bottom of the hill and collected firewood. They walked softly around the napping Kassite, glancing at him with concern.

Deborah cleared the ground of rocks and dry leaves. She felt pain in her fingers and noticed the sharp edges of the leaves. As she stood up, her shoulder brushed against a branch, and she yelped as a thorn pricked her skin. Looking closely, she saw that many thorns covered the branches. The leaves were shiny green, with pronounced veins. Little yellow flowers, the size of her pinky nail, nestled in the base of the leaves. There were also fruits, small but numerous enough to weigh down the branches, ranging in color from green to dark purple. She plucked one and looked at it closely.

"It's good," Antippet said, tying his horse to a nearby branch. "You can eat it."

"Tastes like an apple, doesn't it?"

He nodded, smiling. "You've tried one before?"

She shook her head while placing the fruit in her mouth.

"Careful," he said. "There's a—"

"A hard pit," she said. "I'm not sure how I know this, but I do." The fruit interfered with her speech, which came out funny, making them both laugh.

The flesh of the fruit was sweet and juicy. Deborah spat out the pit, finally remembering. "My mother told me about this tree! She called it juju-bah!"

"We call it jujube." Antippet gave his horse water.

Deborah touched the tree carefully, pronouncing the name the way he did. "Juju-bee?"

"Yes. Jujube. It grows all over the land of Edom, wherever there's water. My grandmother used to send me out to collect a basket full and cooked the fruit in water over the fire until it was pasty and sweet."

"Like bees' honey." Deborah ate another one and spit out the pit. "There are no jujube trees in the land of Ephraim. My mother missed it."

Sallan returned with a large basket of fruit and bread, pulling along a chubby animal with short reddish fur and a flat nose, about the size of a sheep.

"This town sends tribute to Bozra," Sallan said. "I found out that the young king is away on the road, searching for his sister, who was abducted by Hebrew tribesmen."

The Edomite men converged on the animal, which protested with nasal cries that sounded almost human.

Patrees went to Kassite and touched his shoulder. "Master, look!"

Kassite lifted his hat, saw the animal, and smiled.

Seeing their master smile for the first time since Ein Gedi, the Edomite men cheered. They carried the animal to a flat rock where wood had been piled for a fire.

Deborah was embarrassed, but she asked anyway. "What is this animal?"

"A pig." Sallan wiped his lips. "The best meat there is. Eighteen years I've waited to taste it again."

Under the tree, Kassite nodded and covered his face with the hat.

"That's a pig?" Deborah was amazed. "Really?"

She had always imagined the forbidden animal as something of a giant rat, with large teeth and beady, mean eyes, as well as pointy ears, a fat belly, and a long, snakelike tail that ended with a red plume, the same red as the robes worn by condemned or impure women.

"Once it's cooked," Sallan said, "you'll taste it and see how good it is."

"Yahweh forbids us to eat pigs."

"No one will know. It'll be our secret. There are no Hebrews left here, I'm told, except for a crazy old woman, a healer, who never leaves her house anymore."

"She lives here alone, with no other Hebrews?"

He shrugged. "That's what I heard."

Deborah's curiosity was aroused. Why would an old Hebrew woman live alone in an Edomite town? "Do you know where I can find her?"

"In one of the ruins on the other side of town." He pointed. "You can't miss it—walls are still black from the fire, but there's a good roof over it."

Deborah walked across the hilly town, passing between the ruins, and found the house Sallan had described. The stone walls were singed black, like many of the ruins, but the roof had been rebuilt and the windows were covered with fabric. The door was open. On the right-side doorjamb, about two-thirds of the way up, a small scroll rested in a fitting cavity. She touched the mezuzah and kissed her fingers.

"Come in," a hoarse voice said from inside.

Pulling off her leather helmet, Deborah entered a dark room that smelled of incense.

"Don't be afraid, child."

"I'm not a child," Deborah said.

"To me, you're still a child." The woman was sitting on floor cushions. "Come, sit with me."

Deborah unbuckled the heavy sword, put it aside, and sat down. Her eyes adjusted to the dark, and she saw that the woman was wrinkled and without teeth, but her eyes were large and watchful. Glancing around the room, Deborah saw long shelves with many jars and small baskets, but no effigies of false gods.

The woman grinned with bare gums and took Deborah's hand in hers, which was gaunt, the fingers crooked with age, the nails long, but clean. "You came back, child."

The words made no sense, and Deborah tried to pull her hand back.

The woman held on firmly. "You dressed up like a soldier," she said. "Clever. Did it fool the Edomites?"

"Most of them."

"Didn't fool me," the woman said. "I always knew that one of you would come back one day to calm my worries and give me peace, but I didn't expect it to be you."

Going along with the woman's rambling, Deborah asked, "Why not me?"

Her gums showed again. "Pretty girls are married off early and have children, or die giving birth. I expected one of the ugly ones to come back."

Obviously, the woman was delusional.

"I'm not ugly enough?"

The woman clicked her tongue and reached over to caress Deborah's head. "Did the Edomites cut your hair? At least not your neck, as they did to our men and boys."

An idea came to Deborah, and she asked, "Do you remember my name?"

"How could I forget the most beautiful girl in Tamar?" She laughed, for a moment sounding like a young woman. "Silly question."

"What's my name?"

"You are Raquellah."

Inhaling sharply, Deborah covered her mouth.

"What's wrong, child?"

Unable to speak, Deborah got up, went to the window, and pulled aside the fabric. It all made sense now—the burned ruins, the jujube trees, Sallan's words, "There are no Hebrews left here, except for a crazy old woman, a healer."

"This town," Deborah said, "is it called Tamar?"

The woman cackled. "I still call it Tamar, but the Edomites have another name for it."

The realization was both devastating and exhilarating. This was Tamar, the Hebrew village the frontier of the land of Judah, where her late mother, Raquellah, had grown up until it was captured by Edom!

"Tell me, child, did you make it to Shiloh?"

Again, Deborah was shocked. How did the old healer know about Shiloh? "Yes," she said. "I did. How do you know?"

"As a little girl, you heard travelers from Ephraim describe the Dance of the Maidens, and an idea was planted in your pretty little head to go to Shiloh and dance in the vineyards on the fifteenth of the month of Av." The woman smiled toothlessly. "So? Did a good man pick you for a wife?"

Deborah nodded. "A very good man. Harutz of Ephraim."

"A man of Ephraim, same as the prophet Joshua. That's good."

"Why did you stay here?"

"I had to stay," the woman said. "It was the bargain I struck with the evil men of Edom."

"A bargain?"

"They were going to send you, the prettiest of our maidens, to their great city as a sacrificial offering to their copper idol, Qoz, and take the rest of the girls as concubines. But our men had put up a good fight before they died, and there were more than fifty injured Edomite soldiers lined up on the ground with crushed bones and open wounds, bleeding and moaning. I agreed to treat their battle wounds on the condition that they release you and the other girls. It was a good bargain, because your childbearing days were ahead of you, and mine were over."

"I don't understand."

"One man can have a hundred babies in a year, but a woman can bear only one at a time. If we didn't save our maidens, who would give birth to the next generation of Hebrews and fulfill Yahweh's command?" The woman smacked her lips and poked Deborah's side with a crooked finger. "Do you know which command I'm talking about?"

"Be fruitful and multiply and fill the earth."

"Good girl." She nodded. "I'm at peace now. You see, the Edomites swore to me by the greatness of their divine Qoz that they'd deliver our maidens safely to the Judah tribesmen in Arad, but I've always worried."

"You saved us," Deborah said.

"Yahweh saved you. I was only his instrument." The old woman got up with great effort and shuffled to the door. She reached up to the cavity of the mezuzah, poked in with her crooked finger, and fished out the small scroll. She kissed it and gave it to Deborah.

Deborah also kissed it.

"Take it with you, Raquellah, and put it on the doorjamb of your home in the land of Ephraim. Yahweh will see it and protect you and the children you'll bear in His honor."

"But you need it." Deborah reached to replace the scroll in the cavity.

"Not anymore." The woman pushed her away. "Go now, before the men from Edom see you. Go!"

Deborah collected her sword, replaced her helmet on her head, and left while the old woman shuffled back to the cushions, mumbling, "They're safe. They're safe. They're safe."

29

Roasting pig gave off a smell that was sweeter than a roasting sheep, goat, or cow. Deborah found it at once tempting and repulsive. Sallan served the first cut to the effigy of Qoz and the second to Kassite. The Edomite men kept turning the pig over as they sliced off the outer layers of the meat, eating it with bread and cheese. Local men and other travelers came by to share in the food and wine.

Deborah stayed away from the men, sitting in her secluded spot next to Rogez, and ate bread with olive oil.

The men remained around the fire for a long time, eating, drinking, and singing Edomite songs. Deborah was tired, but sleep evaded her, not because of the noisy men, but because she couldn't stop thinking of the old healer and the bargain she had made with the invading Edomites. Deborah found the mezuzah scroll in her pocket and put it in her sack. One day, she decided, the scroll would adorn the door to the house at Palm Homestead in memory of the woman who had sacrificed everything to save Raquellah and thereby give life to Deborah.

Daunting questions began to pester Deborah: Was her rejection of womanhood a betrayal of the old healer's sacrifice? Was her denunciation of childbearing a betrayal of her own mother's resilience, suffering, and loss? One the one hand, Yahweh brought her to Tamar to learn how her mother had survived in order to fulfill the divine command to "Be fruitful and multiply and fill the earth." On the other hand, Yahweh had also given her father a dream, back in Palm Homestead, foretelling her future as His prophet. Which one was her True Calling—motherhood or prophecy? How could she reconcile the contradiction? How could she figure out what God really wanted her to do?

Later that night, the Edomite men fell into a drunken stupor, and Deborah dozed off. At one point, Rogez shifted restlessly and snorted, and she sat up and looked around. The starry night was filled with sounds of crickets and frogs, rustling leaves, and snoring men, but she saw no one lurking nearby. The smell of roasting pig was still strong, though the fire had died down. Perhaps the smell had attracted a coyote or a fox that had disturbed her horse. Deborah covered her head with the blanket and slept fitfully for a while longer, but woke up in a fright when she felt Hashkem's hands on her neck again. She threw off the blanket and inhaled deeply, but the terror of suffocation clung to her for a long while.

Deborah was relieved to see first light over the horizon. Everyone was still asleep. Keeping quiet to avoid disturbing the men, she led Rogez downhill to the stream and tied him to a tree. No one was around at this early hour. She entered the fresh, cool water wearing only her undergarments. It was quiet and peaceful, and she stayed in the slow-moving water until the sun shimmered through the trees.

Sitting on a rock to dry, Deborah watched the water and thought about the odd chain of events that had started in Tamara with the old healer saving the beautiful Raquellah from being sent to Edom as a sacrificial offering to Qoz, making it possible for Raquellah to realize her dream of going to Shiloh to dance in the vineyards, marry a good Hebrew man, and bear Hebrew children—two girls, the younger of which was now back here among the ruins of Tamar on her way to Edom. Was Yahweh playing a game to amuse Himself?

Behind her, the horse shifted about and made noises as he'd done during the night.

"Enough, Rogez," she said. "Give me a little peace."

The stream water was as clear as air, and she saw little fish dart between rocks. They were too small to eat, but she wondered whether larger fish might be found. After a night of smelling the roasted pig, the idea of throwing fresh fish on hot embers made her salivate.

A branch broke behind her.

Deborah jumped away just as a hand tried to grab her. She turned and saw Antippet, dressed only in undergarments, his hands still reaching forward over the large rock she had been sitting on, which now separated them. His reddish hair was messy, and he stank of roast pig and wine.

Rogez whinnied and pulled on the reins, shaking the tree.

She stepped backward to the water's edge. "What are you doing?"

He grinned, bypassed the rock, and slowly advanced toward her. Behind him, Patrees and the other men came down the hillside, also in their undergarments.

Deborah tried to step downstream along the bank, but two of the men circled around to block her way, and two others did the same in the upstream direction. She considered crossing to the other side, but wasn't sure how quickly she could get there before they caught up with her.

Antippet took another step.

"Stop right there!" Deborah's voice came out with an anxious edge, which even she could hear. "Leave me alone!"

Her distress bolstered their confidence. They kept coming, and Rogez whinnied louder, struggling to get free.

Antippet reached within two steps of her. "We won't hurt you," he said.

"What do you want?"

A few of the men laughed.

"Not much." Antippet reached forward with his hands, his eyes falling to her chest, where the wet undergarment stuck to the contours of her breasts. "To touch you."

Rogez neighed and stomped the ground. The other horses, tied at the campsite up the hill, whinnied in response.

Deborah knew she had to distract them long enough to reach her horse.

"Fine," she said. "I'll trade with you."

Antippet's eyes lit up, and Patrees made a funny sound, something between a snigger and a sigh.

She pointed at her chest. "You can touch my breasts."

Antippet stared, mesmerized.

"And I'll touch your eyes." Deborah lunged forward, both hands striking like venomous snakes, index fingers drawn like fangs, and poked him in both eyes, which felt like raw eggs.

He screamed and fell back, colliding with Patrees, and the two of them tumbled to the ground. Deborah stepped on them and sprinted to Rogez. The other Edomite men were momentarily stunned, enough for her to grab the belt, which hung from the saddle horn, unsheathe Seesya's sword, and turn to face them, her back to the horse.

Six men confronted her while Patrees dragged the howling Antippet to the water and rinsed the blood from his face. The men picked up sticks and tree branches. Their mouths were slightly open, and their gazes focused on her chest as if they were under a spell. Deborah gripped the silver hilt with two hands and swung the heavy blade from side to side to keep them away. One of the men tried to get through when the sword pointed the other way, and she swung it around, making him jump back. The others laughed. They spread in a wide semicircle and crept closer while her arms grew tired.

Patrees left Antippet moaning at the water's edge and came back, his face twisted in fury. "You blinded him! I'll kill you!"

The sound of rolling rocks made them all turn to look. It was Kassite, making his way slowly down the slope.

"Master!" Patrees ran over and took Kassite's arm to support him. "She hurt Antippet's eyes!"

Kassite walked to the water, leaned over Antippet, whose howling had reduced to moaning, and made him remove his hands from his face.

Sighing, Kassite shook his head. "Very bad," he said.

"You're speaking!" Patrees clapped. "Master is speaking again!"

Kassite looked at Deborah, his gray eyes cold. "Did you do this to Antippet?"

"He attacked me," she said. "I was only defending myself."

Rogez neighed and pulled on the reins.

Kassite turned to Patrees. "Is it true?"

"Yes," Patrees said. "We want to have her."

"What is not yours," Kassite said, "you cannot have."

"She's a Hebrew woman, and this is Edom. We have the right to take her."

The other men voiced their agreement while Antippet moaned by the water.

"Master," Patrees pleaded, "she's only a woman."

"This is Borah!" Kassite raised his voice, pointing at her. "We are free only because of Borah! We are alive only because of Borah!"

"But Borah is a woman—"

Kassite slapped Patrees across the face.

Everyone froze. Even Rogez stood still.

"You brought shame on me," Kassite said.

Patrees fell to his knees and cried, "Master, I'm sorry."

"I am not your master anymore. All of you—leave me!"

They looked at him in shock, unable to comprehend. He had been the source of order and food, of life itself, for as long as they could remember.

Collapsing on the wet ground by the stream, Antippet sobbed like a little boy.

"Master, no!" Patrees kissed the old man's boots. "Forgive us, please!"

The other men dropped the sticks and tree branches, their faces pale and fearful.

"Go back to the camp," Kassite said. "Get dressed, take your horses, and leave."

"Master—"

"Go!"

Their heads low, the Edomite men climbed the hillside, Patrees leading Antippet by the arm.

Kassite stepped to the water's edge and watched the stream in silence. Deborah strapped on the belt, sheathed the sword, and patted her agitated horse.

After a long while, Kassite took Deborah's arm, and they started up the slope slowly, Rogez following behind.

"I am sorry," he said. "I should have taken steps to prevent this from happening."

"Now you understand why I don't want to be a woman anymore."

He chuckled. "A man's life is not exactly a walk in the Garden of Eden, either."

The return of his humor gave Deborah new hope. The Elixirist was back, and by standing up for her against the Edomite men, he had shown where his priorities rested. In a few more days, they would reach Bozra, where he would obtain the needed ingredients and mix the third dose of the Male Elixir for her.

At the campsite, the men and their horses were gone, leaving only Sallan and his boy-servants.

"They left in a hurry," Sallan said. "With not as much as a word. How did Antippet injure his eyes?"

Deborah gestured at Kassite. "He can tell you."

Sallan turned to Kassite. "Can you?"

"I can," Kassite said.

"You're talking!"

"I was angry, and the words came back, just like that." Kassite clicked his fingers.

"Ah!" Sallan rushed over and hugged him. "Didn't I tell you?"

"Yes, you predicted it," Kassite said. "The innate human abilities of hearing and speaking always come back."

Sallan laughed, beaming with joy. "I knew it was going to be easier this time!"

They hugged and kissed on both cheeks.

"This time?" Deborah looked from one to the other. "It's happened before?"

They stepped back and glanced at each other, their smiles fading.

"Wait a minute," Deborah said, trying to grasp the tail of an elusive thread of memory. "I've heard this term: 'innate human abilities.' When did I hear it?"

Neither of them responded.

"The story you told me," she said to Sallan, "about the guard who helped the Elixirist." She turned to Kassite. "The guard who helped you escape—he was deaf and mute, right?"

Kassite grunted as he sat down with his back to the tree trunk.

"I remember now," she said to Sallan. "In Emanuel, when I asked you if the story about the Elixirist was true, you confirmed it. You said that the Elixirist had turned the women of Edom into men, and they'd formed an army and succeeded in scaring away the Egyptian attackers. But the people's adoration of the Elixirist upset King Esau, who had him locked up and invented an official story about an Egyptian abduction."

Sallan nodded and sighed.

"You were jailed," she said, turning to Kassite. "Deep inside a mountain with no human contact, except for a guard, who was deaf and mute, but you cured him." Deborah closed her eyes, trying to remember. "Sallan told me: 'Cure is a big word. Let's just say that he helped the guard rediscover those innate human abilities of hearing and speaking. It was an easier task than turning all those women into men before a battle.' That's what Sallan said!"

"Easier?" Kassite chuckled. "It was not easy at all, was it?"

Sallan shook his head. "Three years of daily sessions, but in the end, we succeeded, and you were able to carry a conversation as well as any man."

Both of them became teary.

"I don't understand," she said to Sallan. "Were you locked up with him?" She turned to Kassite. "And I've noticed, ever since I met you, that you hear better when you look at my lips. At night, you can barely hear anything. Were you also deaf like the guard?"

Kassite put his hand to the side of his head. "What?"

Sallan laughed.

"It's not funny," Deborah said. "What's going on here? Tell me the truth for a change."

Kassite took off his hat and used it to fan himself. "My hearing was very poor from birth. At the isolated homestead in the desert hills, where my family scooped up copper from a small mine, no one bothered to teach me how to use what little hearing I did have. As a result, I grew up mute. One day, when I returned from a week of herding our sheep in the hills, I found my family dead—must have been the red fever. I buried them and remained on the land, a lonely, deaf and mute young man, until the king's guards brought a prisoner for me to watch."

Deborah was stunned. "You were the guard?"

"And a good student," Kassite said, "who was lucky to have an excellent teacher."

Turning to Sallan, Deborah pointed at him. "The Elixirist—it's you?"

He nodded and smiled. "At long last, you found the man you've been looking for. Congratulations!"

Deborah swayed, almost losing her balance. A rapid series of images flashed through her mind from her harrowing quest to find the Elixirist: the nighttime escape from Emanuel and the lonely trek on the dark road north, Seesya's chase and Zariz's deadly arrows, the slave warden in Shiloh and the wedding procession, Seesya's violent attempts to possess her in bed and the taste of bloody chunks of flesh from the waterskin, Seesya's nighttime attack and the journey with the lepers, the abusive guards in Aphek and the backbreaking slave labor in the tannery, and worst of all the vicious flogging under the Weeping Tree and the travesty of a trial before hundreds of hateful men—all those horrible experiences could have been avoided had Sallan told her the truth, that he was the Elixirist!

As if this weren't bad enough, a worse realization hit her. If Kassite wasn't the Elixirist, then the two doses of the Male Elixir he had given her had been nothing more than nauseating, rotten junk!

"You cheated me!" Rage exploded inside her, and she screamed, "Liar!"

Lunging at Sallan, her hands clenched, Deborah drummed him with her fists until the two boy-servants pulled her back.

She tore out of their hands and ran from the campsite, down the slope, and plunged into the stream, facedown, hoping to drown. Everything had been for nothing—the fear, the loneliness, the suffering, and the blood she'd spilled—all for nothing!

Deborah kept her head underwater, her mouth open, trying to inhale the water, but her body refused to do it. She crawled out of the stream, her muscles limp, curled up on the warm sand and wept.

30

Deborah woke up and found a pig licking her face. She pushed the animal away and sat up. The stream gurgled beside to her, masking the noise from the campsites up the slope. Judging by the position of the sun, she had slept for a while. Her body felt refreshed, but her mind filled with despair. What was she supposed to do now? Continue on the journey with the two crooked old Edomites? That would be a waste of time. Go back to Emanuel and submit to Seesya? That would mean death, or a servile life even worse than death. Return to Ein Gedi and accept Ramrod's offer of marriage? The idea of living with him on his relatives' small plot near Bethel, washing his dirty clothes and bearing his skinny children, made her sick. What else could she do?

With a bitter groan, Deborah recalled the inspiring Hebrew proverb that the blacksmith in Shiloh had shared with her: "When you pursue your True Calling, God provides the shortcuts." Having learned that Kassite wasn't the Elixirist, Deborah now knew that all the progress she had rejoiced at making wasn't progress at all, but a sad chain of futile sacrifices and needless suffering. How could God have let her pursue her True Calling on a false path? How could He have let her exult in divine shortcuts over events that in truth were no better than unlucky coincidences that took her further away from her goal? She recalled wondering the day before whether Yahweh could be playing a game to amuse Himself, but who was she to blame God for what must have been her own errors? Perhaps it wasn't her path that was false, but her very quest? Could she have been wrong altogether about her True Calling?

The possibility was too upsetting to consider.

Deborah sprang to her feet, pushing the idea away, and ran up the hillside.

Back at their campsite, she found Kassite, Sallan, and the two boy-servants ready to go. They had packed up her sack and gotten Rogez ready, too. Ignoring them, she strapped on the heavy sword, mounted her horse, and trotted off. She could tell they were following her, but she didn't look back.

Unsure where to go now, Deborah directed Rogez through the half-ruined town to the old healer's house.

Her knocks on the doorjamb produced no response. Deborah entered and paused, letting her eyes adjust to the darkness.

The old woman was lying peacefully on the cushions in the corner, where she had sat the day before. Her eyes were closed, and her creased face wore a peaceful expression. Deborah put an ear to the healer's mouth and felt no breathing.

The finality of death ended any hope of speaking with the old woman one more time, of asking about the past or seeking advice for the future. The thin thread of connection to her mother, Raquellah, was now severed. She was alone again.

Shaking off the fog of sadness, Deborah stood, took a deep breath, and exhaled with a sigh. There were no Hebrews left in Tamar, so it was up to her to give this brave woman a proper burial.

She poked her head out and beckoned the two boy-servants. They helped her wrap the dead woman in a blanket, carry her outside, and lay her down under a jujube tree with her feet pointing north toward Yahweh's temple in Shiloh. They covered the body with rocks.

Unsure what else to do, Deborah held her hands over the pile of stones, her fingers parted in pairs, and recited the priestly blessing: "May Yahweh bless you and protect you. May He show you kindness and grace. May He illuminate your path and grant you peace."

The boys got back on their horse.

Deborah touched the stones one more time. "Thank you," she said quietly, "for saving my mother and giving me life."

Outside the town of Tamar, just before the intersection of the major trade routes, Deborah stopped Rogez. To the left was the road back north to the Sea of Salt and Canaan, right was the road south to Bozra, the capital of Edom, and straight toward the rising sun was the road east to Moab, Arabia, and Persia.

"Come with us," Sallan said.

Deborah turned her horse and glared at him.

"You're right to resent our dishonesty," he said, "but it's in the past, and our friendship is sincere."

"Friendship? Sincere?" She groaned with frustration. "You manipulated me into leaving Emanuel on a quest to find the Elixirist while you—the actual Elixirist!—were right there in front of me in the basket factory! Everything I've gone through was in pursuit of a lie!" Her voice was rising. "I had to kill a man! And poke out another man's eyes! Do you realize what you've done?"

"Yes," Sallan said. "I could tell you that I regret lying to you, but that would be another lie, and we're done lying. The truth is that I don't regret sending you off to search for Kassite, because the result is that we're here in Edom—you, Kassite, and I. Do I wish it hadn't required lying to you? Of course I do, but it did. I had no choice and I would do it again. That is the truth, but it's in the past. Let us all focus on the future now, together, as each other's most loyal friends."

Kassite nodded.

"Loyal friends?" Deborah was dumbfounded. "How can you expect me to trust you?"

"Trust is no longer an issue," Sallan said. "You know the whole truth. I lied to you because it was the only way to find Kassite and obtain our freedom. And it worked. We're free, all three of us. I'm forever indebted to you for your courage and sacrifice."

"Me too," Kassite said.

"You know the truth now," Sallan said. "The only issue is your anger, which is wholly justified."

"Exactly!"

"But you've forgiven us already."

"Have I?"

Sallan smiled. "Do you remember what I said at the campsite on our first night out of Ein Gedi?"

"Yes," Deborah said. "You told me that, from the beginning, you and Kassite had been focused on unshackling yourselves from slavery and getting back home to Edom, even when it required making me risk my life repeatedly."

"Correct. And you forgave both me and Kassite, true?"

"Yes, but I didn't realize the extent of your deceit—that Kassite wasn't the real Elixirist and that the two doses of the Male Elixir he gave me were fakes, just like him!"

Kassite shifted on his horse but said nothing.

"You don't have to worry about that," Sallan said. "During the years of my isolated incarceration, I taught him many things. The first two doses he gave you were real, as good as if I had prepared them."

"Is this another necessary lie to keep me around until you make it back home to Bozra?"

Sallan held up a hand. "In the name of Kothar-wa-Khasis and the great Qoz, I swear that the two doses of the Male Elixir you have consumed were as good as and as potent as anything I could have prepared."

Looking into his eyes, Deborah was inclined to believe him, but he had lied to her so successfully before that she didn't know how to judge him accurately. Instead, she asked the single question that mattered: "What about the third dose of the Male Elixir?"

"In my opinion," Sallan said, "you are ready."

"I agree," Kassite said.

They watched her, waiting for her decision.

Deborah was torn between her reluctance to trust the two men again and the realization that she might not have a better option. She pressed her heels to Rogez's ribs, urging him to go, but dropped the reins, providing no direction. He snorted and sprinted forward, but at the middle of the four-way intersection, stopped and turned in place several times, impatient for Deborah to indicate her wishes. When she persisted in her silence, Rogez stopped turning, swayed his large head this way and that, and took off down the road south to Bozra.

The others caught up with her.

"You made the right decision," Sallan called over the drumming of the hooves. "As soon as we reach Bozra, I'll prepare the third dose."

"I didn't make the decision," Deborah yelled, collecting the reins. "Rogez did."

Sallan laughed. "The elixir will be ready—if you still wish for manhood!"

31

They traveled south for four days through the arid land of northern Edom. Once in a while, they ran into a caravan of merchants heading north, who invariably moved aside respectfully to let Deborah and the group pass. At first, she was bewildered by it, but soon she realized it was the sight of Rogez, whose great size and pure white color made the travelers assume the rider was a wealthy and powerful man.

Each night, they camped by a village or a small town built around a natural spring or deep well. Deborah slept poorly, wary of dangers lurking in the dark every time Rogez made a sound. Worse yet, her dreams kept taking her back to the killing of Hashkem and the panic of suffocation, leaving her with a foreboding expectation of God's harsh punishment for her grave sin.

In the middle of the fifth day, the road crested yet another barren ridge, and at the top, a vast green valley appeared before them. The group stopped and gazed at the view. The valley was divided into hundreds of square fields and mature orchards, dotted with farmers and livestock. Up ahead, at the opposite end of the valley, the entire mountainside sparkled with countless copper roofs reflecting the sun. Massive defense walls surrounded the city. The walls and the houses were painted white, resembling the snow Deborah had seen once, a few years back, on an aberrant winter day in the Samariah Hills.

"We're home," Sallan said, his voice cracking. "Praise the gods!"

Kassite sniffled and cleared his throat.

"Welcome to Bozra," Sallan said. "Have you ever seen a more beautiful city?"

Deborah shook her head. It was true. She had never seen such beauty.

They followed the winding road down to the valley and began to cross it. The city gradually came closer. Deborah was surprised to see that the streets didn't go straight uphill as in Emanuel, Shiloh, and Aphek, but followed a horizontal pattern. The lowest street went left across the city, then turned fully to the right and went above the lower street all the way to the opposite perimeter wall, where it turned left, and so on, back and forth up the hill. The houses were built on the horizontal strips of land between each street and the next one up, facing the vast green valley below.

"A unique design," Deborah said. "What's the reason for it?"

Sallan chuckled. "What do you think?"

She contemplated the view for a while. The first answer that came to her mind was "Because it's pretty," but such a response would sound too feminine. The Edomite must have had a practical reason for building their great city in this manner.

"I can think of two reasons," Deborah said. "First, the difference in height between each row of houses and the one above it lets everyone see the views of the valley. The scenery must be incredible from up there."

"It is." Sallan laughed. "It absolutely is."

Kassite grunted. "And the second reason?"

"It's very hot here," she said. "By having each row of houses on a different level, everyone can enjoy the breeze when it comes along."

"I am disappointed," Kassite said. "You still think like a girl."

Deborah stopped her horse. "What do you mean?"

"Views, fresh air." Kassite waved his hand dismissively. "Things that occupy the feeble minds of women and primitive Hebrews from Canaan, not the brilliant men who build great cities in prosperous kingdoms like this."

Her face flushed. "My people may not have built great cities yet, but we have divine laws that came down from—"

"Here is a hint," Sallan said. "Think of the city in terms of our discussion about strategy. Do you remember it?"

She quoted from memory: "Strategy is what men of power and wealth use for self-preservation. When a situation comes up, they look at all the facts, figure out what they can use for their advantage, and come up with solutions that promote three things: their safety, their fortune, and their power. Strategy is the reason they rule the world, whereas everyone else submits to them, works hard for them, and pays them taxes."

"Perfect." Sallan clapped. "Now, look up there. Do you see the king's palace?"

Deborah shielded her eyes with her hand and gazed. Near the top of the city, surrounded by its own set of white walls, was a massive palace. She tried to think rationally. Why would a king build a city with horizontal streets, rather than streets that go straight up the hill? The answer came to her in a flash. Safety!

"It's all about defense," she said, keeping her voice calm. "All these horizontal streets of houses and the people living in them would stand in the way of an invading army trying to reach the king's palace."

"Very good," Sallan said.

Kassite prodded his horse forward. They followed him.

Riding beside her, Sallan said, "Even in my dreams, Bozra hasn't been as stunning as it is in reality."

"Eighteen years is a long time," she said.

"Longer. I was a prisoner for three years before that."

They rode in silence for a while, the glistening city growing larger before them. Deborah counted the houses in the lowest row, just inside the gate, reaching seventy-eight before the street made a sharp upward turn near the massive perimeter walls. The street above it was even longer, and there were at least forty or fifty more streets. Calculating in her mind, she was shocked by the result—over five thousand homes, which translated into tens of thousands of residents.

"It's so big," she said. "How do they get all the water and food for that many people?"

"Good planning and efficient administration." Sallan smiled proudly. "Now you can see how primitive the land of Canaan is in comparison— the Hebrew tribes fighting each other incessantly, the pompous little judges ruling their grimy towns while abusing the tradesmen, merchants, and homestead farmers, and the Canaanites playing favorites with one tribe against another while gradually subjugating more and more of the Hebrews under their king's yoke."

His disparaging words were hurtful, but she had to admit that Bozra put to shame the Hebrew cities of Aphek and Shiloh. She recalled what Obadiah of Levi had said to her at the temple in Emanuel: "Too many Hebrew men have turned their backs on the one true God. Even our ruler, Judge Zifron, holds up the effigy of Mott at trials, while his women kneel before Ra when the sun rises. That's why God is punishing us, sending one tribe to fight against the other and allowing the Canaanites to oppress the northern tribes—and it will get worse unless we repent and correct our ways!" Deborah wondered if things would ever change. Would her people one day realize their errors, throw away the false gods, and stop fighting each other? Would the Hebrews ever manage to build great cities like Bozra?

Near the entrance to the city, the large fairgrounds had a cloth roof, supported by dozens of tall wooden poles, providing shade for the vendors and customers. Numerous soldiers manned the city gates and the perimeter walls. They wore helmets with copper-colored, horsehair rooster combs. Sallan took the lead and greeted the soldiers, who allowed them into Bozra.

At the bottom of the hill, long storage buildings backed up to the inside of the perimeter walls, and merchants sold food supplies from stalls. There were also several wells, where women filled plump jars with water and carried them on their heads. What was missing, Deborah immediately noticed, were the crowded huts and tents of the poor and the stench they produced in Emanuel, Shiloh, and Aphek. Looking around, she saw none of those.

She asked, "Are there no poor people in Edom?"

"Not in Bozra," Sallan said. "Living inside the walls here or in any other Edomite city is permitted only to homeowners, their families, and their servants. Outside the cities, living on the land is allowed only to landowners and their household. It's the same rule all over Edom."

"What about the rest of the people?"

"Those who don't own property or work for someone who does?"

"Yes."

"They're lazy beggars and idle vagrants, and we don't indulge them as the Hebrews do."

"It's charity, not indulgence," she said. "Yahweh commands us to be generous to the poor, give them food and clothes, and leave a corner of every field for them at harvest time."

"And in return for your charity, they give you filth and stench. Look around." Sallan waved. "Our city is clean because those who would tarnish it are sent away."

"Where to?"

Sallan glanced at Kassite before answering. "To the king's copper mines."

"All of the poor?" Deborah was incredulous. "Women too? And children?"

"It's the law."

"It's cruel and unjust."

"Perhaps," Kassite said, "but let me ask you something. When you lived at your father's homestead, did you see him leave trash out for the coyotes to feed on?"

She shook her head.

"Exactly, because if they got used to handouts, they would lose the ability to hunt for food and try to steal it, or bite the hand that had used to feed them. It is the same with the poor."

"But they're people, not animals!"

"Everyone should work for their bread," Kassite said. "It is the law, and it is good for them."

"Let's go." Sallan turned his horse. "My father's house is halfway up the hill."

As the small group rode along the lowest horizontal street, Deborah noticed that the houses were small, built close together on narrow lots, but with each higher street, the houses grew larger, many sporting two stories and generous front gardens with trees and flowers, as well as roof balconies with unobstructed views.

Halfway up the mountainside, they reached a great house with a line of jujube trees along the front of a spacious garden. Many horses and donkeys were tied to the trees outside, and guests filled the garden. Lively music sounded, and smoke from cooking fires drifted to the street.

The group dismounted and tied the horses.

"There's a party." Sallan's hands shook as he unplugged a waterskin and washed the dust off his hands and face. "Maybe a child was born." He fixed his hair over the missing ears. "Or a wedding."

"You look fine," Kassite said.

"For an old man." Sallan straightened his leather armor and adjusted the belt and sword, but changed his mind, unbuckled, and put the sword on the saddle. "I don't want to scare them."

Kassite smiled. "They will be happy that you have come back, alive and well."

"Twenty-one years." Sallan took a step toward the house, but paused. "Maybe you should go in first and tell them. If my parents are still alive, seeing me might shock them to death."

"You are home." Kassite made him turn. "Go in there and hug your family—whoever is still alive will delight at seeing you."

The two boys stayed with the horses while Kassite and Deborah followed Sallan through the line of trees into the crowded garden. Men and women mingled together, chatting and laughing. The women wore colorful robes and jewelry, but no headscarves over their long hair, which was light brown or orange. The men wore fine coats and leather sandals. A group of men played musical instruments.

The guests stepped aside, opening a path for the three strangers.

The front of the house featured a wide, elevated terrace. On the right stood a large copper statue of Qoz, a bowl of fruit and cakes at its feet. Around the rim of the bowl stood several smaller figurines of other gods, made of clay or wood. Deborah recognized Baal, Ashtoreth, Ra, and Kothar-wa-Khasis with his myriad bronze tools.

On the left of the terrace was a canopy decorated with flowers. The rest of the terrace was taken up by a line of chairs, occupied by men and women who conversed amiably with guests.

Getting closer, Deborah noticed the chair in the center, larger than the others, with a tall back and padded armrests. Expecting a man to sit in it, she was surprised to see a woman.

With her plain black dress, black shoes, and lack of jewelry, the woman seemed out of place among the colorful outfits and chattering guests, but her bearing radiated authority as if she owned the place. Her white hair fell around her shoulders in thick locks, and her gaunt face had perfectly drawn features and pale skin that seemed too tight to wrinkle. She had Sallan's gray eyes, and her gaze was focused on him.

Sallan climbed the steps onto the terrace and knelt before her. She looked at him, her expression unchanged for a long moment. Finally, she smiled, revealing perfect white teeth, took his hands, and pressed them to her bosom.

The musicians ceased playing, and the guests quieted down.

"Blessed be Qoz," the woman said, "for answering my prayers."

Sallan kissed her on both cheeks. "I'm sorry, Mother, that it took so long."

"Time has stopped for us since you were taken." She glanced upward. "Your father cried your name with his last breath."

The men and women in the other chairs got up and circled them. Everyone broke down in tears, hugging and kissing Sallan.

Kassite nudged Deborah. "His five sisters," he explained quietly. "The men are probably their husbands and sons."

When calm was restored, a chair was placed next to the matriarch, and Sallan sat in it, his hand still in hers. The crowd of men and women that filled the garden stood quietly, waiting for her to speak. Deborah had never before seen such respect accorded to a woman.

"My dear family and friends," Sallan's mother said in a voice that was tremulous but confident. "Today we give thanks to the gods for a gift that has been long in coming. The years have tested my faith many times, but my prayers have never ceased. We gathered here today to celebrate my great-granddaughter's wedding, but our joy is a hundred times greater. My son, the hero who saved this kingdom more than two decades ago, is back from Egyptian captivity!"

Everyone cheered, the music started again, and the chattering resumed. Waiters walked around, serving wine and fruit. Sallan's family gathered around him, asking questions about his captivity and escape, which he deflected with vague responses.

Kassite leaned toward Deborah and covered his mouth while speaking. "They repeat the lies of the old king, who accused Egyptian spies of abducting the great Elixirist and claimed that the Pharaoh refused all offers of ransom."

"The old king is dead," Deborah said. "Sallan should tell everyone what really happened, how the old king jailed him—"

"Hush." Kassite pulled her further back from the guests. "We have to stick with the Egypt story. If we tell the truth, the young king will hear about it when he returns and accuse Sallan of slandering his grandfather."

"Maybe the young king knows the truth."

"Then he would be even more eager to perpetuate the lie."

Sounds of metal clinking came from the direction of the street, and the crowd parted to let through a huge, gray-bearded man accompanied by several soldiers in full armor, swords, and long spears, their helmets adorned copper-colored, horsehair rooster comb.

An attendant announced, "General Mazabi!"

When the general came closer, Deborah saw that his left arm was missing below the shoulder.

"He was a young officer," Kassite whispered in Deborah's ear, "when the Egyptians ambushed our army and destroyed it near the Sea of Reeds. Lost his arm, but still, he managed to save the king, get back to Bozra, and prepare the army of women that Sallan created to scare off the Egyptians."

"Greetings, Umm-Sallan." General Mazabi had a deep, sonorous voice. "Congratulations on the marriage of your great-granddaughter, the beautiful Leola."

Deborah understood that "Umm-Sallan" meant "Mother of Sallan."

The general bowed before the matriarch, who nodded and smiled. He signaled to his soldiers, and they brought forward a box made of wood and copper, placing it at the foot of the terrace.

"Thank you," Umm-Sallan said, "for your generosity and good wishes."

He bowed again. "May the mighty Qoz bless your family."

"Indeed," she said, "the gods have been generous beyond our greatest expectations and brought back what we've missed the most."

"General Mazabi," Sallan said, rising from his chair. "It's been a long time."

Deborah saw apprehension on people's faces as they waited for the general's reaction. Apparently, the king's version of Sallan's disappearance had not been accepted without doubts.

"Be ready," Kassite whispered to Deborah. "We might have to run."

General Mazabi burst out laughing, threw his only arm around Sallan, pressed him to his giant chest, and roared, "Praise the gods!"

Everyone laughed with relief, and clapping erupted.

When the noise subsided, General Mazabi held Sallan away and looked at him. "By Qoz, you've gotten old, my friend!"

The guests laughed.

"Indeed," Sallan said. "But you haven't aged at all."

"Ha!" The general tugged on his gray beard. "If I could only go back in time and place guards around you. When you disappeared, I wanted to march on the Egyptians right away, but our wise king, who's now with the gods, put sense into my head. You saved the kingdom with the army of women, but we needed them to go back to making babies to replenish all the men we'd lost."

"Which we did," Umm-Sallan said. "My five daughters gave birth to sixty-seven children since then, and almost thirty of them survived to adulthood."

General Mazabi raised a clenched fist. "Edom is rising, and now we have the Elixirist back with us!"

The guests cheered.

"It's good to be back," Sallan said. "I was starting to lose hope."

"The old king offered great sums to the Egyptians," General Mazabi said, "but they always denied holding you. How did you get out?"

"A local rebellion broke out, and we took advantage of the chaos to escape into the desert."

"We?" The general looked around. "Who else?"

Sallan waved dismissively. "A few fellow prisoners. No one important."

Kassite leaned closer. "What did he say?"

Deborah faced him so that he could see her lips. "A few fellow prisoners. No one important."

Kassite smirked. "How true."

"Tell me, General," Umm-Sallan said. "Any news from our king?"

"A messenger arrived yesterday. The king is on his way back from the Negev Desert without his sister. The leader of the Simeon tribe denied Needa's abduction. He said she had joined his son willingly as an honored guest on a hunting expedition in the desert."

Umm-Sallan clicked her tongue. "The king must be worried for his sister."

"Worried and angry. Those Hebrew tribesmen are clever and elusive, always on the move—here today, gone tomorrow."

"May the gods bring Needa back as they brought our son."

"Or there will be war." General Mazabi bowed, turned, and marched away with his entourage, his voice reverberating through the large garden. "Come see me soon, Sallan—danger is on the rise again!"

When the general was gone, Umm-Sallan gestured at the musicians, who began to play a slow, soft tune. Little girls in colorful dresses spread white flower petals along the front of the terrace from the corner of the house all the way to the decorated wooden canopy. The young couple appeared and followed the path of white petals. They were about fifteen years old, dressed in matching white robes and crowns of woven flowers. The bride had inherited Umm-Sallan's regal stature and perfectly sculpted features. Her wheat-colored hair, woven with golden threads, cascaded over her shoulders and down her back.

The couple knelt before Umm-Sallan.

She placed one hand on each head and said, "I give you my blessing."

The soft music continued while the couple kissed Umm-Sallan and stepped over to the canopy.

An attendant announced, "High Priest Qoztobarus!"

The guests parted to make way.

The High Priest wore only a black loincloth, his skin was painted to look like copper, and he was completely hairless—not even eyebrows or eyelashes. His entourage of six boys resembled him completely, except for their small size and young age. Deborah noticed that the guests lowered their eyes as he passed through, except for Umm-Sallan, who watched him with an unflappable expression. He made a quick bow, which the matriarch acknowledged with a nod, and continued to the canopy.

The six boys lined up behind the canopy and chanted a monotonous hymn while Qoztobarus sprinkled copper dust on the couple. The two shared a bowl of ripe jujube fruit, drank in turns from a wine goblet, and exchanged rings. Leola knelt before her groom and sang a song filled with hope and innocence. When she finished, the guests wiped tears and applauded.

Deborah could see that the young couple was truly happy together. Their eyes were locked through the whole ceremony, and when the ceremony was over, they clung to one another as if there were no one else around. Deborah imagined kissing Zariz that way, and being kissed back by him, but the image disappeared when she remembered his horrified rejection when she visited him in her dream. The only other young man with whom she had ever felt such kinship was Barac, son of Abinoam, the blacksmith in Emanuel. For a brief moment, Deborah imagined kissing Barac like that, but she shook her head sharply to chase away the image. Barac was dead, murdered by Seesya, and there was no point in longing for him or for their friendship, which had died with him.

"Young love." Kassite elbowed her gently. "How pure and innocent, is it not?"

"It won't last," she said.

"You are too young to be a cynic," Kassite said. "Sometimes, love does endure."

Qoztobarus departed with his entourage, and as he passed by, his eyes caught Deborah's gaze. It was only a brief glance, but it chilled her. She regretted not lowering her eyes like everybody else.

The couple went back to the house, accompanied by music and showered with fistfuls of wheat and barley grains. Sallan tossed the grains with one hand while wiping his eyes with the other.

Deborah turned to Kassite. "Was Sallan married before he was jailed by the old king?"

"When he was young, there was a girl he loved and married. She died, and Sallan blamed himself. Even now, a lifetime of many misfortunes later, Sallan cannot talk about her without crying." Kassite chuckled sadly. "You see? Love does endure, even beyond death."

Sallan beckoned them over.

"Mother," he said, "this is Kassite, my dearest and most loyal friend."

Kassite bowed. "An honor to meet you, Umm-Sallan."

"Welcome to my home," the matriarch said.

"And this is Borah." Sallan placed his hand on Deborah's shoulder. "He's young, but braver than ten grown men put together. We wouldn't be here if not for this special boy."

"Girl," his mother said. "I'm old, not blind."

Sallan shifted uncomfortably, but didn't argue.

"Come closer, girl." Umm-Sallan curled her finger. "And take off this foolish helmet. I want to see you."

Deborah pulled off the leather helmet.

"Thank you for helping my son." Umm-Sallan touched Deborah's cheek with her long fingers. "What is your real name?"

"Deborah, daughter of Harutz and Raquellah."

"A Hebrew?"

Deborah nodded.

"Not from the Simeon tribe, I hope."

"Ephraim. Our tribe lives in the Samariah Hills, north of Jerusalem."

"That's better, but until Needa is back safely, it would be safer not to tell anyone that you are a Hebrew."

"My father taught me that Edom descends from Abraham, who is our forefather as well."

"True, but our king is very young, which means he cares little about the past, whereas his passions run hot for today's pleasures and animosities." Umm-Sallan took Deborah's hand in hers. "You've done a man's job recently, very hard work."

"Yes."

"But not long enough to ruin your skin. My son used to make a magical potion called the Youth Elixir. It restored our skin to the smoothness of silk." Sallan's mother turned to him. "Will you make some for Deborah?"

"It's been a very long time since I mixed any potions."

"We've kept the workshop as it was on the day you disappeared, with all the jars, bottles, and urns. Your father was too upset to continue."

Sallan's eyes moistened.

Umm-Sallan noticed the sword on Deborah's hip and touched the line of red rubies along the crossguard. "That's a beautiful sword," she said. "And expensive."

"It belonged to a man who tried to kill me. Now it's mine."

"Carrying a man's weapon is forbidden for a woman in this land."

Deborah recalled the soldier she'd killed in Ein Gedi. "In the desert, even a woman needs weapons."

"Perhaps, but in Bozra, a wise woman can get her way without weapons." Umm-Sallan smiled. "I can tell that you would be very pretty after a good scrubbing and a hot bath."

Deborah blushed and looked away.

"Pretty isn't something you want to be, is it?"

Shaking her head, Deborah thought of Antippet, Patrees, and the other Edomite men closing in on her by the stream in Tamar like a pack of hungry dogs.

"I understand, dear." Umm-Sallan leaned forward and kissed Deborah on the cheek. "This is your home now. Rest from your journey, and then we'll talk some more."

32

While Sallan remained at the wedding celebration, a servant took Kassite and Deborah to the guest quarters. The two boy-servants, who were already there, assured Deborah that Rogez and the other horses were being cared for in the stables behind the house.

They washed, put on clean robes, and lay down for the night. Kassite and the boys fell asleep, but Deborah remained awake. The music continued to play outside, and she thought about what she had seen and heard since arriving at Sallan's family home.

In particular, she was troubled by something General Mazabi had said to Sallan: "You saved the kingdom with the army of women, but we needed them to go back to making babies to replenish all the men we'd lost."

The story she had heard from Barac, may he rest in peace, was that the Elixirist had turned the women of Edom into men. Sallan had confirmed the story, and Kassite had also implied as much about the power of the Male Elixir, advising her, "Imitate until you mutate." The old general's words, however, implied that the women of Edom had not mutated into men, but went back to bearing babies, which meant that any masculine transformation had been temporary. Deborah was seeking a permanent and complete transformation, not a temporary masquerade followed by a return to womanhood and childbearing.

Thinking back to the first night at the tannery, Deborah recalled what Kassite had explained to her about the three doses of the Male Elixir. The first would accelerate her acquisition of masculine strength and endurance. The second would help her develop the male attitude and character. And the third would cause her female body parts to change into male. Taken together, those changes didn't sound like a temporary, reversible masquerade. Had Sallan given the women of Edom a watered-down version of the Male Elixir that had caused short-lived changes, whereas Kassite was giving her a more powerful version, infused with the high potency required to bring about an irreversible mutation? Or was the whole thing another lie?

At the other end of the room, Kassite passed gas and mumbled something in his sleep. Deborah resisted the urge to wake him up and ask him about General Mazabi's statement. Surely Kassite would give her a thoughtful, convincing answer, but wouldn't her doubts persist? Had she been naive to trust him and Sallan after discovering their earlier deceit? Had she made a mistake traveling with them to this foreign kingdom?

The music outside had long since ended when soft tapping sounded from the door. The room was dark, the night completely silent. She felt in the dark for the hilt of the sword, which rested on the floor beside her. The door cracked open, letting in the meek light of a small lamp. It was Sallan, wearing a night robe.

"Come with me," he whispered.

Deborah got up and joined him in the hallway. "Where are we going?"

"Back in time," he said. "You'll see."

She followed him down a dark hallway. He paused and raised his lamp to illuminate the wall, where the skin of an adult tiger was mounted. Deborah put her nose close to it and was able to discern a faint remnant—same as her tiger tail.

Sallan touched one of the tiger's paws. "My father hunted it down after it had killed his horse at night as they camped by the road to the Sea of Reeds. I was only eight, but I still remember my father coming back without his horse, which I loved, but with a huge dead tiger, which was dead. He even let me take part in dissecting it—tiger organs are very valuable for potion-making. The whole house smelled of the skin for months after it was put up on the wall."

They reached a side door, which let them out to a small garden, planted with flowers, vegetables, and aromatic herbs. Across the garden was a separate structure, dark and overgrown with ivy. Sallan gave her the lamp and tried to open the door. It resisted. He put his shoulder against it, pushed hard, and the door gave in with a loud screech and a puff of dust. Dogs barked nearby, and a moment later two of them appeared at a sprint. They were huge, almost the size of donkeys.

Deborah froze in fear, but Sallan laughed and petted them. A moment later, they sprinted away, wagging their tails.

"My mother's dogs," Sallan said.

"Your mother owns dogs?"

"She loves them, and they love her—enough to kill anyone trying to enter her bedroom at night." Sallan chuckled. "Even her slaves don't dare approach—"

"She owns slaves, too?"

"Of course. Why not?"

Deborah was shocked. "She's a woman."

"This is Edom, girl, not Canaan. Here, a woman may own land, slaves, and horses. She may inherit property from her father if he has no sons, from her husband if he dies before her, and from her own sons if they precede her in death without wives or children. Our women may sue before a judge, give testimony at trial, and make valid contracts for goods if they have no husband or father to do it for them."

"Your women are lucky," Deborah said. "Has it always been like this?"

"Since the war with the Egyptians, which left us with too few men." Sallan took her arm. "Let's go inside."

He poured oil into two wall lamps, one on each side of the entry, and lit them with his small lamp. As the flames flickered and caught, a large room came into view. The air was musty with a mix of sharp smells. Rows of wooden shelves held countless jars and bottles. Several large work desks held measuring scales, clay bowls, wooden barrels, and mixing utensils. Everything was covered with spider webs and a thick layer of dust.

Sallan's shoes left footprints on the floor. It was obvious no one had been here in many years.

He took her hand, and she felt his fingers clasp tightly.

"Is this your old workshop?"

He nodded.

They proceeded along the rows of shelves. As they reached deeper into the workshop, the light from the wall lamps by the door grew weaker, and the flickering flame of the small lamp took over. At the opposite end, a large oven was built into the wall. Inside was a giant clay pot. Sallan lit two more wall lamps, which caught after a few flashes of hesitation.

"It took six of these," he said, pointing at the pot. "The Egyptian army was marching north from the Sea of Reeds, where they had destroyed our army. There were going to reach Bozra within days and mount an attack. I was working here like a madman while three thousand women lined up outside, each one waiting to drink a goblet of the Male Elixir."

"The same as what Kassite has given me?"

"Not exactly." Sallan touched the pot, his fingers leaving marks. "The situation required something very concentrated but short-acting. Mixing it required all my knowledge and expertise, and hefty measures of speed and audacity."

"The women were audacious to drink it and face the Egyptians."

"Like oil for a fire, my elixir fueled their courage, which in turn fueled my hubris, until the gods taught me a painful lesson whose scars would never heal."

Sallan turned away, and Deborah sensed that he didn't want her to ask him about that lesson. She wondered if it had to do with the death of the woman he'd loved.

The light from the lamp fell on a set of shelves nearby, each lined with jars and bottles.

"There are so many of them." Deborah peered at the first jar on the top shelf, which was at her eye level. "What's in this one?"

"The scalp of a male ape."

She stepped back. "It contains a scalp?"

Sallan removed the jar from the shelf, pried open the cork plug, and poured out fine powder into the palm of his hand.

"Oh." Deborah was embarrassed. "I thought you meant—"

"—that a whole bloody scalp was shoved into this jar?" He laughed and held out his hand. "Touch it."

She did. The powder was soft and cool. A few grains stuck to her fingers. "It's completely dry."

"Every living creature is made mostly of water." Holding the jar under his hand, he carefully poured the powder back into the jar. "Have you ever seen an animal carcass that's been lying in the sun for a few weeks?"

Deborah nodded.

"You could lift it with one hand, because all the water has evaporated, but the good ingredients stay behind. We used to crush the body parts down to fine powder so that the elixirs would come out smooth. Customers didn't want a lumpy elixir for their good silver."

"What Kassite gave me was quite lumpy."

"You didn't pay much silver for it, did you?"

She blushed.

"In his defense," Sallan said, "my dear friend didn't have the tools and staff that I used here. My slaves worked very hard at the millstones." He replaced the jar on the shelf. "A trader brought this ape to us from the land of tall black people, twice as far as Egypt. We paid fifty silver coins for it, but the lotions and elixirs we were going to make from its parts would have brought in a thousand times more."

She noticed a small wooden cutout nailed to the end of the shelf, shaped like an ape. "That's a cute animal."

"With the personality of a rabid dog and the size of a donkey." Sallan chuckled. "It took six slaves to hold it down."

"It was alive?"

"Of course. We never bought dead animals. Merchants don't know how to dissect the carcass, separate the various organs and body parts, and then dry them in the sun while keeping track of what is which."

"How did you kill this ape?"

"Gave it a strong sleeping potion and suffocated it with a pillow over the face—the best way to end a life without causing physical damage. Dissection took a whole day, and the parts stayed on the roof to dry for a week while two slaves chased away the scavenger birds with palm fronds. Once everything was totally dry, my slaves ground the parts down to powder."

"How do you know what's in each jar?" She counted over fifty jars of various sizes on that particular shelf. "There are so many of them, and the powder inside probably looks the same. Have you memorized everything?"

"The secret to keeping track of many items is to devise a system that's logical, consistent, and easy to remember. When separating an animal into its parts, we started from the top and went down." He touched each jar along the shelf while listing the contents. "Scalp, skull, front brain, rear brain, eyes, nose, and so on."

"What about parts that are at the same level?"

"From right to left and from front to back. Does that make sense?"

"Yes."

"Let's test you." He pointed at two jars down the shelf. "Each one contains one of the ape's hands. Which jar has the left hand?"

Deborah imagined facing the ape when it was still whole. Its left hand would be on her right side. "This one." She touched the second jar.

"Very good!" He waved at the rest of the shelf. "Everything else is here—the lips, teeth, tongue, every internal organ and every appendage down to the ape's toes, which look more like our fingers than our toes."

"I've never seen an ape."

"Would you like to?"

"Of course!"

"Then stay here with us for a while. Soon word will spread that I'm back, and the traveling merchants will start to bring me all kinds of wild animals."

Checking the ends of the other shelves, Deborah saw small cutouts for other animals, some recognizable, others unfamiliar to her. She touched one of them. "What's this?"

Looking closely, Sallan's face lit up. "That was a strange one, also from the land of black people. It was a young one, looked like an ox with a single horn. The adults apparently grow twice as big, but with very short legs."

"Only one horn?"

"A huge one that grows on top of the nose."

"The nose?"

"Like that." He demonstrated with his hand above his nose. "In a fight, they lower their head to the ground, get below their opponent, and gorge the underbelly. Their skin was very hard to cut, and the internal organs are similar to an ox, but what's really valuable is the horn."

"For what?"

"For mixing the Potency Elixir. Rich old men always need help to make their young wives pregnant, and no price is too high for that. Do you know what I'm talking about?"

Deborah nodded, thinking of Seesya's inability to possess her on their wedding night and his explosive rage afterward. To change the subject, she pointed at another shelf-end cutout. "What's this? It looks like a mouse."

"The biggest mouse I ever saw. It had yellow teeth and red fur." Sallan smiled at the memory. "Libyan traders brought it to me, but I'm not sure where they got it. One of my slaves reached into the cage to feed it and lost his finger."

Deborah covered her mouth. "That's terrible!"

"And very funny."

She didn't think it was funny, but life among the men at the tannery had taught her that men could laugh at things that, to her, seemed cruel, sad, or downright tragic.

"Now I understand why you loved your work," she said. "All the strange animals and the powers hidden inside their body parts—it's fascinating. How many different animals do you have here?"

"Over a thousand, many of them bought by my father, grandfather, and great-grandfather. Through the decades, foreign merchants learned of our interest in strange animals, and we paid generously for their efforts." Sallan walked along the rows of shelves. "They are in perfect order from large to small, from four-legged to crawlers and snakes, from mountain dwellers to prairie, river, and sea creatures."

"Logical, consistent, and easy to remember."

"Exactly. Have you ever seen anything resembling this workshop?"

"No." Deborah was truly amazed. "Do you need so many ingredients for mixing elixirs?"

"Elixirs to drink, lotions to apply, or aromatic incense to inhale. Most are medicinal, some are for improving life in various ways, and some are still a mystery—an opportunity, really. We'd always experimented with new things to see what results could be achieved."

The windows along the wall had been covered with heavy linen. He tugged on one of the sheets, and it came down with an explosion of dust and dead moths. Coughing, they hurried outside, where they patted the dust off their robes and breathed in the fresh air. Deborah looked around, worried that the dogs would return.

"Don't fear them," Sallan said. "They're good dogs."

"They're like wolves."

"With dogs and with men, if you cower and show weakness, they will abuse you, but if you stand proud and exude confidence, they will seek your approval."

"I'm not accustomed to hiding what's in my heart."

"Sincerity is a precious quality in friendship, but a disadvantage in dealing with dogs and their human equivalents."

Deborah laughed. Sallan locked arms with her, and they crossed the small garden to the main house.

"You left the workshop door open," she said. "And the lamps are still burning."

"I'm going back there," he said. "Thank you for accompanying me."

"I didn't do anything."

"To the contrary," Sallan said. "I was too nervous to enter alone after all those years of absence from the workshop. It's filled not only with shelves, jars, and ingredients, but also with countless memories."

"Good memories?"

Sallan sighed. "My father was a healer, like his father and grandfather before him. The men in our family never strayed from the holy mission of curing illnesses, injuries, and physical dysfunctions. My father disapproved of my experiments with popular elixirs. In fact, he cringed at the mystical flourishes and magical theatrics I brought to the craft. We argued, but he was a gentle man, and time has a way of settling arguments. For every customer with an aching stomach or a pestilent skin rash, there were a hundred customers seeking a cure for the various effects of aging." Sallan paused and gestured vaguely. "People used to wait in the front garden for hours until I could see them and offer the particular elixir for their desired effect."

"And your father?"

"He grew proud of me and my success." Sallan took a deep breath and sighed. "I added flare and glitz to our tradition, but all the secrets of the craft I learned from him. My father was a gifted teacher. Perhaps that's the most valuable skill I learned from him, and one day I'll be able to teach a young apprentice the things I know. It's a heartwarming prospect, especially now that I've reentered the workshop and found it so well kept."

"Why did you call me to join you?"

"I didn't know what to expect when I opened that door and walked in, what ghosts would be waiting for me, what destruction unwelcome visitors might have wreaked on our tools and treasured ingredients." He paused, took a deep breath, and exhaled. "Actually, I was afraid to enter."

"Afraid of what?"

"Of finding the answer to a frightening question. I didn't know whether Qoz had brought me back to close the book on my life peacefully, or to give me an opportunity to launch a fresh beginning, a chance to start a new chapter, a second adventure as the Elixirist. That's why I was too afraid to go in alone."

They reached the door to the guest quarters.

"And?" She rested her hand on the door handle. "Did you find the answer?"

"I'm not afraid anymore." He took the lamp from her. "Good night, and thank you for joining me."

Deborah opened the door. "Why didn't you ask Kassite to accompany you?"

Sallan considered her question for a long moment, and when he looked at her above the lamp, his eyes glistened. "He's as old as I. What's the point of a fresh beginning at my age if there's no one to carry on after me?"

Back under her blanket, Deborah wondered what he had meant by those words. Surely Sallan didn't think that she would make a fitting apprentice for him, did he? A Hebrew girl, masquerading as a boy, to become the future Elixirist and sell skin-softening potions to old women and virility elixirs to old men? The whole idea made her giggle in the darkness.

She curled up, her sack under her head, and fell asleep.

The sense of suffocation had become so familiar that even in her sleep Deborah knew it wasn't real, because a man with a sword stuck in his chin couldn't possibly choke her, surely not a week later and a great distance away. She opened her eyes, raised her head, and glanced around the room, faintly illuminated by moonlight through the thin curtains over the window. She saw Kassite and the two boys sleeping soundly.

Resting her head back on her sack, Deborah wished she could stop dreaming about Hashkem. Wasn't it enough that she thought about the young soldier constantly while awake, filled with guilt and remorse? She would rather dream of flying on the wings of the great eagle, soaring over new places, experiencing new events, and finding new opportunities to interpret the dreams in ways that would help her resolve her nagging doubts about what Yahweh wanted her to do. Should she complete the transformation into a man, go back to fight for Palm Homestead, and serve as God's prophet, or was her True Calling to follow her mother's example and abide by Yahweh's command for the Hebrews to procreate and fill the earth, for which the old healer had made the ultimate sacrifice?

Kassite made a snorting sound in his sleep, similar to the sound he often made to express disdain while awake, and she felt disdain for her new doubts. Hadn't she worked too hard and suffered too much to give up now? "When you pursue your True Calling, God provides the shortcuts." How could she doubt Yahweh's expectations when His divine hand had brought her this far? Here she was, in Bozra, and Sallan was probably measuring out the ingredients right now from jars and bottles in his old workshop, mixing the third dose of the Male Elixir for her. In a few hours, when the sun came up, she would drink it and begin the final phase of her transformation.

Deborah decided to set aside her doubts. Closing her eyes, she imagined she was back at Palm Homestead, lying down for the night at home with her parents and Tamar.

33

The eagle soared over the Sea of Salt. The air was warm and pleasant. They approached the shore, and Deborah recognized Ein Gedi. The eagle swept over the mouth of the canyon. A pile of rocks near the locals' huts told her they had kept their promise and buried Soosie's bones. Completing a full circle, the eagle passed above Miriam's grave by the plum tree and descended very low over the stream. She saw Hashkem lying underwater, looking up, her sword stuck under his beard, the blade glinting through his mouth open. Deborah grasped the feathers on the eagle's neck and pulled hard, making the huge bird ascend sharply and fly away, high over the Sea of Salt. She took a deep breath, and a sense of relief washed over her at avoiding being choked yet again by the man she had killed.

"Do not kill," a voice said beside her.

Deborah turned and saw Hashkem sitting on the wing, his beard fluttering in the wind, the bronze hilt of her old sword sticking out from under his chin.

She scooted away from him onto the other wing, as far as she dared before falling off. "What are you doing here?"

"Where you go, I go." He grasped the hilt and tried to pull out the sword, but it wouldn't budge.

"I lost this sword in the sea of salt," she said.

"Have you also lost your faith in Yahweh?"

"No."

"Have you forgotten his sixth commandment?"

"Do not kill!"

"And still, you did it." Hashkem gave up on pulling out the sword and showed her his red hands. "Look, my blood won't stop pouring out."

She touched her throat. "Are you going to choke me now?"

He tilted his head as if uncertain, and blood trickled from the corner of his mouth.

"I'm really tired of it," she said. "Why do you keep choking me?"

He wiped the blood off with the back of his hand and asked in a boyish voice, "Why did you kill me?"

The wing under her moved down and up as the eagle maintained the altitude. The unfamiliar movement startled Deborah, who wasn't used to sitting on the wing. She moved closer in.

"I made a terrible mistake," she said. "It all started when I sent the lepers to Ein Gedi based on a confusing dream I had. Months later, I ran into Ramrod on the way to Bethel, and he told me how they were suffering. I felt a duty to find them and tell them that I had misinterpreted my dream and they could go back to the Samariah Hills. Worse yet, I foolishly planned to set an ambush, as if I could outsmart the men chasing me, surprise them, and scare them off with a shower of stones from our slings. I didn't expect Seesya to be waiting, attack me with spears, or force me to use my sword to hurt anyone. The truth is, I'm just a foolish girl pretending to be a soldier."

"You weren't pretending when you killed me." He looked down at the front of his leather armor, which was covered in blood. "I'm only nineteen."

"You were a soldier. Fighting was your job. Didn't you expect the possibility of being injured or killed?"

"By a girl? I didn't expect such humiliation."

Deborah was surprised that he cared about this aspect, but who was she to judge? "I've taken your life and your honor. Will you continue to strangle me every time I fall asleep, or can you finally forgive me?"

"For violating God's commandment? Ask Him to forgive you!"

"I've been asking, but maybe He's waiting for you to forgive me first."

"How can I forgive you?" Hashkem's voice grew weak, his face grew pale, and his eyes became sad. "It's too late. I'm dead."

The eagle flapped its wings, and Hashkem lost his balance, rolled backward, and fell from the wing. Deborah looked back and saw him behind the eagle, tumbling through the air all the way to the distant sea below. He hit the water with a splash of red spray. She screamed in horror and woke up.

There was sunlight in the curtained window. The boy-servants were gone already, but Kassite was still under his blanket.

He rose on one elbow. "What is wrong?"

"A bad dream," she said.

"Ah." Kassite sat up and rubbed his eyes. "I am not surprised."

"What's this noise?" Deborah went to the window and moved aside the curtains.

The sun had just risen, the air was still cool, and a mass of people filled the front garden. They wore simple robes and plain sandals. There were men and women, many with gray hair and some stooped with age. They conversed in hushed voices.

Kassite joined her at the window. "That was quick."

"Why are they here?"

"Word of mouth does not always move at slobber's pace. Sometimes it flies like an eagle."

She looked at him. Did he know about her eagle, or was it a coincidental choice of words?

"The great man is about to make his first public appearance." Kassite pointed up. "Listen and learn."

"Good people of Edom!" Sallan's voice came from the edge of the roof above. "What you heard is true—I'm back from captivity!"

The crowd outside exploded with a collective cheer that made Deborah cover her ears. It went on for a few minutes.

"As you can imagine," Sallan continued, "I'm very tired and in poor health, having spent many years in awful conditions and the recent weeks on a difficult and perilous journey. I ask that you leave now and go back to your homes. When our brave king returns, we'll have a reason to celebrate and give thanks to the mighty Qoz for his eternal blessings."

"Thank you, Qoz," a man yelled. "The Elixirist is back!"

Cheering broke out again.

"Quiet! Quiet!" It was a shrill woman's voice from the middle of the crowd. "When will you start making—"

Many other voices interrupted her, pleading for him to resume working as soon as possible.

Sallan must have held his hands up, because the crowd gradually quieted down.

"My good people," he said. "Your pleas and prayers fill my heart with joy and gratitude that I'm finally back among you. In time, with the love of my family, the permission of the king, and the blessings of our gods, I'll find the help and support needed to resume my work."

They started cheering again, but he hushed them.

"I beg of you, please go back to your homes. May the great Qoz bless you and your families!"

The crowd began to leave.

"Very good," Kassite said. "The last thing we need is for the young king to feel threatened."

"We?" Deborah folded her blanket and packed her sack. "I'm not staying here. As soon as Sallan gives me the third dose of the Male Elixir, I'll leave for home."

"Home?" Kassite snorted the way he'd done in his sleep. "I would not go back to Canaan even if Kothar-wa-Khasis himself guaranteed my safety and prosperity with every tool he wields. Canaan is a cursed land of lawlessness, strife, and bloodshed."

His words were hurtful, but he was at home, where he belonged. For her, home was in the Samariah Hills.

"Is your mind is made up?" he asked.

Deborah nodded, keeping her doubts to herself. "I must return to Canaan to realize my True Calling."

Kassite smiled. "There is always more than one way to realize one's True Calling."

They had the morning meal on a cozy patio at the back of the house. Deborah left her armor, belt, and sword in the room. She wore a simple wool robe, with the sling as a belt, and plain sandals. Umm-Sallan did not join them. Kassite and Sallan were quiet, and Deborah was hungry. The table was laden with fruit, bread, and cheese. Everything was fresh and tasty, and she ate quickly, enjoying the food.

"You like the food of Edom," Sallan said, smiling.

"Yes." She swallowed what was in her mouth. "It's delicious. Thank you."

"As my mother told you last night," Sallan said, "our home is your home now."

"And thank you for showing me your workshop."

Kassite glanced at Sallan, but didn't say anything.

"And how about the crowd this morning?" Sallan waved in the

direction of the front garden. "Did you see? Hundreds of them came, starting at sunrise."

"They're very happy you're back," she said.

"A new beginning would be exciting," Sallan said, "but at my age, I'm not sure. How long will I have the strength for it?"

"Long enough," Kassite said, "to train the next great Elixirist."

Sallan opened his arms wide. "Where will I find a person with the talent and the temperament?"

"Ask your mother who among your nephews is smart and capable." Kassite had a smirk on his face, but his tone was even and deliberate. "Whoever joins you will be very lucky, and with all those customers, there will be wealth, too."

Sallan grunted and looked away.

Kassite chuckled. "The complicated allure of a new beginning."

"Speaking of new beginnings," Deborah said, "I'm ready for the third dose of the Male Elixir and the beginning of my life as a young man."

"She is eager to leave us." Kassite's hand fluttered in the air like a bird. "Off she will go as soon as you give her what you promised."

"What's the hurry?" Sallan brushed breadcrumbs from his sleeve. "We haven't even recovered from the journey yet."

"My journey isn't over," she said.

"Going back is not a continuation of a journey. It's a retreat."

"Palm Homestead is my final destination."

"It will be final—your final day alive. That is, if you survive the road, a girl traveling alone."

"Not a girl, not anymore, not after I drink the third dose."

"A boy, then." Sallan pushed away his half-full plate. "Even a young man, riding a good horse, carrying a sword and a spear, would be reckless to go alone. How would you survive on the road through the desert, the wilderness, the heat, and the animals? How would you defend yourself along the empty stretches of roads in the territories of your fellow Hebrews, where men of one tribe don't hesitate to molest those of another?"

Shaken by his harsh tone, Deborah glanced at Kassite, but he offered no support.

"Answer me," Sallan insisted. "I really want to know."

She looked down at her hands, clasped together in her lap.

"Why would you leave this great city and your caring friends?" He pressed a hand to his chest. "And in the unlikely event that you do make it back to Emanuel alive, how in the world will you survive a confrontation with Judge Zifron, his murderous son, and their garrison of trained soldiers?"

Deborah struggled not to burst into tears. He was right. She had focused on the goal of reaching Bozra, where Sallan would obtain the last ingredient and give her the third dose of the Male Elixir, but she had failed to plan ahead.

"Are you listening?" Sallan knuckled the table several times. "Have you thought logically about what's next, or are you blindly following some irrational girlish sentimentality?"

"I'm not girlish," Deborah said. "Or irrational."

"Then answer my question!"

"Yahweh is my answer. He will guide me and keep me safe."

"The god of the Hebrews?" Sallan sneered. "The God nobody has ever seen? He will save your life from countless mortal dangers?"

"Yahweh is the Almighty, present in every place and at every time, with grace and powers—"

"Where was this almighty Yahweh when Seesya killed your parents?"

Her chest constricted painfully, recalling Babatorr's description of her parents' last moments: "Seesya ran his sword through the man's chest. The wife defended herself with a scythe, slashing Seesya's face. She gave him that scar, and he cut her throat."

The images played in Deborah's mind, and tears filled her eyes.

"Maybe your Yahweh was busy that day," Sallan said.

"When you have only one god," Kassite said, "he is always busy."

"That's not true," she said. "Yahweh can do many things at the same time."

"Is that so?" Sallan leaned forward, glaring at her. "How about the day your sister was stoned to death unjustly?"

The image of Tamar's bloody head caused Deborah to let out a muted whimper.

"And when the High Priest handed you to Seesya in Shiloh, to abuse you and kill you as he had done to your sister, where was your Yahweh then?" Sallan's voice was rising. "And when Seesya tore off the armor from your chest at the gates of Emanuel and flogged you like a stray slave, where was your Yahweh then? Where?"

"I don't know." Deborah stood up, her chair falling over. "I'm not a priest—I can't even read or write. Yahweh is not some man whose actions I can try to explain. He is God!"

Kassite put a hand on her arm. "Calm down. You are among friends here, and we also cannot explain our gods' occasional cruelties."

"That's true." Sallan leaned back in the chair, his expression softening. "My questions were harsh not because I wished to upset you. I'm concerned for you."

Deborah righted her chair and sat back down. Her hands shook, and she pressed them together. "It's true. My parents and sister lost their lives, and I've suffered injuries and humiliations, but when I needed Him the most, Yahweh provided help. That's how I kept my promise to you and returned to Emanuel to obtain your freedom." She paused, hesitant for a moment. "And that's how I'll make it back to Emanuel again, win back Palm Homestead, and serve as His prophet."

Sallan must have noticed the hesitation. He looked at her inquisitively.

"That's my True Calling," Deborah said, raising her voice to mask her doubts. "And to do it, I must become a man and be ready to confront Seesya and beat him down for good. Now, are you going to keep your promise?"

"She is right," Kassite said. "You promised to give her the third dose upon reaching Bozra."

Sallan pushed up from his chair. "I will keep my promise."

A few moments after Sallan left, a servant brought sweet cakes and cups of warm milk. Deborah and Kassite ate and drank, but neither said anything. The air was full of scents from the garden and the kitchen, the trees around the house were teeming with birds, and the great city hummed with human activity. Deborah hoped Umm-Sallan would join them. The matriarch intrigued her. How could a woman become the head of a large family?

Sallan returned with a small clay bottle, plugged with a piece of cork.

Deborah and Kassite gawked at the bottle.

"Don't worry," Sallan said. "It won't explode."

Kassite laughed, but Deborah was too nervous. She extended her hand for the bottle.

"Not here," Sallan said.

"Where?"

"It's a surprise," he said. "Let's go."

Deborah gestured at the table. "You haven't tasted the cakes."

"I'll have some later. Come, the boys are waiting for us up front with the horses."

Following him, Deborah asked, "Where are we going?"

"To obtain the final ingredient," Sallan said.

Kassite caught up with them. "Are we going to—"

"Yes," Sallan said.

"Where?" Deborah asked.

"You'll see. It's only a couple of hours away."

"Two hours?" She untied the sling, straightened her robe, and retied the sling more tightly around her waist. "That's a four-hour round trip. I'm not dressed for a long ride in the desert."

"Your reluctance is understandable," Kassite said. "Would you like to wait? It would give you some time to reconsider taking the third dose."

"I'm not reluctant."

"There's no rush," Sallan said. "Changing your sex is a permanent solution to a temporary problem."

"True," Kassite said. "There are many ways to reach a destination."

Deborah resumed walking. "I was concerned only about the ride, but it's fine. If we ride fast, we'll be back before the heat builds up."

The two boy-servants waited outside the stables with five horses, clean and saddled, each with two waterskins hanging from the saddle horn. Seeing Deborah, Rogez neighed and rocked his head up and down. She kissed his nose.

Sallan and Kassite mounted their horses, pulled the hoods of their robes over their heads, and started down the street. Deborah and the boy-servants, who shared a horse, did the same.

They left the city and took the road north. Halfway through the valley, Sallan stopped and turned his horse around.

"Look at this," he said, facing Bozra's glistening copper roofs and stark white walls. "The most beautiful city in the world. Why would anyone want to live someplace else?"

Deborah held the reins firmly as Rogez shifted impatiently. "It is beautiful," she said. "Too beautiful."

"How can anything be too beautiful?"

"Too perfect," she said.

Sallan laughed. "How can perfection become excessive?"

"It doesn't seem real." Deborah pointed at Bozra. "It's like a picture in a dream. For example, there aren't any poor people."

"You miss their smelly huts and dirty tents?"

Deborah felt her face flush. It was true. Compared with Emanuel, Shiloh, and Aphek, Bozra's cleanliness and sweet-smelling air were undeniably appealing, if one didn't think about what had to be done to achieve it.

"I don't miss the stench," she said, "but I feel sorry for the poor when I think that they all have to work in the copper mines—even women and children. Do they get shackled and flogged like slaves?"

"They work willingly," Sallan said, "and serve their king. In return, they get a mat to sleep on, meals to sustain them, and healers to treat their maladies and injuries. You have no reason to feel sorry for the poor people of Edom. They're better off than the poor of the Hebrews, who live in squalor and feed on scraps. There's nothing wrong with Bozra's beauty—you will learn to love it, as we do."

Deborah looked at the great city. Would she still worry about the poor if she lived here and made it her home?

"We are wasting precious time." Kassite turned his horse and resumed riding.

They followed him across the valley and up the hills. After a while, he left the road and took a narrow path. They rode single file through dry streams and crevices, up into the hills. The rocky landscape grew barren, its tinge of red becoming more pronounced. The sun rose higher, hinting at the hot day ahead.

Whenever the trail intersected with another, Kassite paused, looked around, and chose which way to go. At one point, the trail split into three branches, and Kassite stopped altogether. He looked around, raised his eyes to the blue sky, and gazed at the imposing cliffs.

Deborah glanced at Sallan, who gestured for her to be patient. Sure enough, Kassite made up his mind and moved on.

She asked in a low voice, "Is he trying to remember the way, or is he guessing?"

"Probably a combination of the two," Sallan said.

Rogez whinnied, and Deborah rubbed his neck. "Even my horse knows you can't find your way in the desert by guessing. Either you know the way, or not."

"That's true for a horse, not for a man."

"Why?"

"Because a man has a heart." Sallan pressed a fist to his chest. "Navigating in the desert is like finding your way in life. You have to choose among the paths available to you, because staying put means death. If you're paralyzed by doubts, ask your heart which path feels true, and when it tells you, don't be afraid to leap forward and go on."

Deborah remembered a story her father had told her. "Our patriarch, Abraham, once heard Yahweh's voice commanding him to go into the desert and sacrifice his only son, Isaac. While Abraham wandered in the desert with his son, Yahweh kept telling him where to go until they reached a boulder that was destined to serve as the altar."

"It's easier to find the right way when you have god in your heart."

"If it's the true God," she said.

He chuckled.

Following Kassite, Deborah imagined Abraham as a tall, thin, ascetic-looking man with white hair and a contemplative aura—in other words, a Kassite lookalike. But if this were a repeat of Abraham's story, who among them was Isaac—the intended sacrificial offering? In this group, she realized, the natural choice would be her, the lone Hebrew girl.

"But Isaac lived," Sallan said, as if guessing her thoughts. "And that's fortunate for both of us."

She understood what he meant. Isaac had grown up to have twin sons: Esau, the forefather of Edom, and Jacob, the forefather of the Hebrews.

They stopped in the shade of a large boulder to drink and give the horses water. Scavenger birds appeared above, circling and crowing. Kassite told the boys to collect dry twigs and sticks, which they tied in a bundle and carried. He craned his head and watched the birds for a while, then mounted his horse and rode on. Deborah and the others followed.

Somewhere deep in the hills, Kassite turned into a ravine and quickened his pace. After some time, they passed by a clearing that showed signs of past cultivation. On a rock ledge above the fields were the remains of wooden shacks, with most of the walls and roofs long gone. Kassite didn't stop, but he kept his eyes on the ruins until they were left behind.

Ascending slowly, the ravine grew deeper and narrower, forming a canyon. There was no vegetation, and the ground turned to deep, reddish sand, which slowed down the horses. It grew darker between the canyon walls, and the noises they made echoed ominously.

Coming around a curve, they faced a dead end. It was the head of the canyon, where water had once sprung from the rocks, carving the canyon over many centuries. The bottom of the basin was sandy, and horizontal lines in different shades of copper marked past water levels on the walls. Deborah wondered where all the water had gone.

Kassite dismounted his horse near a large pile of stone that covered part of the sidewall. He told the boys to remove the stones. As they did so, an opening appeared, blocked by a wooden door. The opening, wider than the doorway of a house, had been carved into the canyon wall. A wooden frame kept it from collapsing. Kassite pushed at the door, which opened inward. Sounds of running water came from within. He went inside and reappeared with three torches.

The boys started a fire with the twigs and sticks. One of them removed a jar of oil from a saddlebag pocket, poured some oil on each of the torches, and lighted them with a stick from the fire. Kassite, Sallan, and Deborah took one torch each. Kassite took the oil jar as well and went back inside.

Sallan slipped the clay bottle under his robe. "After you," he said.

Deborah hesitated. "Is this where we'll find the last ingredient?"

He nodded.

"Are you coming?" Kassite's voice emerged through the opening with an echo.

She entered.

The dancing flames from the torches illuminated a large cave with a flat floor and a domed ceiling, all of it rough and uneven—the work of men with hammers and chisels. She saw a few baskets containing tools, ropes, and clothing items by the wall near the door, as well as a pile of used torches. The air was cool and musty.

The noise of running water was much louder inside. Deborah took a few steps in the direction of the sound.

"Careful!" Kassite grabbed her arm.

In front of her was a round hole in the floor, about twenty steps across.

"It's a long way down," he said.

Stepping to the edge, she held the torch over the hole. The light didn't reach the bottom. At the opposite side, a spring gushed from a crack in the wall and formed a waterfall that tumbled down the hole. Spiral stairs started from a small landing near the top and descended in serpentine circles, disappearing into the darkness below. At first, it seemed that the hole became narrower as it got deeper, but by moving her torch left and right, Deborah realized that the hole remained at about the same circumference, whereas the stairs were carved into the outside wall with enough standing room to make them usable, but only barely. It was the shaft of an old mine, long out of use.

"Let me guess," Deborah said, turning to face Kassite. "Thirteen hundred and thirteen stairs?"

He smiled. "The prisoner and the jailer going back for a visit." He climbed down to the small landing at the top of the stairs.

Deborah turned to Sallan. "Are we all going down?"

He nodded.

"What's there?"

"What do you think?"

"The last ingredient?"

"That's it."

"You left it here when you escaped?"

"It's not easy to explain." Sallan pointed his torch at the hole, where Kassite could be seen making his way down. "Go ahead. I'll be right behind you."

"What is the ingredient?"

"You'll find out." He pointed with the torch again. "Follow him."

Deborah stepped to the edge. "Can't Kassite bring it up?"

"Only you can do that."

"Why?"

"Questions. Questions. Questions." Kassite's voice echoed, his torch flickering down below. "What are you afraid of?"

"I'm not afraid." Deborah jumped over the edge to the landing, which was narrower than she expected, making her heart stop as she gripped the wall.

"Go slowly," Sallan said. "Gravity shows no pity."

The stairs were narrow and steep, each almost as high as her knee. There was no railing to hold on to. The wall was carved in over the stairs, creating a half tunnel, which made the descent awkward and unnerving even for Deborah, who didn't have to bend over as much as Kassite. Every time they went a full circle, the stairs passed behind the waterfall.

"Don't drop the torch." Sallan's voice echoed over the sound of the water. "You'll need it when we get to the bottom."

"This is dangerous," Deborah said. "Who built these stairs?"

"My ancestors," Kassite said. "I heard the stories as a child. They started digging this mine with their own hands, standing in the canyon basin with water up to their armpits while sifting the ore. After they exhausted the copper at ground level, they started digging the shaft. As the mine reached deeper, they carved out more stairs. Meanwhile, the water drained into the mine. By the time I came along, the canyon had been dry for generations. We had to carry water all the way down to our family's homestead."

"The ruins we saw earlier?"

"Yes. My grandfather owned the mine when I was born, and after him, my father." Kassite paused and pointed into a dark tunnel that went off the main shaft. "They followed every vein, digging slowly, and carrying the copper ore up the shaft in baskets. When a vein ran out, they deepened the shaft to find a new vein."

Deborah looked up to the top of the shaft, where a bit of daylight came in through the doorway. "Must have been backbreaking labor."

"It still is," Sallan said. "These days, landowners aren't allowed to dig anymore. The king owns all the mines in the kingdom and all the copper they produce."

They resumed their descent. On the way down, every thirty or forty stairs, another tunnel went off horizontally into the rock, dark and uninviting. They continued downward, one step at a time. Soon, the light at the top faded into darkness, the noise of the waterfall grew louder, and the air became colder and damper.

Finally, after thirteen hundred and thirteen stairs, they reached the bottom. The two men sat on the last step to rest, breathing heavily.

Deborah's legs felt wobbly, and she put her hand against the wet wall for balance. At the opposite side of the shaft, the waterfall hit bottom with thunderous force, filling the air with a cold mist. The waterfall filled a small pool, which boiled with white foam. The stone floor was rough, uneven, and slippery, but the water didn't accumulate, likely draining into the earth through the bottom of the pool.

Deborah noticed one last tunnel going off into the rock. Unlike all the tunnels she'd seen on the way down, this one was blocked off by a heavy door. A horizontal crossbar rested in wooden slots attached to each doorjamb, securing the door. A porthole the size of a man's face had been cut in the upper part of the door. She stood on her toes to peek inside, but saw only darkness.

Sallan came over and tried to lift the crossbar with one hand, holding the torch in the other. Deborah helped him. They drew the heavy crossbar out of the slots, put it aside, and pulled the door open.

The tunnel was high enough for a man to walk in straight, though Kassite had to take off his hat. About ten steps wide and thirty steps long, the tunnel ended in a solid wall. She saw a wooden chair and a clay lamp, as well as a pair of worn leather sandals. A trickle of water over the back wall was collected in a clay bucket, which was filled to the brim.

Kassite closed the heavy door, blocking off most of the noise from the waterfall, and put the jar of oil on the floor by the lamp.

Sallan lowered his torch. "Do you see the lines on the floor?"

Deborah looked. Two parallel lines showed in the rough rock floor, running down the middle of the tunnel from the door to the opposite wall.

"I used to walk back and forth, on and on. I stopped only to relieve myself." Sallan pointed at a hole in the ground near the far end. "And to eat, when the food came once a day."

"Here," Kassite said, "for old times' sake." He took a folded piece of cloth from his pocket and unwrapped it, revealing a handful of dates.

"Ah!" Sallan picked one and tossed it in his mouth. He shut his eyes and chewed slowly, savoring the taste. "These precious dates sweetened my bitter existence down here."

Kassite put his hand through the porthole in the heavy door. "Like this, every morning, I passed through bread and fruit for my prisoner, then climbed the stairs back to the top. I was younger then, of course, and had two good legs, but still, it was hard. I used to count the stairs, thirteen hundred and thirteen down, and the same number going up, day after day."

Sallan pointed at the wall. "That's how I knew to mark the days."

Deborah looked closely. He had scratched thin, short lines in the rock. Each group of six was crossed by a seventh to make a week. There were many of them, covering a large section of the wall.

"One hundred and fifty-seven weeks," Sallan said.

"Must have felt like an eternity." Deborah looked around at the bleak, narrow tunnel. "This place is like a grave."

"That's what the king wanted—to keep me alive in case he needed me again, yet snuff out my arrogance and fame."

"The higher the rise," Deborah said, "the steeper the fall."

"You don't forget anything, do you?" Sallan chuckled. "Yes, I was riding high after the Egyptians withdrew in the face of the army I had created out of women. My elixir had infused the women with masculine vigor and proactivity. They cut their hair, made leather armor out of coats and wall-decorating skins, and tore up their shoes to make boots with thick wooden soles to raise themselves to the height of men. They fabricated fake spears and swords out of household chairs and tables, as well as flags and unit banners from linen and robes. General Mazabi taught them to march to the beat of drums while growling like bloodthirsty warriors. It was a sight to see!"

"And you got the credit for the victory."

"Yes," Sallan said. "Everyone adored me. A line of customers formed every morning from our front garden all the way down the street. Even my simplest potions sold for silver coins, not to mention the Youth Elixir, which sold for gold."

"The one your mother mentioned?"

"Yes. I left her with enough supply to last a lifetime, which is why she still looks so well. Have you ever seen another ancient seventy-year-old woman with skin like my mother's? Never in a million years!"

"She's a beautiful woman," Deborah said. "Ageless. It's real magic."

"Magic?" He inhaled deeply, shaking his head. "Do you want to know the secret to a powerful elixir?"

Kassite, who had been standing by the door quietly, cleared his throat.

Sallan turned to him. "Why not? She should know it before choosing her path."

"What secret?" Deborah looked from one to the other. "Tell me."

Sallan lowered his voice as if someone might be listening. "The secret to a powerful elixir is true enchantment."

She looked at him, waiting for an explanation.

"You can use the best ingredients, mix the best potion, and preserve it in the best bottle." He pulled the clay bottle from under his robe. "But the effectiveness of an elixir will always depend on the customer's complete, sincere, and true enchantment with its allure."

Deborah's eyes were drawn to the clay bottle. "Its allure?"

"That's right. Even the best elixir works only if the person drinking it is truly enchanted by its allure—if the person wholeheartedly believes in the elixir's powers and passionately desires the changes it's supposed to generate. The more powerful the enchantment in the person's heart, the more powerful the effect of the elixir on the person's body. A funny quandary, isn't it?"

"Very funny," Kassite said. "So funny that the king buried you here alive."

"That's what I don't understand," Deborah said. "Why here?"

"He couldn't jail me near Bozra for fear that people would find out I had not been abducted by Egyptians but locked up by a jealous and ungrateful king. This isolated and neglected copper mine was perfect. Kassite's family was dead, and he'd been left alone, barely able to support himself here, or anywhere else."

"Where would I go?" Kassite shrugged. "This was my family's homestead, the only place I knew."

Deborah could relate to that.

"I was collecting herbs near the city when the king's personal guards appeared." Sallan sighed. "They killed my servants, whisked me here, and ordered Kassite to keep me locked up."

Deborah turned to Kassite. "Did you understand the situation?"

"I was deaf, not stupid," he said. "I knew what they wanted and how good it was for me. Imagine my life beforehand, alone on an isolated homestead, far away from any village or town. I was given responsibility for a prisoner and regular rewards. Every few weeks, the king's guards came back with sacks of wheat and barley, baskets of fruit, as well as a good donkey, a sheep, or a goat. My life was greatly improved after they brought him here, and that was only the beginning."

"He taught you to speak," Deborah said.

"And to listen." Kassite looked at Sallan. "But most importantly, he taught me to be a full person. He taught me life. And friendship."

Sallan smiled. "And in return, he set me free."

"I did." Kassite laughed. "We both had to run away, and we were free, at least for a while."

They punched each other playfully, laughing together about a shared past that, to Deborah, seemed nothing short of horrible.

Sallan raised the clay bottle in a toast. "To true friendship!"

"To truth, in particular," Kassite said.

Deborah went to the door. "We should get back to Bozra before the heat builds up. Where's the final ingredient?"

"Check over there." Sallan pointed at the opposite end of the tunnel. "By the wall, where it's dripping."

Deborah walked down to the end. "Here?" She looked closely around the bucket under the drip. "I don't see anything here."

Behind her, the sound of the waterfall roared as someone opened the door. She turned and saw the door slam shut. The two men were gone.

"Sallan?"

The crossbar thumped as it settled into its slots outside, barring the door.

Deborah hurried over. "Kassite?"

There was no answer.

She pushed the door, but it didn't budge. She looked out through the small porthole and saw the two men standing a few steps back from the door, holding their torches, facing her. Behind them, the waterfall roared.

"What are you doing?"

They didn't answer.

"Is this another test?" She raised her voice. "Is it?"

They shook their heads.

With the torch in one hand, she banged on the door with the other. "Open up!"

Again, they shook their heads.

"You lied to me!"

"There was no lying," Sallan said.

"There's no final ingredient!"

"Maybe, maybe not. It's up to you to search for it."

"Where?"

"Inside yourself," he said.

"What are you talking about?" She pounded on the door. "Let me out!"

"Search within yourself for the last ingredient." Sallan stepped forward and held the clay bottle close to the porthole. "Take this, but carefully. Don't drop it. The ingredients already in it are worth their weight in gold."

Deborah reached with her hand through the porthole and took the clay bottle.

"You may drink it," he said, "but only if you find the last ingredient."

"I don't understand." Her hand shook, and the bottle almost slipped. She put it on the floor by the door.

"Good luck," Sallan said.

"Wait!" She saw them walk to the base of the stairs "How could the last ingredient be inside me?"

"Think of what I told you about the power of true enchantment." His voice echoed through the shaft, barely audible over the noise of the waterfall. "It's up to you to find it and determine if it's real."

"How?" She pressed her face to the porthole. "Tell me!"

"Only you can decide what's in your heart, if you wholeheartedly want to become a man, and for what purpose—"

"Yes! I know what I want!"

"—or not become a man," he continued, "now that you've seen Bozra and realized there's much more to this world than the primitive Hebrew tribes."

"Let me out!"

Kassite began climbing the stairs. "She does not understand."

"Not yet," Sallan yelled back over the noise of the waterfall. "But she will. In time."

"Understand what?" Deborah banged on the door. "Don't leave me here!"

"You'll be fine." Sallan started up the stairs.

"She will not go thirsty," Kassite said. "That is certain."

"Please!" Deborah felt sobs rise in her throat. "Come back!"

The light from their torches flickered.

"I beg you!" She struggled not to cry. "Don't leave me alone here!"

"You're not alone," Sallan called from above. "Your Yahweh is with you."

Kassite laughed.

"Don't laugh," Sallan admonished him. "She needs the—"

The rest of the sentence was lost in the rumble of the waterfall.

34

Her face pressed to the porthole, Deborah watched the glow from their torches grow weaker until there was total darkness outside the barred door. Sallan and Kassite were gone, and she was completely alone, locked up at the bottom of an abandoned copper mine, thirteen hundred and thirteen stairs below the dead end of a desolate canyon. The sudden turn of events stunned Deborah. None of it made sense. Was it a nightmare from which she would soon wake up?

Deborah's knees went soft, and she collapsed to the damp floor. The torch fell from her hand, spraying a shower of sparks that singed her arm and cleared away the fog of numb bewilderment. She picked up the torch, blew on the sputtering flame to revive it, and propped it against the wall. She unplugged the oil jar that Kassite had left on the floor and tilted it over the small lamp. Nothing came out.

The torch sputtered.

Grasping the bottom of the jar, she tilted it further. A thin stream came out. Her hands were shaking, and some of the oil missed the lamp. She put down the jar, tilted the lamp to soak the dry wick, and touched the dying torch to the wick. It took a moment, but then the wick ignited.

The torch died, leaving only the small flame of the lamp.

The enormity of their betrayal began to sink in. Had the invitation to ride in search of the last ingredient been merely a ruse? Had they planned this all along, or only after she had insisted on leaving for Canaan immediately after drinking the third dose of the Male Elixir?

The shaking spread from her hands to her knees, and then to the rest of her body. Deborah leaned back against the wall, hugged her knees to her chest, and struggled to stop shaking. Tears trailed down her cheeks. Sallan and Kassite had become like a family to her, despite their oddities and earlier deceit, for which she had naively forgiven them. Why had they deceived her again?

She felt completely alone. Wasn't Yahweh supposed to be everywhere, all the time, even down here with her? Deborah looked around. She didn't feel any divine presence in this dark, cold, fearful place. Obadiah of Levi had said, "Faith frequently falters under fear." Was she losing her faith?

No, she believed in Yahweh's power and His justice.

Was this disaster her just punishment?

Deborah shuddered at the memory of shoving the sword into Hashkem's chin at Ein Gedi, forcing it all the way into his head while his wide eyes glared at her from under the water. He had the same accusatory expression later, when he sat on the eagle's wing and berated her for violating Yahweh's sixth commandment: "Do not kill!"

Sadness descended on Deborah. If this dungeon was Yahweh's punishment, her fate was sealed. No one would miss her, or even notice her absence. Except, of course, Sallan and Kassite, who had left her locked up for reasons she couldn't comprehend, as Kassite had correctly said, "She does not understand." To which Sallan had replied, "Not yet. But she will. In time."

What was she supposed to understand?

Deborah got up and walked to the end of the tunnel, back to the door, and back again, pondering. What was she supposed to figure out?

Frustrated, she yelled, "Use your head!"

For some reason, hearing her own voice had a calming effect.

"That's right," she said. "Use your head."

She paced back and forth along the smooth grooves that Sallan's feet had left in the floor all those years back.

"Maybe they'll come back," she said out loud, "and have a big laugh about how they scared me and made me beg not to be left here alone. Maybe this is a test to see how I respond. Will I be passive, temperamental, small-minded, and anxious, or will I prove myself proactive, even-tempered, adventurous, and logical? Is that what they're doing—testing my character?"

Recalling the two men's frantic escape from Ein Gedi, she sneered. "Even-tempered! What a joke!"

Her face pressed to the porthole, she stared into the darkness, hoping to see a glow from their torches above in the shaft. There was a great deal of noise from the waterfall, but not even a flicker of light. Recalling how difficult the descent had been, Deborah assumed the climb up would be slow and painful for the two limping men. How likely was it that they'd be climbing down again soon? No, they weren't playing a joke on her, Deborah realized. This was a real betrayal. But why?

Her eyes were drawn to the clay bottle on the floor by the wall. What if there was no missing ingredient? What if the whole thing was a trick? What if that bottle contained the complete third dose of the Male Elixir? It could be the culmination of all her efforts and sacrifices since leaving Emanuel in the middle of the night with the priest's blessing and a fierce determination to find the Elixirist and convince him to help her become a man.

Deborah picked up the clay bottle and touched the cork plug. Should she open it and drink the contents, even if it's missing an ingredient? Was it ready to drink? Was she ready?

When she had accused him of lying about a missing ingredient, Sallan had said, "Maybe, maybe not. It's up to you to search for it. Search inside yourself for the last ingredient." And after he'd given her the clay bottle through the porthole, he'd added, "Think of what I told you about the power of true enchantment. It's up to you to find it and determine if it's real. Only you can decide what's in your heart, if you wholeheartedly want to become a man, and for what purpose—"

"The enchantment!" Deborah's voice sounded hollow in the tunnel. "That's the last ingredient!"

She recalled him saying earlier, "The secret to a powerful elixir is true enchantment. You can use the best ingredients, mix the best potion, and preserve it in the best bottle. Even the best elixir works only if the person drinking it is truly enchanted by its allure."

"That makes no sense," Deborah said as she put the bottle down in the corner. "How could I be enchanted by an elixir when I know that it won't work without my enchantment?"

She started walking back and forth again, repeating Sallan's words in her mind, trying to figure out what she had missed. She noticed that her shadow moved faster in each direction on the wall opposite the lamp. She waved, her hand casting a long, thin shadow on the wall. She stopped and faced the wall, her back to the lamp, and flapped her arms like eagle's wings, but the shadow looked more like a cricket than an eagle.

Deborah sat cross-legged in the middle of the tunnel and stared at the clay bottle. It seemed plain, no different from any small bottle of wine that a man would carry for the road.

"You're not enchanting at all," she said to the bottle. "There's no allure whatsoever."

She reached over, picked it up, pulled out the cork, and sniffed. It had a sour, pungent odor. She coughed, pushed in the cork, and put the bottle down.

"That wasn't enchanting, either," she said.

The lamp flickered as if it was about to go out. She picked up the oil jar and tilted it carefully to make sure the thin stream entered the lamp. The light steadied and appeared brighter, but the jar was almost empty, and her mood grew darker. She lay down on the damp floor, her head resting on her folded arm, and watched the jittery light from the lamp dance on the opposite wall.

35

"Your lamp is about to die," a woman's voice said in crisp Hebrew words. "Better add some oil before we lose the light."

Jolted out of deep sleep, Deborah wiped her eyes and sat up. The oil lamp still burned, but barely, its weak light fading halfway down the tunnel.

"Quick," the voice said from the dark end of the tunnel. "I can't do it for you."

Deborah tilted the jar upside down, and a bit of oil dripped into the lamp. A moment later, the flame recovered.

"Light is better than darkness." The woman sounded old, about Vardit's age, but her voice bore an accent reminiscent of Deborah's mother. "Don't you agree?"

Deborah could make out the outline of a large figure. "Who are you?"

Stepping forward into the dim light, the eagle from her dreams appeared. The long talons clicked on the stone floor, the wings folded in tightly to fit in the narrow tunnel, and the top of the white head touched the ceiling.

"Didn't you recognize my voice?"

Too stunned to answer, Deborah shook her head.

"You assumed I was a male, didn't you?"

Deborah nodded.

"It's understandable, but you should know that, unlike earthbound women, we, female eagles, are much larger and stronger than our mates."

"I've never heard you speak before."

"You found your voice." The eagle chuckled, reminding Deborah of the old healer in Tamar. "That's good."

"I'm confused," Deborah said. "You've appeared only in my dreams, but here you are, even though I'm awake."

"It seemed urgent that I visit you immediately, considering your dire circumstances."

Deborah glanced at the door, which was still shut. "How did you get in?"

"Where you go, I go."

"That's what Hashkem told me when we were flying—"

"On my wings, yes. I heard him." The eagle lowered her head, her hooked beak almost touching Deborah's face. "Why do you think you're here?"

"Yahweh is punishing me."

"Interesting." Her yellow eyes glowed brighter than the lamp. "Punishment for what?"

"My sins," Deborah said. "First off, my heart was filled with hate."

"Feeling hate for those who hurt you isn't a sin. Acting on your hate and hurting another person—that could be a sin."

"I did act on my hate." She took a deep breath. "I violated the sixth commandment: Do not kill!"

"Did you?"

"Yes, I killed Hashkem in Ein Gedi." Deborah looked down at the floor. "I'm a murderer."

"That's a common mistake."

She looked up. "A mistake?"

"Do not kill!" The eagle sighed. "It's an important prohibition, no doubt about that, but it's not absolute. There's an exception for unavoidable situations."

"Unavoidable?"

"When a person rises to kill you, rise first and kill him."

"Who said that?"

"It's written in the holy scriptures."

Deborah was surprised. "Do you know the scriptures?"

"Do I know the scriptures?" The eagle cocked her head and chuckled. "Let's just say that I have an intimate familiarity with the holy scriptures. Trust me on that."

"But still, I killed a man. How could killing not be sinful?"

"It was traumatic for you, I'm sure, killing another person for the first time in your young life, but it wasn't murder."

"Why not?"

"Because Seesya was determined to kill you, and his soldiers were there to help him. All your actions were aimed at saving yourself and your companions, and therefore justified completely. Rest assured, Deborah, that this temporary confinement is not a divine punishment for killing."

"I'm not a murderer? I did not violate Yahweh's sixth commandment?"

"That's correct."

Deborah was relieved to the point of tears. "Maybe now Hashkem will stop choking me in my dreams."

"I think you're safe," the eagle said.

"I've done another terrible thing, though. I blinded a man." She paused for a moment, thinking. "The exception should help me with that, too, because I did it only to protect myself when that man and his friends tried to rape me."

"I'm impressed," the eagle said. "You have the mind of a good judge."

"What do you mean?"

"Most people have a hard time applying a rule to a set of facts, but you seem to do it quite easily." The eagle shifted, her talons grazing the stone floor. "Which brings us back to the first question: Why are you here?"

"Sallan and Kassite tricked me."

"Did they say why?"

"To find out whether I'm truly enchanted."

"With what?"

Deborah pointed at the clay bottle on the floor by the wall.

"Why would you be enchanted with a clay bottle?"

"With what's inside—the third dose of the Male Elixir."

"I hear it smells like rotten meat." Air whistled in the nostrils on the sides of her beak. "Are you sure that's what you should be enchanted with?"

Deborah thought for a moment. "Sallan said that an elixir works if the person is enchanted by its allure."

"That's all he said? Tell me exactly."

Closing her eyes to remember, she quoted Sallan: "Even the best elixir works only if the person drinking it is truly enchanted by its allure—if the person wholeheartedly believes in the elixir's powers and passionately desires the changes it's supposed to generate. The more powerful the enchantment in the person's heart, the more powerful the effect of the elixir on the person's body." She opened her eyes. "That's what Sallan said, but I'm not sure what it means."

The eagle sighed. "It sounds to me like a whole lot of big words that needlessly complicate a very simple question."

"I think it's about the result," Deborah said. "The enchantment is supposed to be with the result, not with the elixir itself. Is that right?"

"What does it mean in your situation? Spell it out."

Deborah considered it for a moment. "For the Male Elixir to work, I should be completely enchanted with becoming a man."

The eagle's big head bobbled up and down while her yellow eyes remained focused on Deborah. "And what is the answer?"

"I don't know."

"What's in your heart? Are you truly enchanted with the prospect of spending the rest of your life as a man?"

"How can I tell?"

"Have you ever tried being a man?"

"Kassite told me what to do at the tannery," Deborah said. "Imitate until you mutate."

"That's clever. I like it. Why don't you pretend now to be a man and see if you're enchanted with it?"

"I'm a man!" Deborah thickened her voice. "I'm a big man, a brave man!" She bent her arm and pressed her biceps. "Strong man!" She touched her face, imagining there was stubble. "Man with a beard!"

Opening her beak, the eagle laughed—a deep, rolling laugh that warmed up the damp tunnel and buffeted the small flame in the lamp.

"See what I mean?" Deborah threw her arms in the air. "The whole thing—it's a joke!"

"The best joke has a grain of truth in it. How badly do you want to become a man?"

"Want? It's not about what I want."

"What then?"

Deborah hesitated.

"You can tell me."

"Maybe I want to be like my mother, not only to fulfill Yahweh's command to procreate and fill the earth, but also as a way to rebuild the wonderful family life I once had, to become a mother, to be as beautiful and kind as my mother was, blessed with a good husband by my side and children who adore me as I adored my mother." Deborah coughed to clear the lump in her throat. "But how could I neglect my duty to become a man and fulfill my father's dream?"

"When facing a tough dilemma in life," the eagle said, "we tend to fixate on an obvious choice and fail to see other, less obvious ones."

"How else could I return to the Samariah Hills, win back Palm Homestead, and become Yahweh's prophet, if I'm not a man?"

"Let's answer one question at a time. Are you enchanted with becoming a man?"

"Not at all. I cringe thinking of hair growing on my cheeks and, you know, the other changes to my body."

"Your private parts?"

Deborah shuddered. "I don't even want to think about that."

"There's much more to a man than the hair on his cheeks and what's between his legs. Do you wish to be like the men you know? To think like them? Behave like them?"

"Lie and cheat like them?" Deborah laughed bitterly. "Lust and rape like them? Fight and murder like them? Or stink like them?"

The eagle was quiet for a moment. "What I hear is not enchantment with the prospect of manhood, but disenchantment."

"I'm even more disenchanted with the prospect of remaining a woman."

"Why?"

"Everything about womanhood is bad."

"For example?"

"Where to begin?" Deborah groaned in frustration. "As a woman, I'd had no say about where I live, whom I marry, how I dress, or what work I must do. My husband may force himself on me in bed, whip me at will, or accuse me of a sin and have me stoned to death based on his word alone. And those are only the things that I've witnessed with my own eyes! As a wife, I'd have to bear as many children as possible until dying in labor or becoming barren. I may not inherit from my father, farm my family's homestead, or carry a weapon, and if I tried to learn to read and write, I'd be flogged or stoned to death. That's a woman's fate, and I don't want it!"

The eagle's eyes radiated kindness. "Have you known any men who treated women kindly?"

Deborah thought of her father, how kind he had been to her mother, making her happy every day. And Barac, who had waited for her with his father at Palm Homestead on the night of Tamara's death, risking their lives. And Zariz, who had treated her as his equal, teaching her how to shoot arrows and learning from her about throwing rocks at targets.

"There was a Moabite boy," she said. "His name is Zariz."

"The one we visited at his grandfather's house in Moab?"

"Yes."

"Soft and cute on the outside, but resilient and valiant on the inside."

"That's right. You should have seen him handle his bow and arrows: Hit! Hit! Hit!" Realizing that she'd let her excitement burst into the open, Deborah stopped talking. Her face flushed. "Looks like I've become enchanted with a boy instead of with my duty."

"It's natural." The eagle winked. "And he seemed enchanted with you, too, until he changed his mind and ran away."

"It wasn't his fault. I had hair growing on my face."

"That would do it."

"I think of Zariz often, but I don't expect to see him again. It makes me very sad." Deborah's voice trembled, and she inhaled deeply to calm down. "Right from the beginning, I liked Zariz. He wasn't afraid of Seesya and the soldiers, just like my friend Barac. I'll never see him again, either."

"Why not?"

"Seesya killed him."

"Really?" The eagle cocked her head. "That's news to me."

Deborah reached across and picked up the clay bottle. "I should just drink it. There's no choice. I must become a man."

"That's hardly an expression of enchantment."

"I might not be enchanted with the immediate result of becoming a man, but my heart is truly committed to the ultimate result—winning back Palm Homestead and becoming Yahweh's prophet." Deborah pulled out the cork plug. "That's my True Calling."

Putting the open bottle to her lips, she started to tilt it.

"Wait!"

She paused.

The eagle shifted, her bobbing up and down. "I have one more question."

"Yes?"

"Did you ever ask your father how you—a girl—could become a prophet?"

The odor from the bottle stung Deborah's nose and she held it away.

The yellow eyes blinked. "Well?"

"I did, and he answered." Closing her eyes, she recalled that sweet day, sitting with her father, the world safe and happy, neither of them having any inkling of the approaching calamity. "Yahweh created the whole world. Don't you think He can create a prophet out of a girl?"

The eagle nodded. "Wise man, your father."

"He was," Deborah said, "but I still thought the idea was outlandish."

"It's natural for fathers to have aspirations for their children, to imagine them doing great things."

"Which are completely unrealistic."

"Not always," the eagle said.

"I told my father that, even if I received a prophecy, no one would listen to a girl."

"What was his answer?"

"To a special girl, they'll listen. You're a true Hebrew, the seed of glorious ancestors. One day, Yahweh will speak to you, and you will sit under your palm tree and deliver His message to the people—to us, the ancient Hebrews. I believe it with all my heart. I pray that I'm still alive to witness it." Deborah took a deep breath and exhaled. "That's what he said, and a short time later, Seesya murdered him."

"Yet his words continue to live in you." The eagle stepped backward, her folded wings scraping against the tunnel walls. "Come, climb on my back. I want to show you something."

Deborah gestured at the heavy door. "There's no way out."

"Indulge me." The eagle lowered her shoulder. "Hop on!"

She plugged the bottle and put it on the floor by the wall. "Is this really happening, or am I dreaming?"

"Why don't you bang your head hard against the wall and see if it really hurts?"

Deborah laughed and climbed onto the eagle's back, bending forward to avoid the ceiling.

"Hold tight. It'll be a rough ride."

Deborah put her arms around the thick neck. "I'm ready."

The eagle lunged forward and rammed the wooden door. There was a loud cracking sound, but the door remained in place. Deborah expected the eagle to collapse, but instead, she took a few steps back and rushed at the door again. This time, a long, vertical crack appeared in the door.

"It's locked with a crossbar outside," Deborah said.

The eagle reversed all the way to the back wall, took a deep breath, and raced forward along the narrow tunnel, striking the door and shattering it to pieces.

Deborah pressed her cheek to the feathers as the huge bird squeezed through the doorway and stepped to the center of the floor at the bottom of the shaft. The waterfall roared, engulfing them in a cold mist. The eagle tilted her head upward, spread her wings, and took off.

They ascended through the shaft, slowly at first, then faster. Higher up, the darkness softened, and Deborah could see the serpentine chain of stone-carved stairs circling them swiftly. They rose through the whole height of the shaft in a fraction of the time it would have taken her to climb all thirteen hundred and thirteen stairs.

The entrance had been left open. It was narrow, but the eagle forced her way out through the wooden doorjambs into daylight and stepped to the middle of the dry basin. Deborah glanced back and saw large, four-pronged footprints in the copper-tinged sand.

After the damp and cold mine, the heat outside was pleasant. The small fire that the boy-servants had started in the morning was reduced to smoky ashes. Deborah wondered where the men and horses had gone, but before she managed to say anything, the eagle took off again.

They flew low above the ground, the wings spanning the width of the canyon, and then soared into a vast blue sky. A turquoise spot appeared in the distance, growing into the kidney-shaped Sea of Salt. The light-brown peaks of the Judean Mountains appeared on the left, and the dark Moab Mountains on the right. She saw Ein Gedi by the salt-crusted shore below, and Jericho, surrounded by countless palm trees. The eagle followed the Jordan River north for a while before breaking west, over the ridges of the Samariah Hills.

Deborah noticed a dramatic change in the land below. The hills, which she remembered as barren and barely inhabited, now supported many towns, villages, and homesteads. The slopes were terraced and cultivated, the valleys cleared of stones and divided into fields. When they flew over a village, she looked carefully at the livestock in the corrals. There were horses and donkeys, oxen and cows, sheep and goats, but no pigs. She was filled with joy and wonder. Overnight, her people had populated and filled the land, which was blessed with the abundance Yahweh had promised!

The eagle veered northwest. The familiar hilltop structure of the Holy Tabernacle appeared, surrounded by pilgrims carrying offerings, priests in white robes, and columns of smoke from the altars. Shiloh had grown to three times its former size, and the fairgrounds outside the city gates had expanded into the valley, busy with vendors and caravans.

Turning westward, she saw hundreds of maidens in white dresses, dancing in the vineyards while young men packed the hillside. Deborah realized it was the fifteenth of the month of Av again, but how? She had been to Shiloh only recently. Could a whole year have passed without her noticing? Was she still fourteen, or was this her fifteenth birthday? It made no sense, especially because the changes she was seeing had taken more than a single year to materialize—a decade or two, more likely.

Further west, the road was busy with pilgrims in both directions. When the eagle turned south again, the road below became even more crowded, but most of the travelers were heading in the direction of Emanuel. Deborah wondered where they were going.

The answer came a few minutes later, when she saw Emanuel in the distance and the eagle turned east, leaving the road before it reached the town, following the column of travelers, which soon arrived at Palm Homestead.

The slopes surrounding the verdant valley of her childhood were filled with Hebrew men and women, too many to count. Palm Homestead was thriving, its fields thick with wheat, its orchards heavy with fruit, and its pastures dotted with cattle. There was no trace of the canal Judge Zifron had used to steal the water of the cistern. A two-story house with a sizable courtyard and spacious livestock corrals had taken the place of the small house she remembered. In one of the corrals, a man walked a pony with a young boy in the saddle. The man wore a wide-brimmed hat on his head, hiding his face from above. As the eagle circled the house, Deborah tried to see the man's features, but couldn't.

The eagle hovered above the great palm tree near the house, the one her father had named Deborah's Palm. Under the tree, a woman sat, her back against the trunk, her bearing proud and imposing. She was dressed in leather armor and held a long sword with a silver hilt, red rubies decorating the crossguard, a black gem on top of the pommel. The woman didn't cover her head, as Hebrew wives usually did, and her orange hair was long, wavy, and magnificent. She raised the sword, and the thousands of Hebrews quieted down.

"Hear, O Israel!" Her voice was clear, sonorous, and very familiar. "Yahweh is our God! Yahweh is one!"

"Yahweh is our God!" The countless voices joined together, reverberating like thunder. "Yahweh is one!"

"The King of the world has spoken," she continued. "If you follow my laws and keep my commands, this land shall give you its full harvest, and every field shall be heavy with bounty. But if you break my—"

The flapping wings drowned the woman's voice as the eagle ascended, heading south. Deborah looked over her shoulder, catching a last glimpse of Palm Homestead and the multitudes of Hebrews. She finally understood what the eagle had wanted to show her, and she was filled with awe and anticipation for the future.

The sun went down, and they flew in silence between the dark earth below and the starry sky above. Deborah leaned forward against the thick feathers, her arms around the eagle's neck. She closed her eyes and rested.

A sudden drop in altitude made her sit up.

The eagle descended into the canyon and flew between the dark walls until the final curve came, and they faced the dead end. Folding her wings tightly, the eagle squeezed through the entry, dropped down the shaft, and landed at the bottom beside the waterfall.

Deborah dismounted and stepped over the broken door into the tunnel, where the small lamp still burned. She heard a commotion behind and turned to see the eagle standing outside the tunnel and repairing the door, which came together and stood solidly as if it had never been broken. A loud bang told Deborah that the crossbar had settled into its slots, locking the door.

She pressed her face to the porthole. "What I saw in Palm Homestead, was it the future?"

"The future isn't certain until it becomes the present." The eagle's voice easily overcame the roar of the waterfall. "What you saw is possible—if you make wise choices along the way."

"Nothing is possible while I'm locked down here. I'd like to get out."

"That's a wise choice."

"But you barred the door."

"You noticed?" Chuckling, the eagle knocked on the door with her beak. "As good as new."

"Won't you let me out?"

"Freedom must be earned, not collected as a gift."

Deborah patted the door with an open hand. "How? It's impossible to open this door from inside."

"Defeatism is self-fulfilling, but so is the determination to win."

She understood. It was up to her to find a way out.

The eagle's yellow eyes glowed warmly. "I hope our aerial expedition illuminated your path and granted you peace."

Her last words echoing over the noise of the waterfall, the eagle spread her great wings and flapped them powerfully. Deborah caught a glimpse of the pronged talons as the eagle disappeared upward in the dark shaft of the mine, sending gusts of air that puffed on Deborah's face through the porthole, carrying the sweet scent of Palm Homestead.

36

Deborah added the last of the oil to the clay lamp. How long before the lamp would die? Not long, she thought, and the ensuing darkness would be bleak and final, like death. She shuddered and sat down, her back against the wall. The eagle had said she must earn her freedom, but the heavy door was barred from the outside, and she had no tools with which to tackle it. Sallan had spent three years locked up in this tunnel, and if the Elixirist himself couldn't find a way out, what hope did she have?

Closing her eyes, Deborah realized how tired she was. A quick nap wouldn't make a difference. Would Hashkem return to choke her again? Killing him had been no sin, and she would tell him he had no right to torment her anymore.

When Deborah woke up after what felt like a short time, she checked the oil in the lamp and discovered that only a thin layer remained at the bottom. Most of the oil had been consumed, which must have taken a few hours. Now the prospect of darkness was close and real, and Deborah's dread was mixed with anger at herself for wasting time on sleep. She had to find a way out!

Pacing back and forth between the door and the far end of the tunnel, she poked the walls in search of hidden cracks, stared at the rough-hewn ceiling for signs of weakness, and racked her mind for insight on how to earn her freedom. She could see only a single way out—the door—but it was almost as solid as the surrounding rock.

From memory, she visualized the door on the outside. The crossbar was a thick plank of solid wood, a bit longer than the width of the door. It was secured in two slots, one on each side of the door, about a third of the way up each doorjamb. Could she reach out, hook her fingers under the crossbar, and pull it out of the slots? She suspected that her arm wasn't long enough, but it was worth a try.

Deborah pulled the chair over, placed it next to the door, and mounted it. The wooden legs creaked and trembled but held her weight. She put her arm all the way out through the porthole, her shoulder pressed against the edges, and reached down, searching for the crossbar with her fingers. As she suspected, whoever built the door had considered this possibility and placed the crossbar low enough that even a man with long arms couldn't reach it. She needed a tool that was long enough to reach down and hook on the crossbar, but there was nothing even remotely useful in the tunnel.

With a sinking heart, Deborah realized there was no solution. She had plenty of drinking water in the bucket by the back wall, and the dates Kassite had left would last her a few days if she nibbled sparingly, but the prospect of spending even one more day in this soon-to-be-dark tunnel was intolerable. Pacing back and forth, she stared into every corner, searching for something useful. Anything!

Eventually, she gave up, collapsed to the floor, and buried her face in her hands. "Freedom must be earned, not collected as a gift." The words rang with wisdom, but in reality, she was stuck here until the two Edomite men came back and gave her the gift of freedom. Otherwise, she would die here, never to be free again. Which brought to mind the other lofty proverb the eagle had shared after barring the door: "Defeatism is self-fulfilling, but so is the determination to win." Was it defeatism to accept defeat at the hands of reality—a solid door, a well-designed crossbar, and a total absence of tools? How was she supposed to muster determination to win empty-handed against this unyielding and impassable barrier?

The flickering light gave her an idea. She carried the lamp carefully and placed it beside the bottom of the door, tilting it until the burning wick touched the wood. If the door caught fire, she might be able to break it. On the other hand, the smoke might kill her before the door budged, but right now, she was willing to risk death rather than give up.

What she got, however, was neither freedom through a burning door, nor death by smoke inhalation. Instead, the mist coming in through the crack under the door extinguished the small flame.

Deborah froze. She stared in every direction, seeing nothing. She held her hand in front of her face, and her white skin didn't show at all in the black void. This wasn't the normal darkness she was used to at night, when the light of the moon, the flickering of the stars, and the glow of a nearby fire gave shape to her surroundings. The darkness in the tunnel was complete and absolute.

Slowly, Deborah got down on all fours and proceeded until her head banged on the wall. Her breathing quickened as she sat with her back to the wall and began to tremble. The scabs on her back began to itch, and she leaned forward away from the wall, staring into the darkness. She thought she saw shadows and shapes. Was there a large figure standing before her? The eagle?

"Are you here?" Her tremulous voice sounded like a stranger's. "I need you to come back!"

There was no response.

"Please! Help me!"

The constant noise of the waterfall outside sounded louder now. Was someone coming through the door?

"Who's there?" She waved her arms in front of her to ward off whoever, or whatever, was about to attack her. "Go away!"

Panting hard, her body shaking, Deborah felt her chest tighten, and a lump formed in her throat. It was a terrifying yet familiar feeling—her own fear tightening its clutches.

She recalled Sallan's words: "Banish your fear and embrace your strength."

"There's no one here," she said out loud. "No reason to be afraid."

Trying to conjure memories of situations when she had been able to overcome her fear and embrace her strength, Deborah thought of Ein Gedi, when Seesya came down from the cave and rushed toward her with his sword raised for a fatal blow. He would have killed her had she not overcome her fear, primed her sling with a fitting stone, aimed it carefully, and hit him.

The memory made Deborah feel better. She touched her sling, tied snugly as a makeshift belt over her robe. Her skills with this simple weapon were her biggest strength, as long as she could overcome her fear.

Deborah's panting slowed down and her trembling subsided. She untied the sling and shook it loose in the darkness. Forming a fist with her left hand, she pressed it into the leather pouch and raised her arm so that the two cords, attached to the opposite ends of the pouch, dangled along her arm down to her shoulder. With her right hand, she straightened the cords. At the end of one cord she felt the loop, and at the end of the other, the leather tab. It was a modest weapon, yet ingenious and very effective in the right circumstances. It made her feel safe—not that she could use it in this underground tunnel. There wasn't a single stone to shoot, the ceiling was too low for rotating the sling, and in any event, it was useless against a solid wooden door. To break through the door, she would need a giant sling that could shoot a cow-sized boulder. Deborah smiled at the idea of sling-shooting a cow and shattering the barred door to pieces, as the eagle had done. Not that she needed to break down the door to get out. If there was a way to reach the crossbar and lift it out of the slots—

Reach the crossbar!

The idea was so simple—why hadn't she thought of it before? Now she understood the eagle words: "I hope our aerial expedition illuminated your path." Illumination was what she needed most in this total darkness, but without a source of light, illumination would come from her memory, imagination, and sense of touch.

Deborah grasped the sling in one hand and felt her way back to the door with the other. She got onto the chair and felt the cool spray from the waterfall through the porthole. Acting by feel and visualization, she threaded the thumb of her right hand into the loop, coiled the tab end around her pinky and ring finger, and clenched her fist to secure her grasp on both cords. Pushing the pouch first through the porthole, she put her right arm out and shook it to straighten the cords. She felt the cold mist from the waterfall on her arm and imagined the pouch suspended below, its cords separated by the width of her hand.

Next, Deborah tilted her arm sideways to the left until she felt the doorjamb against her thumb. Visualizing the crossbar, she remembered that it was slightly longer than the width of the door, with the end of the crossbar sticking out beyond each slot about as much as the length of her forefinger. With her cheek pressed against the inside of the door, her right arm all the way out through the porthole, she slowly lowered her hand along the doorjamb. She could feel through the cords when the bottom of the pouch touched the top of the crossbar, and began to rock her hand slightly back and forth in order to cause the pouch to swing as a pendulum parallel to the doorjamb while she continued to lower it very slowly until its swinging was blocked by the outer end of the crossbeam. Slightly lower, while keeping one cord close to the doorjamb, she felt the pouch clear the bottom of the crossbar and get under it. She held her breath and tugged upward on the cords, hooking the pouch under the end of the crossbar.

"Got you!" She laughed in the dark. "Got you!"

Now came the next hurdle—lifting the crossbar with one hand. Deborah adjusted her position on the creaky chair, took a deep breath, and pulled hard.

Nothing happened.

She kept the tension on the cords of the sling to prevent the pouch from slipping off the end of the crossbar, rested for a moment, took another deep breath, and pulled again, even harder this time.

It didn't budge.

Her arm hurting from the effort, Deborah struggled to keep disappointment from overwhelming her. She had to think calmly. Having helped Sallan lift it when they had first arrived, she remembered that the crossbar was hefty and the slots tight. Was the pouch somehow hooked on the slot instead of on the end of the crossbar? She couldn't imagine how that could have happened. But what else could it be?

Out of ideas, Deborah steeled herself and pulled up again as hard as she could, gritting her teeth and groaning, the muscles of her arm and shoulder tight to the limit.

No movement, except for the chair, which creaked and rocked under her.

She wanted to keep tension on the cords, but her arm hurt badly from the effort, and she inadvertently lowered it enough for the pouch to slip out from under the end of the crossbar. With her whole body shaking from the effort, Deborah gave up. She pulled her arm with the sling back through the porthole, got down from the chair, and lay on the floor, panting. She was nauseated, and the darkness around her lit up with sparkling multicolored stars that didn't disappear when she shut her eyes. It was a beautiful sight while it lasted.

As she recovered, the stars faded into complete darkness again. Her plan had failed, and she didn't even know why. Perhaps the door itself pressed on the crossbar, which in turn pressed against the slots, making it hard to pull out the crossbar. But what could she do about it? Pull the door inward while trying to lift the crossbar? It seemed impossible, and she couldn't find the will to get up and try. Kassite had said, "Women are passive, temperamental, small-minded, and anxious." Was he right? Were women incapable of doing what men could do in the same situation? If a man was in her position now, would he climb back on the chair, or remain on the floor, defeated, hoping someone would come to rescue him?

Another dreadful possibility came to her. What if Sallan and Kassite were captured or killed while riding back to Bozra? No one else knew where she was. The thought dying in this cell, starved, blind, and alone, enraged her. She had to get out, or die trying. In fact, a quick death would be better than a slow and lonely one.

Repeating the steps as before, she used her left arm this time, and managed to hook the pouch on the other end of the crossbar. However, when she pulled, the result was the same, except that now she was filled with rage. Rather than lose control, she harnessed all that rage and channeled it against the cursed door that was keeping her prisoner.

Continuing to pull hard on the cords, Deborah turned her body sideways and used her hip to hit the door repeatedly, shaking it in hope of releasing the tight fit of the crossbar in the slots. It didn't work, and her rage exploded into fury. Pounding the door harder with her hip, again and again, she pulled on the sling, her left arm and shoulder burning with muscle pain.

"Damn you," she shouted. "Come out already!"

The chair broke under her.

Deborah yelped as she dropped halfway down and hung by her left arm, which remained extended through the porthole, twisted painfully, before the sling tore out of her hand, and her arm threaded back in through the porthole, allowing her to fall the rest of the way to the floor.

The fall knocked the air out of her, and she lay flat, panting. Her arm hurt from being twisted, and her hand burned from having both the loop and the tab torn out of her grip. But Deborah couldn't stay down. She had to find out whether the sling had been torn apart, or had extracted the crossbar from the slots before she lost grip of the cords.

Staying on all fours, she felt her way back to the door, brushing aside the pieces of the broken chair. With a deep breath, she put the palm of her right hand flat against the door and pushed.

The door didn't move.

"No!" Her rage flaring again, she got up and threw herself blindly against the door.

The door budged.

Deborah paused. Was she imagining it, or had the door actually moved?

She pushed with both hands, putting her weight into it. The door screeched and resisted, but edged a bit further. Another push, harder yet, didn't help. The door would move no more.

The roar of the waterfall was much louder, and cool mist caressed her face. Feeling around with her hands, Deborah found that the door was cracked open with enough space to put her arm through. She reached out and felt about with her hand on the outside of the door. The crossbar was there, standing diagonally. It had come out of one slot, but was still set in the opposite slot—the side of door where the hinges were. To loosen it, Deborah lay on the ground, reached out with her right hand, and nudged the crossbar with her fingers, shaking it while applying pressure on the door with her shoulder. Her efforts forced the door a little further, and she managed to put her head through the narrow gap, followed by the rest of her body.

In the darkness outside the tunnel, engulfed by the cold mist from the waterfall, Deborah burst out crying. She had made it! She was free!

Still down on her knees, Deborah searched with her hands on the floor outside the door and found the sling. She ran her fingers on the cords, the loop, the tab, and the pouch. The sling was undamaged. She tied it around her waist. The complete darkness no longer bothered her. She knew where she was and where she was going.

Deborah washed her face in the cold water of the pool at the bottom of the waterfall and drank some, too. Moving slowly along the circular wall at the bottom of the shaft, she found the base of the stairs. Her right foot on the first step, she glanced up, hoping to see the meek light at the top of the shaft—her beacon of freedom. Instead, she saw the glow of torches above.

37

Deborah's first instinct was to start climbing fast and confront Sallan and Kassite over their betrayal. On second thought, however, she realized that the torches above might be carried by persons other than the two Edomite men. Running into a bunch of strangers on the narrow, rough stairs high up in the shaft could be deadly. Besides, even Sallan and Kassite might be dangerous to her. Hadn't they locked her down here in the first place, putting her life in danger?

Feeling her way back around the wall back to the door, Deborah closed it, lifted the crossbar, and secured it in the slots. She proceeded to the pool and stepped into it. The cold water reached above her knees, and the splashes from the waterfall soaked her robe.

The approaching torches began to soften the darkness. Deborah stepped sideways, her back to the wall, and entered the narrow space behind the waterfall. The noise was deafening, but she was safe, at least for now.

She waited.

Through the column of water, the glow slowly grew stronger. Meanwhile, the chill from the water and spray penetrated her body, making her tremble.

Finally, she saw two points of light reach the bottom and go from the base of the stairs to the tunnel door.

She peeked from behind the waterfall. There were two men, their backs to her. One was taller and thinner than the other and wore a white hat. The shorter man had Sallan's bushy hair.

Kassite looked in through the porthole and yelled something. Sallan banged on the door with an open hand. Kassite shook his head, and Sallan thumped the door again.

Deborah retreated behind the roaring waterfall. It wasn't hard to guess what was going on. They had expected her to be inside and to rush to the door anxiously upon hearing them, but despite yelling through the porthole and banging on the door, there was no response. The darkness inside, she knew, made it impossible for them to see that she was no longer in the barred tunnel.

The torches shifted and shook. One of them disappeared, then the other.

Deborah stepped out of the pool.

The door was ajar, and the glow from the men's torches spilled out on the floor. She went to the door. She could hear their voices inside.

"Look in the back," Kassite said. "By the wall."

"I'm looking," Sallan said. "She's not there."

"Impossible!"

With both hands, Deborah edged the door in until it closed. She lifted the crossbar and slipped it into the slots. With the door barred, she stood on her toes and looked in through the porthole.

The two men stood at the far end of the tunnel, facing the wall, the flames from their torches casting jittery shadows.

"She got out." Sallan touched the back wall as if expecting to find a secret passage in the solid rock. "I don't know how, but she got out."

"Someone let her out." Kassite said.

"Who? Nobody knows about this place except my boy-servants, and they've been with us the whole time."

"Obviously, somebody helped her. There is no way she got out by herself."

"There is a way," Deborah said.

The men turned and tilted their torches in her direction.

"Who is there?" Kassite asked.

"It's me," she said.

They approached the door.

"It really is you." Sallan held his torch forward. "Good morning."

"It's a wonderful morning for me," she said. "Not so much for you, I'm afraid."

Kassite pushed the door, testing it.

"It's very solid." Deborah knuckled the crossbar. "How does it feel to be on the inside?"

"Let us out," Sallan said.

"Why should I?"

"Please, open the door."

"Did you open it when I asked you to?" Deborah stepped back and squeezed some of the water out of her robe. She was trembling from the cold.

"It's not funny." Sallan pressed his face to the porthole. "Not for me, not with my memories of this lonely jail."

"You're not alone this time. Isn't that nice?"

"My old friend," Kassite said, "your Hebrew girl outsmarted you."

Sallan turned to him. "She outsmarted both of us!"

"It was not my idea to bring her here and lock her up."

"It's not about outsmarting you," she said. "It's about doing to you what you did to me. That's all."

"I did it for your own good," Sallan said. "Believe me, Deborah, it hurt me to leave you here alone, but I had to do it in order to help you clear your mind and discover what's truly in your heart."

"I'm also doing it for your own good." Deborah adjusted the sling around her waist. "I'll leave you here to help you clear your conscience and discover what it feels like to be on the receiving end of trickery and manipulation by someone you trust."

"Please, don't do this," Sallan said. "It's not in your making to be cruel and vengeful like this. We're old men. We could die here."

"There's plenty of water, and I haven't touched the dates you so generously left for me."

"Look at this." Kassite picked up the clay bottle and shook it. "Still full."

"Is it?" Sallan took the bottle. "Didn't you find the final ingredient?"

"I know what to look for now. True enchantment. As you predicted yesterday, I figured it out."

"Then take it." He passed the bottle through the porthole. "I mixed this Malc Elixir for you. No point in letting it go to waste."

Deborah took the bottle, her hand shaking. "I'm freezing, and the sun is waiting upstairs. Farewell."

"Open the door, Borah!" Kassite pounded the door. "I command you!"

"Master, I'm sorry," she said. "Can't do that."

"You swore to obey me!"

"I swore to obey the Elixirist, but you extracted my oath with a lie, and then made me work as a slave. And even if my oath was valid, it has expired." She held up the bottle. "With the delivery of the third dose of the Male Elixir, our deal is concluded."

"Don't leave us here," Sallan said. "I implore you."

"Do not beg her." Kassite grasped the porthole and shook the door. "Borah! I command you—open up!"

"We're too old for this place," Sallan said, his voice trembling.

"Old and wise," she said. "Surely the two of you together will be able to figure out a way to free yourselves."

Pointing his torch, Sallan made a full circle, looking around at the walls. "How did you do it?"

"Freedom must be earned, not collected as a gift."

The two men looked at each other, their pale faces lit by the flickering torches.

"I'll come back in a day or two," she said. "Unless something happens to me, in which case you'll die here the same way I could have died."

Heading across the floor to the base of the stairs, she took the first two steps.

"Borah!" Kassite's voice rang out over the noise of the waterfall. "Do not kill!"

She paused, and for an instant her throat constricted and she couldn't breathe.

"Please, Deborah," Sallan cried, "have mercy on us."

"Have mercy on yourself," Kassite yelled. "The Hebrew god will punish you."

She groaned, unable to keep climbing.

"I'm sorry." Sallan sounded on the verge of panic. "Forgive me."

Deborah walked back to the porthole. "Why should I forgive you—yet again?"

"Because you're kind. And decent."

"That's why you keep tricking me?"

Sallan covered his face, unable to speak.

Kassite put his arms around Sallan and held him.

Her anger faded. She remembered the eagle's words: "When a person rises to kill you, rise first and kill him." These two old men posed no danger to her—not anymore. If she left the door locked, would she have dreams about Sallan and Kassite dying of hunger and cold, clawing at the barred door until their fingernails broke? Would they come to her in her dreams and choke her?

Deborah put the clay bottle on the floor, hoisted the crossbar out of the tight slots, and dropped it aside with a loud thud. She picked up the bottle and went back to the stairs.

Behind her, Kassite called, "Thank you, the great Qoz!"

"You're welcome," Deborah said as she took the first step.

Climbing the stairs warmed her body, and the monotony of the steps allowed her mind to wander back to the eagle's flight and all the details of the Hebrew prosperity she'd seen in Canaan, particularly at Palm Homestead. That glorious future was worthy of her heart's true enchantment. The eagle had said, "The future isn't certain until it becomes the present. What you saw is possible—if you make wise choices along the way."

Deborah glanced at the bottle in her hand, barely visible in the near darkness. The choice she was facing was the greatest she would ever make: to drink, or not to drink.

From the high perch of the eagle's back, Deborah had seen herself delivering God's message to the Hebrews as a woman, seated under Deborah's Palm, just as her father had predicted. It meant that realizing her True Calling as a woman was possible. At the same time, a voice of reason in her head prodded her to think logically, to question the reality of the flight. Had it been a mere dream, instigated by her fervent hopes and embellished by her fertile imagination?

The two men followed her up the stairs at a slower pace, groaning from the effort. Deborah kept going, the clay bottle in her right hand while her left hand touched the wall for guidance. In her mind, she was also in the dark, unable to see what was real and what was an illusion. Had she been sleeping the whole time, dreaming of the eagle's visit and imagining her wise words? But the eagle had seemed so real, her questions so clever, her advice so insightful, and her gift of glimpsing a possible future so joyous.

One moment Deborah told herself to dismiss the flight to Canaan as a sleep-induced fantasy and stick to her original plan—drink the third dose and transform into a young man. The next moment she changed her mind again. What if Yahweh had sent the eagle with divine guidance?

Her parting words implied that much: "I hope our aerial expedition illuminated your path and granted you peace." Indeed, the trip had done both—illuminated Deborah's path and given her peace—which was the realization of the priest's blessing, wasn't it?

As she approached the light at the top of the shaft, Deborah knew she had to make the choice, which would determine her future, one way or another. How could she choose, when the facts were so elusive? If the eagle had been only a dream, the wise choice would be manhood. Surely, she could become wholly enchanted with the prospect of life as a man—strong, independent, free to inherit Palm Homestead and prepare to become God's prophet. But if the eagle was real, a messenger from Yahweh, then it was possible to win back Palm Homestead and become God's prophet—as a woman! Now, she had no idea how to achieve all that as a woman, but it was a future much more enchanting than any man's life!

Deborah reached the large cave at the top and climbed out of the shaft. She saw the two men below as they continued to climb the stairs. At the doorway, which was flooded with sunlight, she paused and shut her eyes, enjoying the soothing warmth that welcomed her back to the world.

Going from darkness to light after a long climb spent in internal debate, she wished the light would provide the clarity she yearned for.

Had the eagle been real, or a mere dream?

Deborah waited for the hoped-for enlightenment, but none came.

Passing through the narrow door, her elbow rubbed against something soft, and she glanced at it.

A crack in the dry wood of the doorjamb had caught a long white feather. Deborah tugged on it gently until it came free. Having held on to the eagle's neck each time they flew, she recognized the long white feather. It came from a great eagle, that was certain, but was it the eagle she knew?

Outside, in the copper-tinged sand of the dry basin, she saw familiar footprints. They were the four-pronged talons of a large eagle, but the same question persisted: Was it her eagle?

Deborah felt the white feather between her fingers. It was soft, yet its spine was firm. She put it to her nose, sniffed it, and froze, stunned by the unmistakable smell that came from the white feather. It was the sweet scent of Palm Homestead.

All her pestering doubts suddenly perished. Deborah sank to her knees. Raising her arms, the elixir bottle in one hand, the eagle's feather in the other, she inhaled deeply and shouted, "Thank you, God!"

The sound of her voice echoed from the narrow canyon walls as if answering her. No longer burdened by indecision, she got to her feet and ran back into the large cave. Stopping at the edge of the shaft, she saw Sallan and Kassite approaching the top of the stairs on the opposite side. They noticed her above and stopped, breathing heavily.

"I found it," she yelled. "The final ingredient."

They looked at her.

"Where?" Sallan asked.

"In my heart. I discovered my true enchantment."

"Congratulations," he said. "What is it?"

"The future."

Kassite turned to Sallan and said, "What does she mean?"

"I'm enchanted with the future. It'll be a long road, but I'm determined to succeed!"

She kissed the clay bottle, extended her hand over the edge of the shaft, and let it go. The bottle dropped, the men following it with their puzzled eyes until it disappeared in the dark shaft. After what seemed like a long time, the pop of the smashing bottle returned from the distant bottom.

38

Rogez neighed happily at seeing Deborah, and the boy-servants greeted her with smiles and a chunk of bread with goat cheese. She placed the eagle's white feather in the pocket of her robe for safekeeping, kissed her horse on the nose, and ate the bread and cheese with great relish. Sallan and Kassite waited for the boys to stack up the stones over the entrance to the mine before mounting their horses.

Heading down the canyon, the group reached a point where the walls were wide enough for direct sun to reach the bottom. Turning her face up, Deborah closed her eyes and enjoyed the warm rays. Her robe was almost dry, and she was no longer cold. Her time underground had made her realize how much she loved being outside, free to ride and enjoy the fresh air. If she could help it, Deborah decided, she would never again step into a mine.

When the ruins of Kassite's family homestead appeared, she noticed the smoky remnants of a campfire. Had the men spent the night there? She turned to ask, but Kassite sped up, trotted by her without a word, and took the lead, navigating the way back to Bozra.

With the sun approaching its highest point, they rode over a hillcrest, and Kassite stopped. The vast green valley stretched below, separating them from Bozra with its white walls and glistening copper roofs.

"It's getting hot," she said. "Let's go."

"What's the rush?" Sallan patted his horse's neck. "I thought women were inclined to be captivated by nature's beauty."

"You mean, when we're not busy being small-minded and anxious?"

Kassite chuckled, but Sallan wasn't amused.

"As a woman," he said, "you'd be wise to watch your mouth. Talking back to a man could earn you a good flogging, or worse."

"The last man to flog me ended up getting a good flogging himself."

Kassite laughed. "A veiled threat for a veiled threat!"

"I wasn't threatening," Sallan said.

She glared at him. "It sure sounded like a threat."

"I was giving you good advice, now that you've chosen to remain a woman." Sallan's voice softened. "You should stay in Bozra, at least for a while. My home is your home. You'd be safe here."

"My home is in the Samariah Hills, at Palm Homestead. That's my true enchantment."

He sighed. "You're very young and deeply scarred by all the misfortune and cruelty of the past year. It's natural to feel the urge to right the wrong, to recover what's been taken from you, to win back the grace of the gods before they rain more trouble on your head. It's understandable, but you may feel different a month from now, or a year from now. Why rush into a decision now?"

"Didn't you lock me up for the night in order to force me to discover my heart's true enchantment?"

Sallan sighed again. "I had to do something to stop you from leaving us and going back to Canaan. I feared for you. The result, however, is disappointing."

"What did you expect?"

"I expected you to realize that there was nothing enchanting about your family's little homestead, nothing enchanting about the endless fighting with the wicked judge and his violent son, and nothing enchanting about the impossible religious role your father dreamed up for you."

She looked at him, baffled. "You expected me to realize what I'm not enchanted with?"

Sallan glanced at Kassite, who nodded as if saying, "Did I not tell you?"

"Be honest with me," Deborah said. "What was in your heart when you locked me up down there? What did you truly expect to gain from it?"

Shaking his head slowly, Kassite frowned at Sallan.

"I'll tell you," Sallan said. "I expected the solitude to cause you to reflect on your life, think of all that's happened to you since your parents' murder, and realize that your only friends on earth are right here in Bozra—a city that rules a great kingdom, a city worthy of your talents, a city where you could have a safe and prosperous future—even as a woman."

Deborah was dumbfounded. "You expected me to become enchanted with the prospect of staying here?"

He nodded.

"How could I live in Edom? I'm a Hebrew."

"By what measure? You have no living family left among the Hebrews, who murdered your parents and sister. You have no right to own property or a chance to find safety in Canaan. You have nothing there but deadly enemies. Here, on the other hand, you have friends and a sanctuary and the right to own property when you become prosperous, even without a husband. Besides, your appearance could easily pass for an Edomite."

Deborah shook her head. "I could never be enchanted with a future in Edom."

"Never say never," Sallan said. "Even a feeling of absolute certainty is only temporary, subject to a change of mind."

"I will not change my mind."

"Have you not changed your mind about becoming a man?"

She wanted to answer, but to explain her recent decision would require describing the eagle's visit and the flight they had taken to see the future she could achieve through determination and wise choices. Deborah knew that Sallan and Kassite could not possibly comprehend the reality of the flight and the truth of what she had experienced.

"You have no answer," Sallan said. "That's an admission that there is a chance of another change of mind. You should not have destroyed the third dose."

"That's exactly it," Deborah said. "I destroyed it because I don't want the possibility of changing my mind."

Rogez whinnied and rocked his head up and down.

"Typical female foolishness." Kassite took off his hat and used it to fan his face. "That is what you should have expected."

"Don't rush," Sallan said. "Enjoy the grandeur of this city, appreciate the greatness of this kingdom, see how much the people need the skills that I possess. You saw the crowd yesterday morning, didn't you?"

"Yes, I did," Deborah said.

"And the people's appetite will only grow. Don't you see what's happening here?"

"You're a great man, but I—"

"How can you not become enthralled with such prospects?" Sallan cleared his throat. "Don't you understand what I'm implying? Don't you realize that, one day, I will pass on to be with the gods and someone will to take over my work?"

"Me? The Elixirist?"

Sallan nodded, his eyes moist.

"Why me? You have such a large family here, many young men to choose from and teach your craft."

"It's not a craft," Sallan said quietly. "It's an art, and none of them possesses what you possess."

Deborah patted Rogez, who was getting impatient. "I have nothing."

"Do you not understand, girl?" Kassite tilted his hat, glancing at her. "The Elixirist, the great man himself, has become enchanted with you."

Sallan turned to Kassite. "You mock me? What did you whisper to me in Emanuel? 'She is a gift from Qoz.' Weren't those your words?"

"I readily admitted it." Kassite raised his hands. "But you denied it."

"I admit it now." Sallan turned back to Deborah. "It's true. I couldn't believe my heart at first—a Hebrew girl, poor and uneducated—but there's something about you that captivates my heart."

Deborah looked away, embarrassed.

"It's not lust," he said. "I'm too old for that. It's a different attraction that I feel for the unique gift that the gods have endowed you with."

"What gift?" She felt her face burning. "The gift of bad luck? Of sorrow and loss? Of sworn enemies and needless killing?"

"You have strength, radiance, quality of mind—and your spirit is only going to rise and strengthen." Sallan pressed his hands together. "Stay here and let me nurture you to your full potential. You could be my son, or my daughter—it doesn't matter. Either way, I can teach you everything I know about old and new elixirs, about bringing relief to the sick and joy to the needy."

The intensity of his emotions and the enormity of his offer moved Deborah deeply. She longed to accept this opportunity of a life filled with wealth, adventure, and service to countless people, but her future wasn't hers to give away.

"I can't." Her voice trembled. "I must go back to Palm Homestead."

"Why must you?" Sallan pointed at the sky. "Yahweh? Is that why?"

She nodded.

"Your loving god wants you to go back into that den of Hebrew coyotes? To fight a lost battle? To bare your chest to their spears and your back to their whips? Is that what you believe—that your god is cruel and unjust?"

"Of course not."

"Then maybe it's the opposite. Maybe your god brought you here intentionally." Sallan waved his hand at the view of the city across the valley. "Maybe your god wants you to stay in Bozra and flourish. Isn't it possible for you to believe that your god is merciful, generous, and kind?"

Deborah didn't answer.

"See? You can't tell for sure. Stay here, and in time you'll have all of Edom at your feet."

After a long moment of silence, Kassite said, "Enough already. Her heart is in Canaan. Stop humiliating yourself."

"Think about it, Deborah," Sallan insisted. "You saw how the people admire me, beg for my help, adore my powers—and I've just arrived back after two decades. Imagine what the future holds! You could be as great as I am, or better than me, my heir! The Elixirist!"

All Deborah could do was shake her head.

39

They rode across the valley without exchanging another word, though in her mind Deborah argued, reasoned, and explained her duty to her family and to Yahweh. Sallan had been correct about the risks awaiting her in Canaan. Going back now to confront Seesya and Judge Zifron would surely bring about her quick and bloody demise. To win the first battle against her enemies and to continue winning every battle after that—for she was certain the House of Zifron would keep fighting her—she had to learn how to fight real battles with swords and spears against well-trained and fully equipped opponents. She had to learn the art of war as a professional soldier preparing to fight and to lead others in fighting and winning.

Could she acquire the skills of a warrior?

As the eagle had said, she would have to make wise choices along the way, and her first choice was to put all her talent and determination into succeeding. There was no fear in her heart, knowing that God would watch over her, but the prospect of loneliness weighed heavily on her. If only she had a friend ready to stand with her against Seesya—someone brave like Barac.

Deborah recalled how the eagle had reacted when hearing of Seesya's murder of Barac. She had tilted its head and said, "Really? That's news to me."

Deborah slowed down to let Sallan catch up with her. "Are you angry with me?"

Sallan shook his head.

"You were right to warn me about the dangers ahead. Before going home to fight my enemies, I must learn to be a warrior. May I stay with you until I'm ready?"

He thought for a long moment. "You may, but better you continue to be Borah, or your weapons will be taken from you."

"Your mother saw through my disguise."

"Umm-Sallan can see through walls, but she's your friend. With her help, your disguise would be more believable."

"Thank you," she said.

They rode past an apple orchard in the middle of the valley. The farmer, his wives, and his children were busy picking the fruit from the trees and filling large baskets. They stopped working as the group passed by and bowed respectfully, their faces serious. The farmer came over with a basket of apples. He bowed before Deborah and raised the basket to her. She took an apple and bit into it.

"It's sweet," she said. "Thank you."

The farmer bowed again and offered the basket to Rogez, who picked out an apple with his teeth and chomped on it noisily. The farmer held the basket up for the other men, but not to the other horses.

The group moved on at a slow pace, Deborah rising beside Sallan.

"I was wondering about Barac," she said, "son of Abinoam, the blacksmith."

"The boy who lived," Sallan said. "He was braver than all the men of Emanuel, defying Seesya in public during your sister's stoning."

"Unfortunately, that's not the end of the story. Later on, in Shiloh, Seesya bragged that he had caught and killed Barac." She thought of Seesya's description: "We chopped off his head and kicked it around like a ball." A tremor went through her. "Do you know if it's true?"

"I don't remember anyone mentioning it in Emanuel. Unless Seesya told the soldiers to keep it a secret, they would have told others, and I would have heard about it."

Deborah exhaled with relief. She had feared that Sallan would confirm Barac's death, but he didn't, allowing her to maintain a small hope that Barac was alive. She imagined seeing him again. How wonderful that would be!

As they approached the city, trumpets sounded. Two large flags, copper-colored with a golden tiger, were raised to the top of tall poles and fluttered in the wind. The sentries ran out and lined up by the gates.

Sallan straightened up, sitting tall in the saddle, and sped up to take the lead ahead of the group. He raised his right arm in greeting. Riding behind him with Kassite and the two boys, Deborah was impressed that Sallan's arrival had prompted such honorary commotion, though the large crowd in the garden had already shown her that his fame was indeed great.

General Mazabi emerged from the gates, riding at the head of a contingent of soldiers, and galloped down the road toward them.

Sallan stopped his horse and kept his arm raised in a greeting.

The general and his soldiers didn't slow down as they bore down on the group. In the last moment, Kassite urged his horse forward, grabbed Sallan's horse's bridle, and pulled both horses off the road. Deborah and the boys did the same while General Mazabi and his soldiers flew by at full speed.

A trumpet sounded from the west, where a military convoy was approaching. The general and his soldiers welcomed the convoy in a cloud of dust.

As it came closer, Deborah saw a gold-plated chariot, drawn by a pair of black stallions, followed by twelve iron chariots and a few hundred foot soldiers. The soldiers wore the same tall helmets, decked with rooster combs of copper-dyed horsehair on top, and carried the same flags as the ones by the gates. General Mazabi rode beside the golden chariot.

The vendors and their customers ran over from the fairgrounds and lined up along both sides of the road.

Deborah was surprised at how young the king looked. His freckled face was smooth, his body was slim, and his lips were thin and red. He drove the chariot with one hand and held a spear in the other. His leather armor was etched with intricate designs, his helmet was the color of gold with a crown-like ridge but no horsehair comb, and his gloves glistened with precious stones.

Everyone dismounted, went down on their knees, and bowed as the king's chariot came to a stop.

"Is this our long-absent Elixirist?" King Esau the Twentieth had a thin voice, which fitted his physical stature, yet contrasted with his opulent regalia.

Sallan stayed kneeling, but looked up and smiled. "Yes, my king."

"The news of your return delighted us immensely."

"Praise the gods for bringing Your Excellency home safely."

"We've been away for only a few weeks, but Edom has missed you for a lifetime. And now Qoz in His divine wisdom has brought you back to us, because we need you more than ever." The king pointed his spear at Sallan's bandaged hand. "What happened?"

Sallan held it up. "A setback during our escape. I lost a finger, but the rest of my body gained freedom."

Deborah looked at the king. Up close, his face seemed even younger.

King Esau tapped Sallan's shoulder with his spear. "Stand up. Let us look at you."

Sallan stood, a sigh escaping his lips.

"You've become an old man." The king grinned. "You should drink your famous Youth Elixir—or better yet, bathe in it!"

The men nearby laughed.

"Yes, my king." Sallan bowed again. "May I take this command as permission to resume my work and provide the people with the elixirs they desire?"

Murmuring broke out as his question was repeated for those who were too far to hear it.

The king's grin faded. "Not yet. We shall think about it."

More murmuring sounded, tainted with resentment.

Sallan bowed. "I'm grateful for having lived long enough to see the precious child who once bounced on my knee grow up to wear the crown of Edom. My heart swells with unbounded happiness."

"Good. We are pleased." The king looked at Rogez, measuring him up and down with admiration, and his eyes dropped to Deborah, who was kneeling by her horse.

"These men escaped with me." Sallan placed a hand on Kassite's shoulder. "This good man is an expert in treating cowhides, making wonderful leather—"

"This one!" The king pointed his spear at Deborah. "What's his name?"

"This is Borah," Sallan said. "He's just a boy."

"A boy on a rich man's horse." The king stared at her. The blue in his eyes seemed unreal, as if painted with the dye used to color the threads on the Hebrew priests' robes.

Sallan nudged her, and Deborah lowered her gaze.

"The world is out of order," the king said. "The cursed Hebrew tribesmen of Simeon abducted our beloved sister, Needa. We demanded her safe return, but they play hide and seek with us, those roving outlaws!"

"May Qoz strike them down where they stand," Sallan said, "and bring Princess Needa home."

"You are right," the king said. "We shall make an offering to Qoz, and then, with His blessing, we'll raise a new army and make war on our Hebrew enemies."

Hearing his words, Deborah could hardly breathe.

The king shook the reins, and his horses pulled the golden chariot forward, followed by General Mazabi, the twelve chariots, and the hundreds of foot soldiers, who marched with renewed vigor to the open gates of Bozra.

The vendors and their customers lingered near the road, discussing the return of the young monarch without Princess Needa and his refusal of Sallan's request.

Kassite mounted his horse, but Sallan didn't. He looked at Deborah, shaking his head.

"I know," she said. "I shouldn't have stared at the king, but his eyes—they're so blue."

"Drawing attention to yourself is very dangerous," Sallan said. "If he finds out you're a Hebrew, we'll both lose our heads."

"Why?"

"Should I have told him you're a Hebrew like the tribesmen who abducted the princess?"

"I'm of the Ephraim tribe, not Simeon."

"Do you think the king cares about your tribal affiliation? In his eyes, you're all roving outlaws."

Kassite chuckled atop his horse. "The king is right. I would give my right arm to see all the Hebrews cut down by the sword."

Deborah looked up at Kassite. She was hurt at first, but remembered that both he and Sallan had spent almost two decades in Hebrew slavery.

"If you want to live," Sallan said, "you must hide your Hebrew roots. Imitate our Edomite ways—even if you don't wish to mutate."

She didn't argue.

"It won't be hard." He gestured at her. "Your hair, your skin, your height. No one will doubt you're an Edomite. We escaped from Egypt together, and I've made you a member of my household for as long as you wish."

"You have my complete gratitude," she said, "but please remember that one day, when I'm ready, I'll have to follow the path laid down for me by my ancestors and my God and return to Canaan."

"I won't hold you prisoner," Sallan said, "but continue to hope that your heart will eventually accept the futility of returning to Canaan and rejoining the primitive Hebrews."

"My people aren't primitive. We are sinners, and Yahweh has turned His back on us, but when we repent, He will smile upon us again and make us more prosperous than before. One day, we'll build cities greater than Bozra."

"That is what you get," Kassite said to Sallan, "for begging a Hebrew girl as if she were Pharaoh's daughter."

"I'm not a king's daughter," Deborah said. "God forbade us from anointing kings and queens, but He told my father in a dream that I was destined to become a prophet, and that's a greater honor than being royalty."

"It's tempting," Sallan said, "to believe that the gods marked you for greatness, but what if your father's dream was just that, a dream?"

"It was true," she said. "I'm sure of it."

"Then you should have drunk the third dose. A man's path is much safer in this world, especially in Canaan."

"The path is never safe," Kassite said, "for one claiming to speak for a god."

"God created me a woman," Deborah said. "He expects me to pursue my True Calling as a woman. And to succeed, I'll have to be better than any man."

"Why?" Sallan smiled as he asked it, for it was usually she who asked why.

"Because I'll have to do battle, not once, but repeatedly, and I'll have to win every time. For that, I'll have to learn not only how to fight, but also how to lead others in fighting."

"That's an impossible goal for a woman."

"My time in the tannery taught me that I could do everything the men did."

"You compare my tannery to war?" Kassite waved his hand in dismissal. "Perseverance might be enough to survive the tannery's stench of rotting animal flesh, but a battlefield reeks of rotting human flesh."

His words caused her to catch a whiff of the terrible stench coming from the lumps of rotten, bloody meat she had swallowed in order to survive her wedding night in Shiloh.

"I'll do what's necessary," Deborah said, "become a trained warrior and learn to win battles as the best general."

"There's an Edomite saying," Sallan said. "To make a great general, start with a witless recruit."

"I'm not a complete novice," Deborah said. "I've killed a man."

"Winning a scuffle isn't the same as winning a battle, which isn't the same as winning a war."

"Will you help me?"

"Do I have a choice?" Sallan sighed. "I'll speak with General Mazabi."

"Good timing," Kassite said as he urged his horse forward. "The king wants to raise a new army."

Deborah held the reins of Sallan's horse while he mounted it, before getting onto Rogez. He whinnied happily as she settled in the saddle.

They rode through the gates into Bozra. The king and his entourage were already halfway up the first street, moving slowly through a cheering crowd.

"Look who is here," Kassite said.

A familiar group of men stood by their horses inside the gates. They had cleaned up and wore new robes, but Deborah recognized them at once and felt a cold wave of dread. Antippet was wearing a bandage over his eyes, while Patrees and the other Edomite slaves from the tannery stared back at her.

Kassite waved them over. They came and knelt before him.

"Master," Patrees said, "we beg forgiveness."

"Do you have my silver?"

There was a long silence, and Deborah looked at Kassite, wondering what silver he was speaking of.

Patrees reached under his armor, pulled out a heavy purse, and handed it to Kassite. "I forgot to leave it behind when you banished us. I was too upset."

Deborah watched Kassite put the purse under his robe. The missing purse was news to her, and she was impressed that the Edomite men were honorable enough to return it.

"Master, will you forgive us?"

"Only if Borah does," Kassite said.

They turned to her.

"Why would I forgive them? They attacked me and forced me to poke out a man's eyes." She pointed at Antippet. "They deserve no forgiveness."

"It's not simple," Sallan said. "You're sentencing them to harsh slavery."

"Me?"

"They need a place to live and work, or they'll be arrested and sent to the king's copper mines. Kassite's patronage is their only hope."

Now she understood why they had returned the purse.

"Tell me who am I," she said.

They didn't respond.

"Speak up," she said. "Who am I?"

"You're Borah," Patrees said. "Borah, the boy, our group leader."

The rest of them nodded.

"Fine," she said. "You're forgiven."

Their faces broke into smiles.

"Master," Patrees said, "we want to serve you again."

"My family's homestead has been neglected," Kassite said. "There is water, but it has been diverted into an old mine and needs to be redirected. Will you work hard and obey me?"

They chorused, "Yes, Master!"

"Get your horses ready." Kassite turned to Sallan. "Be well, old friend. I will come back to visit you soon."

The two men edged their horses closer and hugged.

Things were happening too fast, and Deborah suddenly felt alarmed. From the moment he had agreed to let her stay at the tannery, Kassite had been her guardian and mentor. Despite his occasional sharp tongue, she knew his heart was warm and caring.

"I don't understand," she said. "Why are you leaving?"

Kassite smiled and tugged at his horse's reins to get closer to her. "As you are attached to Palm Homestead, I belong on my forefathers' land."

She nodded, a lump forming in her throat.

"Before I go," Kassite said, "you must tell me something. How did you get out?"

"Yes," Sallan said, "I also want to know, having been locked down there for three years, constantly trying to find a way through that heavy door to no avail!"

Deborah untied the sling from around her waist and held it by the loop and tab, the pouch dangling below. "I put my arm out through the porthole, swung the pouch until it hooked under the end of the crossbar, and pulled—"

"Ah!" Sallan clapped. "That's why the chair was broken!"

"Brilliant." Kassite laughed. "Just brilliant!"

"There was nothing brilliant about it," she said. "In fact, because of my stupidity, the lamp went out and I was left in complete darkness. Then, by coincidence, I fumbled with my sling and got the idea to use it as a lever. That's all."

Kassite shook his head in wonder. "I must admit, when you first arrived at the tannery and told me your story, I thought of you as a foolish girl with a big dream that would surely get you killed."

"But you helped me."

"Because I felt pity for you," Kassite said. "Now, I pity your enemies."

Tying the sling back over her robe, Deborah felt her face flush.

Patrees said, "Master, we're ready to go."

Kassite leaned over and pressed Deborah's forearm. "You will always remain in my heart, Borah."

"Farewell, Master."

"Say a good word to your Hebrew god for me."

She smiled through her tears. "Shall I give you a blessing?"

He removed his white leather hat and lowered his head.

Letting go of Rogez's reins, Deborah held her hands over Kassite's head, the four fingers in each hand spread in two pairs. "May Yahweh bless you and protect you. May He show you kindness and grace. May He illuminate your path and grant you peace."

Kassite put his hat back on. "And may He do the same for you."

With Patrees leading Antippet's horse, the Edomite men trotted behind Kassite through the open gates of Bozra and broke into a gallop on the road across the valley, raising a dusty wake.

Sallan wiped his eyes and urged his horse up the street. Deborah caught up, followed by the boy-servants.

They made the sharp turn to the next street up. Everyone had come out of their houses to cheer the king and his soldiers. When the people saw Sallan, they cheered again. In front of one of the houses, Deborah saw a woman holding a young boy, who pointed and yelled, "Look, Mother! A white horse!"

To be continued ...

A NOTE TO THE READER

Deborah's dramatic quest for freedom continues in the third book in the series – *Deborah Slaying*.

While the *Book of Judges* describes Deborah's stunning success as a prophet, a judge and a military leader, who liberated her people from Canaanite oppression, it says nothing about her youth and upbringing. How could a girl, growing up in a world controlled by men, rise to rule over them? What hardships fueled her tenacity? What setbacks steeled her resilience? What battles transformed her into a formidable leader? These are the fascinating mysteries unraveled by the *Book of Deborah* series.

To ensure accuracy in describing how people lived in the ancient Mideast, I consulted countless books and articles. They are too many to list here, but I am particularly indebted to the scholarly works of William F. Albright, Yigael Yadin, Avraham Biran, Israel Finkelstein, Benjamin Mazar, Amihai Mazar, William G. Dever, Joyce Salisbury, Carol Meyers, Thomas E. Levi, George Hart, Bruce Routledge, Richard Elliot Friedman, Geraldine Harris, Richard Wilkinson, Boyd Seevers, Gale A. Yee, Brian Schmidt, Alan Dickin, Monroe Rosenthal, Isaac Mozenson, Diana Vikander Edelman, Hershel Shanks and Claudia Valentino.

We are blessed with wonderful friends and family members, who read my manuscripts at various stages, provide insightful observations, and offer enthusiastic support. They include (in alphabetical order) Margie and Arie Adler, Sarai Azrieli, Talya, Ben, and Elan Azrieli, Hagit and Michael David, Rabbi Dr. Israel Drazin, Don Eddins, Monica and Prof. Michael Finkelthal, Risa and Dr. Opher Ganel, Rachel and Joel Glazer, Prof. Sharon Glazer and Tamas Karpati, Julie and Hanan Gur, Dr. Jennifer and Nir Margalit, Linda and Dr. Bernard Rosenbaum, Glenna Salisbury, Wendy and Avner Skolnik, Stephen J. Wall, Stephanie and Ernie Wechsler, and Carol Wilner.

As always, this novel would not have come to life without the tireless support of my wife, Fiona, a dedicated physician who finds time to read the first draft of every new novel and provides astute critique, perceptive comments, and inspiring encouragement. Fiona and our children fill my life with love and laughter, which sustain me daily.

Last but not least, I owe a debt of gratitude to you, my readers, for choosing to spend your precious time with my books, for recommending the books to your friends, and for posting thoughtful insights and reviews on social media. There is no greater joy for a writer than a supportive community of readers. Thank you!

ABOUT THE AUTHOR

Avraham Azrieli is the author of books and screenplays. His first novel was *The Masada Complex* (a political thriller), followed by Israeli spy novels *The Jerusalem Inception* and *The Jerusalem Assassin*, as well as *Christmas for Joshua* (an interfaith family drama), *The Mormon Candidate* (a political thriller), *Thump* (a courtroom drama featuring sexual harassment and racism), and *The Bootstrap Ultimatum* (a mystery involving the commercialization of Memorial Day). Most recently, he has written a series of novels inspired by the true story of the first woman to lead a nation in human history, starting with *Deborah Rising* (HarperCollins 2016), and continuing with *Deborah Calling*, *Deborah Slaying* and *Deborah Striking*.

Beside fiction, he has also authored *Your Lawyer on a Short Leash - a guide to dealing with lawyers* and *One Step Ahead – A Mother of Seven Escaping Hitler's Claws* (an acclaimed WWII true story, which inspired the musical By Wheel and by Wing).

While growing up in Israel, Avraham received extensive Talmudic education, before attending law school and serving as a law clerk at the Israeli Supreme Court in Jerusalem. He later earned an advanced law degree from Columbia University in New York City, served as a law clerk for the Federal District Court, and started his legal career with Davis Polk & Wardwell. He has represented clients in numerous complex court cases before trial and appellate courts, including the United States Supreme Court. He currently lives near Washington DC with his wife and children. Like Ben Teller, the protagonist in *The Mormon Candidate* and *The Bootstrap Ultimatum*, Avraham often rides his motorcycle in the mountainous forests of western Maryland. To learn more, please visit www.AzrieliBooks.com

BOOKS BY AVRAHAM AZRIELI

Fiction:

The Masada Complex
The Jerusalem Inception
The Jerusalem Assassin
Christmas for Joshua
The Mormon Candidate
The Bootstrap Ultimatum
Thump
The Elixirist
Deborah Rising
Deborah Calling
Deborah Slaying
Deborah Striking

Nonfiction:

Your Lawyer on a Short Leash – A Guide to Dealing with Lawyers
One Step Ahead – A Mother of Seven Escaping Hitler's Claws

Author Website:
www.AzrieliBooks.com

www.ingramcontent.com/pod-product-compliance
Lightning Source LLC
Chambersburg PA
CBHW030415180626
46812CB00005B/2024